Farewell
from
Nowhere

Farewell from Nowhere

by Vladimir Maximov

AUTHORIZED TRANSLATION FROM THE RUSSIAN
BY MICHAEL GLENNY

DOUBLEDAY & COMPANY, INC.
Garden City, New York, 1979

All of the characters in this book are fictitious, and
any resemblance to actual persons, living or dead, is
purely coincidental.

Library of Congress Cataloging in Publication Data

Maximov, Vladimir Emel'ianovich.
  Farewell from nowhere.

  Translation of Proshchanie iz niotkuda.
  1. Maximov, Vladimir Emel'ianovich, in fiction, drama, poetry, etc.
I. Title.
PZ4.M2354Far [PG3483.2.K8] 891.7'3'44
ISBN: 0-385-09569-4
Library of Congress Catalog Card Number 76-42374

CONTENTS

Farewell from Nowhere

Part 1

CHAPTER 1

Israel, Israel! Sun-parched and tawny land, bearing yet the faint touch of His long footprints, heat-blurred mountain chain eroded by scorching winds, whose every hilltop might be His Golgotha! How many times since then, cleaving through time and space, have you been conjured up in Russia's snowbound confines like some mirage, hallucination, recurrent dream that lurks forever in the deepest recess of our historical memory? Your mysterious charm entranced the gentle heart of a priest of Novgorod, Luka Zhidyata; and for your sake suffering souls went forth from countless settlements of Slavdom toward the City of Redemption and of the Temple, trailing behind them the lamentations of Kolyma and Babii Yar. And is not this the reason why ". . . bowed down beneath the cross's burden, the King of Heaven walked your length and breadth, my native Russia, blessing as he went"?*

Vlad lay on the half-unmade divan bed, staring vacantly ahead of him into the snowy night, and the feeling of emptiness filled him with a deceptive sense of calm. Outside the uncurtained window

* Quoted from a poem by the Russian lyric poet Fyodor Tyutchev (1803–73). An English translation of the complete poem is to be found in Zeldin, J. (tr.), *Poems and Political Letters of F. I. Tyutchev*, University of Tennessee Press, Knoxville, Tennessee, 1973. (Tr.)

snow was drifting slowly down into a darkness barely penetrated by the light of street lamps. In the empty, destitute room there still hovered the ghost of that spirit of home which had so lately reigned over the house, but the mark of decay lay upon everything the eye could see. To one side of him, a razor-thin strip of light sliced into the darkness through the crack of the door. There, in what used to be the dining room, Vlad's relations, the five people closest to him, were lightly dozing the night away before flying to Vienna, whence they were bound for Jerusalem. He could see them now, all five of them, as a cluster of tense silence in this frail, worldly abode of theirs; he saw them, too, as five individuals, each wrapped in their own ripening cocoon of expectation, ready to burst and be sloughed off with discovery and hope.

"And so Maria Mikhailovna, my dear . . . after two famines which decimated your kith and kin, after four wars which left only anonymous stars over the dead young men who might have married you and over the tribe of their unbegotten offspring; after your ten decades, so generously rewarded by half a dozen medals, stamped out of ersatz bronze at the Mint . . . where will your sixty-first winter find you, after you have flown over the hills and far away? What awaits you in the sands of Sinai, you old, old maid from the village of Sychevka, that forsaken little dot on the map somewhere between Moscow and Tula?"

"Don't pace up and down so, don't smoke so much and so furiously, Katya, my sister! It's no easy matter, I know, to wrench yourself away from the lace-like snow that covers Krasnaya Presnya, away from the thirty-year-old web of ties and friendships, losses and gains, meetings, partings, talk, quarrels and loves, from the charmed circle of familiar thresholds and half-forgotten graves. No, it's not the smoke of a stubbed-out cigarette that's giving you a tickle in your throat, Katya, but the gray-brown dust of a shabby suburban backyard in Sokolniki and the bitter-tasting fluff from its poplar trees."

". . . How little, how slightly I knew you, Yura, son of Polish refugees and grandson of an American Jew who still heads a clan scattered over the five continents! Of all the mysterious ways of the Lord, perhaps the most inscrutable was that which brought you into this half-extinct Moscow working-class family of erstwhile peasants, to marry a girl, still almost a child, with whom you founded a new branch of the family tree, a fierce symbiosis of Slavic and Hebraic blood . . ."

"If only I knew what may become of them, the two smallest twigs to sprout from the Samsonov stem, far away in the Promised Land, that polyglot home of hope and longing! The older one is already prepared; she has resigned herself to the inevitable and is already in the power of that age-old female instinct of acceptance in the face of the mysterious or the unknown. But for the life of me I cannot imagine *you*, little Alexei, beyond the reach of my touch and my sight— you, with your childishly blurred version of the family looks, and the gift of pure blue in your relentlessly questioning eyes."

The snow fell in slanting streaks across the wan light of the street lamps, and as the darkness and silence around him thickened almost to tangibility and shut him off from the surrounding world, Vlad felt himself being steadily filled with the sickly sweet pangs of loneliness. He suddenly had the feeling that he had been buried alive in the snowbound darkness and deafening silence, and that he had been lying like this—arms folded on his chest and knees up—for years and years in unassuageable grief and with a silent cry on his lips: who am I, whence have I come and why?

CHAPTER 2

Yes, whence did you come and why are you here on this earth, my child? What shaped you? Was it the wind? A swirling agglomeration of dust in a random light-beam amid the darkness? Or the fading echo of distant ancestors, thrusting through time and made incarnate in you, only to vanish with you into oblivion at the last? All around was the void and in that void, on a tiny sphere compounded of water and clay, iron and blood, memory and forgetfulness, on the outskirts of any one of innumerable cities, a place grew up with the cheerful-sounding name of Sokolniki, and there you suddenly became aware of your own presence, of the dimensions of reality around you, of your shortened first name, Vlad, and of your more complicated last name, Samsonov . . .

"Vlad!"

"Vla-ad!"

"Vla-a-di-ik!"

"Samsonov!"

That was his sign, branded upon him by fate, the nonnegotiable bearer-bond with which he was to spend a lifetime in search of his mysterious Lord and Master, his Creditor. Many times in later life, as he changed his biography to suit the occasion, he would come to wear the label of a borrowed alias, but that first name, like a blade of grass under asphalt, would force its way through him to the surface again and again, bringing him inexorably back to his original state, his primal identity. Only when he was well on in years would he grasp the arcane significance of that inevitability, its purpose, its pre-destination. As it later transpired, the Creditor had not slept and had overlooked nothing; he had merely been biding his time until the due term when he should be paid his debt in full and, as they say, at the fixed rate of interest. Subconsciously, of course, Vlad had always felt that he was bound one day to be called to account, to pay the price of some long-standing and still unknown transgression, but only too late did he discover exactly what it was . . .

CHAPTER 3

The world impinged upon his consciousness in abrupt and unusual
fashion: a courtyard flooded with May sunshine in a capricious mixture of light and shade; the laughing face of old Sasha Shilov, the
janitor, standing over a pile of broken brick; and bustling back and
forth between the front door and the gate, the house manager Itkin,
who looked as like Karl Marx as two peas in a pod—a fact which at
first helped to win him favor with all his official superiors, but was
later to cause him to end his days immured as a political prisoner
"without privilege of correspondence."

At all events, that was the day from which Vlad subsequently
reckoned his sentient existence. On that day Solomon Itkin took
what was, in its way, the historic decision to lay a brick pathway
from the gate to the front door—a pathway which was to last the
best part of forty years and along which, one by one, the entire first
generation of tenants of that apartment house were to be carried out
feet first, including the wife of the man who was the double of Karl
Marx—Sarah Itkin, who did not survive to await her husband's return from his enforced absence at government expense.

While old Sasha stood chuckling beside the heap of broken brick
and the house manager dashed up and down the courtyard with his
tape measure, planning the outlines of the highway-to-be, Vlad, with
a builder's hammer over his shoulder, watched them keenly and
awaited the order to go into action.

"Right," said Itkin at last, thrusting the tape measure into the pocket of his government-issue, belted blouse.

"That's it, I think. You can start now, Sasha. And you, Samsonov"—the kindly sparkle, like a goldfish in the depths of his brown eyes, was all the reward Vlad needed—"you will be his right-hand man. I'm relying on you."

His graying beard billowing out like a square-rigged sail, he floated out of the courtyard, and old Sasha, still chuckling into his tobacco-stained whiskers, nodded indulgently to Vlad:

"Let's go!"

And he laid the first brick . . .

Ah, that brick pathway from the front door to the wicket gate! Even now Vlad still occasionally passes by and goes into that courtyard. The path is still creaking underfoot, still doing its duty, although naturally it no longer looks quite like the highway for Caesar's legions that it seemed to him on the day of its completion. Only scattered islands of it have survived intact. Nowadays the rest of it can only be guessed at by slivers and fragments that still protrude from the trampled soil. But just think what it has endured through all those years! How many drunken foreheads have struck sparks from it, how many boot heels, how many bare feet have imperceptibly ground away its surface, what piles of household junk have rumbled over its ribs! It has borne them all without complaint. Still functioning, still holding out to this day, that pathway has greeted and buried enough people to fill much more than one house. Though endless new tenants have pounded its remnants into dust, ironically it may yet be that at the end of all your earthly strivings one thing and one thing only will remain: the memory of that brick path that ran from the front door to the gateway of the house where you were born.

Starting from the front door, the path lengthened slowly but surely. Every day, as soon as his homework was done, Vlad went out to help the janitor, who would nod to him with silent approval as he took the next half or three quarters of a brick from his hands. Toward evening Itkin would come and inspect the construction site; sweeping the day's work with a fiery glance, he would usually give a grunt of satisfaction and immediately evaporate into the chill air.

Old Sasha's only comment was to give a sarcastic wink after him as he disappeared and mutter:

"Crazy old fool . . ."

But the house manager was not the only one who took an interest in their construction: the whole courtyard followed the progress and quality of the work. Everyone in the house had to have their say about it. Whenever Vlad's neighbor, Ivan Kudinov the carpenter, came home from work, usually half drunk, he would stop beside them and always say the same thing:

"Mustapha built a road and Zhigan walked on it . . . You're a real couple of workers, God dammit . . ."

Every evening Weintraub, the man from the fourth floor who supplied the material, would carefully count up the bricks they had used and say to Sasha:

"No, Shilov, this won't do. You're wasting state property. For each meter's length you're using six more bricks than you should. If you don't look out, I'll have to fetch the police inspector and search your shed. You're stashing away the extra bricks to sell them on the side."

Nikiforov, who worked in the secret police, saw the whole thing as a matter of high principle:

"That's the way to build socialism: brick by brick, until you've built a palace in honor of Lenin. Keep your eyes skinned, though, Shilov—remember the enemy is everywhere and he never sleeps . . . What's young Samsonov hanging around you for?"

Old Mrs. Durova, who lived in the single-story annex to the main building and who always had the last word to say about the goings-on in the courtyard, would sigh despairingly, causing the whole of her monumental frame to shake, and say:

"It's all so much dust and ashes . . . What good is it to anyone?"

The nearer the job drew to its completion, the more fully and tangibly Vlad perceived the world around him. Life for him took on content and significance. For the first time he felt aware of his sinews and muscles, the easy resilence of his own little body, the taste of his own sweat and of the blood from his cut fingers, the sweet lassitude of rest after work. Like a kernel shelled from a ripening nut, there came forth from him a person, an individual, a man, ready now to bear fruit in his turn.

Later, when fate was to drag him brutally through the thorny undergrowth of reality and fling him aside more dead than alive, he was often to remember that brick path and to give thanks to Providence for arranging his life to begin just there.

CHAPTER 4

On a window ledge bathed in the sunlight of a May afternoon, Vlad sat reading and rereading a tiny news item in the very corner of page four of *Pravda*, under the heading "Events":

Yesterday a heavy, thunderous rainstorm burst over Moscow. On Second Novotikhvinskaya Street the overhead power cables snapped and fell down. A horse stepped on the bare ends of the broken cable and was electrocuted on the spot. On Mishin Street, severed cables fell across some trees. Kostya Butylkin, aged ten, who was trying to climb a tree, received an electric shock. A similar accident occurred to the six-year-old Yasha Samsonov on Mitkovskaya Street. First-aid vans administered medical assistance to the two injured children.

He studied the text this way and that, from the end, from the middle, and then again from the beginning, spoke it aloud in every tone of voice and learned it by heart, reveling in the intoxicating magic of print. The horse and the luckless Kostya Butylkin only interested him insofar as they formed a preface to the most important passage in the report: the news about himself, Vlad Samsonov—even though for some reason they had called him Yasha. His mild annoyance at this, however, was more than outweighed by the absolutely accurate naming of the location of the incident. The printed letters, like notes on a stave, made music in Vlad's heart. In his overflowing rapture with himself he was ready to sing, to dance in anticipation of the thrilling changes in his life that this foreshadowed.

The newspaper in Vlad's hands flowed, vibrated, glowed with life; menacing, exclamatory headlines flew at him off the page like great black birds:

"Death to the Betrayers of the Motherland!"

"Call the guilty to account!"

"Sweep the hirelings of fascism from the face of the earth!"

The names of the sadistic Doctor Pletnev and of several erstwhile marshals of the Soviet Union—only recently lauded as the conquerors of the tsarist hordes and the armadas of the Entente—together with the name of the vigilant People's Commissar who had instantly divined their sinister intentions, were displayed in all the most conspicuous spots in the newspaper. Awareness of his own fame stimulated Vlad's imagination. He vividly pictured to himself a fanatic in a white coat torturing Stakhanovite workers under orders from the underground headquarters of the marshals, whose dearest wish was to undermine the country's defense capacity on the labor front. He chiefly pictured the torture weapon in the form of an enormous hypodermic syringe, and an ember of sacred wrath would glow furiously in his ardent young heart: "Death to them!" he repeated, fervently clenching his fists. "Call them to account! Sweep them from the face of the earth!" His own presence among this medley of printed adjuration suffused Vlad with a feeling of being part of the campaign. "Foes, don't dare to harm our Motherland!" The spark of rhyme touched his soul, conjuring forth the sacred fire of divine inspiration. "Or you will die by our avenging hand!" He was even a little stupefied when he realized what had happened. "But that's poetry"—a thrill of delight seized Vlad and bore him onward—"like in a book!" There was no stopping him now; he was in the triumphant grip of writer's mania, strong enough to provide work for all the printing presses of his native land:

> Each loyal Soviet worker knows
> We'll settle scores with all our foes.
> Great Stalin's promise we shall keep:
> All traitors from the earth to sweep.
> Our mighty leader will not fail
> To mow them down with leaden hail.

The limitless possibilities offered by the standardized vocabulary of official abuse and a heady whiff of the lucrative potential of character assassination struck his keen nostrils. The enticing prospects made him dizzy, opening up a succession of vistas, each one more seductive than the last.

Listening to her son gulping with self-admiration, Vlad's mother pursed her lips in thought and said dubiously:

"Listen to him—making up poems at his age! Spouting all that nonsense about 'enemies,' when I have to stand in line to take food parcels to his father, who's in jail for just that." But then she relented and gently mussed his hair. "All right, Mr. Poet, keep it up —who knows, we may get some sense out of you yet, and you may even bring an extra kopeck or two into the house. Run along and play."

Coming from her, this was gracious praise, a sign of approval, a payment in advance on future account. She never gave up hope of a miracle, for which she always made suitable allowance in her vague, chimerical plans for the future. Her flabby, limp body was apparently only kept going by these fantasies, by her irrepressible ambition and her desire to have her revenge on life. She awaited the turning point in her fortunes with the obsessive faith of a cardplayer who has staked life itself on a single card. Again and again reality shattered her intricate calculations, playing tricks on her of ever-increasing cruelty; yet no sooner had she recovered from one disappointment than she regained her former certainty of a rapid and—this time— inevitable change for the better. One could only speculate in amazement on the source from which this lethargic and impractical woman derived such almost mystical, dogged persistence. After her fatal accident Vlad was convinced that even then, at the Kazan Station where she fell down between an electric train and the platform, she had still regarded what had happened to her as an annoying but temporary misunderstanding that heralded some great stroke of good luck. Obviously, while there's hope there's life . . .

The first person whom Vlad met in the courtyard was old Mrs. Durova, to whom he was bound by a feeling of mutual gratitude. He maintained a taciturn friendship with her only son, Leonid, a melancholy schizophrenic who worked as an extra in the theater, and whom the neighbors avoided as though he had the plague; Durova, in her turn, defended Vlad against the righteous anger of the tenants whose windowpanes he had broken. The old woman remembered better times, but without self-pity. She now lived in one tiny room in the wooden annex to the apartment house, and spent her time in wearisome calculations to spin out the family budget, which consisted of her son's far-from-regular earnings and her own niggardly pension. Her inventiveness in this respect knew no bounds, and she was only able to make ends meet by the financial miracles which she achieved through trotting around all the local shops with her ancient shopping bag. The riffraff of the courtyard, who could not forgive her social origins, called her "Lady High-and-Mighty" behind her back, although they never dared to offend her openly. This hereditary noblewoman had a masterly command of obscene abuse, and when the occasion called for it she could deliver a stinging clout on the ear. As a result, their servile instincts preserved even the boldest of them from the temptations of class antagonism.

Vlad's poetry produced a visible effect on Mrs. Durova.

"I'm sorry, my dear, but it sounds like crap to me," she said with a mournful sigh. "Where on earth did you pick up all that claptrap?" Her dust-colored eyes stared at some point above his head. "Lord, they've even managed to poison the minds of young children!"

"But mine's no worse than what's in the newspaper, is it?" An author's touchiness was already beginning to make itself felt. "It's exactly the same, in fact."

"That's just the trouble, my dear, that's just the trouble." Fastidiously, she turned away. "So much the worse for you."

The old woman waddled away into the dim twilight of the annex porch, leaving Vlad with a sense of bewilderment. In years to come he was to hear much harsher judgment from critics of all sorts, but he was never to feel so stricken and discouraged as on this occasion.

But Vlad was irrepressible: his amazement at his newly revealed talent was too great. Wounded amour-propre obligingly suggested the reason for his first failure. "The old lady's envious," he grumbled behind the retreating old woman's back, "because a working-class boy like me can write poetry too!" Mediocrity will always take comfort from having made enemies.

Nor did he have to wait long for recognition.

"You've got a head on your shoulders, Vlad, you'll go far," said old Sasha, spreading his arms in admiration before Vlad even had time to finish. "Just like your father. He was going to be a great man too. Pity they stopped him short . . . They give people medals for writing things like that nowadays. You've heard about Mamlakat—

only knee-high to a grasshopper she was, but she got to meet Stalin. You ought to show your poetry to someone in the Party, like Nikiforov, for instance—he'll give you a helping hand."

"I'd rather try Itkin." Vlad did not relish the prospect of reciting his verse to his chief foe in the courtyard. "Itkin has a lot of influence."

At once the janitor's face seemed to freeze from within, turning dull and expressionless:

"Itkin's gone." He started to edge away. "He was here, then next day he vanished as if he'd never been born."

"But where is he?" Vlad inquired automatically, although he had already guessed what had happened: the male half of the courtyard's population was thinning out daily before his eyes. "I saw him from the window only yesterday."

"Yesterday!" The janitor shook his head mournfully. " 'Yesterday the priest had a wife, but she upped and ran off with a gypsy . . .' You've said it yourself in your poem: 'We'll settle scores with all our foes.' There's your answer!"

So saying, old Sasha slipped out through the gateway. That day everyone kept clear of Vlad, avoiding him with inexplicable haste, as if there were something—though exactly what, they didn't know—which embarrassed them in his presence. The realization of what it was only dawned on him years later and filled him with belated repentance. But before this could happen, he too had to traverse the same hell through which others had gone before him and taste himself the full measure of retribution for his gullibility.

CHAPTER 5

"Pistol" glared at Vlad as though studying him intently or sizing him up. Vlad did not feel frightened; rather the reverse—he even found it amusing, because he simply could not work out why the school principal had been nicknamed, of all things, "Pistol." The principal was tall, gaunt, and straight-backed, with bushy eyebrows and a sharp, jutting chin; he looked, in fact, exactly like an upside-down exclamation mark.

"So you are Vladik Samsonov, are you?" He stood up in profile and relaxed into a stoop, which at once gave him the appearance of an enormous upright fishhook. "Why don't you say something?"

"I . . ."

"Well?" The principal flashed a look at him as though to make sure that he was still there, and immediately turned away again to stare at the wall.

"I . . . I don't know . . ."

"But I know." He continued to look at the wall. "You take rather a lot of liberties, Samsonov." The principal appeared to be talking to someone on the other side of the wall. "If I were you, I would try to behave a little more discreetly. That is my advice to you, Samsonov." He swung sharply around, came out from behind his desk, and came straight toward Vlad. "I trust you understand me?"

Vlad understood him all right. There were too many things that he had been made to understand too early in life. Long before Vlad had even crossed the threshold of school, a vigilant society had ensured that he knew his place and made no false steps. The saying about the apple never falling far from the tree even haunted his dreams at night: his father in the shape of an apple tree and himself —Vlad—at his father's feet, looking like a tiny crab-apple sapling. His limited but bitter experience had taught him to maneuver cautiously between the treacherous reefs of silent sympathy and open hostility. Painfully, with the keen perceptions of a small, hunted animal, he discovered that his only salvation was to act as though nothing had happened: *tout va très bien, madame la marquise!* So now, too, the evasive caution which he usually deployed on such occasions came instantly into play:

"Yes . . . I mean, I don't know."

"I'm told that you're a bright boy." Pistol moved almost right up to Vlad, his eyebrows swooping menacingly down toward him. "You learn easily and you catch on quickly. And you have an excellent memory, isn't that so?"

"I don't know . . ."

"Why do you keep on harping on one note all the time, 'I don't know, I don't know'?" The principal's thin palm descended protectively on to Vlad's shoulder. "You should know; you must know. Understand?"

"Yes, I understand."

"Do you love Pavlik Morozov?"

"Yes . . . I do . . ."

"Now there's an example for you to follow." His voice took on a note of sincerity—the sincerity of the predator. "Loyalty to the cause of Lenin and Stalin comes before all else. The enemy is sly and cunning, he will worm his way in through any crack, so we must all be on the alert—understand?"

"Yes, I understand."

"I knew you were a sensible boy." His voice rang with a winning note of trust and complicity; Vlad even thought he heard the principal give a slight sob. "You must be especially vigilant—understand?"

"Yes."

"Good boy!" The principal's words vibrated with an emotional thrill. "If you hear anything, or feel anything going on, don't be shy but go to your class teacher and tell her. If it's urgent, come straight

to me—we won't let you down. You're on our side, you're one of us—
understand?"

"Of course . . ."

"Of course!" Imbued with the solemnity of the moment, both had
involuntarily straightened up and were standing at attention. Vlad
was intoxicated by a feeling of communion with an esoteric mystery,
with the holy of holies, of initiation into something vast and unknow-
able in its transcendent significance, into something about which
one could either speak only in a whisper or keep a proud, aloof silence. Henceforth he no longer existed merely for himself, merely as
an entity called Vlad Samsonov: his *I* was now merged into an exciting yet comforting *we*. At this moment he was not just a small and
defenseless creature who had to struggle alone against the demands
and inroads of the surrounding world; behind him there had suddenly arisen a force capable of smashing, of pulverizing anyone who
might dare to threaten him. From now on he no longer needed to be
torn between the menacing alternatives of "yes" and "no"! Henceforth his every "yes" and his every "no" were predetermined by what
was needed and best for the Common Cause and the Single Goal,
into which he had been initiated. The buoyant thrill which had
seized Vlad made his head spin; never before had he felt so self-assured and so free. Poised on his new eminence, he was beckoned to
by exciting prospects from the distance. Just let anyone like Nikiforov or Weintraub from the fourth floor try nagging or lecturing
him now! As for the riffraff who made up the rest of the courtyard's
inhabitants, he could no longer think of them with anything but
condescending scorn. Let tyrants quake!

The principal's somewhat cramped office seemed to grow brighter
and more spacious. His ink-stained desk beneath the portrait of
Stalin acquired an inexplicable solemnity. Even the dusty fig plant in
the corner, if one peered at it with half-closed eyes, began to resem-
ble the spreading palm tree from an illustration to Lermontov's famous poem: anger stimulates the imagination.

"Yes, Samsonov, I believe in you." The principal was clearly sharing the emotional upheaval that Vlad was experiencing. "Soon it
will be time for you to join the Pioneers."

"Yes." If at that moment the principal had asked him to jump out
of a fifth-floor window, Vlad would have flung himself earthward
without a second thought. His throat contracted in a spasm of self-
abnegation. "I'm ready."

"But before you can join you must prove yourself, Samsonov. It is your duty, your entrance fee, as it were."

"I'll try . . ."

Of course he would try! Henceforth there was no stronghold on this earth too mighty for him to storm. His hour had struck—forward, march! Now he would prove himself!

An opportunity arose on the very next day. During the lunch break, Vlad's deskmate Mishka Rabinov, having first glanced around to make sure the classroom was empty, leaned over toward his friend's ear and said:

"What does U.S.S.R. stand for?"

"Well, what?" Vlad asked warily, expecting a trap.

"Don't you know? You dumb peasant!"

"Peasant yourself."

"I'm telling you 'cos I'm your friend, but if you . . ."

"All right, tell me."

"It stands for 'Uncle Stalin Starved Russia'—see? U-S-S-R . . ."

You're in luck, Samsonov—he's played right into your hands! Vlad felt a triumphant pounding in his temples: fate had dealt him a trump card, a chance which might never be repeated. He had always felt slightly irritated by Mishka's arrogance and by his success in the boys' choir—he was considered the best soloist in the whole school. Furthermore, while the portraits of the "enemies of the people" in everyone else's history textbooks had been enthusiastically defaced with ink, or had at least had their eyes pierced with pencil points, Mishka's were untouched. Admittedly he said it was because he didn't want to spoil the book, but you could never be sure that this was the real reason.

"Did you think it up yourself?" Vlad nudged him cautiously. "Bet you didn't."

"No, the kids on our block told it to me. So what?"

"Nothing . . . just curious . . ."

He did not miss the slight flicker of fear in your eyes, Mishka, but it only spurred him on: it was a sign that he had not been mistaken, that the moment had come to prove his loyalty to the Common Cause and the Single Goal. God knows where you are now, Mishka, but you have a right to know who first sneaked on you.

When classes were over Vlad hung around the school for a long time, waiting for his class teacher, Iraida Vladimirovna, to come out. When at last she appeared in the doorway, radiant in her peaches-

and-cream youthfulness, he rushed toward her like a new convert to a hallowed priestess. At first the teacher could not understand this young Enthusiast for the Great Cause. His muddled story could scarcely penetrate the barrier of her triumphant, pristine innocence, but no sooner did she realize what he was saying than her eyelashes started to blink in perplexity and she blushed hotly.

"But he's your *friend*, Vladik!"

"But what if he did say that?"

"Then you should have told him off."

"What—me?" Vlad literally gulped with indignation: who would be fool enough to show his hand to the enemy? "I couldn't tell him."

"Why not?" She was already close to tears and she convulsively bit her full lips, barely able to control herself. "Who taught you to sneak on your friends?"

"The principal said . . ."

"Oh, the principal did, did he?" The teacher fixed Vlad with her angry stare. Scarcely ever again in his lifetime was he to experience such a look of mingled pity and contempt. "So that's it!"

Disgust suddenly seemed to reduce her in stature, making her seem even younger and more defenseless. For a moment or two, as though collecting her thoughts, she paced back and forth beside him, then angrily clenched her fists and with a determined look marched back into the school building.

Staring after her in alarm, Vlad genuinely could not imagine what had upset her so much. Not long afterward, however, trailing behind his mother into a store, he saw his former teacher sitting behind a cash register. It was then that something silently snapped inside him and he hurriedly scuttled out of the store to avoid catching her eye.

CHAPTER 6

Under the cloudless sky a bugle rang out. Ringing and enticing, the bugle call's pure sound filled the surrounding countryside and then shattered into silver fragments in the faraway dawn. Instantly the camp responded to this clarion with a banging of doors and windows, the shuffling of many feet, the hum of an awakening swarm of children. A new day had begun at Vlad's first Pioneer summer camp. In the two weeks that he had spent here he had imperceptibly adapted himself to the measured rhythm of communal living. He enjoyed leaping out of bed at the sound of reveille, racing the others to the wash-house, and then standing to attention at morning parade. He enjoyed marching everywhere in ranks, proud to feel himself a useful little cogwheel in a smoothly functioning machine; he enjoyed the solemn mystery of the camp fire, where he first exultantly awoke to a joyous awareness of group solidarity; he enjoyed the war games, in which for the first time he discovered the heady taste of being on the winning side. He was all set to hatch out into the brave little drummer boy, ready for self-sacrifice.

Vlad's life in camp was only spoiled by his troop leader's distaste for him. She had, it seemed, taken a dislike to him on first sight. Everything about him displeased her: the way he walked, the way he looked, the way he ate, and the way he dressed. Her round eyes, that

looked like dusty spectacle lenses, sought him out wherever he might
try to hide from her.

"Come here, Samsonov." So saying, she would invariably grab him
by his shirt button. "Your bed's in a mess again and your appearance
leaves a great deal to be desired, so that once more, thanks to you,
the troop has lost marks." She pursed her lips meaningfully. "I wonder, now—why do you do it?"

Her favorite occupation was to conduct literary quiz sessions, the
questions for which she herself composed in verse. It was strictly
compulsory to take part in them: the troop leader pursued absentees
with a vindictiveness that equaled her boundless self-esteem as a
poet. The children in her troop spent all their spare time racking
their brains over their mentor's intellectual riddles. At times her inspired imagination reached positively dizzy heights.

"Who's a man of many parts?" In the throes of composition her
fantasy knew no bounds. ". . . And wrote his plays for the Moscow
Arts? Whoever wins the most points in our quiz will get a prize—a
twelve-kopeck piece of Tula gingerbread!"

The piece of gingerbread was her chief invention, and she was as
proud of it as if it were a scientific discovery. No such piece of gingerbread ever existed in reality, and each one of them knew it, for although the quizzes were repeated practically every day, the winner
never did receive the promised reward; but hope always proved
stronger than logic, and time and again the little intellectuals would
join battle for twelve kopecks' worth of delight—just suppose, one of
them might be lucky today!

A fierce tussle developed between the partisans of Chekhov and
Gorky, which was finally resolved in solemn arbitration by the
game's grown-up instigator:

"Chekhov, children, Anton Pavlovich Chekhov!" Now there was
no stopping her. "Next question. Who was a writer and a count, the
scourge of vice and virtue's fount? Now try hard, children, that one
will give you something to think about . . . Who wrote a poem
about Vlas, to entertain the ruling class? See who can guess *that* one
. . . Who boldly cursed the feudal lords and suffered for his stinging
words? . . . Think, children. Here's another one that'll tickle your
brains, though it'll make you laugh, too . . . Whose verses angered
Nicholas the tsar? Who was both poet and hussar?"

Unable to withstand this hours-long ordeal, Vlad escaped to the
river, but she found him there.

"Running away from the healthy Pioneer collective, Samsonov?"
Her voice rang with unfeigned indignation. "Fostering in yourself
the alien spirit of individualism, are you? Bored with camp life? You
can't hide from us, Samsonov, we proletarians have sharp eyes . . ."

The troop leader did not explain why proletarians had such good
eyesight, nor how to acquire it, but from the steely timbre of her
voice it was not hard to guess that anyone who came under proletarian scrutiny was in for a hard time. Argus-like, society was driving
Vlad into a corner.

On top of it all, Vlad had fallen in love, and as happens to those
in love he lost both his sleep and his peace of mind. How many
times in the future was he to lose them, and then regain them—until
the next time! A great inclination to fall in love was to become a
scourge and a curse to him, the source of countless misfortunes and
disappointments, the cause, too, of not a few morbid complexes. But
in the third quarter of life's journey, before the threshold of his
declining years, when the passions of his heart would abate a little
and his memory would recall the past, freed of transient vanities, he
would remember each of them with lucid gratitude and take any
blame in each separate instance upon himself.

Vlad's first ardor was unrequited. Its object—a sprightly slip of a
creature who wore, as he now recalls, a blue beret on her short,
bobbed black hair—reacted to his silent worship with magnificent
disdain. In his efforts to impress her he started going in for all kinds
of activities, which resulted in his being a disastrous flop as a solo
dancer at the camp concert; one fine day, although unable to swim,
he threw himself into the water before her eyes, but was fished out in
time and brought to the bank by some older children. Even this act
of self-sacrifice left the fair young damsel indifferent.

But fate was preparing to deal him another and even crueler blow.
It happened during one of the regular war games. On the "Red" side
Vlad was allotted the role of scout, with the task of observing the
movement of the enemy's forces. Lying in a hazel bush, he already
saw himself as the hero of the day, destined to be the chief architect
of the coming victory and honored in front of the whole camp at
evening parade. *Then* she would see just who it was that she had
dared to reject! She would, of course, come to him on her knees to
beg his forgiveness, but he would walk proudly by without so much
as a glance in her direction.

Vlad even half-closed his eyes in anticipation of this delightful prospect, and when he looked up he could not believe what he saw: coming across the field straight toward him was his goddess, his fairy-tale princess, his fair lady, in her light blue beret and wearing the dark blue armband of the opposing side tied around her snow-white sleeve. She was moving fast and confidently, as though she had no doubt that he was sitting in the bushes and waiting, ready to do whatever she wanted. He could not disappoint the seductive creature in her expectations. He walked toward her, having momentarily forgotten all about his forthcoming triumph, and submissively bowed his head to her.

"Surrender," she said. "You're my prisoner."

"No," he mumbled. "I won't surrender."

"Then I will kill you," she said, and reached for his armband. "D'you understand?"

"All right." He bowed his head lower still. "I understand."

"Come on." Wrenching off his badge, she gave him a contemptuous push. "You're dead."

With that she vanished, melted, faded like a dream, like the morning mist . . . Even before reading Gogol, he had betrayed his cause for a woman and did not regret it. May that faithful warrior, the unbending Taras Bulba, forgive him!

Bewildered and depressed, he wandered about the forest, staring apathetically at the thickets around him; at that moment he saw his life as completely useless, and thus devoid of meaning. He did not come to his senses until he reached the bank of the river, where, at a spot a little removed from the camp, he had a secret refuge: the sewage pipe of an unfinished outdoor toilet. Here he used to come at difficult moments, and here, in a dry gulley overgrown with juniper bushes, he gave himself up to gloomy meditation on the imperfection of life, staring up at the sky through the hole cut in the pipe. Where can fate's victim find a place of solitude to brood?

Once more he came to that forsaken spot and, like a sorrowing demon, his injured spirit soared above the vanity and pettiness of life. Sweet daydreams were already starting to transport him to heights of fantasy beyond the clouds, when he heard above him the sound of someone expelling wind. The sound was sharp and peremptory, and it signaled the firm intention of its perpetrator. Trumpets were sounding the alarm.

Vlad jerked into life and immediately went cold with horror: above the opening in the pipe there swayed an enormous, pimply bottom, and between the wide-open knees loomed the goggle-eyed features of the troop leader. His terror was so great that from an involuntary urge somehow to excuse his desertion from the field of battle, he raised his hand and froze in the gesture of the Pioneer salute. Be Prepared!

The vast posterior hovered above him in the sky like a white flag of surrender.

CHAPTER 7

When Vlad first saw his grandfather Saviely, it never entered his head that the time he was to spend with him would be that part of childhood of which people generally cherish their fondest memories.

Opposite Vlad sat a gaunt, clean-shaven old man, intent and unsmiling as he looked him up and down with his weary, slightly protuberant eyes that were the color of dried fish scales. Vlad knew of his grandfather by reputation, since he had been the subject of interminable discussions at home. He was well aware that his grandfather came from a family which had always worked on the railroad, that for a short time during the civil war he had held a high-up job in transportation and had then spent two years in prison for negligence in his duties. Out of numerous fragments of indirect information and his own guesswork, Vlad's imagination had constructed an image of his grandfather as some kind of grim-faced commissar in buttoned-up leather tunic and patent-leather boots, something in between Maxim of the popular trilogy and the familiar portraits of Furmanov. But here sitting at the table, bent and stooping, was an ordinary, unremarkable old man, whose railroad uniform tunic, discolored with age and long wear, looked as if it were hanging on the crosspiece of a scarecrow.

"Here he is, here's my treasure." As she came in from the kitchen,

Vlad's mother roughly mussed his hair. "Here he is—looking quite clean for once."

She was clearly trying to ingratiate herself with their visitor, her father. As Vlad guessed, he used to help her with money from time to time, although he was considered miserly by his relatives. For this reason she was now making a great effort to please the old man to the best of her ability, anticipating his every word and wish.

"How are you doing in school?" His grandfather finally opened his bloodless lips. "Getting lots of bad grades?"

"He's almost at the top of his class." Vlad's mother hastened to his rescue. "Only he does get up to mischief."

"Like his father." The old man brightened up slightly and drew the boy to him. "Alexei's always getting into trouble too."

Coming from him, this remark was more than a little careless. Any reminder of her husband, Vlad's father, invariably threw Fedosya off balance. She genuinely thought that by being sent to prison on a political charge her husband had deceived and betrayed her, had barred forever her access to those higher spheres of life to which fate had predestined her. All her complexes, normally repressed by more immediate, everyday concerns, all at once burst out into the open like a horde of disturbed ghosts.

"That's just the trouble!" Fedosya started off, her voice immediately rising to a wail. "His father was always poking his nose in where he had no business, and now his son's doing the same. I've had to put up with one man always in trouble, soon I'll have to put up with the other too. He just disappears and leaves me with these two on my hands." Vlad's mother's indignation knew no bounds. She made it sound as if he was not serving his term in a remote Siberian prison camp but skulking in some fashionable resort on the French Riviera. "You can see for yourself . . ."

"All right, that'll do." Her father checked her gruffly but kindly. "Not in front of the boy."

Without even noticing it, Vlad had quietly leaned his head on his grandfather's shoulder, and this first trusting contact with the old man established a closeness between them that was to be permanent. With his free hand the old man gently stroked his grandson's hair, saying in a teasing voice:

"Like to come to Uzlovaya with your granddad?"

"M'hm." Excitement roused Vlad from his drowsiness. "Yes, I would."

"But suppose I won't take you?"

"You'll take me . . ."

"Listen to him—cheeky boy!"

"Will we go soon?"

"Yes."

"When?"

"We'll go when you've finished school."

"Aha . . ."

"Go to sleep now."

With what intoxicating ease they flew by, those remaining days until the summer vacation! Hardly waiting for the bell to mark the end of school, Vlad would rush headlong home, eat his meal with feverish speed and then, having hastily dealt with his homework, urgently beg his grandfather:

"Can we go?"

Uncomplainingly the old man would lay aside his newspaper and put on his inevitable tunic, after which they would set off for Sokolniki Park. There was nothing particularly exciting or memorable about those walks of theirs, yet how often, with what burning clarity, would he dream about them at hard times in his later life! The Maytime woods opened up hospitably before them, revealing the countryside around Moscow in the blue haze of the distance. Striding along beside his grandfather, Vlad would trustingly press his cheek to the old man's sleeve.

"Are there woods at Uzlovaya?"

"We'll find some for you . . ."

"And a river?"

"Yes."

"Is it far to go?"

"We'll take the morning train and we'll be there by evening."

"And shall we bring Nina with us?"

"What do you think?"

"I'd like to . . ."

"Very well, we'll take her."

"Aha . . ."

Your features have almost been effaced from his memory, Nina, yet he has kept some recollections of you: your look, the turn of your head, the faint shadow of a smile. From these he has inwardly recreated and memorized your image, your long-since disembodied essence. Who knows what wind it was that wafted you into their family, or why, to reward what virtues did the good Lord contrive to bless that selfish, contentious brood with your presence? You held sway over the strife of a communal apartment like an auburn-haired angel and your mere presence calmed the surrounding world and restrained it from slipping into ultimate insanity. When he realized this, it was already too late; the mound over your grave had already disappeared, swept from the face of the earth by winds and oblivion.

On the day of their departure the house was given over to frantic bustle. As she dressed him, Vlad's mother was unusually lively and affectionate, and plied him with goodnatured advice:

"You must do what Granddad tells you and help him about the house. He's really quite a sick old man, and you should make things easy for him. At home you're used to doing what you please and you don't give a thought to others—you never listen to me or your aunt. But if you start playing your tricks with Granddad, whatever will he think of you?"

His aunt, wholly occupied with getting Nina ready, chuckled softly to herself as she fussed around the little girl, her favorite.

"Our Nina is going away, away, our Nina shall have a new dress today . . . Is that too tight?"

"No."

"And what about there?"

"Just a bit."

"How's that?"

"That's better," said Nina, with a little giggle of gratitude.

Grandfather only grunted with disapproval as he watched the general commotion: the old man hated fuss and always complained about it . . .

As they walked out of the gateway to a chorus of farewells and parting words, Vlad turned around. As though seeing his home for the first time as an outsider, he was struck by its wretched, pathetic look: two boxes—one of stone, one of wood—stood huddled together, framed by a few gnarled and stunted poplar trees. But something in its meager appearance pierced Vlad's unfledged soul with such delicious intensity that his heart came into his mouth.

CHAPTER 8

Uzlovaya! A little cluster of buildings around the railroad station, a grain elevator and a bakery alongside the tracks. Dusty acacias bending outward over picket fences; a motionless pond, the edges overgrown with duckweed; unpaved streets with a ribbon of weeds growing along the dry ditches; chickens fussing around wellheads; sleepy cats atop garden walls; boxlike official buildings streaked with the faded traces of yesterday's slogans. An ideal setting for Russian provincial novels of that time. A touching copy of countless other dull, God-forsaken country towns. A barely noticeable pimple on memory's sensitive features.

Why, then, does Vlad's heart feel such an overwhelming twinge of delicious pain at the mere sound of the name of that insignificant, unsung little town? What power still makes him shudder and thrill with excitement whenever he chances to hear the word "Uzlovaya," wherever he may be? What does that name mean to him? The human heart, of course, will always fill with tearful longing for the hearth to which it can never return. The image of home, be it ever so humble, will rise before his mind's eye like a mirage, a fata morgana, a waking dream, and all his life he will swear to return in pursuit of that blurred vision, stumbling on the way and picking himself up again, his parched lips muttering prayers and imprecations. But he will never make the journey; he will grow weary and short of breath when only halfway there, and his eyes will close. His beloved Uzlovaya may sleep in peace.

His grandfather lived on the very edge of town, where every little street and alleyway ended in the adjacent fields. Wisps of smoke from neighboring villages were all that could be seen across the wide-open, treeless, surrounding plain. The shell of a decapitated church floated like a captured flagship amid that flat, imperturbable expanse, and to keep it company on its sad voyage was the rumbling cube of the local flour mill. The sharply tapered pyramid of a lonely slag heap followed in their wake on the blue horizon.

His grandfather's house—a semidetached, slightly moss-grown brick house with a sheet-iron roof—was indistinguishable from the dismal row of identical houses, strung out in two parallel straight lines from the market square to the town's outskirts. One half of the house was shared by the old man with his eldest son, Mitya, while the other was occupied by his brother, Tikhon, and his numerous brood of children and grandchildren. All around the house was a garden, fenced off into two halves, with toolsheds by the gateway. The brothers lived in a state of alienated indifference to one another. Having worked all his life as a conductor on express trains without ever being promoted higher, Tikhon treated his brother Saviely with good-natured derision, an attitude acquired in their childhood. He regarded Saviely as slightly touched, and he condescendingly tolerated his brother's enthusiasm for politics as though it were a temporary if somewhat long-lasting whim. Saviely reciprocated in his own fashion, considering his brother to be part of the "ballast" of the proletariat, an irritating liability to the cause of the revolution, a sterile offspring of the class struggle. For all this, however, the family atmosphere within the house did not lack equilibrium.

Almost the entire clan descended upon the house to mark the visit of their Moscow cousins. First to arrive from nearby Stalinogorsk, driving up with a noisy flourish in a smart official droshky, was Saviely's brother-in-law—Uncle Fedya, who ran the personnel office of one of the Stalinogorsk coal mines.

"Just look at them now, my little niece and nephew!" The cheerful gleam of his gold teeth seemed to expand the cramped room and suffuse the mean surroundings with confidence, health, and prosperity. "How thin and peaky you are, like famine children." This was a dig at their mother, of whom he secretly disapproved because of her

superior, big-city manner. "Well, we'll feed you up. We don't have
to count the crusts down here . . ."

Uncle Fedya, Uncle Fedya, you irrepressible jack-in-the-box! Like a
devastating plague you swept through a dozen or more jobs, leaving
behind you empty cash-boxes and empty bottles, illegitimate children and ruined organizations, hoodwinked auditors and repentant
accomplices. Then after serving a short sentence for one of many em-
bezzlement jobs, you were to settle down peacefully on a pension
under the fully insured roof of your own cottage. Having spent a lifetime pilfering government property, what need had you to count the
crusts? Hands up—your money or your life! Expropriate the expropriators!

Aunt Lyuba, his wife—who was, as they say, as broad as she was
long, with a disproportionately small, close-cropped head—took one
look at her niece and nephew and snorted venomously:

"Huh! So much for Moscow food—look at them both: nothing
but skin and bone."

She would live to a ripe old age, this aunt, and give birth to droves
of children, of which only three daughters would survive, all as generously built and fertile as herself. War, the death of her grown-up
son, her husband's checkered career—all this flowed over her like
water running off a duck's back and without ruffling her monumental imperturbability by so much as the twitch of a muscle. Like all
the Mikheyevs she was naturally competitive and ambitious, but having failed to reach the pinnacles on which she had set her sights in
her youth, in the end she took to consoling herself with the misfortunes of her relatives. She throve on disaster, the more complete the
better.

Mitya, Saviely's eldest son who shared half the house with him,
showed up noticeably the worse for drink, and began teasing his
brother-in-law before he was through the doorway:

"What a surprise! The bosses are honoring us with their company
today!" He ruffled the hair of Vlad and his sister as he went past
them, shaking his tightly curled head at everyone as he strode around
the room. "What's the matter with you and your dear comrades?
Can't you even do your job properly? The stores are empty
again—there isn't even any flour to be had."

"You just eat too much." Not to be outdone, Fedya hit back at
him, grinning cheerfully. "We've brought down the price of bread
and so you gobble all you can, can't get enough. We'll make you see

sense, though, Mitya—and if you don't, we'll knock it into your head the hard way, for your own good."

"Oh, leave him alone!"

"Give him a drink."

"No—not that!"

"Shut up."

"Look out, or you'll scare him so much he'll wet his pants with fright."

"You'll be the one who's scared . . ."

Amid their cheerfully insulting banter, a tall woman with a printed calico shawl around her shoulders came into the house and stood leaning against the doorpost. Unlike the Mikheyevs, she had big round eyes, and looked like a large, brightly hued bird with wings folded in exhaustion. As she entered, she began to weep soundlessly, radiating pity in the direction of the children. In that moment of silence, her childless heart was to pick out as the object of its love not Vlad, alas, but his little sister, Nina, though this did not prevent him from later growing very fond of his aunt and retaining his affection for her until his hairs had turned gray.

Somewhere at the level of her shoulder, in the shadows of the porch, there bobbed impatiently the ugly face of her husband and namesake, carrying a battered accordion under his arm.

"My hands are freezing, my feet are freezing, it's time we started raising our elbows . . . Stop wasting time in gossip and let's sit down at table . . ."

And that will be the story of your life, Uncle Sasha—lurching from party to drunken party with your accordion, until that night in the depth of winter when the misery of a hangover will push you under the wheels of a switching engine. Railroad men die on the tracks.

As the noise around the table reached its height, Saviely's youngest son, Misha, arrived with his young wife, a schoolteacher. These two newlyweds were a distinctly ill-assorted pair. He was dressed in the uniform of a re-enlisted Red Army soldier, and his face wore the perpetual, slightly imbecilic smile of the deaf. She was the typical provincial bluestocking: there was something desiccated and colorless about her figure, tightly encased in a gabardine suit. If not exactly ice and fire, these two were at least the personification of wax and stone.

Immediately the slightly deaf Misha broke loudly and inconsequentially into the general conversation:

"I remember when we were in Bessarabia they used to offer us wine like it was water, in pitchers: drink as much as you like. You'd down a couple of pitchers, then eat some semolina or whatever they call it. I remember Marshal Timoshenko himself . . ."

He looked around proudly, but immediately realized from the expressions on the others' faces that he had spoken out of place, fell into an embarrassed silence and lowered his gaze to the plate in front of him. As he did so, his wife only snorted contemptuously and looked around with a fishlike stare.

"Say what you like," Uncle Sasha piped up mischievously, "our Misha's an example to us all. A soldier in the cause of freedom. If it wasn't for him, look what a mess Bessarabia would be in now. He lent a hand to help the working class. You don't even have to feed Misha—all he asks is to be able to stand up for the right. No people will ever be downtrodden when Misha's around, Misha'll always get them out of trouble." Sasha could not resist another dig at his brother-in-law, Fedya. "He makes a good pair with Fedya. Our Fedya will beat up anyone you like, and Misha will save them."

But it was not so easy to make Fedya rise to the bait. A flap-eared peasant from Epifanskoye, Fedya Grishin cared not a whit for Bessarabia, for the downtrodden working class, or for the right. These concepts were only of interest to him insofar as they made it easier for him to live a carefree and idle existence under their broad protection. As he listened to his brother-in-law he only grinned provocatively and attacked the food with increased gusto.

Seeking sympathy, Misha glanced miserably toward his father, who was just making an effort to come to his son's rescue with a reply when Uncle Sasha, obviously judging the moment to be pregnant with discord, pulled out the tattered bellows of his accordion:

"Come on, Fedya, give us a song . . ."

Uncle Fedya had a tenor voice that was light but tuneful. He began softly, as though testing it out, but gradually his voice gathered strength until soon it was in full and steady flight. Loud and ragged, the family joined in singing the chorus of a song about "What wouldn't I have given for the glances and the charms, Of the one who me, and only me, embraces in her arms." In years to come, Uncle Fedya would climb many golden mountains of government property, and would drink, if not rivers, then streams of wine without ever exchanging them, in the words of the song, "for an ill-fated love," but remaining instead faithful to his elephantine Lyuba. Even

so, as he sang the closing bars of the song he wept hot tears of genuine pity and regret for his abortive passions.

Vlad then and there conceived a great liking for Uncle Sasha. Listening to him, Vlad already saw himself grown up and resembling
his uncle—cheerful, blessed with good luck, simple and kindly, with
a mouthful of gold teeth. Like him, Vlad felt, he too would sing in a
light but melodious voice about golden mountains, and like him he
would weep as he sang—though not forgetting, either, to put away
his share of food and drink at the same time.

Even amid the temporary unison engendered by the singing, old
Saviely did not forget the conversation that had been started, nor its
contentious undertone. No sooner had another round of drinks been
poured than he pushed his glass aside and said impatiently:

"Mitya, we know you haven't any brains and you don't often hit
the nail on the head, but why do you let that brother-in-law of yours
get away with it? Why don't you answer? Or did they just give you
your Party card as an ornament?"

A total, awkward silence followed. The brother-in-law in question
strove to pretend that he had nothing to do with it, and merely went
on eating in a noisy, careless manner, his head well down into his
plate. Misha stared around in perplexity with a vacant, questioning
look. Mitya's short, restless figure shriveled with embarrassment. The
bellows catch on the accordion slipped obstinately free of Uncle
Sasha's fingers, and his instrument let out a long, squeaky moan.
Knowing the old man's quick temper, the women fell silent. The
first to break out, with an expressive, reproachful glance in the direction of the children, was Alexandra, who said:

"Now, father . . ."

In reply, old Saviely only grunted with annoyance, gave an irritated shrug of one bony shoulder and stood up:

"All right, I'll go out for a breather . . ."

No sooner had he gone out than everyone started talking at once.

"Father's at it again!"

"Always talking out of turn."

"What is this—a meeting, or what?"

"When can we ever sit down and just enjoy ourselves?"

"He's old, you ought to show him some respect . . ."

"Well, *you* show him some respect, then . . ."

"We've said our say, and that's an end of it."

"How about another glass all round?"

Vlad took advantage of the general hubbub to slip out into the fresh air after his grandfather. The May twilight was seeping through the frothy white blossom of the surrounding gardens. From the pond opposite came a noisy chorus of frogs. The monotonous hum of the flour mill at the edge of town was occasionally punctuated by the mooing of cows and the whistling of locomotives. From a bench beneath the windows, shaded by a lilac bush, could be heard the muffled sound of two plaintive voices, one of which was his grandfather's:

"You bring them up, and then they . . ."

"That's life, Saviely, that's life."

"Might at least show some respect."

"What do you expect?"

"They're old enough to know better."

"They have their own interests now."

"I know what their interests are, Tikhon: sleeping and eating, that's all they're interested in."

"They're legitimate interests."

"And you're just as bad!"

"We're ordinary, simple people, Saviely, we don't care much about politics the way you do."

"Huh!"

How agonizingly clear, how ineffaceable to this day is his memory of that evening, that haze of apple blossom above the roofs, that lilac, and the protracted, interminable conversation beneath that window!

CHAPTER 9

Toward the end of that summer, Uzlovaya was drenched with persistent rain. The low-lying clouds, unseasonably big and bulky, scudded over the rooftops and soaked the earth in a heavy drizzle. The surrounding fields were blotted out by a blue-gray, water-saturated mist. Everything swelled and grew visibly bloated, quivering with the penetrating damp. All living creatures disappeared and huddled under cover to await better times, and only desperate swallows occasionally darted through the sodden air in search of their daily provender. In the whole town life barely flickered, crushed to earth by the prolonged bad weather.

For days on end Vlad sat on the ledge of the stove, devouring book after book and listening intently for the sound of footsteps outside. Grandfather's return from his train journeys slightly brightened the cheerless monotony of the wetness. The old man never came home with empty hands. His conductor's satchel invariably contained some present for his grandson—lemon drops, gingerbread, a poppy-seed bun. Although long past the age when he could have retired on a pension, he could not bring himself to retire, fearing boredom and loneliness at home. Jealous of his grandfather's attachment to his work, Vlad nevertheless patiently endured his absences, and even pandered slightly to this weakness of the old man's, engaging him in endless talks about railroad affairs. Vlad's periods of waiting were made tolerable by books and by his Uncle Mitya, who lived with his family on the other side of a partition wall.

"Vlad!" Waking, he would thump on the wall with his fist. "Enough shut-eye, time to start building socialism. Run out to the privy and put some fertilizer on the fields, then we'll eat. Today it's best-grade soup, special rye rusks and sunflower oil, the revolution's gift to the working class, then some fresh carrot-top tea with no lemon and no sugar, the government's gift to the toiling masses . . ."

He was unquenchable in this vein. His cheerful, malicious banter, like fresh caustic soda, instantly corroded away the frail equilibrium of reality and laid bare its crude seams and its gaping deficiencies. Apparently unshakable truths suddenly became absurd, resounding words shriveled into pettiness, grandiloquent slogans began to smell of mustiness and falsehood a mile away. Uncle Mitya was smoldering inwardly with some burning, suppressed pain which, as soon as he had enough drink inside him, would gush forth into the open:

"And what about that old fogy of yours, Vlad?" he would start, his voice rising. "I'd like to show him up for what he is! You don't think I would? Do you really suppose the old man's going to start the world revolution on a passenger train? One foot in the grave, God damn him, the old crackpot. We poor workers have spawned too many pig-headed, big-mouthed fools of his sort—you can't get away from them. They make our life miserable, the parasites. You can't hear yourself think for their chattering. The time'll come when we can't bear it any longer and we'll kick 'em in the teeth . . ."

But Mitya was not destined to survive his father. Before the year was out, he would lay down his curly head when his unit was surrounded by the Germans near Smolensk and the first waters of the spring thaw would wipe even the memory of him from the face of the earth.

From a sense of family obligation, Great-Uncle Tikhon would now and again make a visit. He would come in, ease himself down onto a bench near the door, and bring out a pouch of snuff; take a pinch and noisily inhale the greenish dust into both nostrils. After sneezing a few times, he would inquire:

"Still reading?" He did not expect an answer. "Well, maybe you'll grow up to be a great man like Saviely. But don't forget, my lad, the higher you go, the harder you fall. That's something your granddad doesn't understand to this day. Life's a lot easier if you just keep going steady and don't stick your neck out. All those people who write books keep telling us different things—so how are *we* to know what's right and what to believe? Best thing to do is to work things out for yourself without any of them books . . . Are you hungry?"

"No thanks. I'll wait till Granddad gets home."

"All right. My old woman's just made a nice pot of soup, though. You can have some whenever you feel like it." He rose ponderously, turning to go. "If you change your mind, drop in any time, I know how hungry young boys can get."

And Great-Uncle Tikhon would go out, painfully dragging one ailing leg after the other. Many were the miles of prison-camp pathways along which his feet were to shuffle when he served a sentence for his enforced service under German occupation as a street warden, although fate in the end was to be kind to him: he would return and live to a ripe old age in his own house, surrounded by his numerous progeny.

One dull wet evening, only a few days before he was due to go home, Vlad was drawn back from the borderland between waking and sleeping by anxious voices coming from the porch:

"Under his legs, pick him up under his legs . . ."

"Carry him over here . . ."

"Sshh! Not so much noise!"

"The boy's asleep, isn't he?"

"Bring him in here . . ."

At once Vlad's spirit seemed to fly out of his body, and as if floating somewhere amid the twilight shadows of the room, he saw himself for the first time from the outside: a dark huddle of fear on the white surface of the stove.

As his grandfather was carried in, undressed and put to bed, Vlad, squeezing himself into a corner of the stove ledge, felt himself slowly dying with anxiety as he waited for some irreparable disaster. "I couldn't, I couldn't bear it, I couldn't!" a voice wailed inside him. "It mustn't be, it mustn't, it mustn't!"

Uncle Mitya appeared and immediately took charge, fussing and clucking like a rooster:

"Good for you, old man! Acting like a human being at last. Got so drunk you lost your class consciousness—so you didn't let us down in the end, you kept up the family reputation. It's all right, Vlad, it's all right—a drunk will always sleep it off and come to his senses, but a fool never does. Your old granddad has a head on his shoulders, he got where he did on his own—overdid it a bit, mind you, but still he did it on his own. Maybe he had a bit of help at the beginning, but after that it was all on his own." He positively breathed triumph and exultation. "Well, Dad, I'll never forget this as long as I live—it's done me that much good to find you're a human being after all. I needn't be ashamed of you in front of other people anymore, even if they do keep on calling you 'that old commissar.'"

Only then did it dawn on Vlad that his grandfather was simply dead drunk, and this brought him partly to his senses. Vlad had never seen the old man drunk before, so it was all somewhat bizarre, but it meant that the worst was not to be: the old man's condition was not fatal.

After a short spell of unconsciousness, the old man started to babble, and gradually a logical sequence of events began to emerge from his disjointed raving:

"Young puppies! I started on that line as a greaser, I knew every tie on those tracks, risked my life for that railroad—and now I'm no more use! It's the scrap heap for Saviely Mikheyev . . . I don't want your damn gold watch, keep it as a souvenir . . . I've got my own watch and it'll go for a hundred years without winding . . . After all these years, after all the times I've wiped the snot off your young noses—and now I'm good for nothing but the junk yard . . . Why, everyone on this line knows me . . ."

Vlad rejoiced: it was goodbye to the railroad. Vlad felt about the railroad as though it were a living being; he was deeply and passionately jealous of his grandfather's loyalty to it, regarding it as solely to blame for the old man's short but agonizing spells away from home. It had robbed him of a part of what by rights was his and his alone, and now at last it was going to have to concede it to him!

Now old Saviely belonged wholly to Vlad alone. Life was worth living.

CHAPTER 10

After the squat, dusty, provincial sprawl of Uzlovaya, Moscow struck Vlad as particularly elegant. Yellow, dappled with brown, circling in the resilient and almost bluish-tinged air, the leaves were settling into a layer of rustling lace on sidewalks and pavements. Cyclops-eyed streetcars charged across street intersections, filling the surroundings with their protracted, high-pitched screech, the brass discs on janitors' white aprons flashed with a joyous gleam, the clattering hooves of bay carthorses echoed down Mitkovskaya Street and gray-brown pigeons circled over the chill metal of sheet-iron roofs. Dusted over with fallen leaves, the courtyard was bathed in an even sunlight the color of egg yolk. The clear sky promised a long, cold, bracing fall.

Their mother met them with her usual repertoire of remarks, slightly mollified by their comparatively long absence:

"Here you are again, my little darlings!" She turned them around, inspecting each one in turn from all sides. "Well, now that her children are back home, it's time for mother to get back into harness again for some hard labor. Still, at least you're looking a bit healthier. Of course your neck looks like a chimney sweep's, obviously you never washed at all while you were with your grandfather. Oh, the trouble you cause me . . ."

As their aunt embraced his little sister, she could not conceal her joy and purred gently to her:

"She's back, bless her little heart, my little helper's back. Auntie's been quite exhausted without you, it was like being without a pair of hands. And she missed you more than she can say. You didn't forget your auntie, did you?"

In honor of the occasion there was no stinting of good things to eat. On the table, alongside his favorite fruit pudding, there towered a mound of pale rennet apples, crowned by two heavy bunches of grapes. The lunch turned out to be well up to the standard of the dessert: two separate kinds of soup—noodle soup (his sister's favorite) and pea soup (an enforced concession to Vlad's taste)—preceded a dish of really meaty meatballs with fried potatoes. A salad of stewed dried fruits crowned this culinary orgy.

After the ritual of mealtime, mellowed by food and her own display of good nature, their mother graciously allowed the children to go down and show themselves in the courtyard:

"Only no shouting, please . . ."

The age-old, familiar rhythm of life in the courtyard had not changed. Kitchen aromas and bad-tempered abuse floated skyward through wide-open windows. Assorted sets of family laundry fluttered in the wind like bunting; the neighboring stables still reeked of delicious horsy smells. From somewhere up above (judging by the volume, it came from the cheerful Kuptsov clan) a waterfall of sound flowed down from a phonograph: "Farewell, my campfire, my gypsy campfire, I sing to you my last farewell!" Like it or not, life went on in its accustomed rut.

Old Mrs. Durova, beating a threadbare carpet against the fence, greeted Vlad with her usual goodnatured banter:

"Hullo there, young Samsonov, you've been away long enough. We've all missed you very much, especially my son, your friend Leonid."

At that moment Leonid himself appeared at the window as though in a portrait frame, holding a smiling baby in his arms.

"Take a look at him . . . This is my nephew Boris, your future faithful henchman. You must love him and be kind to him. Come on in, there's lots to tell you . . ."

And that, Boris, was how he first met you, at the very beginning of the fall of 1940, on the brink of memorable events and great changes. After many years and much travel, his fate and yours were ultimately to be tied together by a subtle knot, and only God knows who is to untie it and when.

In the gateway Vlad bumped into Maria, the eldest of the Khleb-
nikov women from the third floor. Myopically, presaging her even-
tual blindness, she ran her hands over him, recognized him, and said:

"Why don't you come up and see us, Vlad? I've put aside some
very interesting books for you."

Ah, those books of the Khlebnikovs', in two antique bookcases in
their corner room looking out on to a blank wall of the next-door
house! It was from them that he drew the "little learning" that "is a
dangerous thing"; it was there that he stuffed himself silly with
names and dates, events and situations, climates and latitudes, there
that he first developed an addiction to the heady drug of idle fantasy. His imagination was given disturbing stimulus as a vast number
of other men's dreams passed through him and took root. His head
buzzed with them as he walked the earth and lived all the adventures of a Till Eulenspiegel character. The Khlebnikovs felt a sense
of solidarity with Vlad: the head of their family had been arrested
on almost the same day as Vlad's father, but he had perished, by all
the signs, "without privilege of correspondence." His widow Maria
and her two children—Lera (or as everyone called her, Lerusya) and
Slavka, who was slightly older than Vlad—somehow survived by giving private lessons and with help from their numerous relatives. He
knows now that this woman was to survive her son and end her days
in total blindness together with her unmarried daughter in that same
corner room looking out on to a blank side-alley; but that day, on the
threshold of that fall, no such thoughts entered his head.

That day stands out from his past as a special one, clearly separate
from the endless succession of similar, routine, and unremarkable
days of early fall. Vlad even remembers the colors of the ball which
he and his sister used to play with at the time: it had a blue half and
a green half, divided by red and yellow stripes—a farewell present
given to them in the spring by the tenants who moved out of the
wooden annex to the apartment house. It was their last game together.

Next morning his sister did not get up. What at first seemed an
ordinary rash, the slight aberration of a healthy organism, a passing
indisposition after the holidays, developed by evening into a bluish-
purple flush with a fever. The doctor, a colorless little old man with
a gray beret above his haggard face, after prodding the patient a few
times with his stethoscope, diagnosed erysipelas and prescribed some

medicine, but twenty-four hours later she was driven off to the Botkin Hospital with a diagnosis of "blood poisoning." Later, their mother was often to curse that ill-omened doctor, but who knows in what form, under what guise the grace of God manifests itself?

The house grew empty. Their mother spent all her time at the hospital, and when his aunt came home from work in the evening she simply collapsed prone on the divan and gave no sign of life until the next morning. All this time Vlad existed alone, outside the radius of their sight and consciousness. It was probably during those days that he realized with stunning clarity his own utter loneliness in the surrounding world and vaguely perceived that he was fated to spend his life in singlehanded combat against that world.

At the weekend, loafing aimlessly about in the courtyard, Vlad suddenly saw his mother standing in front of him. Vacant, without a drop of blood in her pinched face, she moved toward him like a sleepwalker, whispering thickly and passionately:

"Why wasn't it you? . . . Why wasn't it you, instead of her? . . . Why are you still alive? . . . Why?"

Grief made her speak her true feelings, and she was quite sincere. Probably for the first time in her life.

CHAPTER 11

"You know," Leonid said to Vlad, shivering as he wrapped himself up against the cold in a flannelette blanket thrown over his shoulders, "this earth is probably just a station in our life where we change for somewhere else. We still have to fly on and on until we reach our destination. Each stopping place for us is a new life in a new guise. Here, for instance, you're a human being, but on another planet you may be a plant or even a stone. Our death is simply a farewell to one of many stopping places, no more than that. A farewell from nowhere, so to speak. It's just a pity that this time we happen to have been allotted such an uncomfortable waiting room. Let's hope we have better luck next time. What do you think?"

Under its mantle of nebulous starlight, the night around them was alive with the rustle of dead leaves, foretelling a sharp frost next morning. The few lamps along the street shed a timid bluish light into the dark; the air smelled of coal fumes, dry leafmold, and the dusty topsoil of cooling earth.

"But where is the end of the journey?" Vlad inquired anxiously, chilled by the delicious horror of this newly revealed prospect. "Do you know, Leonid?"

"There is no end," the latter answered sadly, wrapping the blanket tighter around himself. "There is none and never can be."

"What do you mean—there is none?"

"Just what I say."

"Everything comes to an end." Vlad shook his head obstinately, dissatisfied with this outlook. "Everything has a beginning and an end."

"You're little and stupid," Leonid declared fastidiously. "You live in your pathetic little three-dimensional world and you're glad of it. But fortunately there is another, a fourth dimension, which you are not fit to attain."

"What's the fourth dimension?"

"God." The word dropped almost soundlessly from his lips and slowly rolled away into the night. "But that's not for you."

Vlad forgave his friend for his sharpness with him. Leonid had just been through his latest amorous crisis and had still not recovered. One had to put up with a great deal from someone who was unlucky in love, and Vlad tolerated the unfortunate Leonid, treating him with magnanimous condescension. He already knew that this emotion was stronger even than Goethe's Faust, that it could conquer death . . .

From the pitch darkness of the front doorway loomed the vague outline of old Mrs. Durova:

"Are you boys planning to spend the night out here?" Lovingly she patted her son's shoulder. "Aren't you cold?"

"We boys are talking about God, mother." Leonid frowned. "Please don't disturb us."

With an aggrieved sigh Mrs. Durova obediently vanished back into the gloom, leaving them alone again with the night. The word of any of her offspring was as law to her; she had long since reduced the scope of her own interests to the limits of their hopes and fears. No other life existed for her. Fate had been unkind to her: of her two sons—one a sports journalist, the other an actor—both had turned out to be failures, her daughter-in-law spent almost all her time in the lunatic asylum, her grandsons were growing up timorous and sickly, yet despite all this, like a carthorse she continued to pull this wagonload of pain and lamentation, scorning malicious gossip and with her head held proudly high. A potent mixture of the blood of soldiers and circus artistes flowed in her unwithered veins.

"But what is God?" It was hard to put Vlad down; he had inherited his grandfather's obstinacy. "Is God a man or not?"

"Samsonov, you ask questions which could easily cause trouble for you one day. In this day and age curiosity is a criminal offense; beware of superfluous knowledge, Samsonov."

"You haven't answered my question, Leonid."

"Why are you so obstinate, Samsonov?"

"I want to know what God is."

"You'll come to a bad end, Samsonov."

"Leonid!"

"All right, all right!" He held up his hand in a defensive gesture. "Only don't curse me later; you're setting out on a dangerous path. As they say—you asked for it, Georges Dandin!"

"Well?"

"God is love."

"What else?"

"God is freedom."

"What sort of freedom?"

"The freedom to love."

"To love whom?"

"God—and therefore everything and everyone."

"Even fascists?"

"God doesn't know what they are. He only knows people, and to Him they are all equal."

"But is he a person?"

"That's more than enough for today," Leonid snapped wearily. "I've already given you plenty to think about, so shut up . . ."

He was silent, drawing his head into the blanket like a snail into its shell. I doubt, Leonid Vladimirovich, whether this conversation with you would have done him any good, had it not been for the meals, obtained on your special ration card at the actors' canteen in the Hermitage Gardens during that hungry year of 1942, which you shared equally with him like a brother. Those meals were probably his first communion with the Blessed Sacraments. He is still being drawn to his Faith and still seeking it, but that bread which was shared between the two of you will never be forgotten by him . . .

Suddenly the darkness at the end of the street was thrust aside, the bright light of a car's headlights and the hum of an engine came rushing toward them, lighting up in its path the rickety fences and darkened boxlike houses, the gnarled patterns of leafless trees, the dull patina on the gray cobblestones of the road. Soon a black Emka car braked almost soundlessly and pulled up at the gateway: Tselikovsky, a tenant from the second floor who was chauffeur to a

People's Commissar, had returned from his demanding work. During his several years in government service he had seen five bosses disappear into oblivion, and was now about to say farewell to the sixth. Tall, wiry, always flashily dressed and self-assured, he was regarded in the apartment house as an enviably good family man and provider.

"Hi, fellers!" His slim figure was sharply silhouetted in front of them, and an open pack of Kazbek cigarettes came floating toward Leonid. "Have a smoke, neighbor."

"You know I don't smoke."

"Go on, they're not mine, after all—I got them as a present."

"No, but thanks all the same."

"You're welcome . . . So long, fellers."

The chauffeur vanished through the doorway, and only the sound of his jaunty footsteps marked his progress upstairs.

How Vlad envied Tselikovsky in those days! If only *he* could grow up and get a job as chauffeur to a People's Commissar, drive home in a black Emka, offer Kazbeks to his neighbor, feeling himself smart, confident, handsome! He could not have foreseen it at the time, but the object of his envy would end his days, almost in Vlad's arms, as a miserable alcoholic, having drunk himself into a stupor on polishing fluid (or "Paulina Ivanovna," as it was ironically called), and that his wife and two sons would see him buried at the expense of the housing cooperative.

"There," announced Leonid gloomily, "goes a perfect example of the modern troglodyte. 'Clear the way—here I come . . .' that's his motto. He'll eat anything, not excluding human flesh."

Leonid fell silent and did not open his mouth again all evening.

Above them, at unimaginable heights, shone the autumn stars. Vlad stared up at their enigmatic twinkling and tried to guess which one of them was destined to be his next abode.

CHAPTER 12

On Soviet Constitution Day, in honor of the Most Just Constitution on Earth, Vlad was given twenty kopecks. Anyone who grew up fatherless in Sokolniki, as he did, will know that in 1940 twenty kopecks was a fortune. In those days a vast number of temptations awaited a nine-year-old with a capital sum of that size in his pocket. Of all the possibilities—two visits to the movies, three ice creams with wafers, or a piece of Tula gingerbread—he chose tangerines. Clutched to his chest, still slightly green around the stalk end, the four big fruits with their taut, pimply, aromatic skins shone through his fingers as he ran home through streets dusted by the first snowfall.

Ah! Tonka, Tonka, how many times afterward were your paths to cross, until that fall day when, on a tipper truck that happened to be going that way, he bore you away to the Preobrazhensky Cemetery, where you shared the fate of all Moscow's alcoholics—burial in an unmarked grave. But on that morning, like the neighborhood busybody that you were, you came rushing toward him and his tangerines, and he will never forget that meeting:

"Vladik, your father's come home!"

His twenty-kopeck present seemed to break into four equal, bright-orange parts, which rolled away across the first fall of December snow. And there was no power on earth which could gather them into his hands and into one whole again.

From the corner of the street to the doorway of the living room he was borne through space in a single gust of frosty air. And there, frozen into dumb silence on the threshold, he saw a man with graying hair, wearing a government-issue tunic, seated beside the radiator. The man was hunched up alongside the radiator as though he could never get completely warm, pressing himself against the ribbed cast-iron as though he wanted to melt into it.

Each of them had long since forgotten what the other looked like. But only too well did Vlad remember how, not long ago at a Council Meeting of his Pioneer Troop, in a voice ringing with self-importance, he had firmly announced: "I have no father!" If only he could have realized then, on that December morning, as he stood in the doorway and stared wordlessly at the visitor sitting by the radiator, how much that denial was to cost him, what price he would pay for his first betrayal! How was he to know that he too was already poised for the descent, through all its nine circles, of the same downward spiral that his father had just traversed? Out there, on prison-camp bunks in Eastern Siberia, in the savage cold of forced-labor logging camps, under an inhospitable sky in unsuccessful attempts to escape, he would remember it all and would weep for his sin in tears of blood, paying for it a threefold price.

As his father sat pressed against the warmth, his mother, without a trace of color in her face, fussed around the table and kept glancing imploringly toward Vlad's aunt as though trying to appease her. Like a stone statue his aunt sat rigidly on the edge of the divan, staring into space with dry eyes, and her stony look was charged with unconcealed accusation, challenge, and reproach. She and Vlad's mother knew everything about each other, but in his aunt's knowledge there lurked a violent force, and that force threatened to explode at any moment and to bury beneath it the first timid shoots of hope that were beginning to sprout in their home.

And the explosion would undoubtedly have occurred if, at the very moment when the first word was about to shatter that fragile silence, the door into the room had not been flung open and Tonka's Uncle Stepan appeared on the threshold—a big, bony man of about thirty with the look of a horse thief, not only visibly tipsy but clutching a bottle:

"From what I hear, seems like Alexei Samsonov has come home!"

Although unease flickered in his drink-blurred gypsy eyes, Dutch courage forbade him to show that he was afraid of being seen to associate with this dangerous visitor. "So I thought, if that's the case then a bottle's called for."

Stepan was in any case the only neighbor who dared to pay a call on them that day, and probably because of this, Vlad's mother, who had never harbored any particularly kind feelings toward him, was sufficiently moved to go out and fetch another bottle, followed by a third; on top of this she joined the men's drinking party and eventually even persuaded her sister to join in too. Temporary peace was restored within the family.

The cheerful conviviality gradually reached the point where it overflowed in song. When Stepan struck up his favorite song about the old robber chieftain Khaz-Bulat, Vlad's father chimed in with his faint but pleasing tenor, and in two-part harmony they began to lament the fate of the old man who had a young wife, but who refused to give her up to his young rival—not even for a horse, still less for his dagger and his rifle. They wept in sympathy for the old man, all unaware that six months later a piece of German lead would cure them of hangovers forever, one in the fighting around Sukhinichi, the other somewhere in the region of Lozovaya.

That night, for the first time, a separate bed was made up for Vlad on the floor. Until then he had always slept in his mother's bed. Above him, in the stuffy darkness atop the box spring, something went on which made his throat constrict with frenzied asphyxia. Still ignorant, he could only guess vaguely at what was happening up there, but the worm of latent hostility, even hatred, toward his father had crept into his tiny heart and was to lodge there forever. Vlad began to feel upon himself the burning armor of Oedipus, and his puny hand reached out, for the first time, to the ever-ready sword.

And thus, Katya, he was made a witness to your conception. Who could have guessed on that December night, when your spark first gleamed amid the dark of a shared apartment of fifteen square meters, in that apparently God-forsaken Moscow suburb, that thirty years later you would settle, never to return, in the sandy, stony kingdom of the Holy Land!

After a short silence, Vlad heard the muffled sound of their almost inaudible voices over his head:

"Won't you come with me, Fenya?" Then, beseechingly: "Won't you, Fenya?"

"No, Alexei, I'd rather put my head into a hole in the ice than go back to Uzlovaya. There's no life for me there."

"What's so special about Moscow, Fenya? We can make a life anywhere, if we just have our hands and a head on our shoulders."

"You can see for yourself where *your* head has got you. Be thankful that you're still alive."

"I wasn't the first and I won't be the last—they arrested everybody, one after the other."

"Not everybody. Others survived by keeping their mouths shut, but you always had to open it once too often."

"Let bygones be bygones, Fenya; it's time to start living now."

"You go by yourself, until your residence restriction is lifted, then when you come back we can live like human beings again."

"It'll be hard for me to have to live alone, now that I'm out . . ."

"You'll have your relations all around you."

"They're *your* relations, Fenya—they're Mikheyevs."

"The Mikheyevs have never had any quarrel with you, they'll look after you for a while."

"Won't you come, Fenya?" Then more softly and still more imploringly: "It was *you* I came back to, all the way from the Far East, not your relations."

"No, Alexei, I won't move out of Moscow."

"Oh Fenya, Fenya!"

"That's how it is."

"All right." Vlad's father's voice slowly filled with a hopeless weariness. "You know what suits you best, I suppose . . . Don't you get tired of living alone? You didn't manage to keep our little girl alive."

"I'm not a magician."

"You should have looked after her better."

"I did look after her . . ."

"Will you let me take Vlad?"

"Take him."

This was said inertly and without a trace of expression, as though they were discussing something absolutely worthless and trivial, and for that reason it cut Vlad to the quick. Vlad knew his mother well enough—a flabby, cold-blooded creature who all her life had imagined herself worthy of some better fate, and who invariably did her best to brush aside all superfluous care and exertion; yet the ease with which she agreed to be rid of him came as a shock even to Vlad. He was never able to forgive her for that. Life was soon to separate them for a long time, but when at the end of his unimaginable odyssey he saw this woman shortly before her death, she aroused in him nothing but bewilderment and pity.

Thus Vlad's fate was decided, and by the following evening a train was carrying him and his father toward the town of towns, that smoke-grimed graveyard of superannuated locomotives, that cradle of the tough and insatiable Mikheyev clan—Uzlovaya.

Outside the frost-covered window lurked the impenetrable night, in the niche above the door leading into the next car a lantern flame slowly flickered, giving off a faint, cosy crackle from its guttering wick. There was a smell of sheepskin, stale bread, and tobacco. Immediately opposite Vlad sat his father, awake but pensive; in the unsteady, reflected light of the lantern flame his expression seemed softer and easier to comprehend than in daylight.

"Go to sleep . . . go to sleep," he would murmur from time to time, and as he spoke his lackluster eyes would liven a little. "It won't be long now."

"Shall we go straight to Grandpa when we arrive?" To Vlad this was the most important, the most agonizing question of the moment, which gave him no rest and kept him awake. "Shall we, Dad?"

"Yes, we will . . . Go to sleep now."

Vlad fell asleep and dreamed of his grandfather Saviely, in his railroad uniform with his conductor's satchel over his shoulder. The old man was walking down the gangway of their car, but instead of his ticket punch he was holding a piece of brown Tula gingerbread the size of a briefcase. "Dear old Grandpa," Vlad thought gratefully as he plunged into unconsciousness, "I wonder where he got such a big one?"

CHAPTER 13

Hail and farewell, my beloved grandfather Saviely Mikheyev! Everything in me that is human I have from you, a priceless gift for which no means of payment has ever been devised.

So tell me now, dear comrade Saviely Mikheyev, how it happened that from you, from a rootstock in which there would seem not to be the slightest blemish, there grew forth that disgusting, reptilian brood whose name is now legion. When did it happen—and what was it that you failed to give them of those qualities which, beyond all measure, you passed on to others? Or were they simply spawned like maggots, without inheriting a single one of your genes, a single hereditary characteristic? Sloughing off their sweaty cocoons, they hatched out and crawled about the earth in the guise of prison-camp guards and wardens, idle big-mouths in safe jobs, bureaucratic hair-splitters, jacks-in-office, and professional stool pigeons; all those rail-road officials, checkweighmen, fixers, hustlers, bathhouse attendants, ticket collectors, policemen, and police informers. Among them were some rare mutants with traces of humanity, but they invariably ended up in prison or victims of delirium tremens. Where does this all connect with you, Saviely Mikheyev? How does it square with any laws made by man or God? After your death, this horde descended for just long enough to divide up your few modest possessions and to fight at the wake over your half-tumbledown cottage. That done,

they felt their duty to you had been discharged, and lurched drunkenly back to their homes, leaving your grave to the tender mercies
of the first spring floods. Your burial place has long since ceased to
exist, Saviely Mikheyev. Twenty years later I spent a great deal of
time searching for it among the bushes in the cemetery, in the hope
that by some miracle I might find traces of it; but my cramped heart
had no room for a miracle; I could not hear your call, and I found
the usual way of escape from awareness of my own fated impotence:
I drank myself stupid and made no further efforts to find you. God
forbid, grandfather, that I should count myself in any way better
than those others! There is not much of the Samsonovs in me. I am
a Mikheyev—another vile descendant of that clan, an exact copy of
their besetting sins, barely touched by God's grace; but there is one
thing to which I can swear without fear: I want to be better and I
will be better, no matter what it may cost me. Now as I draw up a
balance of the past, I realize that each of us Mikheyevs bears a cross
according to his deserts; that full retribution is exacted from us for
each hidden sin, each overt transgression—and may the judgment of
the Almighty be wrought upon us to the full! But as long as I live
there is one thing I shall never comprehend: when He inflicted us
upon you, my dear comrade Mikheyev, my unforgettable grandfather, what was He punishing you for?

Now and again, I admit, I catch some flicker of a meaning, like
twilight through a glass darkly, but no more than that, no more . . .

CHAPTER 14

The old man met his unexpected visitors with no particular enthusiasm. The long-standing fondness which Mikheyev Senior cherished for his grandson did not mollify his even longer-standing dislike of his own son-in-law. Nowadays it may seem absurd—our country is slowly but surely coming to its senses, thank God—but in those days leanings toward syndicalism in the trade unions or, at the other end of the political spectrum, sympathy for the Workers' Opposition could make even close relatives into sworn enemies. It is true that the initiative in this perennial feud was always taken by the old man: Vlad's father, compliant by nature, would only ever defend himself, but in one way or another their every encounter turned into a merciless duel.

It might have seemed that there was nothing to choose between them: both men, each for his own deviation, had served his sentence awarded by the courts and had retired from political activism, but even so the conversation at table was sticky.

"Yes," mumbled old Saviely, staring fixedly into his half-empty glass of cooling tea. "Your lot went too far, so you copped it. They know what they're doing in Moscow—wouldn't put people behind bars for nothing . . ."

"Yes, plenty of them were rounded up," Vlad's father agreed listlessly, but there lurked a profound sadness in his vacant look as he stared at the frost patterns on the window. "And so many who went with me will never come back . . ."

"They know what they're doing." Saviely continued to stare at the bottom of his glass. "The Soviet people has a good head on its shoulders."

"I suppose so . . ."

Like a borzoi dog scenting its quarry, in a flash the old man pricked up his ears and fixed his visitor straight in the eye with a demanding stare:

"And just what do you mean by that, son-in-law?"

"See here, father-in-law"—Vlad's father turned on old Saviely with unexpected ferocity—"you spent a couple of years in the local cooler, I hear, and all it did to you was make you go bald. Well, you try taking a trip out to Siberia in cattle cars and barges before you start laying down the law about who should be put behind bars and who shouldn't."

"I can see"—Vlad recognized the tremor of intransigent obstinacy that was causing the old man to shake—"that you can't straighten a hunchback . . ."

"Don't you hunchback me!" Cutting him off, Vlad's father stood up. "Start scratching your own back first, you may find a bump there. Have you ever been made to stand 'statue' for twenty-four hours in a box cell? Were you ever the hundred-and-eighteenth to be shoved into a cell meant for twenty men? Were you ever shipped in a cattle car for a week without water? Don't you think, maybe, they've been finding too many 'enemies of the people' lately?"

"Now see here, Alexei, God knows I . . ."

"I'm not staying here, old man, and that's that." His father was already tugging at Vlad. "We've lived a lifetime without you, and we'll manage for the rest of our days without you, too. Come on, son; we're done visiting here and now it's time to go. We'll go to Sychevka, you can finish your night's sleep there."

Vlad felt so warm and comfortable in the familiar depths of his grandfather's vast walnut-wood bed that he had no wish to go out into the snowy gloom of a December morning; but his father's rough hands were exerting their implacable control over him and in submission to their firm will he obediently got up, allowed himself to be encased in his winter wrappings, and set off behind his father toward the door.

At once his grandfather's bad temper of a moment ago disap-

peared without a trace. With a nimbleness uncharacteristic of his
bulky frame, he leaped out from behind the table to block their
path, saying in a breaking, tremulous voice:

"Don't, Alexei—stop, stop . . . We're not children, we had a spat,
and now let's make it up—it's all in the family, after all . . . Have a
heart, Alexei, you can't take the child out in weather like this!"

"No, Saviely, old fellow." Pushing his son in front of him, he had
already reached the porch. "I'm fed up with listening to you. I've
had enough. It's someone else's turn to put up with you now. It's
been nice meeting you, but I have other fish to fry, as they say."

As they emerged into the freezing cold of a wintry sunrise and
crossed the front yard, Vlad could not help turning around. His
heart stood still, suspended on a thin, thin thread above a yawning
abyss: his grandfather was standing in the porch—tall, hunched, his
bare feet in felt slippers above which dangled the dirty tapes of his
long winter underpants, and from the way he stood, leaning in a
slightly lopsided stance against the doorpost, it was only too plain to
see how sick and old he was . . .

Nowadays, "at midpoint on the pathway of my life" and more, I
am not ashamed of sounding sentimental. Saviely, my grandfather,
whom I remember with such pain and sadness, many burdens since
then have weighed down my soul, but the one which you laid upon
me that December morning has remained to this day the heaviest of
them all.

The morning light was gathering over the town in a gray-blue
mist, through which the dull crimson disk of the sun shone toward
them. The earth, covered with the first snow, breathed gently and
mysteriously. Here and there the first sled track was spattered with
dark-green knobs of horse dung, around which sparrows were already
swarming and quarreling for possession. The immediate pain had
abated and withdrawn to somewhere in the very depths of Vlad's
soul, and as he strove to measure his stride to his father's steady,
slightly bow-legged gait, Vlad gradually thawed out and was filled
with a sense of mischievous adventure. He filled his lungs with the
frosty dawn air, and everything around him—the roadway smelling of
horse dung, the cold sunlight—became linked, too, with the delicious
proximity of the man walking beside him.

"Dad, is it far to Sychevka?" Having spent every summer at his
grandfather's house, Vlad knew, of course, where Sychevka was and

how long it took to walk there, but talking to his father was fun, and
so he used any excuse to ask a question. "Is it about five kilometers?"

"Not much more . . . we'll be there soon."

"And which ones of our family are there?"

"Your uncle . . . your aunt, too . . . and your great-uncle, who
keeps bees."

"Are they all Samsonovs?"

"Almost all—about half the village."

"Are there that many Samsonovs?"

"Yes, lots."

"And I'm one too . . ."

"Of course you are!"

"I like that!"

"And so you should . . ."

Chatting inconsequentially as they followed the winding sled
tracks, this first experience of male companionship between them
created something which suddenly made the grim, lowering outside
world into a less threatening place, and one which for a while became kinder and more welcoming.

The first cottage of Sychevka, a village straddling a ridge above a
deep gully, floated toward them out of the thinning mist, and here
Vlad's father stopped and caught his breath:

"Wait, son . . . Let me stop and think for a moment."

But he did not have long to think. Out of the dark, wide-open
doorway of a cowshed in front of the cottage there came toward
them a thin, unshaven peasant in a ragged sheepskin jacket. The
nearer he drew the more hesitant became the movement of his legs
in their tattered felt boots. About five paces short of them he
stopped, pulled the scrap of sheepskin from his head, and stood
stock still. Tears poured silently down through the stubble on his
face, and from his chapped lips the hot, breathless words flowed out,
tumbling and confused:

"It's you . . . Cousin . . . Cousin Alexei . . . Alyosha . . . you're
. . . you're alive!"

CHAPTER 15

Carefully and fastidiously the horse beneath Vlad lowered itself into the water. In the transparent mirror of the lake, the July sky, dotted here and there with feathery clouds, rocked and quivered in faint ripples. The horse was a chestnut, almost red, and its bright color blindingly outshone the matt gleam of the lake surface underneath it, the rarefied sky-blue above, and the triumphant green of the surrounding grass.

One day, an eternity later, in an empty, sun-drenched exhibition hall he would be confronted by Petrov-Vodkin's gorgeous painting "Watering the Red Horse"; he would feel time break off and spiral backward up the funnel of the past and, for one solitary but rapturous moment, find himself back there, on that July day by the lake, riding the obedient Orlik . . .

It was a day like any other, resembling the previous day down to the smallest detail, but a spider's web of alarm had overlain its deceptive serenity, leaving a foretaste of impending loss on Vlad's lips. In the first days of war the male half of the town and its environs had noticeably thinned out, and by the middle of July it was the turn of the wagon-train drivers to be drafted, of which Alexei Samsonov was among the first to receive his mobilization order. On that morning he returned earlier than usual from the mine where he worked as an assistant on the surface, and avoiding the boy's gaze he announced to Vlad:

"I'm going away to join the Army, son. You must go back to your mother."

"I don't want to," Vlad objected. The mere thought of having to go home, to the stinking bedlam of their communal kitchen, to his mother's hateful lectures on his behavior and to his aunt's hostility, produced in him a sharp attack of revulsion and nausea. "I'll stay with Grandfather."

As Vlad said this he stopped short. His father stared hard at him, radiating such bitterness and condescending scorn that his resistance faltered and he capitulated:

"All right, I'll go . . ."

And at that moment he was seared by the panic-stricken certainty that his father knew everything about him. Everything, including his rejection of his father at school. And that sudden guess somehow flattened, crushed Vlad. He saw himself like an insect pinned to the spot, racked through and through by intense pain: suddenly, in his still immature body, he was physically feeling the price that had to be paid for treachery. Bearing it proved to be beyond his powers, and then all the agony that filled him overflowed in one long, despairing cry, followed by collapse into unconsciousness.

Vlad came to his senses in the village of Bibikovo, whither all the mobilized wagon drivers from the entire region had been ordered to report, each one bringing a horse. He was lying in a cart on top of a sheaf of new-mown hay; a cloudless sky arched above him, and in the very middle of it a skylark was singing a paean to summer. Life went on, and it was worth living.

"Had a good sleep?" His father's embarrassed face shut out the sky above his eyes. "Like to come and water the horse with me?" Calloused hands picked him up and held him high over the ground. "You're not afraid?"

"No." In an ecstasy of gratitude and excitement, he felt the warm leather of the saddle beneath him. "Not a bit."

"Let's go then . . . Giddap, Orlik."

His father walked alongside, his rough palm touching Vlad's foot, and that ride to the nearest pond outside the village reconciled them forever. As they passed through the broad, flat countryside, it flowed away before them in the heat, giving the surroundings a smoky, unsteady look. The thatched roofs of distant villages, framed in the dark-green lace-like foliage of apple trees and acacias, looked like yellow boats on green lakes as they bobbed on the waves of the July heat haze. An invisible whirring swarmed in the grass, sawing through the dense motionless air from all sides. At every step the path narrowed and grew smaller until finally it merged into the foreshore of the lake.

"Now you go ahead on your own," said Vlad's father, "and I'll watch."

The horse under Vlad advanced toward the water, took one step, then another, and a third, until it was up to its belly in water. A faint shiver rippled across the horse's rump, then it gave a snort and at once set off, fast and smoothly, to swim across the little lake. First the water flowed over Vlad's ankles, his calves, and then reached his hips, at which his heart almost stopped with excitement and suddenly began to leap very rapidly and unevenly. The shore ahead seemed to recede unexpectedly, but the next minute it started to move toward him again. Drums started to beat a tattoo in his temples for his first victory over Fear and the Unknown. His own soul had submitted to his bidding and, in being tamed, became conscious of itself and its own might.

He was thrilled with himself, and the excitement at his own fearlessness made him proudly turn around: how am I doing? He had never seen his father looking like this before. Arms akimbo, he was standing up to his knees in the water, and his shoulders, suddenly looking much younger, were shaking with laughter.

"Well done, Vladka!" he shouted, breathless with laughing so much. "Hold tight, don't be scared! D'you hear?"

"Uh-huh." Vlad's teeth chattered triumphantly. "I'm holding on."

"You okay?"

"Uh-huh."

"Want any help?"

"No . . ."

"Will you make it on your own?"

"Yes . . ."

"Be brave, Vlad—death or glory! Up the Russians!"

"Uh-huh—sure thing . . ."

They reached Bibikovo as bugles were sounding the "Assembly." The village was nothing but a babel of confused noise and weeping, counterpointed by the neighing of horses. From the steps of the village soviet building, a captain from Military District Headquarters was peering shortsightedly at a notebook and calling out names in a hoarse voice:

"Grishin, Pyotr Nefedovich?"

"Present!"

"Zaitsev, Grigory Philippovich?"

"Here!"

"Skakalkin, Nefed Parfyonovich?"

"Yes."

"Samsonov . . ."

"Here, here," his father called out hastily as he backed Orlik between the shafts. "Where must I go?"

Wriggling his rump, Orlik snorted restively, and in his nervous, velvety eyes were reflected the cloudless sky, acacias in front of the cottages, and the seething herd of horses all around. Pushing between the wagons came Uncle Tikhon, Vlad's father's cousin, the same one who had greeted them at the edge of the village last winter. He made his way toward them, holding in his outstretched hands—as if bearing bread and salt to offer to guests—a peaked cap full to the brim with eggs. On his unshaven features was an embarrassed smile, as though he were ashamed of his fragile burden.

"There you are." He carefully placed his hand on the side of the cart and winked ingratiatingly at Vlad. "You may like these for the journey. Straight out of the nest."

Still bearing traces of chicken dung on their warm shells, the pile of eggs loomed large to Vlad, and his memory stored away the sight, never to be forgotten. Long afterward his inward eye would catch occasionally glimpses of those eggshells, their matt surface spattered with bird droppings, held by two gnarled hands crisscrossed with a mesh of prominent veins.

"Now you must do what your uncle says, Vladka." Vlad's father went over to his cousin and put an arm around him. "He'll put you on the train to Moscow tomorrow." Then warmly and confidingly he added: "I'll be back and I'll come and fetch you again."

From the village soviet the captain's voice shrieked out on the highest note he could muster:

"Move off!"

The whirlpool of horses slowly straightened itself out, surged off toward the road at the end of the village, to be followed by a loud wailing sound arising from every house and yard: the countryside was bidding farewell to its breadwinners. Ahead, mounted unsteadily on a skewbald stallion, bobbed the puny figure of the captain, who glanced backward from time to time to shout a hoarse command:

"Don't spread out! Don't spread out—how many times must I tell you! Keep in line, damn you, keep in line!"

The ride and the loading up that followed left only a vague impression in Vlad's mind. Occasionally the mingled smells of horse dung and hay will stir up blurred recollections of that departure. But the moment when the train started to pull away from the platform has remained imprinted on his soul with indestructible clarity. The figure of his father leaning over the railing at the end of a passenger car stood out for a few moments, bathed in copperish red by the sunset, only to vanish and fly away around the first curve. The last thing that Vlad remembered was his father's smile—fleeting and somehow slightly guilty.

Nowadays it is hard for Vlad to remember what his father looked like. Time refuses to give back what is dearest to us from the past, in order to accustom us to the silence of our ultimate aloneness. But something of Samsonov Senior remained in his son; as an unspoken parting gift he had bequeathed to Vlad one simple, divine truth: when a man betrays another, first and foremost he betrays himself. And that truth is a worthwhile legacy . . .

"Come on, let's go"—Tikhon's stiff fingers touched Vlad's shoulder—"or we won't be back before dark."

As they emerged onto the station square, amid the motley crowd Vlad saw his grandfather. He was standing with his back leaning against a billboard, and from his unusually pronounced stoop it was easy to guess that he had already been standing there for a long time, alone and disregarded.

"All right, off you go." Tikhon turned away understandingly and let go of Vlad's hand. "I guess you two are pretty well inseparable, even though one's old and the other's young . . ."

Filled with happiness and pity, Vlad rushed headlong across the square and, in full flight, buried his head in the old man's stomach:

"Granddad . . . I don't want to go home . . . I want to stay with you, Granddad!"

Unsteadily his grandfather stroked Vlad's freshly shorn crew-cut, calming him in a hoarse, wheezing voice:

"Of course . . . of course you can stay . . . Did you think I'd let you go? I'll never let you go, you silly young thing."

Firmly holding hands, they set off, and that evening life to Vlad seemed full of hope and great significance. Oh, how he loved you, grandfather Saviely!

CHAPTER 16

Abandoning towns and villages for purely strategic reasons, the Soviet forces successfully pushed deep into the continent. The Army's gallant commanders, the heroes of Eastern Poland (occupied without a shot being fired), of Moldavia (ditto) and of Khalkhin-Gol (six Soviet divisions against two Japanese divisions), galloped full speed ahead of their troops, well provided with optimistic communiqués and a suit of civilian clothes "just in case." "Our armor's tough, our tanks are fast" . . . "We'll smash the enemy on his own territory" . . . "Any day now a proletarian revolution will break out on the enemy's home front" . . . *"Die rote Front!"* . . . *"¡No pasarán!"* . . .

And in those days thousands of hastily mobilized youths clustered like puppies around the few regular soldiers—themselves hopelessly lost—as they wandered through the woods and forests of Western Russia in the vain hope of breaking out and getting back to their own lines. Many, many of them, caught in German encirclement, will soon enter upon their fated ordeal in prisoner-of-war camps between the Vistula and the English Channel, later to be scattered abroad over five continents in search of the uncertain rewards of an émigré's life; even so, they will be the envy of those who do return to the Soviet Union, huddling for warmth over inadequate fires in the forests of the Far North or slowly dying in the wooden huts of innumerable exile settlements.

But that was yet to come; now the country was facing its first winter of war, in which Vlad and his grandfather were being carried away along the circuitous, tortuous routes of the Great Evacuation in a freight car, loaded with the archives of the Uzlovaya railroad depot and hitched on behind a string of locomotives.

Moving at a snail's pace, the extraordinary train—eight locomotives and two cars—crawled across the snowbound wastes, stopping for days on end in the blind alleys of nameless sidings. At big stations the car was besieged by refugees who offered everything they had, even piles of gold, for a ride; they wept and abased themselves, but old Saviely was adamant: no unauthorized passengers could travel along with government property. Sometimes, as though ashamed of his enforced harshness, he would excuse himself:

"Be reasonable—there won't be a general retreat, but I'm carrying secret documents, and if anything happens to them my head will roll, old man though I am. Or supposing, which God forbid, that some infection broke out and you got sick? What would I do with you then? If I take one, how can I refuse the others?"

In Penza they got well and truly stuck. Vlad's grandfather disappeared from morning till evening, leaving no stone unturned as he besieged the railroad offices with requests for an unscheduled dispatch order, but his efforts were clearly unsuccessful, because the string of engines with its two heated freight cars at the tail end did not move for two weeks. Left to his own devices, for days on end Vlad loafed despondently up and down the length of the train in an agony of boredom and inactivity. His only amusement—climbing on the locomotive footplates—had long since lost its attraction, and he was usually at a loss to know what to do with himself at their stopping places.

One foggy frosty morning, however, wandering aimlessly around the train, he saw a young girl, muffled up to the eyebrows in an old angora shawl. Tall, shod in felt boots that were too big for her, she was standing near the car used by the locomotive crews, stamping her feet for warmth and looking around her with interest.

"Who are you?" Vlad was so surprised that he spluttered as he blurted out his question. "What train are you from?"

"We've come from Ozherelye." Her snub nose was tilted challengingly upward. "So what?"

"Oh, nothing . . . I was just asking."

"Curiosity killed the cat." She gave a cheerful laugh and launched into eager explanation: "My daddy got sick here, so they took us off the train. We might have sat here for ever and ever, only my daddy met some railroad engineers he knew, and they put us in their car . . . You must be the boy who's traveling with the old man. The engineers told us about you. Your name's Vladka, isn't it?"

"Yes, that's right . . . What's yours?"

"Tanya. I'm Tanya Sirotkin."

"What grade are you in?"

"Sixth grade. What's yours?"

"Fifth," Vlad lied. It would have been too humiliating to admit that he was two grades below her. "I missed a year, 'cos I got sick."

"You're very small for your age!"

"Just because you look like a bean pole," he spluttered, "it's nothing to brag about!"

She was not offended, and even seemed a little flattered:

"Yes, I am tall. We're all long and thin in our family. It's hereditary, and that's that."

"Oh, I didn't mean anything." Vlad was mollified by her relaxed response. "I wasn't teasing—you're just tall, that's all."

"Is there just the two of you in one whole car?"

"Uh-huh." Vlad adopted a slight air of importance. "No one's allowed to travel with us, because we're carrying secret documents."

"Do you have any books?"

"No . . . Just papers, ledgers, and suchlike. They're sealed, too."

"Can I have a look?"

"Sure, if you want to."

"Suppose your grandfather turns up and finds us?"

"No chance, he won't be back till evening . . . Come on . . ."

How irrevocably far away it is, that pallid winter's day, reeking with the acrid stench of coal smoke. Even now there are still times when that smell tickles his throat . . .

Beside the cheerfully roaring stove she peeled herself out of her cocoonlike shawl, and turned out to be a girl with boyishly short-cropped hair and the features of a grown woman—at once gentle and mocking. Between her thin fingers, spread out toward the fire, could be seen the remaining scabs from a recent attack of chickenpox. The little mounds of her incipient breasts were clearly outlined under the faded cotton dress that showed beneath the open front of her short, padded overcoat. Like a blue thread, a vein throbbed steadily in her thin little neck. The flickering light and shade of the flames played over her, giving the girl an enigmatic, disembodied look.

As Vlad cast furtive glances at her, he was alarmed to notice his inability to stop himself blushing and growing hot, which made him feel slightly dizzy and took his breath away. The temptation to touch her—her chickenpox scars, the bumps under her dress, the vein in her neck—became unbearable. He tried to force himself not to look in her direction, but in the end, in spite of himself, he could not help constantly glancing at her.

"Isn't it rather crowded for you, sharing a car with the engineers?" After a protracted silence, this was the first remark that came into his head. "After all, there's an awful lot of them."

"Yes, it is crowded, but we don't mind," she answered cheerfully, tossing her head. "Besides, it's fun."

"I'm afraid of men when they're drunk." Talking brought him no relief, and he felt himself choking. "They shout so much."

"Let them shout—I don't mind."

"They fight, too."

"I like it when men fight."

"You might get hurt."

"The man isn't born yet who'd do me harm."

"I wouldn't be too sure of that."

"Just let 'em try."

"Aren't you just a little bit afraid?"

"No."

"Aren't you afraid at night?" He suddenly stared hard at her and immediately turned away, dazzled by the look of her. "In the dark?"

"Not a bit."

"Not even looking down from a bridge?"

"Course not!"

"You're funny . . ."

"How am I funny?"

"Well, you're not like a girl . . ."

"What a thing to say!" Flattered, the girl blushed, and as she caught Vlad's glance she unexpectedly grasped his hand. "I suppose you haven't been friends with girls before, have you?"

"Why do you think so?" He almost fainted. "I'm not a little boy any more, you know."

"Oh yes, you are." She lightly placed the palm of his hand on her

knee. "You don't know how to play with girls yet." He felt himself
collapsing, falling into an abyss. "Come closer."

She drew him confidently to her, and at once the waking world
around him melted into a fog of delirium. Like a blind kitten, moan-
ing slightly and drenched with sweat, Vlad crawled over her in a vain
attempt to find the source of his longing, an unquenchable ache
throbbing under his heart and somewhere below the belt. He groaned
aloud. His flesh exploded and melted like lava stirring within the
tiny volcano of his puny body. Countless multicolored rainbows
floated in an endless succession before his eyes.

When finally he fell away from her, unassuaged and half-
suffocated, racked by the shame of his still unspent chastity, he could
only find the strength to burst into soundless but devastating tears:

"Go away."

"Why, what's the matter?"

"Go away, I say!"

"What a little fool you are, to get so upset."

"Go away, go away."

"What's wrong—are you sick, or something?" A note of condescending scorn came into her voice. "I didn't force myself on you—it
was you who asked me in." A cold blast blew in through the open
door. "Your mother's milk's still wet on your lips, you'd better go back
to her . . ."

The noise of the door being slammed and the crunch of her rapidly departing footsteps came to him as though from oblivion . . .

How he wept then—wept at having been hurt and humiliated,
wept at his own fear and weakness. Never before and never since was
he made to feel such disgust at himself and at life in general. And
for years the agony that he went through then left in him a
suppressed though deeply painful mistrust of women, of their inexplicable power over him, of that incompatibility which lurked menacingly in every one of them.

CHAPTER 17

Through barely open eyelids, the first thing that Vlad could discern from his bed on the top bunk were the crowns of two gray heads, bent over the dying stove. One, with a crew-cut, was his grandfather's head; the other, fringed with an untidy cluster of matted curls, belonged to a stranger. Gradually the sense of the conversation that was going on below him began to penetrate his consciousness:

"Ah, Saviely, I gave up thinking about all that long ago!" In a voice muffled by a cold, the curly-haired man was making a thinly veiled effort to be ingratiating. "I'm no fighter. When you're young you'll do anything, and not give it a thought, as you well know, but by the time you've acquired grandchildren, it's time to stop tilting at windmills, believe me."

"You mean you think the revolution was just tilting at windmills?" The old man did not care for jokes on such a sensitive topic. "Or what *do* you mean?"

"God forbid, Saviely, God forbid that I should suggest any such thing!" He clasped his small hands. "I just meant that there's a time and a place for everything, and we old men should know what our place is."

"Yes, Lazar, I can see you really have given up—in every way. But when I think what a tiger you once were, how much counterrevolutionary blood you shed! What's become of the Lazar I once knew?"

"Gone with the wind, Saviely." The visitor sighed miserably. "Yes
. . . our enemies were real enough in those days . . . But I was the
hunter then; now I'm the one they're hunting. It makes a slight
difference, you know."

"Who on earth would want to hunt *you* down, Lazar?"

"Ever heard of Hitler, Saviely? That's who." Lazar had leaped to
his feet in an excess of emotion. "He swore to hang all Jews and all
Communist Party members, so I stand condemned on both counts.
I'm not alone, either; I have three children, you see, not to mention
grandchildren. And I'm just tired of all the shooting."

"Where are you and your family headed?"

"We're going to try and settle somewhere in Central Asia, then
we'll see what turns up. Right now the main thing is to hold out
through this winter; after that things will get easier. In a warm cli-
mate my wife will get back to her old form again. She's a remarkable
woman—you remember her, I hope?"

"I should think so!" the old man grunted. "Thanks to her, I was
almost put up against a wall myself."

"Ah, Saviely Anufrievich, we should let bygones be bygones!" The
visitor made a point of calling Vlad's grandfather by his full name
and patronymic, as if on purpose to emphasize his dependence upon
him. "We were all maximalists in those days. Believe me, Rosa my
wife has paid dearly for the emotions of our youth; she can hardly
move, and I have to push her everywhere, like a child, in a wheelchair
. . . If you could only take us with you, even if only as far as
Kuibyshev!"

"You don't need to persuade me, Lazar," the old man sighed
glumly. "Of course I'll take you, I'm not a monster."

"But Savva, you said"—as he relaxed the visitor slipped imperceptibly into the familiar form of address—"that you were carrying
secret documents."

Wheezing, Vlad's grandfather stood up:

"That's enough, Lazar, let's stop fooling around. You weren't playing marbles when you were in the Cheka. Don't you realize that
these so-called secret documents are half a joke and half a load of
trash? Go ahead and bring your horde in here."

"I knew you would, Savva . . ."

"Go on, before I change my mind."

"I'll be back before you can turn around."

A moment later it was as if the visitor had been swept out of the car—a gray blur of tousled hair, spurred on by the wind of success . . .

Did Vlad know his grandfather? He thought he knew him. Having spent all his summer holidays with the old man, Vlad had grown used to the unsociable manner with which he fended off the importunate demands of those around him. Having settled on his own particular way of treating people, he kept to it firmly and undeviatingly, often even against the promptings of his conscience. He practically never had any dealings with his children, limiting himself to short visits at holidays. He possessed no friends, and showed no desire to acquire any. The only chink in his psychological armor was his weakness for Vlad, which the latter, with typical childish egotism, exploited to the full, regarding his grandfather almost as his personal property. Now, for the first time since Vlad had known him, the old man had clearly broken what had always seemed to be a lifetime's rule; in this Vlad sensed a threat to his own undivided power over his grandfather, and for this reason he took up in advance an attitude of barely concealed hostility toward their new traveling companions.

They were not long in coming. Although their irruption was almost noiseless, it was impressive. They burst into the car like some natural disaster, spread themselves everywhere, and filled the whole place with their presence. From every corner a pair of melancholy eyes shone in Vlad's direction, burning him with their look of piercing reproach.

The place beside the stove was firmly occupied by the wheelchair of Lazar's paralyzed wife, Rosa Yakovlevna, a peevish old woman with a tight bun of coarse gray hair, who looked like a reanimated mummy. She spent her days ceaselessly knitting and bickering with her husband.

"That, of course, is beyond your capability," she would say to him in greeting when he returned empty-handed from a long search for food. "Naturally it is something that only I could manage to do. You can't even piss without someone to help you."

"Rosa!" Rushing to her side, he whispered imploringly: "Control yourself—there are children here!"

"Yes, producing children is all you *can* do; you're incapable of feeding them. My God, if only I had known what I was letting myself in for when I married you. And to think that for you I gave up my youth and innocence."

"Rosa, I took you when you already had a child. So what on earth do you mean by 'youth and innocence'?"

"I always knew you were a petty bourgeois at heart, and that you only joined the cause of the revolution to save your own skin."

"Who recommended you for Party membership, Rosa—remember?"

"That was pure self-interest on your part. You did it so that I would live with you—you bourgeois egotist!"

"It was *you* who wanted to live with me, Rosa."

"More fool you, in that case."

"Where's your logic, Rosa?"

"The hell with logic!" she burst out. "It would be more to the point if you would kindly tell me how you're going to feed this horde!" Like a general reviewing the troops before a battle, she swept her brood with a demanding glare. "How, I ask you?"

"Somehow, Rosa, somehow. Our comrades will help us."

She seemed only to have been waiting for this remark, which reduced her to ultimate fury:

" 'Comrades'! Ha, ha, ha! And where are they, these comrades of yours? I can assure you that they are already far in the rear, enthusiastically defending the achievements of the revolution in government canteens, while you and your children are dying of hunger."

"Rosa, why do you exaggerate so much?"

"I ask you—just look at him!" She turned to Saviely for support. "Acts as if he was Croesus, or at least a Rothschild. He thinks they'll put up a monument to him for going hungry. What do you think, comrade Mikheyev?"

In reply the latter only coughed in embarrassment and turned away, but she needed no answer.

"Oh, I forgot, you and he are two of a kind." She rounded on Saviely. "It was a pity, dear comrade, that I didn't complete that investigation on you and have you put up against a wall. You deserved it, when all's said and done."

"That's all past and forgotten, Rosa Yakovlevna," said the old man evasively, sidling toward the door. "Why bring it up at a time like this?"

"Ah yes, my dear comrade Mikheyev—you deserved it all right! You were not only concealing sabotage, but you were playing along with the aristocrats of the railroad trade union, you miserable liberal!" Having dealt with his grandfather, she turned to Vlad. "Wretched child, to be related to a degenerate like that." Squinting at him appraisingly, she sighed heavily. "You have an interesting face, my child. You'll either be a rogue or a politician—which incidentally is one and the same thing."

She was silent, as though withdrawing into herself. The knitting needles in her fingers clicked unceasingly, looping stitch after stitch, and one might have imagined that she was profoundly satisfied with herself, had it not been for the mocking grin which hovered about the furrows around her lips, and which contradicted everything that she had just said: inscrutable are the ways of female logic!

Looking like a round, goggle-eyed loaf of bread, Rosa's eldest grandson Lyovka waddled over to Vlad with his inseparable chessboard under his arm:

"Shall we play?"

Chess constituted the meaning of existence for Lyovka. He went to bed with it and got up with it in the morning. At any time of the day he could be found either carrying his chessboard or sitting in front of it, and would constantly be playing innumerable variants against himself. No sooner had he taught Vlad the moves than Lyovka made him his obligatory partner. In fact, Vlad was more of a spectator at the game than a player. Logically and pedantically Lyovka would correct every one of Vlad's blunders, and was particularly satisfied when, in this way, he lost to himself.

As they set out the chessmen, Vlad could not restrain himself and said in a malicious undertone, which fortunately could not be heard down below:

"She's vicious, your grandma—like a snake."

Lyovka shot him a brief, withering glance and immediately looked down again:

"Your move."

"She's vicious, I tell you."

"You mustn't say that, Vladik."

"Well, she is."

"You can see she's sick."

"My grandpa's a very sick man, too."

"Your move, Vladik."

"You haven't answered me . . ."

"She's in a bad way, Vladik, very bad."

"Fancy that!"

"You . . . you . . ." Tears choked him, his hands shook and

twitched. "How could you!" Nervously he knocked over the chessmen and jumped down from the bunk. "I'm not going to talk to you again!"

Vlad merely shrugged his shoulders and turned over onto his side, as much as to say, "Please yourself."

That night Vlad was woken up by a sharp jerk: the car was moving, and jolting slightly over the track joints. Outside the small window the freezing December fog was flowing past, pierced here and there by stars. The feeble flame from the stove threw out a fan of flickering shadows. Made indistinct by the movement of the train and the half dark, a whispered conversation was in progress around the stove:

"You know perfectly well, Lazar, that I won't survive the journey," sighed the old woman, with uncharacteristic gentleness. "We're not children. Why deceive ourselves?"

"You need warmth, and then everything will be different." His voice expressed the utmost pain and tenderness. "And then—the war will be over soon."

"Do you think so?"

"Of course!"

"You always were an optimist, Lazar. Only don't forget that the Germans are just outside Moscow."

"All will be well, you'll see."

"The chief thing is that all should be well for our children."

"And that's exactly why you must hold on."

"What about you?"

"I must too . . . for your sake."

"Oh, Lazar, Lazar, we're already old!"

"You're not."

"You're incorrigible."

"For your sake, Rosa."

"Forgive me, Lazar"—her voice broke off—"but this awful pain!"

"I know, Rosa . . . I know . . . If only I could suffer it instead of you! Try and go to sleep."

"How I love you, Lazar . . ."

"Go to sleep . . . I'll sit awhile beside you."

"Lazar . . ."

"Go to sleep . . ."

As the words floated past Vlad they disturbed him in a way that he had never experienced before, and as he fell asleep he could not throw off a feeling of guilt whose source was as yet beyond his power to determine. Vlad dreamed about old Sasha, the janitor, standing in the scented shade of the lime trees in the courtyard at home. "Now the Yids"—the janitor's vague features floated transparently in front of him—"they're a *cunning* people! No matter what happens, they always land on their feet. Russians, poor fools that we are, end up doing the dirty work, but the Yids always land the cushy jobs. That's the way it is." For the first time, Vlad found his ingenuous features repulsive.

In Syzran the news reached them that Uzlovaya had been liberated. That evening Vlad's grandfather returned from the station in a noticeably merry state.

"This is it—our troubles are over," he announced solemnly from the doorway. "It's our turn to celebrate at last. Uzlovaya's been taken, we're going home."

Having said this, he broke off, aware of the tense, sticky silence which greeted his words: the news aroused no enthusiasm in his traveling companions.

"Congratulations," the head of the family said perfunctorily. "Have a good trip back."

The others only lowered their eyes in dismal foreboding: the prospect of finding themselves out in the cold again, amid the flood of thousands of other refugees who stormed every passing train, evoked in them nothing but oppressive gloom.

"See here, we'll go back together, Lazar." The old man tried to cheer them up. "It'll be more fun for all of us."

"Unfortunately, Saviely," Lazar smiled weakly, "that's impossible. We have other, quite different plans."

As a sign that she agreed with her husband, Rosa Yakovlevna gave only a regal nod.

Farewells were short and silent. They slipped out of the car as precipitately as they had arrived. Only Lyovka lingered behind, held out his hand to Vlad, and perplexed him by saying:

"Because of you I had a quarrel with my grandmother."

"So what?"

"She told me to make it up with you."

"But I didn't . . ."

"My grandmother said that you looked a lonely soul and needed sympathy. Goodbye, Vladik. No hard feelings, eh? No hard feelings?"

"No." A spasm made his throat contract. "None at all."

"We'll play chess again some day . . . Goodbye."

As Lyovka went out of the door, he vanished into the darkness of a cold wartime winter, and, as the saying goes, from the face of the earth . . .

Lyovka, Lyovka, brave fellow voyager with the chessboard under your arm! Where are you now, in what incarnation, whither has fate led your footsteps?

He will never forget the lesson you taught him, just as he can never forget your scorching reproach. Later, often among people who bore only the faintest resemblance to you he was to discern your features, and whenever he did so it would awaken in him a nagging memory of his still unexpiated guilt toward you.

CHAPTER 18

Their return journey went even more slowly, and they reached Uzlovaya when the first streams were already cutting runnels in the dirty snow. The smell of rotting horse dung, piquantly combined with locomotive smoke, floated along the streets. Flocks of hungry crows flew cawing over the town, spying out the environs from bird-height in search of nesting places and food. Thatched roofs exuded the smell of moldy dampness, and mists rolled in from the fields. Gradually spring was undermining winter's fastness and laying bare the ubiquitous scars of war.

They saw almost no ruins as they arrived, except for the burnt-out skeleton of a grain elevator, but the stamp of decay and desolation lay on everything in sight as they walked home: in those short months the latent decrepitude of the town had been, as it were, suddenly laid bare and made starkly evident. The town—really a village with an accretion of railroad workshops, sheds, and offices built around it—suddenly revealed its inherent unsoundness. The houses were still whole and standing in their places, but behind the dark eye sockets of their windows, crisscrossed with strips of paper, life seemed to have expired, giving way to cold and neglect. The spirit of oblivion hovered over the town.

A letter from his mother was waiting at home for Vlad. The letter had been brought by Aunt Klasha, Saviely's daughter-in-law, who was living in misery in the other half of the house with her two children by Saviely's eldest son, Mitya, of whom nothing had been heard since the first day of mobilization. Tall and given to flamboyant gesture, almost from the doorway she flung the already opened and distinctly tattered envelope onto the table in front of her father-in-law:

"There—letter from your Lady Snooty. She wants her brat back." There were times when the blood of the Vikings—her father had been German—made itself felt in the extreme pithiness of her remarks. "It seems that the pudding's gone cold 'cos there's no one there to eat it, so dear little sonny boy's wanted back home." Unable to keep up her bantering tone, she modulated into a shriek. "Here am I struggling with two kids, they're lucky to get bran meal on high days and holidays, and no help from anywhere, try as I may. You do everything you possibly can for your Moscow beauty and her little bastards. But mine aren't any grandchildren of yours, it seems—they might as well be just somebody's wild oats. You sit on your pile, with a scowl on your face, keeping it all for this little tadpole—your favorite. I s'pose you imagine he'll show gratitude for it! He'll show his gratitude all right—just open your pockets wider and you'll see! When Mitya comes home I'll tell him everything . . ."

The old man only had to turn a weary eye in her direction, and she immediately dried up and faded out: as she knew from experience, tempting fate in this way was likely to cost her dear.

"Give me your dirty clothes, dad, and I'll wash them for you." She switched at once to bustling concern, as if nothing had happened. "Take off your things, Vlad dear, I'm sure the lice have made a meal of them . . ."

"Stop making such a noise." He cut her off sullenly. "The boy needs sleep. I'll come and see you later and we'll have a talk."

With uncomplaining obedience Aunt Klasha disappeared, and Saviely, placing his spectacles on his nose, started to read the letter. Vlad fixed his eyes intently on the old man, and his little rabbitlike heart beat agonizingly fast: his fate, already ordained, was rustling in those exercise-book pages held in his grandfather's hands.

Steadily the clock on the wall measured out the silence. As always, the place smelled of dried raspberries, an aroma which had never been dissipated even while the house had been standing desolate and empty. And those bright calico-red geranium petals against a background of frost-encrusted windows! No—he could not, would not think of returning to Moscow! As far as he was concerned everybody in Moscow could drop dead, and along with them the whole hateful atmosphere of wrangling in the communal kitchen and the family internecine warfare.

"You've got to go, my lad." With every word that he spoke, Vlad's heart was filled with desolate panic. "It seems you now have a little sister."

Even this news did not jerk Vlad out of his numbed misery. He was incapable of taking it in. Mentally he was already at home, in the overcrowded world of shouting and swearing, in the stinking nightmare of their single room. Have mercy on him, O Lord!

"Oh yes?" he said mechanically, not noticing his own tears. "How big is she?"

"Come along, you'd better go to bed." As he pulled off Vlad's felt boots, his grandfather guiltily looked away: the old man knew and felt exactly what was going on in his grandson's mind, and he could not stop his hands from trembling. "Everything looks better when you've slept on it . . . Now, now, that will do—you're acting just like a baby . . . I can't bear to see you like this . . . There, come here . . ."

His grandfather lifted him up in his arms and at this Vlad let himself go. Burying his head in the old man's shoulder, he gave way uncontrollably to his misery. Through the tears he could just hear his grandfather trying to comfort him:

"There now, that'll do." The voice grew hoarse and broke off. "I'm not made of iron, you know—if you go on like this, I'll start howling too. And then there'll be two of us howling like hyenas, and what good will that do? You'll come back here in the summer, and we'll go over to Aunt Lyuba's cottage in the woods and pick mushrooms. We'll pick so many, we won't be able to eat them all. There, there now . . ."

The old man's tunic smelled of homegrown tobacco and sweat. His harsh bristles gently scratched Vlad's temple, and the boy gratefully pressed himself against them as he sank into a deep sleep: children's troubles are short-lived. And Vlad dreamed of the woods in front of Aunt Lyuba's house: the tall, straight pine trees rustling in the wind, the ceaseless cawing of rooks above them, and the warm soil of the cobweb pattern of paths leading away into the green twilight. And wherever Vlad looked, mushrooms were sprouting: red-capped boletus, smoky-blue russula, and brown boletus with big, nodding heads floated past his feet, thrusting through the undergrowth and grasses. "There you are," his grandfather's hoarse bass voice boomed above him. "I told you—and you just cried!" "I did it on purpose," he laughed in reply. "I knew all along!" Great pine trees swirled majestically overhead and the sky between them seemed toylike . . .

When Vlad awoke, his grandfather was no longer there, but his Aunt Klasha was at the stove, wielding the fire tongs. The room seemed to have come alive as it absorbed warmth from the heated brick; the first patches of melting frost were trickling down the windowpanes, the geranium looked noticeably more cheerful, and the spiders' webs in the corners of the room had regained their tautness. The human spirit was forcefully reasserting itself after the temporary neglect.

Aunt Klasha greeted her nephew's awakening quite peaceably.

"Alive, are you?" Arms akimbo, she grinned ironically. "You haven't melted clean away?" But she hastily softened her tone. "Did your auntie upset you? Pay no attention, I've a devil of a temper these days—that's life!"

"I don't mind . . ."

"Want a bite to eat?"

"Where's Grandpa?"

"Goodness only knows! Gone to the station to hand over his papers and all that junk. His Party conscience won't let him rest, and he'd work night and day, only they won't let him. Course, all the work he does is wag his tongue, though it keeps him busy . . . But you'd better look over there—there's a whole bunch of visitors come to see you and their mouths are watering."

She nodded toward the other side of the stove, and almost instantaneously, as though awaiting the order to emerge, two children appeared, their heads shaven bare and wearing identical fur-trimmed jackets, so that at first sight it was hard to make out which was the girl and which the boy.

"Hello," they said, almost in chorus, and shyly came forward. "Here we are . . ."

Ah, Slavka, Slavka, Margot-Margarita! Do you remember that single pair of ragged felt boots between the three of us, those pancakes made from a starchy paste of rotten potatoes, that feast of the gods when we shared a cast-iron saucepan full of boiled nettles? Vlad still had some time before he was due to leave for Moscow, time enough to eat with you that obligatory peck of salt which is needed, they say, for kinship to be truly indissoluble. How could he have foreseen then that Slavka, with whom he spent more than one hungry night together under a blanket rotting with their own urine, would be fated to follow the same progress through the prison camps as Vlad himself? And that Margot-Margarita, a fragile butterfly of a child with questioning eyebrows like a pair of flaxen wings, would turn into a smug, colorless heap of fat, enthroned dully on a pile of fiber suitcases crammed with synthetic goods? When he met his cousin after the age of thirty, Vlad, who had once been reverently in love with her and who, in all the years of his odyssey, never forgot that erstwhile infatuation, could only feel condescending sympathy for her husband. And only Aunt Klasha, only the indefatigable, unfading Aunt Klasha, even after a whole geological age had elapsed, would remain as furiously militant as ever in her battle against the united forces of the rest of the world.

"There you are," she said as she handed Vlad a farewell present of baked potatoes wrapped in a bundle. "If there's any left when you get home, you can share it with your family—and madam your mother can sample our caramel soufflé."

And out of habit she dabbed her dry eyes with a corner of her head scarf.

"Will you come back next summer?" Slavka said, sniffing. "The Germans will be beaten by the summer, and your dad will come home."

Hopping from foot to foot, Margarita proferred him a sweaty little palm:

"And our dad'll be back too, and we'll all go to Torbeyevo for the haymaking."

Morosely, Grandfather Saviely hurried them up:

"All right, that's enough, or we'll miss the train . . ."

Vlad felt that the walk to the station was literally the last journey he would take with his grandfather. Even without this depressing thought, the dull sky seemed to him even more lowering and ill-omened than ever. The surrounding world had shrunk to the dimensions of the street leading to the railroad station, and it was slowly drawing him, as into a funnel, toward the opening at its end, at the center of which was a raised barrier. Vlad had the feeling that after every step he took the earth behind him was collapsing and giving way to form an impassable abyss. He was being wrenched away from a familiar environment. He was walking out of his own childhood.

He neither looked about him nor turned around. He already knew that he would not return to this place again.

They walked the whole way in silence, and only when they were on the platform, in front of the steps up into the car, did his grandfather impulsively press Vlad's head against his hip:

"Don't forget your grandpa . . . He's an old man now . . ."

In answer Vlad could not even cry, because he was now nothing but tears: touch him, and he would have simply melted into the ground, whole, without a trace.

As the train started to move, a timid strip of sunlight from above broke through the ragged gray clouds and caught the stooped figure of Vlad's grandfather in its focus. And that Bergmanesque vision—a lonely old man lit by a chance sunray—like a stopped frame in a movie, fixed itself on his mind forever, for the rest of his life, and followed him beyond its visible confines . . .

CHAPTER 19

Spring in Moscow turned out to be unusually dull and chilly. The greenery in Sokolniki Park had to force its way out against frosts at night and damp winds by day. Hungry sparrows huddled in little blobs of puffy feathers along gutters still bulging with ice. Windows, sealed up since the fall, blinked damply out at the world from panes crisscrossed with strips of paper. In places of persistent shade, the snow lay almost until the middle of May.

"This weather!" grumbled old Sasha, as he hacked away at frozen heaps of snow with a crowbar. "At least let's hope it buries Hitler. Work like a slave for days on end, and you know what the food's like nowadays—it's not exactly filling. My stomach's like a sack full of holes, can't seem to make this ration food stay in it. I go out to work feeling like I've been eating nothing but chopped straw, dammit."

Since Vlad's return home, he seemed unable to settle down to a normal life. He was supposed to go back into the fourth grade, but after somehow sticking it out for less than three months he arranged to have himself taken on as apprentice to a carpenter in a woodworking factory, a position he barely managed to keep till the end of the year. After that came jobs working for a bookbinder, in a papier-mâché workshop, and in a candy factory. He really enjoyed making candies. It was pleasant to feel oneself an inhabitant of a tiny island of sweet abundance amid the gray ocean of wartime food shortages.

He was employed as a piece-worker, and his chest swelled with pride
as he watched himself pulling out a hot ribbon of liqueur-flavored
caramel, called "Benedictine" or "Heroes of the Arctic." When he
left work he would purposely not clean off the caramel mixture sticking to the soles of his shoes: it was proper that the rest of mankind
should recognize one of the lucky ones. Before his eyes, capricious
fortune had lifted a corner of the veil over another world, another existence.

But Vlad's happiness was short-lived. One morning his card was
no longer in its slot alongside the time clock. For an instant his heart
contracted to the size of a microscopic icicle and then immediately
swelled up like a fireball, making him so hot that he felt faint. Harsh
reality had again brought Vlad back to his previous condition; his
wings were crushed, broken. Walking along the street, the little boy
turned blue and shivered all over.

"Lord, what have I done to deserve this punishment?" his mother
wailed, shaking with indignation. "How much longer are you going
to suck my blood?" The charge of bloodsucking was an obvious exaggeration, but in every other respect his mother genuinely deserved
sympathy: Vlad was far from being the ideal son of a Soviet
mother. "You'll drive me to an early grave, you little horror! Either
you come to your senses or I'll hand you over to a reformatory. I've
reached the end of my tether!"

His aunt, her lips pressed sternly together, said nothing. Her dislike of Vlad was now equaled by the sense of triumph over her sister-
in-law: like father, like son, she implied; as ye sow, so shall ye reap.
The birth of her niece had noticeably mollified her, for she had a
maternal weakness for little girls, but her jaundiced attitude to Vlad
had not diminished; if anything it had grown worse from the direct
comparison.

Vlad's salvation at such times was the street. Its course ran
straight through his heart—unforgettable Mitkovskaya Street! The
mighty hooves of carthorses have long since ceased to thunder over
your cobblestones; the raucous cry of the glazier and the screech of
the knife grinder's spark-spitting wheel have not been heard for years
in your courtyards, and your wooden houses, windows framed in
lace-like fretwork, have been demolished. But memories of you, no
matter how harsh, could neither be erased from his memory nor
supplanted by any visions of faraway abodes of paradise. Leaving the
main city highway to follow a zigzag course, the far end of the street

ended at the gates of suburban Sokolniki Park, where the local children spent the best part of their free time. Sokolniki was their Mecca, their Promised Land, their Siberia and their Patagonia, their Klondike and their Colorado. Here they acquired the difficult arts of living: here they were initiated into the Solemn Mystery of Tobacco, the Great Magic of Strong Drink, the Falsehoods of Careless Love. From hence, armed with practical and manly experience, they went out into the wide world, where they were awaited by barracks and concentration camps, informers and police narks, pure girls and railroad-station whores, hopes and disappointments, lone burial-places and mass graves.

In Sokolniki, Vlad had his own, private hiding places and secluded corners. On expeditions hunting for acorns or maybugs he crawled over practically every inch of the park, swam back and forth across all of its ponds, knew all the remotest trails and paths. Whenever life grew particularly hard he would creep into the trench of an abandoned shooting range behind the children's playground, and there he would brood in solitude on the world's imperfections and on his own luckless fate. Ever since those years, marked as they were by the call of the flesh, the names "Deer Ponds," "May Avenue," "Shiryayev's Meadow," heard in passing amid a thronging crowd, have always sounded to him like a password, a symbol of mutual understanding and trust. Wherever he may go, a reminder of his native heath will always bring him a dizzy sense of pleasure.

From the beginning of the war the street also became for its inhabitants one of the basic sources of existence. Right across the street, behind a straggling row of two-story wooden boxes, was the Mitkovo freight depot, with its adjoining lumber yard and storage warehouses for vegetables. These two places kept the neighborhood supplied. The unfit and wounded veterans who guarded them were incapable of withstanding the round-the-clock siege mounted by the rapacious, fearless, locustlike hordes of the local street urchins. Wood and coal from the depot burned in all the stoves of Mitkovskaya Street, and potatoes from the vegetable warehouses formed its staple diet. From dawn to dusk Vlad was engaged in shuttling furtively back and forth between the source of supply and the consumer. Since there were always buyers for his goods in the apartment house, he had no complaints about his standard of living, but this relative prosperity was hard-earned. Each log, each potato tuber were paid for by him with the fear of imminent capture. It is not surprising that for the whole of the rest of his life he was to dream of being pursued.

In the courtyard Vlad acquired a solid reputation as an inveterate tearaway and a future habitué of the country's prisons. The court-yard wiseacres only shook their heads and sighed as they watched him go past, while he proudly passed through the scorching fire of his own fear, and the ominous thunder of the Criminal Code rumbled over his head.

As he unloaded his regular share of goods stolen from the very depot entrusted to his care, Fyodor Weintraub from the fourth floor, a supply official saved from front-line service by his rank of sergeant in the Quartermaster Corps, would invariably greet Vlad with the same question:

"Still thieving, Samsonov?"

Old Sasha, on the other hand, was thoroughly approving:

"Take it, Vlad, if they can't look after it. They all steal, and we're only human. Nowadays being a thief is a trade too."

Whenever old Mrs. Durova saw him she would say sadly:

"Such promise—and you're already a little crook. What's to be-come of you? The mind boggles!"

Nikiforov, the secret-police officer, did not conceal his intentions toward Vlad:

"I see you haven't been caught yet. It's time to put you where you belong—in a reformatory."

With this Vlad firmly disagreed; he had other plans for the future, and although he could not describe these plans, even to himself, their total nonconformity with Nikiforov's plans were obvious to him. He knew, he sensed that his present way of life could not last much longer, that his fate was bound to take some sharp turn in the near future, and it was easy enough to guess that a long and hard road lay ahead of him.

At home Vlad was just tolerated but no more. His mother, apa-thetic and visibly going to pieces, accepted his booty as her due, ask-ing no questions and showing no interest in anything. His aunt scowled in silence, but his contribution to the household's meager budget, which had now devolved entirely onto her shoulders, forced her to come to terms with the inevitable. She even began to treat him a little more kindly: necessity condemns us to coexistence.

It was the hell that reigned outside their room, in the kitchen, that had become more intense and vicious. Crazy Katya, a rag

wrapped around her hair, would hoist a two-handled wooden tub
onto her head and parade up and down the corridor uttering furious
curses:

"Stop hammering nails into my head! You filthy devils, can't you
leave a person in peace? I hate you, damn you! You can all drop
dead! Help, murder! Save me, miserable orphan that I am!"

Vlad only grinned maliciously as he listened to her tirades: let the
idiot rant if it makes her feel better. He could not have known that
exactly fifteen years later he would be a fellow patient with her in
Block Three of the Troitsky Hospital, or, as they still call it, the
Central Asylum. She would not recognize him and would pass by,
but he would stare after her for a long time, his heart aching as he
recalled the past.

The next turn on the program might be a duet between Lyuba
and Vanya. He would begin it, starting up from a distance as though
taking the range and working out what the coming battle would cost
him; but gradually, with each glass that he downed, his voice would
harden, taking on a metallic edge as the obscene abuse began to
flow:

"What the hell do you think you are, Lyuba? You walk around,
God forgive you, you slattern, in a filthy bathrobe, looking like nothing on earth . . . you're repulsive. Why don't you go to the
hairdresser and get a permanent wave, and a manicure too, so I don't
have to feel ashamed to be seen with you. As it is, it makes me throw
up to look at you. Somebody ought to put you in their garden instead of a scarecrow, you disgusting slut. I'm stuck with you now,
and the two brats you spawned are just a couple of parasites—one
looks like a frog and the other's a cretin, never stops slobbering.
Ugh!"

No sooner did he draw breath than Lyuba would start yelling back
at him, and her piercing shriek would echo around the apartment
and spill out into the courtyard:

"Stuffing himself, the filthy slob! Our stallion's getting the itch
again—I'll give him a permanent wave. Just look at him, mangy
devil. He's got the sort of mug you want to throw a brick at—one of
his eyes is always chasing the other. You ought to be ashamed, insulting your own children like that. At least they don't look like you,
thank God. They're lovely kids and I'm proud to show them to anybody . . ."

Ah, Lyuba, Lyuba, if you knew that you were to die in the state poorhouse, two streetcar stops away from your home, and that your "lovely kids" would not even bother to get up from the table on a Sunday to go and see you buried. In vain would the messenger from the poorhouse beg them at least to come and attend the funeral. Your eldest son—Boris—would only find the strength to say, through a drunken haze:

"She'll last the winter without us—get digging!"

And his younger brother would just grunt wordlessly in agreement.

Vlad's day began and ended to the accompaniment of a noisy chorus of voices outside in the lobby and the crying of his six-month-old sister. She exerted herself with a persistence that was worthy of a better cause. In her little birdlike lungs was concealed such power that she even managed to drown out the noise of the air-raid siren: obviously dried-milk baby food is not conducive to inner equilibrium. At first he tried to pacify her by singing, cooing, and pulling what he thought were funny faces for her, but in the end he gave up, and when it became absolutely unbearable he would simply cover her baby carriage with a quilt and run out of doors: sleep tight, dear comrade!

Do not blame him for this, Katya, in your distant Sinai; in any case, you grew up into a fairly taciturn and thoroughly suitable companion.

CHAPTER 20

The book came into his hands quite by chance, among an uncounted host of other books which he devoured without discrimination. *Alexei Svirsky*, it said on the cover: *The Story of My Life*. On rereading it much later he was to be appalled by its small-town sentimentality, its prolixity and literary mediocrity, but there is no getting away from it—this particular book was due to play a decisive role in his destiny . . .

The weather that morning was so dull and colorless that the windows seemed to have been daubed all over with gray paint. The stove was exhaling thick smoke, a bluish swath of which had spread out beneath the blackened ceiling; a large spider's web was dangling from the shabby wallpaper and the whole room bore an astonishing resemblance to the picture of a cave in the sixth-grade zoology textbook. But in the book that lay in front of Vlad, a little Jewish boy was traveling light and carefree, wandering through the towns and villages of the sun-drenched South, the thirst for experience glowing in his anxious eyes. The boy suffered beatings, starvation, and insults, but none of this caused the account of his tortuous journey to forefeit any of the charm of immediacy and exhilaration. This was certainly the first, though not, as Vlad was later to discover, the ultimate price of freedom.

The decision came to him suddenly, and at once caught him up and swept him along. He was fed up with his smoky room, fed up with the ceaseless bickering in the passage outside, fed up with "meatballs" made of potato peelings and seasoned with his aunt's barely concealed hostility or his mother's weary indifference. The world was big and there was bound to be a place for him in it. "I'm not chained to them, am I?" The thought burned in his mind as he feverishly threw everything that came to hand into a duffel bag: his own cast-off clothes, one of his mother's skirts, and the family's entire stock of soap. "Let's just hope I don't fall on my face!"

His packing was interrupted when his aunt unexpectedly returned home from work. One glance was enough for her to size up the situation.

"Where d'you think you're going?" Her disgruntled features hardened into severity. "Perhaps you'd like to take me with you?"

"I wasn't . . . going anywhere . . ."

"So, little boy, you want to fly away, do you? If you're going to be a tramp, though, you don't have to take all our soap. Or don't you care about us? I'm all right, to hell with the rest of you, is that it?"

Do you remember our brief conversation, Maria Mikhailovna, on that miserable morning of a belated spring? Your life has been so hard—oh, how hard!—that you probably don't recall it. But he remembered it, and it etched forever into his memory the truth which you let fall in passing: Freedom is not bought at other people's expense . . .

Next day his sister was sent over to the neighbors, while Vlad was stripped to his underpants and locked into his room. But once the urge had taken hold, there was no stopping him. He did not need long to think. From the bottom drawer of the chest of drawers, where his mother carefully stored their old, discarded belongings, he dug out a moth-eaten winter jacket made of plush, a pair of torn silk stockings and some canvas sneakers, all of which comprised his first traveling outfit. Having climbed out of the window into the courtyard, he moved immediately to raid the storage shed and extract from it the last of their birch logs, which he took straight to old Mrs. Durova.

Looking Vlad suspiciously up and down, the old woman muttered skeptically:

"You're a fine one, and no mistake!" She had obviously guessed what was afoot but gave no sign of it. She paid him with three five-ruble bills and then, staring into space, sighed reflectively:

"Well, who knows, it may be for the best. No one can tell what fate has in store for them . . ."

Vlad's journey from Moscow began on a fully laden coal train, stung by a biting wind, in the company of several black-marketeers who were setting out for Morshansk to buy up homegrown tobacco. His appearance caused them no little amusement. They had great fun at the expense of the twelve-year-old traveler's bizarre outfit:

"Looks like the kid's copied his gear from a fashion plate."

"Silk stockings and all!"

"Don't you feel a draft up your knickers, my lord?"

"Off to take the waters, he is . . ."

"Where's your hat, my lord?"

"Ought to have his portrait painted, he did."

"Now there's a posh suit!"

Having no idea where he was being taken, he surrendered passively to the human tide, and it carried Vlad to a station called Nizhny Chir, a God-forsaken spot somewhere between Donetsk and Stalingrad. There it cast him up, leaving him lying under a station bench to await death or better times. There, too, he was found by a kind soul, a cleaning woman, to whom he spun a yarn about his parents' dying and leaving him an orphan. She gave him—she had nothing else to give—a pair of felt slippers, and, being on friendly terms with the conductresses, she was able to put him on a train to Stalingrad.

Lying on the luggage rack beside the heating pipes in a car crammed with people, for the first time for days Vlad was able to get really warm. From below him came the buzz of long-familiar talk about the war, about bread, and about the sicknesses brought on by hungry times. When he closed his eyes he could imagine that he had never left home at all, that he was still lying in his corner of the room at Sokolniki and his mother gossiping with the neighbors about their common, everyday problems. But he dreamed of an open road and above it ice-encrusted telephone wires . . .

When Vlad awoke the car was flooded with morning sunlight and was almost empty, except for a young soldier beneath him—his face freckled from ear to ear, his mouth soft and wet, like a calf's—who was entertaining a couple of silent girls with a story about his feat of daring in the front line.

"There I was, crawling along, hellish noise all around me—Lord save us, I thought—bullets buzzing like wasps . . ."

It was at that very moment—Vlad was never to forget it . . . may he be forgiven—that he felt something hard under his foot, wrapped in thin material: a package or a small bundle of some kind. His heart began beating harder and faster, his palms grew wet. By carefully using the soles of his feet Vlad managed to pull the treasure trove within reach. With a hand trembling with excitement he thrust it under his jacket, then he jumped down and slipped along the corridor to the lavatory.

God, he had never seen so much money in his life! Crisp and new, as though just off the printing press, squeezed into a tight wad, the hundred-ruble bills burned his fingers. There were exactly a hundred of them. Ten thousand rubles. Even for those times this was an impressive sum. Also wrapped up in the bundle was a pocketbook, in which alongside some small bills he found a passport, a military identity card, and a collection of certificates. Vlad was not troubled by second thoughts as he flushed the certificates down the toilet bowl. He was in no state to wonder about whom he might be depriving of their rightful property. In his hurry to destroy the evidence, it did not occur to him to find out the person's name. Nor did he even feel the thrill of wrongdoing. At that moment he was guided only by the animal instinct of self-preservation and securing his prey. How he was to pay for it later, though, when he recalled that day and the deadly temptation of that money—though it is hardly a consolation to the victim to know that the cause of his misfortune eventually repented.

In the Stalingrad junk market of 1943, that seething ant heap of poverty and hunger, for twelve hundred rubles Vlad acquired a winter overcoat, boots, a well-worn ski suit, and a completely useless turnip-shaped French pocket watch. That same night, in the sweating melee of the railway station, a youth with protruding eyes, who was slightly older than himself and wore a dirty but well-cut army greatcoat, sidled up to him:

"Where are you heading?"

"To my auntie in Kharkov." Vlad lied from habit now, as he tried to move away from his inquisitive neighbor. "I'm waiting for my train."

"Tell us another." The youth gave a knowing grin. "I've got X-ray eyes, you can't fool me. I was a scout in the Army. There aren't any aunties left in Kharkov, except German ones. Better come South with me. They're living in clover there, you can pick up all you want."

His popeyes glittered mysteriously in the semidarkness of the barely lit waiting room, and his wink was enticing. Giving in to its charm, Vlad, to his own surprise, agreed:

"Okay. Let's go . . ."

Vlad was to see the inside of more than one lock-up and juvenile detention center on the way before reaching their goal, but when the South finally spread out before him in all its lush greens and blues, he never regretted that journey.

CHAPTER 21

Seen from high up on Cape Zeliony, Batum looked like a highly decorated cake, swimming in thick lilac-colored jelly. Through the sticky, sultry heat of an August afternoon, Vlad trudged along the shore toward the town stretching away into the distance. The sea lay spread out to the horizon, green and flat as a vast billiard table. Not knowing what lay in store for him here, a faint ember of hope for food and some kind of shelter still glowed within him, and this alone led him on and kept him going. It was when he had been taken off the train at Kobuleti and almost sent back in the direction of Samtredi, that Vlad had decided to make the final spurt of his journey on foot. Fortunately the police sergeant on duty had been too idle to carry out his threat, and in the end had simply told Vlad to clear off anywhere he liked—provided he stayed out of the sergeant's sector. By this stage of his long and tortuous journey from Moscow to Transcaucasia, Vlad had acquired a firm grasp of the rules for dealing with authority. Giving the sergeant no cause to repeat his command, he vanished from that officer's precinct within half an hour.

Quivering in its heat haze, the town floated majestically toward him, first enveloping him in the semicircular complex of the oil refinery, then cutting him off from the sea by the dockyard wall, and finally leading him into its labyrinth of shady streets by way of a bazaar . . .

Lord, the Batum bazaars of 1945! I often dream of them at night
—those soy-flour pancakes, those *chadolobiani*, that gastronomic
realm of beans and sweet corn. The smell of rotting fruit on the
street makes me shudder in reminiscence and starts rainbow-colored
circles swimming before my eyes: I have had to swallow so much of
it in my time that nowadays, in this era of packaging and sterility,
half of that quantity would be enough to lay low a medium-sized
town or give chronic diarrhea to a whole generation . . .

The bazaar fed Vlad until the end of summer, until the coming of
the first rains. By the late fall, when cold and fog were blowing
inshore from the sea, much of the noise and color had faded from
life in the marketplace. The army of stray and homeless children had
mostly dispersed for the winter to orphanages and juvenile detention
centers, before descending on the town again in the first days of
spring like a voracious swarm of locusts. It grew daily harder to find
somewhere to doss down at night; the places that could always be
relied upon in summer—empty railroad cars at the oil refinery, warm
corners in the station, secluded park benches—grew bare and unpro-
tected, open on all sides to the inquisitive stare of the guardians of
law and order.

Finally Vlad spent several nights in the best traditions of vagabond folklore: under an upturned boat on the beach. Here he
chanced to be caught by a policeman whose beat included that
stretch of the seashore. Gently but insistently the toe of a police
boot was thrust under the planking of the boat and a voice said in
Georgian:

"Come out of there, my lad . . . and look sharp!"

Vlad's abode was a classic trap: there was no way of escape and
he could only surrender himself to the mercies of his captor. He
crawled out and trudged obediently along in front of the watchful
officer, who followed him in silence, occasionally steering him in the
right direction with careful prods in the back. But strange to say,
they walked right past police headquarters and the police duty room
at the railroad station, with his escort continuing to guide Vlad
straight ahead. They left the town center far behind, and the dim
outskirts enveloped them in pitch darkness until they stopped somewhere in the gloom. Rapping on the knocker of an invisible gate, the
policeman abruptly disturbed the quiet of a house which could just
be seen looming up behind a high fence. A light gleamed in the

house, then footsteps were heard crunching down a gravel path, and a low, slightly hoarse voice said:

"What do you want?"

"Open up, boss . . ."

A chain rattled, the gate was opened, the officer pushed Vlad into the opening and two silhouettes merged confidentially. They held a short, whispered conversation, after which the policeman vanished into the night and the other man turned back toward his house:

"Come with me, kid."

With trepidation and hope Vlad followed him into the first-floor room of a private house, which was lit by a kerosene lamp fastened to the wall. The place was something between a storeroom and a summerhouse: blankets and mattresses were piled in a heap beneath strings of onions and corncobs, garden implements were stacked in the corners, and there was a strong, pervasive, spicy smell.

The owner of the house—a stocky man of about thirty, wearing a string-mesh undershirt over his torso—spent some time studying Vlad intently with his dark, yellow-flecked, protruding eyes. Then briskly but kindly he asked:

"Want something to eat?"

In reply Vlad merely gulped down his saliva. The man went behind a plank partition and soon reappeared with a bowl of bean soup, a pancake, and a can of *matsoni*, which he placed on a small table in front of Vlad. In the same friendly tone he said casually:

"Eat up."

While Vlad luxuriated in his meal, the man deftly extracted a mattress and blanket from the general heap, laid them out in a corner, and stared again at his visitor with an appraising look:

"Where are you from, kid?"

"Moscow."

"How old are you?"

"Fourteen."

"Father and mother alive?"

"No," Vlad lied as usual. "They were killed in the war."

"Listen here, son." The Georgian spoke Russian practically without an accent, and no doubt for this reason Vlad felt that there was something not quite real, something stagy about him. "I have work for you to do. You'll get plenty to eat and somewhere to sleep, you won't come to any harm, and I'll even pay you as well. Tomorrow we'll drive out into the country, and when we get there I'll tell you what you have to do. My name's Bondo. Bondo—got it? Same as Boris in Russian." He blew out the lamp and called back from the doorway:

"Not afraid of the dark, are you?"

"No."

"That's good."

And he went out, melting into the darkness.

For the first time for many months Vlad fell asleep in the quiet security of a house. He had, of course, no idea that this was only a breathing space, a period of grace from above, granted to him on the threshold of far greater ordeals than those which lay behind him. Perhaps this was why his dreams were happy and serene, and why, when he awoke, he did so instantly and with a sense of well-being.

CHAPTER 22

Bondo was on the binge again. He went on a spree every time he pulled off a successful deal, and when Bondo celebrated he did so fiercely, expansively, and recklessly. Vlad had long since become accustomed to these drinking bouts, and to the fact that against his will he was always made to take part in them. God alone knew what it was that made the Georgian drag the boy along with him to all the taverns in and around the town, but no sooner did the minions of Demon Drink sound their clarion call than Bondo would remove his young helper from his home in the village, seat the boy alongside him in the most expensive horse cab in Batum, and set off on a methodical round of the best dives in the city and round about. Wherever they went they were accompanied by the wild music of Bondo's favorite shawm players and by the approving grins of policemen and tavernkeepers alike:

"Bondo's at it again!"

"He knows how to live."

"Bondo's a *man* . . ."

"They'll catch him one day, though."

"Bondo's no fool. He has all the police in his pocket."

"He's a generous man, God bless him!"

Almost a year had passed since the night when they had first met,

and in that time Vlad had grown used to his boss's capricious whims
—and to much else besides.

At first it was simply fear—sticky, numbing, panic fear. Fear of a
mountain stream at night, fear of a treacherous silence in the undergrowth along the riverside, fear of the unknown on the far bank. But
gradually Vlad came to regard the monthly sorties across the border
as an unpleasant but normal part of life. He had an accomplice, one
Nikola Lastik, a lazy, clumsy youth of the same age as himself, with
a dazed, perpetually sleepy look on his face—which was like a lump
of almost shapeless dough, sprinkled from ear to ear with freckles
like amber-colored raisins. Lastik only woke up in order to eat, to
answer the calls of nature, and to carry out his regular trip across the
frontier. In all the time they knew each other, they hardly exchanged
more than two consecutive words. Bondo had recruited Nikola two
years previously and since then he appeared to have forgotten about
him, entrusting him to the care of his assistant, Giya Shanava, who
never left the village. Only occasionally, when carried away by the
fumes of alcohol, would Bondo let loose on Nikola a torrent of
cheerful abuse:

"Oh, Lastik, *momadzaglo,* you weren't born of a mother! You
were born of idleness and your father was a passing fireman or a
kinto. God sent you to me to save you from dying of hunger in the
snow. Tell me, why do you stay alive, Lastik? Why pollute the air to
no purpose? If you were to have one good shit, old son, there'd be
nothing left of you . . ."

In reply Nikola would only sniffle and flop down to sleep again as
soon as his boss had gone out.

In Bondo's drinking bouts, however, through the haze of gener-
osity and good cheer, there was always a lurking hint of some powerful, suppressed anguish. It was as if his flow of drunken talk and
laughter was a way of trying to smother something within him
which, if he had to face it alone, would have driven him out of his
mind. At times, when the carousing was in full swing, his face would
be darkened by a shadow, a faint cloud, an obvious stab of memory,
and he would lean toward Vlad with a ghastly look on his face:

"Listen, son . . . I know I shall die like a dog. You'll all forget
Bondo—you, Nikola, Giya. You'll all forget me. I'll die in the cellar
of a prison with a bullet in the back of my neck. And you'll all
squeal on me, all of you. There's only one person who wouldn't
squeal on me, and that's Ashkhen. And she won't forget me. She

loves me, Ashkhen does. She has a heart of gold . . . Let's go and see Ashkhen!"

Vlad would sigh with relief: this meant the end—an end to lurching from tavern to tavern, an end to debauchery and nights without sleep. When Bondo decided to go to Ashkhen, a widow who worked as a dressmaker, it was the signal that there would soon be a long respite. In the tiny room of her shabby little apartment, the boss would collapse face downward on the bed in its curtained alcove, and for a week the devoted Armenian woman would minister to his hangover with special decoctions of her own making.

Many years were to pass before Vlad was to learn the leaden torture of a hangover, but once having done so, he was fated time and again to crawl toward that agony through pitch-black labyrinths of oblivion and delirium. In that state he was to live through hundreds of lives, to see countless momentary visions which shook his soul to its foundations, to experience with destructive frequency the sickening horrors of passing out and coming to; finally, in mature years, he was to sense that this was the foretaste of the hell, the retribution, the fiery Gehenna which awaited him beyond the confines of this life.

Having seen to the needs of the sleeping Bondo, the Armenian woman made up a bed for Vlad in a corner of the lobby, sat down beside him on a little stool and started to bemoan her fate:

"What sort of a life is this, Vladik? What have I done, what sins have I committed, for God to punish me with a life like mine? I've never hurt a fly. Where's the justice in it, Vladik? Tell me—where?"

Unfortunately, Vlad had no idea either of what had become of justice or why it seemed to shun any contact with the harsh reality of life, and the only answer he could offer was the silence of a fellow sufferer.

"I love him Vlad, but he's doomed! Sooner or later they'll catch him and shoot him. He's had three convictions already, and all for smuggling *plan*.* Oh, that accursed *plan*, may the man who invented it never rest in peace! Leave Bondo, Vladik, he'll do you no good— or don't you know what you can get for smuggling *plan*?"

As if he didn't know! From five to ten years, and in the case of a reconviction—anything up to and including the death penalty.

Bondo's calculations, however, were simple and foolproof. He him-

* *Plan* is the vernacular name for an opium-based narcotic. (Tr.)

self never crossed the frontier. Thanks to their age, Vlad and Nikola ran practically no risk. The Frontier Guards were forbidden by law to shoot at minors, and if they were caught, as homeless orphans the worst that could befall them was to be sent to a reformatory. Sha- nava managed the transportation into Batum. Even with all his graft and connections, Bondo might one day, of course, be arrested for contraband and for involving juveniles, but *plan* was worth the risk: one "joint" alone sold in the taverns for ten rubles. And there was no counting the number of ten-ruble worths of that compressed, dark green, liberating drug which they had brought over the frontier to their boss inside the linings of their "workman's" quilted jackets, whose quilting had been ripped out and replaced by "merchandise"!

A few days later, having finally come to his senses, Bondo took Vlad to the bazaar, put him on a peasant bullock cart which was going the right way, and sent the boy back to the village, where Vlad would stay until the next binge and the hangover that would follow it. As he said goodbye, Bondo stuffed a few crumpled ten-ruble bills into Vlad's pocket and, turning his haggard face away, muttered through gritted teeth:

"Tell them I'll be coming soon."

And he walked away, vanishing into the crowd.

Nowadays it is hard for Vlad to imagine where and how his erst- while savior and boss Bondo Shoniya, the notorious Batum drug ped- dler, had ended his days: in a prison lime pit with a lump of lead in his skull or at home in his bed.

CHAPTER 23

Outlined against the starry sky, the dark mountaintops seemed so close that Vlad felt he could stretch out his hand and touch their stone roughness with the tips of his fingers. In single file, Giya leading, followed by Lastik with Vlad immediately behind him, they made their way through the scrub of gorse and juniper bushes deeper and deeper into the mountains. The night enfolded them with a sultry, almost tangible silence. Having left the pathway far behind, they were moving entirely by the guidance of Shanava's wolflike instinct; on each trip he led the boys to the crossing point by a different route, known only to him. Bringing up the rear of the file, Vlad tried to catch from the darkness the long-awaited sound of water splashing over stones, but time passed and the surroundings remained as hushed and airless as ever, the quiet broken only by the sounds of their movement. The earth breathed and pulsated, exhaling the heavy, spice-laden aromas of its fertile, subtropical soil.

The noise of water was heard suddenly and, so it seemed, at their very feet. Vlad parted some bushes, looked down and involuntarily screwed up his eyes: below, in the depths of a ravine, with a tinny flash whenever its waters reflected the starlight, there gleamed a river —distant, inaccessible, fascinating. It made Vlad want to sit there motionless, eyes closed, at the very edge of the abyss, to listen to the

timid gurgle of the water, to savor the sourish taste in his mouth and
the dizziness brought on by the sheer precipice beneath his feet.

But Giya, from the darkness, was already urging them on:

"*Chkari, chkari, bicho . . .*"

A minute later they were gathered around a familiar pothole,
whose other end led them to the mouth of a cave, camouflaged with
bushes, that opened right above the water. From there Giya usually
lowered the boys on a rope down into the shallow, rushing stream.

Now the roles were changed: Vlad was the first to squeeze into
the pothole. The first few meters had to be traversed by lying flat
and crawling, then the passage widened, enabling them to rise on to
all fours, while in the cave itself they could stand fully upright. It
smelled of caked dust, bird droppings, refuse, and mice. The stars
could be seen twinkling cheerfully through the branches of the bush
which masked the exit. The river down below burbled expectantly as
it rushed over the rocks.

"Hang on," Giya whispered as he handed Vlad an end of the rope.
Then to Lastik: "Take your bit."

No more words or explanations were needed. The familiar operation had been worked out down to the smallest detail and was carried out almost automatically. Vlad tied the rope under his armpits
firmly, yet with sufficient freedom not to hamper his movements;
Giya pushed aside the concealing bush and gave him a curt nod in
farewell:

"Off you go."

With emptiness yawning beneath him, Vlad steadied himself for a
moment with the sole of his foot against the rockface, and then Giya
began slowly to pay out the rope and lower him steadily downward.
One step down, a second, a third . . . another, another, and another.
Then his shoes were dipping into shallow water and with a gasp of relief he could feel the bottom:

"Oof!"

The important thing now was not to look down, but only ahead;
this was a rigid rule, for to disregard it was to run the risk of giving
way to the magic lure of the water and to slither away downstream.
Vlad picked his way carefully over the slimy rocks, feeling Lastik's
heavy, jerky breathing behind him. When intense cold began to grip
his feet, somewhere near midstream, he quickened his pace, and soon
the opposite bank reached out to their rescue with a familiar spit of
shingle.

They were expected. Noiseless shadows came to meet them and immediately set to work on them. Everything was done in silence. They were given ready-prepared quilted jackets, whose linings had been tightly stuffed with "merchandise," they took off their own jackets and placed them in willing, outstretched hands. As soon as their rapid change of clothing was made, they stepped back into the water again.

Vlad had already touched the shingly surface of the opposite bank when from the mouth of the cave above them the powerful beams of two flashlights converged on him:

"Stop! Hands up!"

At first Vlad froze, mesmerized by the blinding light, unable to move from the spot, but Lastik's sudden and plaintive cry from behind brought him back to reality:

"Run for it, Vlad . . . aaahh!"

Vlad flung himself prone into the water and gratefully surrendered to its power. As the stream carried, dragged, and pulled him over rocks and through deep pools, he heard the barking of dogs and the shooting as if through a wall—muffled and distant. When at last his hand felt the dry, cool sand of the bank, Vlad lay motionless for a while, dazed by the bell-like clangor of his experience.

Then he ran—stumbling and falling, his face scratched and bleeding from the thorny undergrowth, throwing off the constricting weight of his clothes as he went. He ran faster than a deer, along a narrow path made by wild animals. Yet the air of freedom did not hearten him; instead, he shriveled into a state of numbness. Vlad did not want freedom; it meant hunger, and he was afraid of it.

CHAPTER 24

Tung. The magic of that ringing word fascinated Vlad. It was as if resonant little hammers were striking an invisible tambourine: tung, tung, tung! But the word also had a smell, heady and suffocating. And the color of bright green, shot with darker tones. And a shape: something midway between a fig and an onion. Tung, tung, tung! The evenly spaced rows, the branches spreading like apple trees, thickly hung with the strange, bell-like fruit. Amid these serried, military ranks of oil-bearing trees stood the dazzlingly white boxes of the farmstead, with the drying sheds like yellow beehives ranged alongside.

At the Djikhandjursk Tung Oil State Farm, whither Fate or Chance—whichever you prefer—had borne Vlad after long ordeals in the coastal towns, he gradually rested and recovered. At first he was put to herding fourteen head of short, stumpy little donkeys; but if by evening he managed to drive as many as three of them into the stableyard, he would return to the farm bunkhouse with a sense of victory. No sooner did they leave their stalls in the morning than they cantered off in all directions, and no power on earth could induce them to gather into a herd. Obstinate individualism was the only thing they had acquired from their contact with man. In every thing else, each one of them was a living refutation of the theory of conditioned reflexes. They had never acquired such reflexes, because donkeys have no need of them.

Vlad would chase after his donkeys all over the plantation, cutting his bare feet on thorns and stones. He swore and wept, but to no avail; every evening he would return to the farmstead with the same result. Gogoberidze, the farm manager—an unhealthily fat man with "Marshal Budyonny" mustaches—would greet Vlad every time by wagging a massive, threatening finger under his nose:

"Ah, *djipkir, momadzaglo!* Soon the jackals will have eaten all my donkeys! What do you look at when you're working? At the grapes? Or the figs? But who's going to look after the donkeys? Me? Or the director, Levan Avtandilovich, God give him good health and a long life? I'm a sick man, boy; I can't answer for myself—my heart won't stand it. That's the state you've brought me to . . ."

In the end it was obvious that Vlad would never make a herdsman, so he was attached for training to Ivan Ostapenko, the furnaceman in the farm kitchen. Ostapenko, a glum, elderly Ukrainian, who wore the ribbon of some obscure medal in the lapel of his torn and filthy working clothes, took on his new apprentice with a sullen and suspicious look:

"What the hell are they doing? What do they think I am, a nursemaid or something? Haven't I got enough to do as it is? Look at you —you're nothing but skin and bone. What good will you be as a worker? All you'll do is waste oil. In any case, safety regulations don't allow kids to work the furnace. Well, now that you're here, I suppose we may as well see how you make out."

How that furnace terrified Vlad! The fear of everything connected with machinery, engines, technology, and the combustion that goes with them was to remain with him thenceforth for the rest of his life. His timid fingers only had to touch the furnace and it would go mad. If it was burning with a steady flame, it would immediately go out and either emit a shower of sparks like a firework or run hissing with the jet unlit. Its voracity knew no bounds; he would pour bucket after bucket of fuel oil into its insatiable maw, but it constantly demanded to be replenished. He would walk around the farm smeared from head to foot in diesel oil, wistfully recalling the charm and obstinacy of his erstwhile friends of the stableyard.

During the short break between three and five o'clock in the afternoon, when the calm of after-lunch torpor descended on the kitchen, Ostapenko came to see Vlad in his shed. Staring dejectedly around

at the traces of the boy's unequal struggle with the furnace, he
squatted down beside him:

"What do they think they're doing? This isn't the work for you,
kid. You should be in school, not toting oil for furnaces. You'll
knock yourself out in this job, and all to no purpose. To think that
we made a revolution in 1917—and young kids like you are still having to go to work! We didn't shoot nearly enough of them in those
days, if you ask me. Hell, though, what's the use of talking about it.
Here, have a bite."

He reached into his pocket, handed Vlad a few warm, bruised
pears and immediately turned away again, pulling his shabby cap
down over his eyes. When he did this, his comical medal ribbon pro-
truded noticeably in Vlad's direction.

One day Vlad plucked up courage to ask him:

"What did you get that medal for, Ivan Kirillich? Did you fight in
the Civil War?"

"Nosy, aren't you? I don't suppose there's more than five of us left
alive who held the Arsenal and got this medal. Yes, I fought all
right. Went through the whole of that damn war." He half-closed
his eyelids and whined in a thin falsetto: "'Attention, comrades!
There's a war on! Leave your jobs and go to the front . . . !' Can't
think what all the fuss and bother was about. Things only got worse
afterwards . . ."

In the open doorway to the kitchen appeared the skinny figure of
the head cook, Revaz Gabuniya, with his inevitable ladle stuck into
the belt of his greasy apron:

"Now, now, Ivan, stuffing the boy's head with trash again?" Clasping his hands behind his back, his teeth bared in a good-natured
grin, he stood rocking back and forth from heel to toe. "You'll answer for it to God, you know."

"There ain't no God." In self-defense, Ivan sullenly withdrew into
his shell. "Old wives' tales."

"Now, now, Ivan," Gabuniya continued his lazy teasing. "Mind
what you're saying, or God will strike you down on the spot!"

In fact Revaz cared neither for God nor the devil. The chef combined in himself both God and the devil—at least within the
confines of the farm kitchen—but the opportunity to tease the furnaceman, especially with someone else present, was a welcome relief
after the enervating, abuse-laden din of the kitchen, so he took to
this form of recreation with wholehearted delight. Gabuniya had be-

come a cook by chance—by the irony of fate, as it were. For by voca-
tion he was a thief. When he stole, he did so as though in a kind of
inspired trance. He stole impudently, openly, and greedily everything
that came within his reach. If, for instance, two vats of macaroni or
pea soup (one of which alternately comprised the daily menu in the
farm's dining hall) were supposed to require two three-kilogram cans
of lend-lease margarine, one and a half cans of it were regarded as
the chef's legitimate booty. Nor did he spurn lesser prey. A bowl, a
spoon, a spare iron ring from the kitchen stove, a squash from the
plantation, a new apron—they all flowed in a silent stream to the
house that he rented on the edge of the farm settlement.

Like some devastating hurricane, Gabuniya had cut a swath
through the kitchens of most of the restaurants and canteens along
the coast between Batum and Natanebi before he wearied of audit
inspections and interrogations, and finally settled down in this out-
of-the-way state farm, which offered the broadest possible scope to
his thieving imagination. By only stealing things of trivial value, he
remained wholly unpunished, while giving ample play to his well-
nigh maniacal bent. But his restless soul longed for aesthetic pleasures too, and in this respect the old furnaceman exactly answered his
need. The shrewd chef probed and found the other's weaknesses
without difficulty, and from then on he constantly played on them,
skillfully spinning out his enjoyment.

"I s'pose that's what they taught you in school," Ivan growled
morosely. "Next you'll be telling me the world rests on the backs of
three whales."

"God sees all, Ivan, and hears all." The chef kept on at him. "The
devils will roast you in hell, like shish-kebob."

"There aren't any devils either."

"Oh yes there are, I've seen them myself."

"You see all sorts of things when you're drunk . . ."

"I don't drink, Ivan, you know that."

"Well, where did you see them then?"

"There aren't any more where I saw them," said the cook with a
crafty wink. "But they'll call on you one day, Ivan, just you wait and
see."

"Huh—you're just ignorant and superstitious." The furnaceman
stood up and started to go. "There's no God and there's no devil either."

"There is, Ivan, there is." The chef's triumphant laughter followed him as he went. "There is a God. And there's a devil too."

"You're a fool," snapped the Ukrainian from around the corner, "and a thief."

"Now, now, Ivan"—the taunt came after him in pursuit—"you know it's a sin to say such things. Where did you get those pears from anyway?" Still laughing, he turned to Vlad. "Light the machine, kid, we must start cooking the supper . . . ."

The only relief in Vlad's life was provided by books, of which he had discovered a small and completely untouched cache in an office closet of the farm's clubhouse. Random volumes of Brockhaus and Ephron's Encyclopedia rubbed shoulders with Tolstoy's *The Cossacks* and brochures of government and Communist Party ordinances; *The Brothers Karamazov* lived peacefully alongside Stalin's *Problems of Leninism*, while the great Georgian epic poem, Shota Rustaveli's *The Knight in the Tiger-skin*, was not ashamed to stand beside textbooks on farming methods. Vlad devoured them all one after the other, and his head was soon a fantastic mixture: concepts beginning with the letters "E" and "Z," the logical sophistry of the Grand Inquisitor, rigid precepts on a son's degree of responsibility for his father, Yeroshka's drunken outpourings, and the rules for cultivating citrus fruit. And above it all could be heard the divine precision, the sweet-toned magic of Rustaveli's poetry:

Wax is to fire akin. Inflamed, it burneth bright;
In water groweth cold and pale as sunset rays at night.
Through grief thou better learnst the grief of man, thy fellow;
For know: I too must burn away, as burneth tapers' tallow.

As soon as his shift was over, Vlad would hurry to take refuge in the dry but cool semidarkness of the clubroom, and there, as he opened the cover of his current book, he would plunge into a world of illusory passions and abstract truths. While thus occupied he was found one day by the farm's chief ration clerk, David Khukhashvili, a young, hunchbacked Georgian with the sad eyes of an ailing dog:

"Can you read, son?" he asked in amazement as he turned the light of his suffering gaze toward Vlad. "Can you write, too?"

"Yes, I can." Vlad's heart leaped: the unseen wing of Fortune was fanning him with a refreshing breeze of expectation and hope. "I finished four grades, and was in the fifth."

"I have a job for you. Were you good at free composition?"

"Yes, I was." Vlad's compositions had won the hearts of all the teachers of Russian language who had taught him during the short years of his schooling. "I always used to get a five . . . sometimes even a five plus."

"Come with me . . ."

His new job brought out the potential writer in Vlad. It was probably his first essay in the free use of his imagination. At the time of the hay harvest, the farm would unofficially hire a gang of Armenian seasonal laborers. By the unwritten law of those times, each able-bodied migrant worker had to be given three ration cards; they simply refused to sign up on any other terms. This meant, however, that every year there was a need for someone able to conjure up, by pen and ink, a double quantity of "dead souls"—a job which the ration clerk himself was pathologically incapable of doing. Vlad was his hope and salvation. From morning till evening the boy sat in David's little room, barred on all sides, where he would gaze up at the ceiling for inspiration as he soundlessly mouthed the surnames, first names, and patronymics of a legion of fictitious Armenians: "Karapetyan, Avetik Gurgenovich . . . Dovlatyan, Stepan Arshakovich . . . Akopyan, Suren Karapetovich . . . Ovanesyan, Ovanes Akopovich . . ." The muse of prose hovered over him with her iridescent wings, while impatient Pegasus pawed the ground somewhere just outside the porch. The six-winged seraphim of Pushkin's poem had parted his breast to wrest his heart from thence and in its place to set a glowing coal. His ears perceived the tremor of the heavens, the soaring angels' flight, Leviathan's course beneath the waves, the very movement of the vine-stock as it grew. And in him the prophetic Word was poised to fire the hearts of men.

Vlad's life changed noticeably for the better. Soon he was able to throw away the now louse-ridden woollen sweater given to him by Revaz Gabuniya, and to acquire, thanks to the efforts of the ration clerk, a nice new satin shirt. Then he moved into a separate room in the farm bunkhouse, since a dozen or so single rooms were vacant, and by the end of the season he had managed to trade an almost new pair of sneakers for extra food. In his free time he undertook to cross the mountain pass to the village, where he bought fruit for the farm's technicians and mechanics, which also earned him a certain profit. Life, in the words of Stalin, was getting better, life was getting to be more fun.

When the hay-cutting season came to an end, and with it the looming threat of being sent back to tend the hated furnace, it was David himself who called in his smart young assistant for a decisive talk:

"You should go to school, son." In his sculptured face the doleful eyes seemed to live some kind of secret life of their own. "Go to Tbilisi. I'll fix you a permit." With his suffering air, he shone a martyred smile at Vlad. "You'll be a great man one day, I tell you . . ."

These first prophetic words in praise of his writing talent encouraged Vlad and filled his heart with gratitude toward the kindhearted hunchback:

"Thank you, David Anzorych . . . If it hadn't been for you . . ."

To obtain a release permit from a state farm in those days, when every worker was worth his weight in gold, was not an easy matter, but by hook or by crook David Khukhashvili succeeded in making the farm director comply with the law and sign Vlad's release papers. Afterward he himself took the boy to the nearest crossroads to see him off.

"That road will take you straight to Ochkhamuri; you can make it there in time for the evening train." In the twilight the tall, candle-like trunks of eucalyptus trees looked even straighter and more solemn than usual. Although from there the sea was out of sight, the distant sky above it appeared to glow softly and hazily with the light reflected from the water. The road seemed to give off an almost audible hum as it exhaled the heat of the day into the air. "Write to David when you get fixed up."

"Yes, of course I'll write."

No, Vlad never did write to him, neither then nor later. But often afterward, in dream or delirium, in a far corner of his memory there would appear the stocky little figure of a gnome with wistful eyes, and that twilight, and that sky above the sea, and that road as it breathed out the breath of daytime.

Tbilisi! In the years to come Vlad was to see many cities and in most of them he was to leave behind some portion of his destiny—his hopes, his work, a woman—but none of them were to leave their mark on him with such force and pain as this one. Again and again he would return there, each time to taste once more the bitterness of his first encounter. Having on that first occasion treated Vlad as the worst of outcasts, later this city was to recompense him a hundred-fold with its warmth and hospitality; but between them no trust was to grow, forever poisoned as it was by that initial hostility. He was to freeze with cold and shiver with damp in the labyrinths of Navtlugi, to grow dumb and deaf with hunger and malaria under the steep banks of the river Kura, unaware that somewhere close by, in solitary confinement as a political prisoner, his future guide to these parts, Shura Tsybulevsky, was waiting to hear his sentence pronounced; while the man who was one day to be his friend, Bulat Okudzhava, then still a student, was writing his first song:

> Furious, relentless,
> Burn, fire, burn.
> Decembers are not endless—
> Come January's turn . . .

The cold drove Vlad toward the sun—to Baku, where at that time, walking to school past wharves and the torture chambers of Bagirov, lived that delightful giant Volodya Levin; later, the rough and tumble of the newspaper world was to throw them together for many years. From thence—by sea to the ever-burning sands of Central Asia.

On the dockside in Baku, while waiting for a steamer, he dictated to a chance passerby a letter to his mother:

"Dear Fedosya Savelievna, On the way from Tbilisi to Baku your young son Vladik Samsonov died in my arms from hunger and privation . . ."

As Vlad dictated, he was choked by tears of self-pity. Ah, how he loved fine words!

CHAPTER 25

He had as yet seen no vision of his Galilee, but without knowing it he was already moving toward it in his peregrinations along the labyrinthine roads of Russia, from one tramps' hideout to another, to the sound of police whistles and shouts of prison guards, of prisoners' songs and the barking of tracker dogs. Onward he went, through cities and through the years of his life, along a trail of reformatories and juvenile detention centers, fingerprinting and expulsion orders, encounters, insults and disappointments. He does not regret the episodes which went to make up his past, for each one of us has his cross to bear; but more than once, when unbearable pain made him gasp for breath and the sky looked black, he would cry out, turning his eyes heavenward:

"What for?"

At such moments there came something—he did not yet perceive what it was—that would raise him up and carry him forward, despite darkness and despair. Later, many years afterward, he would come to understand that this was a reward from on high, an advance against future account, the gift of love and forgiveness. How many times was that priceless gift to save him on his long wanderings!

He remembers how, one dull wet autumn in Kutaisi, as he lay on the roof of a public lavatory in his own filth, eaten by lice and racked with hunger, his collarbone broken during a police raid, he was ready

to throw up the sponge and give way to despair; his weak lips opened
in a curse, his fingers clenched bitterly into a fist, yet he could not
raise it in a threatening gesture. At the last moment, through a gap in
the building's pediment there appeared the high-cheekboned face of
the pickpocket Misha Mishadibekov: two gimlet-like eyes beneath a
small, neat, new peaked cap.

"Feel like turning your toes up?" the visitor inquired as he eased
his supple little body into Vlad's lair. "Hey, we can't have that . . ."

Vlad lacked even the strength to reply to him.

For many days and nights this vagrant Tartar watched over Vlad
until he was able to get to his feet and realize that he had survived.
Who, what power, whose will was it that prompted or obliged a social outcast, a thief, to nurse a chance-met tramp, to provide him
with food and drink and change the filthy rags on which he lay?
Later he was to ask himself that question and, in replying to it, he
was mentally borne back into the past:

"There is no way I can thank you, Misha, except by these few
words I have said about you. I would be truly happy if ever you were
to hear them. No, I do not flatter myself with the hope that these
words are sufficient to repay my debt to you—that is beyond price;
but it would make it much easier for me to live on this earth and my
burden lighter to bear."

Part 2

CHAPTER 1

Deer Vladik i got yore letter thanks a lot you cant immagin how glad i was becos i got one from tanya with yors and that was luvly too i cride like a baby wen i red them im very homesik here and cry a lot everythings so strainge and i dont no a sole i feel so lonly and i dont no wot to do with miself becos i dont seem to fit in arround heer my helths not wot it was eether my livers paining me deer Vladik dont wurry about me il be alrite and il last out wile the kids are groing up they ofen ask after you wen alyosha gets up in the morning he asks wot time is it in Moscow now and hows my unkle Vova he sais wen i gro up il go and see him sumtimes he even cries and sais i wanna go to moscow his sister ira cant remmember ennything shes just like her grandma dosnt seme to like annybody in pertickler shel probly be very hard wen she gros up but never mind wel see. deer Vladik dont wurry about me too much i trust in god praps hel help us to see you agane you no wot my lifes bin like nothing but teers i never had a hapy day in my hole life but that cant be helpd i spose its just my fate il stick it out and then wel see. thats all for now so long Vladik deer lots of luv and a big kis rite me soon . . .

Lord, Lord, oh Lord! Where can I hide from that voice, that supplication? Forgive me, my aunt Maria Mikhailovna, and again forgive

me! Sinner that I am, I bless you in your far-distant Sinai—and that
is my act of contrition . . .

My dear brother,
It's ages since I wrote to you, but then I haven't heard from you
for a long time, either. Our salvation is the telephone—Yura can either talk to you or to his friends, who always have some news to tell
about you. I do realize how difficult it is for you to write, but I hope
you haven't forgotten us. In late July and early August I was
furiously busy, taking exams to qualify for the Ministry of Education
certificate to teach school. Taking the exams put me in a horrible
mood. As you know, this August I shall be forty; back in Russia I
had already achieved some kind of settled position in my job and in
life as a whole, I was even quite respected, yet here I'm made to feel
like a child again. With great difficulty I manage to stammer something in Hebrew, and they just smile condescendingly. However, I'm
now beginning to get over my depression. Some time between the
15th and 20th of August we are going to move to Haifa. I'm placing
great hopes on this move, especially where aunt Maria Mikhailovna
is concerned. Personally I want and need nothing—I only pray that
she will recover her health. I actually think she has reached the end
of her tether. The atmosphere at home is awful; she realizes it, but
seems simply unable to do anything about it. I'm particularly upset
by her incessant carping and bad temper. She was never like this before. I'm sure it bores you to death when I keep on writing about
this, but I assure you I will be the happiest person in the world when
I no longer have cause to complain about it to you. Perhaps you
could write and ask her to tell you quite frankly just what it is that
she doesn't like here; perhaps there is something in the way we behave, or in what we do, that upsets her.
Otherwise everything seems to be more or less normal for the time
being. The children are fine and run about all over the place. As of
1 August, Ira has been going to Hebrew classes, Alyosha is already in
kindergarten. His birthday was a great success. We bought him lots
of toys—from Uncle Vova, from Grandma, Grandpa, and from all of
us. He was delighted with them. He has grown a lot, he's sun-tanned,
he climbs up walls and poles with his bare hands like a little mon-
key. And he's very funny and affectionate, but also terribly naughty.
All his American and Israeli relatives are crazy about him. Ira, they
all say, has grown very serious and independent, very self-possessed.

She can already speak good Hebrew, Alyosha understands practically everything, although he doesn't talk much—but then he is only just starting. Lots of photos will be ready soon, and of course we'll send them to you. Yura's relatives from the States have helped us a great deal; they gave us the money for a down payment on the apartment. At last I have seen our apartment. Compared with what we always used to have, it's lovely. It's in a nice and very pretty suburb on a hillside, with a view over the city and the sea. And it's not so hot up there as it is down below, although it is fairly humid—because of the sea. When we move in I'll take some photos of the house and the apartment, and send them to you.

Well, that's about all, I think. I do beg you, Vladik, to give Yura's parents a call now and again. Absolutely no one ever goes to see them or calls them up. And they're old, sick and lonely. Please—even if you only do it occasionally.

I think about you a great deal, and I miss you a lot. I can't say that I always understood you, but I do know that you always understood me—and without many words from me to help you. It's hard for me here, very hard, but believe me, I shall try to stick it out. Apart from you, I haven't told anyone else that I find it hard; Yura mustn't know, because I don't want him to feel guilty in any way.

Well, take care of yourself, keep well and don't forget us.

A big hug and kiss.

Katya.

How can I forget you, my own flesh and blood? I could as soon forget myself . . .

Vlad closed his eyes and tried to imagine that country, that vaulted sky and that city draped like a Bedouin's white burnous over the steep hills and the burning heat haze above the sea. He could almost swear that somewhere, sometime he had seen something like it. Only an approximation: a blurred facsimile of the original, a negative of an undeveloped, amateur snapshot, a clumsy copy of a splendid, full-scale model.

But when was it, and what were the circumstances?

Stop!

CHAPTER 2

The white Caspian Sea faintly tinged with blue; yellow hills bare of
trees; a huddle of gray boxes around a wretched little railroad station
—Krasnovodsk. And heat; sultry, humid heat. Heat laden with the
prisonlike stench of hot asphalt and carbolic. Heat which threatened
to dry out your brain and coagulate the blood in your veins. And
sand, which even after traveling as far as Orenburg—a distance almost equal to a quarter of the earth's circumference—you could still
feel in your teeth.

As Vlad climbed uphill into the town amid a motley crowd of
newly arrived travelers, he was bewildered and scared. Out there, beyond the low hills around Krasnovodsk, lay the hidden menace of
the infinite sands. He felt that in their hot, pulsating breath he could
sense countless beasts and reptiles, weaving the eternal web of their
hidden life. Snakes and lizards, spiders and scorpions, mice, mon-
gooses and jackals, all savagely devouring each other—and sometimes
themselves—and in doing so fertilizing the arid, sandy soil with their
dead remains and their new seed. The grim Karakum desert surrounded the town with multiform legions of enchanted images, and
the town huddled close to the sea, desperately clinging on for safety
to the very edge of the plateau.

From the quayside the road climbed upward, and along it, drifting
off in various directions, there flowed like a funeral procession the

riffraff of that hungry year of 1946. Every morning a crowd of them would land, and set off by the first train across the sands toward the blessed green valleys of Central Asia in search of warmth and bread. And what a mixture they were! Haggard Moldavians, their clothes patched and repatched, features conspicuous by their thick eyebrows and the look of a horse thief on the run; Ukrainians so hungry that they were ready for anything; whole clans of Tartars, dazed by their own incessant shouting; and Russians, Russians, Russians—of all ages and aspects, perpetual rolling stones, mindless vagrants, pilgrims in search of a land of milk and honey, wanderers branded from birth with melancholy and loneliness. Having sucked them all into its fire-breathing maw, the desert would later vomit forth what remained of them at the farthest points of the continent, as far west as Orsha in Byelorussia or the parched Kazakh steppes of Aktyubinsk.

When the human flood had swept Vlad into the town and then, ebbing away down side streets and alleys, left him standing alone in the road, he suddenly heard the sound of rapid footsteps behind him.

"Hold it, kid, want to talk to you." The hoarse, breathless voice finally drew level with his shoulder. "It's you I'm talking to."

Alongside him stood a thin young man, a whole head taller than Vlad, wearing an oversized railroad uniform tunic and a railroad peaked cap on his short-cropped hair. As he walked beside Vlad, the youth gave him an appraising look from his owlish, half-closed eyes, while trying to adjust his long, gangling stride to Vlad's slower, tottering, weary steps.

"Well?" said Vlad. This unexpected companion aroused little enthusiasm in him. The bitter experience of a vagrant's life had long since stifled any desire to strike up quick friendships. "What d'you want?"

"Been on the road for long? Where are you going? Where are you from?" He fired off his questions without waiting for an answer. Under parchmentlike skin his jaw muscles moved crisply, a sharp-pointed chin hovered inquiringly over Vlad's head. "Noticed you back on the ship. Could tell you'd been around a bit. I need a partner badly right now. Let's head for the bazaar. Know how to act as a 'blind'?"

After the business in Batum, Vlad had sworn never to get mixed up in any adventures likely to be covered by some article of the Criminal Code, but hunger was already making itself felt, and his role of accomplice in the proposed operation involved only a minimum of risk.

"Okay." Succumbing to temptation, he gave a businesslike nod. "If anything goes wrong, you don't know me and I don't know you."

"Teach your grandmother . . ."

The small, almost empty bazaar was unsuitable for their plan. Obviously never too busy at the best of times, the place was almost completely empty of customers that afternoon, leaving the native traders to the mercy of the heat and the flies. On the barely shaded counters they had laid out their modest wares: soggy cottage cheese on strips of much-laundered cheesecloth, sour milk in cans of assorted sizes, some meager piles of raisins, a few chopped dried apricots, and here and there among this pathetic medley, looking rather like prehistoric burial mounds, were dully gleaming animal bladders full of mutton packed in lard. Behind the counters, the stallkeepers kept a vigilant watch with eyes suppurating from trachoma and heat, staring ahead over their veils or from the folds of their robes with the unmistakable message: keep your thieving hands to yourselves!

Now and again a police sergeant, cap tipped down over his eyes, would appear in the doorway of the guardhouse at the gates to the bazaar. Stretching sleepily, he would glance around the territory in his charge and then, obviously satisfied with his inspection, disappear back into the welcome semidarkness of the guardhouse.

"Look, over there—that old woman with the necklace, in the far corner." The victim chosen, it remained for them to wait until the heat abated and a busy crowd in the bazaar made their task easier. "Keep a sharp eye on her, and while we're waiting we can have a smoke in the shade."

"I don't smoke."

"Nor do I." The young man gave a mirthless grin and lay down under the counter of one of the unoccupied stalls. "When it gets cooler, wake me up . . . But don't you fall asleep, and don't you let the old hag out of your sight."

Without taking his eyes off the unfortunate old woman, Vlad loafed around the little marketplace waiting for the busy time of day to start, while ever and again the pitiless sun seemed to explode in his eyeballs in a shower of rainbow-colored fireworks, and a piercing sound split his head, resounding in his temples like a dull hammering. Gritty dust tickled his throat, burned the soles of his feet, and penetrated into every pore of his skin. Warm and as insubstantial as water in a dream, the water he drank from a standing faucet did not quench his thirst but simply gathered in a heavy, nauseating lump somewhere under his ribs.

When at last the fading disk of the sun slowly and reluctantly touched the tops of the surrounding hills, Vlad already loathed the old woman with a deadly hatred. Her veil thrown backward over her head, she was picking out the lice in the folds of her robe and squashing them with such self-absorption and furious concentration that this occupation seemed to hold some higher significance perceptible only to her. Now and again her nearsighted, watering eyes would look up, peering dimly ahead into space, only to flick down again to her unceasing search for lice. Vlad could almost hear the beads of her necklace clicking in time to her every movement.

The bazaar came to life as soon as the afternoon heat began to lessen and the first shadows touched the walls and counters. From every nook and cranny a motley crowd of human flotsam drifted into the bazaar square: legless ex-soldiers, blind men in navy jackets, tramps without identity papers who not long ago had been workmen, crowds of local officials grown shabby during the long wartime evacuation, orphaned children of postwar vintage, pensioners and roving thieves, demobilized soldiers and local nomad tribesmen, blackmarketeers, money-changers. Man must eat, and since demand clearly exceeded supply, everyone was in a hurry.

Returning with relief to their hideout, Vlad gently nudged his partner:

"Time to get going."

Already wide awake, the youth instantly fixed Vlad with a round, bright eye and asked briskly:

"Is the old woman still there?"

"Where else would she go?"

"You won't foul up the job, will you?"

"Think I've never done a 'blind' before?"

"Okay, okay." The other grinned, soothing Vlad's injured pride, as they moved off into the crowd. "Keep your wits about you, though, or they'll catch us. Then blow, and meet me behind the water-distilling plant . . ."

The job that Vlad had to do was not difficult: to distract the old woman's attention while his partner rifled her supplies under the counter. Fading into the bazaar crowd, he began to slowly move toward the target. Like a piece of parchment framed in a striped shawl, the old Turkmen woman's sharp features hovered over her piles of dried fruit and bladders; her little trachomatous eyes squinting near-sightedly, she looked exactly like the evil wizard Kashchey in the fairy tale, gloating over his hoard of gold.

The operation went like clockwork. Pretending to be a genuine customer, Vlad had only to stretch out his hand toward some of the old woman's goods for her to be instantly transformed. Her senile apathy and sleepiness vanished. Starting up in fury like a broody hen that has been suddenly disturbed, she began flapping the wings of her robe and clucking in the only language they both understood:

"Shoo! . . . Shoo! . . ." She even seemed about to take flight. "Shoo, little devil! . . . Shoo! . . ."

Vlad amused himself by playing games with the old woman and teasing her, exactly long enough for his partner to raid her reserves beneath the counter. No sooner had the youth dived into the surrounding crowd with a well-filled bladder under his arm than Vlad lost all interest in her and turned away; he was already passing the gates when an infuriated howl from the old bazaar woman reached his ears. "Go on, shout—if it makes you feel better," Vlad thought maliciously as he ran off in the direction of the sea.

Vlad's partner had not cheated him. After a short search he climbed up the steep bank on the far side of the water-distilling plant, and there the young man was waiting for him, bending over a hastily lit fire and wielding a penknife over their joint booty.

"Sit down, kid." Dripping with fat, the heap of meaty rib bones grew larger as he carved up the mutton onto a piece of newspaper spread neatly beside the fire. "What's your name?"

"Vlad," he gulped, swallowing his saliva. "My nickname's 'Boxer.'"

"You don't say!" The youth gave Vlad a sarcastic look. "Take what you want and shove off." Then more kindly: "Okay, no shit, stick around, kid, and stuff your gut—then blow . . . You can call me Seryozha. Okay?"

"M'hm," Vlad murmured gratefully, completely absorbed in eating. "M'hm . . ."

Vlad was to remember that feast for a long time. For years afterward he would dream of that hungry orgy on the deserted shore of the Caspian Sea. The pile of meat melted before their eyes. They swallowed it almost without chewing. His gums were bathed in a sticky layer of fat, meat fibers lodged themselves in the gaps between his teeth, and his palate ached with the strain. Even when their eyes could no longer bear to look at the food, their jaws kept on moving until at last their stomachs refused to take any more; only then did they roll over onto their backs and take their first proper look at the sea, the shoreline and the evening sky above them.

Vlad lay prostrate in delicious exhaustion. A crimson sunset was burning itself out on the horizon and the waves splashed gently, almost at his feet, while just behind him the machinery of the water-distilling plant kept up a low, mysterious hum. Lulled by the peace and calm of the surroundings, like a saturated sponge Vlad mindlessly absorbed the story that his partner told between long pauses:

"Stick with me, kid, and you'll get by. I've been on the road, brother, since I was twelve, I've been sent down the river five times and all for thieving. What the hell, I can always scrounge enough to eat, and you can't stay free forever. This is my third time round on the trip to Asia. The first time was before the war, when there was plenty to eat, and suckers everywhere—you could really live in those days. Then in the war I was evacuated here to hospital on the *Bagirov*, the same ship that brought us here today, and I stayed here while I got well after being wounded . . ."

"So you fought in the war?"

"Sure I did—and how. Copped it twice—once from a rifle bullet, the other time from shell splinters. I was a prisoner, too, but not for long—I escaped and went on fighting right up to Prague. Then they sent me to school, but that wasn't my scene. I'm a loner, see, I prefer freedom. Stalin can do the thinking if he likes, his head's big enough —but I get by just as well without any of the stuff they teach in school. Since last year, though, I've been having trouble with my chest and started coughing bad—don't have the strength I used to. They say there are some waters here that'll cure you. Some good buddies of mine told me where to find the place, so I'm headed there to try it out. No harm in trying . . ." The long-drawn-out wail of a railroad whistle could be heard on the far side of the city, growing louder. "That's the express from Ashkhabad pulling in. In three hours' time it'll start back again. So let's have ourselves a bit of shuteye and then it's off to the railroad station . . ."

Late that evening the Ashkhabad Express bore them away over cooling sands and into the enticing unknown of the desert. Stretched out on the rods under a boxcar, pierced by the bone-dry night wind of the Karakum, Vlad dozed off to the exultant song of the wheels: "Lie down and sleep, lie down and sleep, lie down and sleep . . ."

Asia—the travelers who fly by night greet you!

Sergei, Seryozha! The bond between you and Vlad is indissoluble, now and for evermore. Perhaps now, in the third quarter of life, those two headlong years may seem at times to have been a mere flash of summer lightning, the brilliant flicker of a falling star against the interminable, dull background of ordinary, everyday life, but whenever he remembers them his heart thrills and opens wide to memories of the past. And he recalls in detail every day, every hour, every minute of those fast-flowing years, from the feast in Krasnovodsk right up to that hot afternoon in the cellars of Moscow's Taganka prison, when a grim escort of guards separated the pair of you to send you to different prisons, a journey on which your paths never crossed again.

Let's hope, though, that your predestined parting also means that you are fated to meet somewhere in the future. Let's hope so.

CHAPTER 3

Spiked with broken glass along the top, the four adobe walls of the reformatory rose almost six feet higher than the surrounding buildings, giving the impression that outside them was nothing—sheer emptiness, sand and sky. The only reminders of the ceaseless life of a provincial capital were the daytime hubbub that came from the saltwood lumber yard alongside the reformatory and the lamentations of mourners arising from the adjacent cemetery.

Until late in the fall, before landing up in the reformatory, Vlad had lived a hand-to-mouth existence, sleeping in railroad stations and shantytowns or freezing in the sands of the Karakum desert between Ashkhabad and Chardzhou, sometimes helping Sergei, sometimes making out alone. For the greater part of the time Sergei kept Vlad by his side, only occasionally allowing him to act on his own initiative. Without being aware of it, Vlad himself soon developed an attachment to the consumptive veteran-turned-tramp. There was something about Sergei which evoked in those around him an instinctive trust. An unquenchable urge for mutual understanding and sympathy was always breaking through his mask of cool sarcasm. Although he hated being alone, indeed found it intolerable, he avoided all gangs and thieves' hideouts, preferring a brick factory, where in the space between the roof and the top of a brick kiln most of the town's shifting population of vagrants usually spent the night. Here Sergei was in his element. He was visibly flattered by the respect shown to him as a professional thief by the begging fraternity, but he never took advantage of it or threw his weight about, trying rather to be as inconspicuous and unobtrusive as possible. He shared the proceeds of his daily haul generously and fairly among them all, and when he presided over this pauper's feast at midnight he would say with a good-natured grin:

"Help yourself, fellows. Go ahead, prices are down, everything here's up for grabs. You won't make a living traipsing from door to door. The people hereabouts won't even spare a curse for you these days, let alone a crust of bread. No, you gotta know how to scalp 'em —expropriate the expropriators! They've been sitting here in cushy jobs in the rear, now it's our turn . . . Dig in, Vlad; there's more where this came from."

It was his sociability that was Sergei's undoing. The brickworks was an ideal target for a raid, and although Sergei was usually given advance warning of a police roundup by certain people in close touch with headquarters, one day the network failed to function, and they all shared a common fate. In the courtyard of police headquarters the victims were sorted out into categories. Sergei and the other adults were taken to the Duty Officer, who made them sign the usual undertaking not to leave the city limits, while Vlad and a bunch of under-eighteens were sent to the Juvenile Detention Center from whence, as a persistent offender, he was transferred to a reformatory.

There he was given scarcely more to eat than he had been able to scrounge when living in freedom, but in compensation Vlad, after a long interruption, was able to read books again. Like a welcome drug, they made his existence more tolerable in this homemade hell à la Makarenko.*

It must have required a truly morbid, sadistic imagination to have invented an institution whose only difference from an army barracks was that in this barracks power was in the hands of brutalized teenagers, whose use of it was restrained neither by the experience that comes with adulthood nor by the law. Encouraged from above, these little fanatics with officers' badges on their sleeves enthusiastically vied with one another in inventive cruelty. They would beat up any-

* Anton Makarenko (1888–1939) was a leading Soviet educational theorist and the founder of a method of reforming juvenile delinquents through work camps, where good behavior was instilled by moral pressure from the "collective" or peer group. (Tr.)

one with and without reason, as an advance on future punishment and for sheer intimidation. Beatings up were, in fact, so normal that they were not even taken seriously.

The slightest disobedience was punished even more severely and mercilessly. To this end there existed a whole gamut of possible forms of execution. The lightest of them all was known as "the seagull": the offender was picked up and tossed many times onto the upturned legs of several stools placed upside down in a row. Next in the series was "the poultice": this consisted of from five to fifteen blows with a pair of socks that had been tightly packed with sand. While leaving no outward marks, it produced painful, long-lasting internal bruising. The supreme form of punishment was called "the pyramid": having first had salt smeared on and around his kneecaps, the victim was made to stand in the blazing sunshine, holding a heavy log in his upraised hands and kept in this position until he collapsed unconscious.

The taste of power turned their close-cropped heads and made their nostrils flare with vice and lust. Flocks of young homosexuals would mince around the precincts of the reformatory with the co-quettish mannerisms of kept whores, exuding bodily stench and creating waves of envy. Hungry informers slouched from hut to hut on the alert for a careless word or a dangerous thought. The inmates' youthful enthusiasm for gambling and trade sometimes reached heights that were worthy of the fabled city of Baghdad in the era of its fame. God knows what the erstwhile juvenile offender from Gori found to grin at through the reproductions of his nicotine-stained mustache that adorned practically every vertical surface in the reformatory, for had he been born half a century later he would undoubtedly have been one of the first to experience the beauties and attractions of this "pedagogical poem".*

The prefectlike "activists" tried to break Vlad during his introductory spell in the Reception Block of the reformatory, known as "quarantine." His police record as an underage vagrant aroused their

---

* The phrase "juvenile offender from Gori" refers to Stalin, who was born in the small Georgian town of Gori; during his youth as a pupil in an Orthodox seminary, Stalin was in frequent trouble both with the ecclesiastical authorities for infractions of discipline and with the police for political offences. *Pedagogical Poem* is the title of Makarenko's major work (published 1933–35), a three-volume fictionalized autobiography, which contained a detailed account of his educational theories and of his fifteen years of practical work in the reform and rehabilitation of young delinquents. (Tr.)

unwilling respect: five separate Juvenile Detention Centers in five towns were competing for the right to claim him, under five different names, as a runaway. When the activists bullied him he responded with a stubborn silence. When they tried to drag him out of the communal cell and into the Duty Officer's room for a special "working-over," he threatened to hang himself. After that they gave him up as crazy, and left him alone. The reputation which he acquired of being slightly mad, withdrawn and abnormal, largely freed him from the importunate attentions of the reformatory instructors and surveillance by informers.

In the repair workshop, to which he was eventually assigned, Vlad continued to hold himself aloof from the rest, steering clear of casual acquaintance and attempts at friendship. The others were obviously somewhat afraid of him: a new inmate who had successfully resisted the temptations and brutalities of "quarantine" evoked an attitude of grudging respect mixed with fear. Even the workshop foreman—his face with its prominent cheekbones and tightly stretched pink skin was tattooed with a "beauty spot" on one sunken cheek—who was a promoted reformatory activist grunted sarcastically as he looked Vlad up and down:

"You look as if they could've snapped you in two, but it seems you're a tough nut. We'll see how long you can keep it up."

He never let Vlad out of his sight and did his best to make life unbearable for him at every suitable opportunity. This onetime gang boss, his self-esteem crippled, was jealous of the obstinate pride shown by the cheeky young newcomer. He persecuted Vlad with the resolute malice of someone bitterly disillusioned with the human race. Oh, wretched humankind! Whenever he caught him smoking or idling, the foreman would grasp Vlad's chin with the tenacious fingers of an old cardsharper and slowly rock the boy's head from side to side:

"So you're one of the professionals, are you? Too high and mighty for us, eh? Oil and water don't mix, is that it? The big boys are missing you, I hear. Maybe you'd like to go and have a little talk with them. Or perhaps your ribs haven't healed up yet after 'quarantine'? Okay, you can go now, but next time I'll fix you—don't ask for mercy, I'm in here for a long time . . ."

Vlad lived like a fully compressed spring, ready to unwind instantaneously and strike a blow. Hostility surrounded him on all sides: the law of collective responsibility tolerated no exceptions to the rules. His fierce obduracy could cost him dear, and he lived in permanent expectation of treachery. The very air around him, it seemed, was saturated with the word "evil." Even when he lay down to sleep, Vlad never put aside the iron rod which he kept hidden in case he was forced into a fight. But just when the tension reached a peak and the inevitable seemed bound to happen at any moment, Vlad's circumstances suddenly changed.

One day after work the foreman stopped him and, avoiding his eyes, thrust a note into Vlad's hand:

"It's for you . . . from Sergei . . . Why didn't you tell me you were his partner? You made me make a fool of myself." His thin, cracked lips twisted into a grimace. "I almost made a terrible mistake with you—and I couldn't have made up for it to my dying day . . . I'll be waiting for you in the clubhouse this evening. We'll put our heads together and think up what to do."

Vlad immediately recognized his partner's bold scrawl:

"Blow the joint. This guy will help you. Sergei."

He almost burst into tears in an overwhelming wave of gratitude and affection. "He didn't forget me, he's rescued me!" He read the note over and over again. "I won't forget this as long as I live!"

That evening in a dark corner of the clubhouse porch, the foreman explained his plan for Vlad's escape.

"You must go straight over the wall on a Sunday night. It's less risky that way. I'll make sure there's a hole where you can get through the inner barbed-wire fence. I'll fix it with the other kids to raise a racket and keep the guards busy. The wall has broken glass on top, so you'd better get a mattress for your own protection. There'll be a plank waiting for you between the barbed wire and the wall; it's better than a ladder. Okay?"

"I'll give it a try . . ."

"Tell Sergei that I didn't touch you, will you?" His fear was stronger than his pride, and he was almost trying to ingratiate himself with Vlad. "You will tell him, won't you? It was your own fault, you know. You should've told me right away, then I wouldn't have given you a hard time. Have a heart, otherwise I'm done for . . . He'll rub me out, and I have a family in town. You will tell him, won't you?"

For a moment Vlad felt a perfidious temptation to get instant revenge for everything that he had suffered in this place, but the foreman was gazing at him with such hope and a look of such doglike entreaty hovered in his pale eyes that Vlad could not withstand it, and he fought off the temptation:

"Okay, I'll tell him . . ."

In the days that remained until the agreed date of his escape, Vlad took advantage of the foreman's complicity and lay from morning till night on the roof of a disused hut, reading book after book from the reformatory's small library. It was there, in that dusty closet filled with a random, unsorted collection of literary junk, that fate played a nasty joke on Vlad by offering him, after the undemanding works of the playwright Lev Sheinin, a copy of Darwin's *The Origin of Species*. Stumbling over the strange words and learned terminology, Vlad strove impatiently to unravel the meaning and logic of Darwin's arguments, and when comprehension dawned his whole being was shocked into protest: he simply refused to accept that he traced his genealogical descent from an ape! The mere thought of one of these creatures—one of Nature's unfortunate practical jokes on herself, all covered in matted fur and with scabs on its bottom—made him shudder with loathing and nausea.

On Sunday the foreman, as though out for a stroll, led him past the barbed-wire fence.

"Here's the place," he said, glancing toward a fence post, slightly shorter than the rest, which stood between the latrines and the dining hall. "The wire here is loose, the kids have seen to that. The plank's lying behind the latrine hut. Lean it up against the wall, take a short run at it, and you're over. By the way, better take a blanket, not a mattress. A mattress is too heavy and awkward. Fold the blanket double. It will do just as well, because the glass here is only in small pieces and it won't poke through a double thickness of flannel . . ."

"What about creating a diversion?"

"The kids are going to start up right after lights-out. It'll all go like clockwork. As soon as the singing starts and the guards begin running, then get up and scram—they won't find you're gone till morning . . . And see here—let's part friends." The foreman turned aside and his hoarse voice trembled at breaking point. "Let bygones be bygones . . . I'm no saint, and anyone else would have acted just the same. You know how the system is—you can't help taking it out on the guy next to you."

And he set off at a hurried, shambling walk, as if he had suddenly aged a dozen years.

Slowly thickening, the dense subtropical twilight blanketed the surroundings. A sultry night began to draw its thick curtain, pierced by sharp points of starlight, toward the zenith. Limp from the daytime heat, the town beyond the adobe wall settled down and grew quiet. If only night would come—and the darker the better!

With a blanket under his arm, Vlad crept out after lights-out and hid himself in a corner of the latrine to wait for the promised signal. The thrill of danger tightened his throat, the blood hammered in his temples, rainbow-colored circles swam before his eyes and even the stench that floated all around him seemed delightful. Clearly, every freedom has its own smell—and it's worth it!

The boys did not let him down. Less than half an hour had passed when the luring decoy of a loud song burst out on the far side of the reformatory grounds:

> Action stations, comrades,
> Every man on deck:
> The last roll call has sounded . . .

The singing was somewhat ragged, but on the other hand it was exceptionally loud—the boys were really trying hard. For a moment the whole reformatory listened in silence, not sure whether to believe its ears. The guardhouse was the first to respond, with the piercing note of a whistle, and immediately the action started. A hum of encouragement and approval spread from hut to hut, as though they were a row of disturbed beehives. The barking of dogs mingled with the clump of hobnailed boots. A classic prison-camp shindy was boiling up. The way was open; no one now was going to pay any attention to a runaway.

Vlad carried out the rest of the plan as though in a dream—shakily and nervously, but purposefully. Having tossed the blanket and the plank over the fence and into the no-go zone between wire and wall, he felt the gap in the wire and wriggled through it, then threw the blanket on top of the wall. Next he placed the plank against the wall at a steep angle, took a run at it and successfully grasped the top of the wall. Hauling himself up, he lay with his chest on the safety of the blanket and with a final wrench of his whole body he flew over to the far side of the wall: he was free!

In falling, Vlad struck his elbow a painful blow on a stone and almost collapsed, but oblivious to the pain he leaped to his feet and ran toward the black outline of the lumber yard, then veered slightly to the right in the direction of the Turkmen cemetery. Dodging between tombstones, he pressed on into the darkness. Behind him, like a war cry and a song of farewell, punctuated with cursing and stamping of feet, there rose the triumphant sound of young voices:

> Our proud ship *Varyag*
> Will never surrender,
> We ask for no quarter . . .

When he had no more breath left and the ground was starting to slither away under his aching legs, a voice arose from out of the inky blackness and floated toward him, a familiar voice that brought tears of relief:

"Vlad!"

"Sergei!"

Expressed in that thankful sigh was the full measure of his admiration and gratitude.

That night a passing freight train bore them away into the depths of Asia and the burgeoning spring.

Farewell, Karakum!

CHAPTER 4

Central Asia is recorded in his memory as one splash of color: pale green on sky blue with dazzling flecks of white. And cities with names that all rhyme with each other: Kokand—Samarkand, Andizhan—Namangan, Tashkent—Chimkent; in them minarets and towers soaring above humble, earthbound, flat roofs; beyond them a land as flat as a tabletop, covered with a network of thirsty irrigation canals. And all of it bathed in a sticky, translucent, sultry heat that makes your head reel deliciously until you nearly faint. Truly, the fabulous adventures of Aladdin could only have happened here.

Bukhara! A termite hill of dried clay with rare flashes of intolerably bright blue from the glazed tiles of ancient palaces, a hospitable abode for the most unimaginable diseases, a paradise for fleas and scorpions. It was indeed hard to believe that in this very city the most beguiling epics of Islamic poetry had been composed, and magical pens had reduced princelings to ecstasy. Words like "sherbet," "kumiss," and "muscat," which had once sounded enticing and mysterious, suddenly revealed their prosaic reality. Sherbet turned out to be a tepid, sickly sweet liquid, kumiss gave off a musty, sourish smell, while muscat, with its cloying bittersweet taste, made the muscles of your face twitch. In dusty, tortuous labyrinths of narrow alleyways, the houses—shut off from prying eyes with high, blank walls—oozed little trickles of evil-smelling liquid, whose acrid stench mingled with

the reek of decaying carrion lying in the street. Raucous beggars
crawled out of every nook and cranny, boastfully displaying livid
scars, which they flaunted openly and cheerfully. There was a quality
of challenging effrontery about these beggars; it was as if the Univer-
sal Order of Beggary had raised its tattered, many-colored flag in this
place, claiming the right to sovereignty and recognition. This gave a
particularly futile look to the shiny glass signboards attached to the
peeling stucco of the houses: PROPHYLACTIC CLINIC, RED
CROSS, MUNICIPAL PHARMACY, EPIDEMIC CONTROL
STATION.

After long, exhausting wanderings among the warren of squalid
houses, the city rewarded the traveler with the noisy hospitality of
the bazaar. Ah, the Bukharan bazaar! Amid a blue, smoky haze from
blacksmiths' bellows and cooks' braziers there floated, bobbed, and
circled an innumerable horde of turbans and skullcaps, fur hats and
head scarves, peaked caps and felt hats. Mixed with the biting aroma
of fires of dried dung, a stink compounded of hay, rawhide, and
sweat hit your nose and numbed your sense of smell for long afterward. Above the cacophony of sound could be heard a man's piercing, plaintive recitative sung to the accompaniment of an accordion:

> In vain the woman waits to see her son's return,
> When they tell her the truth, she will weep . . .

Without pausing to reflect, Sergei dragged Vlad toward that voice:
his underworld instinct was more effective than any compass in guiding him to the beacon that he was seeking.

The voice belonged to a blind sailor, with three yellow stripes
denoting serious wounds sewn on his naval tunic, surrounded by a
sizable crowd of obvious evacuees. As Sergei and Vlad approached
him, the sailor had already put aside his accordion. Opening a thick
folio printed in Braille and placing it on his knees, he ran a gnarled
finger along the page:

". . . He will come back to his Tatyana in September . . . Your
name is Tatyana, isn't it? He has fair hair, a birthmark just under
his ear, and he's thirty years old. Am I right? . . . His name's
Pyotr? . . . There you are, my book never lies, your fate is written in
it down to the last detail. Put down fifty rubles, you can't learn this
sort of thing on the cheap . . . He's been lightly wounded, not hurt
badly, he hasn't lost his manhood. So just wait, my dear, he'll be
back in the fall . . . My book never lies, I got it from a comrade of

mine in the navy. He gave it to me before he died, and his grandfather handed it down to him from the olden days. It's priceless. Fifty rubles is nothing, so if you want to know something—walk up, walk up . . ."

The woman standing in front of him alternately blushed and paled, straining every nerve to divine the meaning of the sailor's fortunetelling. On her gaunt face, the color of melting snow, hope gave way to doubt, followed by another flare of hope.

The surrounding crowd buzzed with interest:

"It's as if he knew it all before!"

"I've known Pyotr since he was a boy. He has light red hair and a birthmark under his ear, so it must be true . . ."

"A blind man sees with his heart."

"It's a kind of gift that came to him after being wounded in the head."

"That woman's in luck."

"Whatever will be—will be!"

"He must be a good man to take the risk . . ."

Sergei only touched the sailor lightly on the shoulder, but that slight contact was enough for the latter to start briskly packing up the tools of his trade: he slammed the book shut, got to his feet, picked up his accordion, and, with careless disregard for the annoyance he caused, pushed his way unceremoniously through the crowd.

"Follow me," he said, nodding to Sergei as he moved out of the bazaar. "It's not far from here."

On the way, the blind man casually shoved his magic book into Vlad's hand and, gripping Sergei confidently by the elbow, strode off boldly down a little winding street. As he hurried along behind the bobbing naval cap, Vlad stole a surreptitious glance at the thick volume and ran his finger along the bumpy surface of the pages, trying however vaguely and approximately to discover its secret. The book remained silent, and he was just about to shut it when at the last moment he caught sight of the publishing information printed in small type on the inside of the cover: "Nikolai Ostrovsky: *How the Steel Was Tempered*. Moscow. Educational Publishing House, 1942."

The street they had turned into took a right-angled bend and led them into a blind alley, where a single doorway was let into an adobe wall. The sailor whistled softly three times, and as though by magic the door opened and let them in.

"You can flop here." As he showed the visitors in, the sailor took off his dark glasses and with a grin of complicity gave Vlad a cheerful wink: "The doctors told me to wear them because of the sun."

They found themselves in a spacious courtyard with a dried-up, moss-grown fountain in the middle. A little gallery, overgrown from top to bottom with a creeping vine, ringed the entire inner wall of the house. A brick pathway crossed the courtyard to the far side, toward a doorway shaded by an awning, which looked like the gateway to the infernal regions.

The veiled woman who had let them in made a sign in the direction of one of the sides of the gallery. The sailor gave a nod of understanding, and set off on the way she had indicated, into the shade of the vine, inviting his guests to follow him.

After the intense sunlight of the street Vlad found the semi-darkness under the awning almost impenetrable. Only partly accustomed to the gloom, he was just able to make out the figure of a pudgy man, half bald, dressed only in underclothes, stretched out on a pile of quilted blankets, who was staring at them from under swollen eyelids.

"Who've you brought this time?" he asked, barely moving his stuck-together lips. "Some more no-good pickpockets, I suppose?"

"It's Sergei," said the sailor, nervously rubbing one leg against the other. "D'you mean to say you didn't recognize him, Vasyuta? He's one of us."

Vasyuta showed slightly more signs of life and even tried to sit up, but immediately slumped back again:

"Aha . . . sit down, pal, and let's have a drink. I've gone nearly out of my mind all alone here . . . haven't stopped drinking for two weeks. My brain's almost dried up with this heat." He blinked his heavy eyelids in the sailor's direction and ordered:

"Okay, push off, and tell Fatima . . ."

The sailor vanished at once, and soon the same veiled woman noiselessly and efficiently placed bowls in front of them, served them with pancakes, dried apricots, and a pitcher of yoghurt, then immediately disappeared without having uttered a word.

They drank and ate in silence. First to speak was their host: "Business is lousy here, pal. The people are so hard up, the only things they've got plenty of is patches on their clothes." The food and drink seemed to have sobered him up, his speech took on a note of hard common sense, and his eyes grew rounder, staring at his visitors with a mocking gleam: "It's gotten so boring, Sergei, that the only thing to do is turn pickpocket and fleece any newcomers coming into town."

"Things are the same everywhere." As usual, Sergei did not get drunk but only grew paler and sharper-tempered from drinking. "There's famine and shortage everywhere. Soon there won't be anything left to steal."

"Say what you like, Russia's at her last gasp. There isn't even enough bread anymore."

"It's the drought."

"Bad workers blame their tools. I'm from the country myself, brother, and a drought shouldn't worry a good farmer. But now instead of a sensible boss we've a great thinker in charge of us, and he doesn't want bread, he wants blood. He only understands human slaughter, and keeps the country in hand with a pack of sheep dogs."

"He's not immortal, and he'll have to die one of these days."

"Huh! You should try carrying water in a yoke on your neck. We're not people, we're just beasts of burden. Whatever we do, we get screwed. I've seen Stalin when I've been on trips to Moscow; the sight of him turns my guts . . ."

The silence that followed this seemed interminable. Evening sunlight streamed through the vine foliage, dappling faces and objects with gold. The distant voices and sounds of the city awakening from its daytime somnolence buzzed in the motionless air. A faint semblance of coolness arose from the ground, from the floorboards, and from the roots of the gnarled vines. It was a time to sit without moving and stare mindlessly at the twilight moving in from every corner.

"Yes, things are bad, pal, so you might as well drink." As Vasyuta reached for the bottle a ray of light flickered across his face, making it look far younger and softer than it had seemed at first sight. "It'll be more fun with the two of us, and two heads are always better than one." Putting down his bowl he stared at Vlad, as though seeing him for the first time. "And who's this you've brought with you?"

"Just a lad . . . He's been going with me. Name's Vlad."

"So that's it!" He laughed coarsely. "Consoling yourself with young boys, eh?"

The blood rushed to Vlad's face: so that was what people thought when they saw him with Sergei! A hot, suffocating lump of anger rose in his throat. The shameful implication of that remark mer-

cilessly laid bare the ambiguity and insecurity of his situation. He
had already caught looks of scorn and disgust cast at him by some of
their fellow vagrants, but until now their meaning had never occurred to him. Now for the first time, taken aback by Vasyuta's
frankness, Vlad realized what kind of reputation he risked acquiring.
Bitter tears of anger started from his eyes: no, no, never—anything
but that; better to be alone, always and everywhere, than to be
thought of as *that!* It was something he could never shake off in a
lifetime.

Sergei obviously sensed his reaction. In the darkness he gave Vlad
a silent and encouraging nudge with his elbow, then said aloud:

"No, that's not my game. Women are good enough for me." He
then immediately changed the subject. "So you think we ought to
blow this place?"

A drawling reply came from the twilight:

"We'll go to Tashkent. Got my eye on a job there. If it comes off,
we'll be set up. Take one of these blankets from under me—and one
for the kid too . . . Hell, he's sniveling! Must have offended him
. . . Don't mind me, kid, I don't mean any harm. My tongue runs
away with me and I say all kinds of junk . . . Let's flop, boys, my
head always works better in the morning."

"Tashkent!" Vlad fell asleep with the word on his brain, and
when he awoke it was early morning, promising a long road ahead
and new things to come.

CHAPTER 5

Tashkent, city of wheat, gave them a very cold welcome. It seethed with the riffraff of countless races, and the Uzbek language was drowned out by a noisy mixture of dialects and thieves' jargon. The time was approaching the worst spell of the extended famine of 1946. Everything that there might have been to steal had been taken before they got there. Every possible hideout was occupied and fiercely defended by existing gangs: leave us alone and we won't touch you, but try and lay a finger on us and we'll give no quarter. We'll shoot, as the saying goes, without warning.

After searching for a long time, the ubiquitous Vasyuta managed to find them some sort of a hangout in the old quarter of the city, but it was so wretched and unsafe that any attempt to mount an operation from there was hopeless.

"Yes," sighed Vasyuta at their first council of war, "we couldn't have landed up in a worse place."

Even so, he set off at nightfall to reconnoiter.

Lying in the darkness on rough planks and listening to Sergei's labored breathing alongside him, with each new recollection that passed through his mind Vlad felt himself gradually filled with sympathy and gratitude for his friend until at last he could restrain himself no longer and poured out his feelings:

"You know, Sergei, I used to prefer being alone . . . It was better

on your own, because there was no one else to let you down . . . But
since I've been with you, I don't want to be alone anymore . . . I
couldn't get by without you . . . I'd just die . . . You're not like all
the others, you're not selfish and you always play fair . . ."

Lying beside him, Sergei muttered sardonically but kindly:

"Go on, kid, let it all out and give me a swollen head." He
touched Vlad lightly with his shoulder. "Okay, kid, I get the message. Don't talk about love. Everything's been said about it already."

"But I mean it, Sergei!"

"I know you do . . ."

With that their confidences ended for the night, but the word had
been spoken, and that word bound them firmly together until that
hot, sultry day in the basement of the Taganka prison, when the
guards separated them once and for all . . .

Vasyuta had returned. Exuding a powerful stench of cheap alcohol, he gave a triumphant guffaw of laughter:

"Time to get up, boys! I've got work for you—special work!"

From behind his back came a drunken giggle, in an almost childish girl's voice:

"Let's go, boys!"

Vlad's heart seemed to bounce up into his throat and swell into a
burning lump. Suddenly the thing which the young vagabonds of his
own age used to describe to each other as they gathered for the night
in some flophouse, with tedious sighs and breathless excitement, had
come within his grasp, causing him to flush with a new and unfamiliar warmth. That shameful, long-ago experiment during the evacuation only served to stimulate his imagination. In a foretaste of the
inevitable, Vlad felt a slight, involuntary dizziness. Somewhere
within him a barely audible voice still wanted to resist, but the rebel-
lious flesh had already gained the upper hand, firmly crushing the
frail, budding shoots of chastity and shame.

Vlad found it so difficult to breathe and move that the darkness
around him seemed to have turned to wadding.

"I'm going to lie down in the courtyard," he muttered as he got
up. "It's as hot as a Turkish bath in here."

"We ought to light a lamp," he heard Sergei say as he went out.
"Can't see a damn thing."

"A hungry man always finds his mouth in the dark." Vasyuta gave
a lewd laugh, which was immediately followed by the gurgling sound
of liquid being poured. "Here, big eyes . . . have a drink!"

The girl's faint, tipsy giggle followed Vlad out into the darkness like a hot gust of wind.

At the threshold, he threw his quilted jacket onto the ground and lay down; in a shower of starry darkness the sky closed over him like a fairy-tale quilt, and beneath that endless calm he slipped passively into oblivion. The fairies of memory circled about his sleeping head. The spirit of Sokolniki bore him away to that land of poplar-lined streets where he was born. Far away in their cramped room, in a house somewhere in the middle of the skies, his mother was at this moment putting his baby sister Katya to bed, while from her place on the divan Vlad's aunt was jealously watching as her sister-in-law busied herself about the task and silently moving her thin lips as she did so: enmity tormented her from morning till night.

From here, at a distance of several thousand kilometers, a distance doubled by nostalgia and irreparable separation, that momentary, incandescent image of home seemed almost idyllic. Lord, what on earth was he doing here, under this immense suffocating sky, in this land of irrigation canals and sand, where the soil of two continents was banked up along the track bed of the great Turksib railroad?

The door creaked, the shadow of Sergei's stooping figure spread out like an uneven stain over the flat surface of the courtyard and hovered around Vlad.

"Are you asleep?"

"No."

"Go to sleep, don't listen."

"I'm not listening."

"Say it again . . ."

"Cross my heart, I won't listen!"

"Mind you don't . . ."

"I tell you, I won't . . ."

"You don't want to get a taste for this, kid." He laid his hand, slightly trembling, on Vlad's head. "You only have to try it once—and you're on the slippery slope. After a drink the first thing they want is a woman, and where there's a woman there's wormwood, a bitter taste in your mouth—and you'll probably catch a nasty disease, too. A man's a proud thing to be, brother—until your nose drops off. A man should have one woman, that's the way nature meant it to be. However many you try, however often you change them, you're just wasting yourself for nothing and you'll lose yourself. The first one is *your* woman, there'll be no other, and that's the law, brother."

"Do you have one?"

"Do I?" His hand slipped nervelessly down onto Vlad's shoulder. "Yes, I have, only she's far away and out of reach." Sergei's voice broke off and quivered with emotion. "To me she's not a woman— she's a queen! The only thing a punk like me has a right to do is blow the dust off her, but she lets me touch her with these mitts of mine! No, she's too good for my kind, I don't want to ruin her life. I may be just a roving thief, but I do have a conscience."

"So you won't go back to her?"

"No, kid, I won't go back to her. I've chosen my way to go, and she has hers. We're like oil and water—we don't belong together."

"Perhaps she's waiting for you."

"She'll wait awhile, then she'll give up waiting. A woman's nature is like water—it stops flowing at the first dam it meets."

"Do you love her?"

"What the hell do you know about that? You're just a kid." He ground his teeth with annoyance. "When you've been through the mill until the hide's flayed off you, then maybe you'll have some glimmer of an idea about it . . . Go to sleep . . ."

"I understand."

"Go to sleep, I say!"

Vlad had an impulse to say something to Sergei that would convey to his friend the full extent of his sympathy and comprehension, something which might put him in a better mood, but at that moment the bulky silhouette of Vasyuta loomed in the doorway:

"Come on, Sergei, your turn." He stood for a while, swaying; then getting no answer, he bent down over Sergei: "You're not asleep, are you?"

Sergei did not even stir. "Don't want to, Vasyuta. No need for it."

"Afraid you won't make it?" The shadow's breath reeked of spirits. "Have a go—she's bouncy as best-grade rubber . . . Maybe we ought to give the kid a treat—it's time he learned."

"Don't touch him, Vasyuta, he's asleep."

"Like hell he's asleep!" He gently prodded Vlad in the side with his fist. "I know these small fry . . . Come on, kid, do your stuff, show her what it's for."

"Leave him alone, Vasyuta. I mean it."

"What!" Threateningly, Vasyuta straightened up. "Who the hell d'you think you are to talk to me like that? Got so big you think you can boss me—*me?*"

Slowly, as though unwillingly, Sergei stood up, and Vlad watched the two shadows instantly merge into one and glide farther away into the depths of the courtyard. Then the single shadow stopped moving, and he heard a half-whispered but tense and bitter conversation:

"Feeling cocky, you lousy little skunk?" croaked Vasyuta. "Bored with living?"

"Don't try and frighten me, Vasyuta." A patronizing drawl crept into Sergei's voice. "Once bitten, twice shy. I don't scare easily."

"Then take what's coming to you, scum."

"Relying on your skull being so thick?"

"I'm going to beat you up proper, for being a wet slob."

"Just you try."

The punch was like hitting water—springy and hard. For a moment the shadows separated, only to merge again into a solid but jerky, moving blur. Heavy breathing was interspersed with the ripping sound of clothes being torn, dull thuds, and the scuffling of shoe soles on sand. But soon the shadow began to slither downward and, after looming indistinctly for some time in the middle of the courtyard, it faded away, now and again revealing in the barely perceptible light of a far-off dawn two bodies locked in savage embrace. Vasyuta was getting the upper hand, gradually wearing down the weakening Sergei. Their strengths were clearly unequal: Sergei's illness was beginning to tell on him, and he was in no shape to tackle such an adversary. Having finally pinned him down, Vasyuta was pummeling him in an absolute frenzy, muttering disjointedly as he did so:

"You asked for it, shit-bag . . . and that's for being a slob . . . You've gotten too big for your boots . . . I've knocked better ones than you off their perch . . . That's for talking back to me . . . you won't forget this in a hurry . . ."

Until that moment Vlad had watched it all happening as though in a daze, believing passionately that Sergei would win. No sooner, though, did Vasyuta get on top of Sergei than he hurled himself into the fight as though propelled upward by the release of a coiled spring. But he had only touched Vasyuta when he was flung back by the sharp blow of an elbow in his stomach, which sent him spinning away across the courtyard like a top, doubled up with pain, nausea, and dizziness.

"You bunch of shits . . ." Vasyuta's voice came to him as if through a glass panel, and through the blood-red haze in front of his eyes he watched the ponderous figure lurch off toward the gate. "Go for your own kind, would you? It's no life for an honest thief any-more—they've forgotten the rules of the game." And from somewhere on the far side of the wall he flung back, with a self-pitying sob: "What the hell were we fighting for anyway?"

Sergei was the first on his feet.

"Okay, get up kid, and let's go." Black bruises were already showing clearly on his battered face. "He's won this time, but we'll get even one day . . . Go on, go and get your things."

His heart still hammering convulsively, Vlad opened the door. The girl was asleep on the only bed in the place, her elbow crooked awkwardly under her head. In the first glimmerings of the dawn the smudged makeup on her childish face looked crude and unreal. She looked like an exhausted schoolgirl, the live wire of the class resting after a hectic carnival or a school concert. As though bewitched, Vlad stood over her, afraid of waking her, and as his heartbeats slowed down a feeling of tenderness grew within him like a timid, burgeoning flower bud. He felt a momentary, overpowering wish to cover her up, to touch her tousled hair, to sit down at the head of her bed; and he would have yielded to the temptation, had not Sergei's voice from outside the door brought him to his senses at the last moment:

"Don't waste time, kid, or we'll miss the Moscow train."

To his dying day Vlad will never forget that dash to Moscow. Hunched up, he lay on the brake rods of the Moscow express, and all the winds of Asia howled their robbers' chorus in his ears. At the bigger stations they were kicked off, beaten, chased down the tracks and not allowed to board the train, but by some miracle they always managed to grab a handrail at the last moment and they flew onward, toward the silent forests of Russia. There was no question of getting any food. For six whole days they only ate once, when a Korean from one of the first-class sleeping cars poured a whole packet of moldy cookies into Vlad's cap. It made them throw up violently for a long time afterward, but the illusion of having eased their hunger for a while helped them somehow to hold out until they reached their destination.

Finally, dirty and emaciated, they saw it—the capital itself—and as they got out at the Kazan Station, for the first time in a very long while Vlad inhaled the air, smoky but so delicious that it brought tears to his eyes. Moscow!

CHAPTER 6

During the day they roamed the city, found somewhere to take a bath and somewhere to eat, and by evening Sergei had discovered a switchman at the Moscow Central switchyards who would give them a place to sleep. The switchman lived alone in an old four-axle passenger car that had been sunk into a permanent foundation and roughly converted into living quarters. One half of the car was taken up with triple rows of bunks, probably dating from the war, while the other half contained the switchman's modest belongings: a table with uneven legs, a trestle bed covered with some rumpled blankets, and two stools. He was tall and thin, and he looked like a Transcaucasian, although his speech left no doubt of his purely Russian origin. The man looked about sixty, although he gave it out that he was forty. When he agreed to take them in, he laid down his conditions without beating about the bush:

"You're to keep as quiet as mice, come home only after dark, don't sing, and don't talk loudly. The place is crawling with guards, and if they catch you I shall be in the shit and you'll be behind bars . . . got it?"

"Okay, dad." Sergei could not help answering back sarcastically: "In other words, one step out of line counts as an attempt to escape, just like in the camps."

"If you don't like it, don't come. I don't have to take you," the switchman replied imperturbably. "It's no skin off my nose . . ."

Thus began their life in a converted passenger car amid the Moscow Central switchyards. It wasn't much of a place, but it was their first fixed abode since the start of their wanderings together. By day they operated a few rackets at the three main stations and managed to make enough for a tolerable existence; at times they even managed to live it up in some canteen with a beer for Sergei and a fruit juice for Vlad as dessert. At night the two friends, exhausted but satisfied, would return to their four-axled home and there, in the silence of the night, broken only by the click of wheels and the hooting of switching engines, they would begin their endless talks in which, as the saying goes, they set the world to rights.

"Ah, Vladka, if only I could get some proper papers and go straight, I'd chuck in this whole game. It's a dog's life, and I'm so fed up with it I could almost string myself up."

"Would you go back to her, then?" Vlad needled him jealously. "To that queen of yours?"

"If I could get cured, I would." At once he grew very serious, and even in the darkness Vlad could sense his friend's consumptive cheekbones tightening. "She couldn't refuse to take me back!"

Conquered by the force of his conviction, Vlad surrendered magnanimously:

"Of course she'll take you back! Who does she think she is?"

The two friends fell silent; their momentary surge of emotion subsided and each one became wrapped in his own thoughts, carried away into regions inaccessible to the other.

Whenever Vlad was alone, he always thought about home. It was a ride of only two stops on the streetcar to his home from those three railroad stations where he and Sergei circulated every day from morning till night. No more than two stops on a No. 4 streetcar. There were times when he was idle and at a loose end, but in spite of a desire so intense that it almost made him dizzy, he was still unable to take the decision and kept putting off the inevitable until later, until another time.

But one day Vlad made up his mind. Seizing a moment when Sergei had met one of his vagabond friends from Ashkhabad and had left Vlad alone, he boarded that ill-omened No. 4, and the streetcar, creaking and ringing its bell, carried him off toward his native hearth. Krasnoselskaya. Gavrikov Street. The brewery. The bridge.

Salitsilovka. And there was the shabby but heart-rendingly familiar little movie theater, The Hammer. A turn, and then down the long, dead-straight, poplar-lined Malenkov Street. Store No. 25. The stop.

Vlad found the courage to get off, but it was more than he could do to walk the length of Staroslobodskaya Street, which joined this street with his home territory—the Mitkovka. He was afraid of himself, afraid that he might give himself away and betray Sergei, betray his past and his future as he saw it in his rosier dreams. Farewell, Mitkovka, farewell once more, you will have to wait until I return in triumph. In triumph?

He could not, though, make himself pass by Sokolniki Park without going in; that would have been beyond his powers. Malenkov Street led Vlad straight to the first side entrance to the park, near which he sought out and found the secret way that he had made himself. From there on Vlad could have found his way blindfold: the whole crazy spider's web of walks and pathways was imprinted on his memory like a large-scale map.

Was it instinct or was it a presentiment that led Vlad at that early hour to the open-air chess tables? For whatever reason, it was there that he went and there, beside a table occupied by chessplayers, that he recognized among the other enthusiasts his friend Yurka the chessplayer from the house next door to his, No. 27, and here his reserve gave way.

"Yurka," he greeted him with soundlessly moving lips, "hello . . . Don't you recognize me?"

At first Yurka stared at Vlad uncomprehendingly, trying hard to discover something familiar in this suspicious-looking tramp. Then a gleam of recognition from a childhood spent together lit up his thoughtful face. Yurka, who came from a family of intellectuals, had always deferred to this plebeian youth from next door, and he moved toward the unexpected visitor on shaking legs:

"Have you come back for good?"

"No, not for good, Yurka."

"Are you going home?"

"You must be kidding!"

"Well, yes . . . of course . . . I understand . . . Can I bring you something? Some food, or something else?"

"No, don't bother." Vlad was filled with pride and gratitude. "How are my folks?"

"They're okay . . . Katya's going to school now."

"Don't tell them you met me, or my mother will go running to the police. It'll only upset them."

"Okay, Vlad, if that's the way you want it . . ."

They stood facing each other for a little while longer, exchanging embarrassed looks, then as if slamming something shut inside himself Vlad turned on his heel, nodding and calling out as he went:

"So long."

From somewhere far away in their childhood, from another world beyond a great divide came the plaintive and somehow apologetic response:

"Goodbye, Vlad! . . . Goodbye!"

For the first time Vlad returned alone to their home in the switchyard, and found Sergei not there. In answer to his question the switchman only answered with a surly grunt:

"Guess he must be at a meeting with some minister, discussing the international situation . . ."

Vlad clambered up to his bunk, and after brooding long and painfully on his recent meeting and everything connected with it, he dropped imperceptibly into sleep.

When he awoke and glanced downward, he turned cold: around the table sat their host the switchman, Sergei, and an unknown soldier from the railroad guard troops. "They've caught us!" He was somewhat reassured by the sight of a bottle in the middle of the table, and the conversation made him freeze. The soldier, sitting with his back to Vlad, was saying:

"Mind you, opening up a freight car is no picnic. But there'll be a truck waiting by the approach tracks . . ."

"You can get twenty-five years for that, boss," Sergei said sarcastically, blinking drunkenly toward the light. "Twenty-five years. Have you ever been inside—even for one year?"

"Don't teach your grandmother to suck eggs, young man!" said the guard angrily. "You can't scare me—I've been around. If you're getting cold feet, we can find someone else. There's plenty who'd jump at the chance."

"Go ahead, then, and find them." Sergei cut him off coolly. "You're in no hurry."

"That's just it—we are." The guard lowered his voice. "Would I be haggling with you otherwise? The stuff's due to be moved out soon."

Tired of playing games of bluff, Sergei switched over to a businesslike discussion of terms:

"Okay—when we've put the stuff on the truck, it's a thousand rubles in cash for us, and we all blow in different directions. You go one way, we'll go another. As for this dumbbell"—he nodded toward the switchman—"you and he can settle up between yourselves." Then, suddenly cautious: "But suppose the stuff in the car is no good? Suppose it's only junk?"

The guard looked offended: "Think we can't read the bills of lading? Or our brains have gone soft? What's this kid of yours for, anyway? We'll push him in through the ventilator hatch and he can check on the stuff. But I know for sure what's there: indigo cloth."

As Sergei pondered, from his bunk Vlad could see his prominent forehead wrinkling with the effort to make a decision on this well-nigh insoluble problem. Then he lowered his head, and as though talking to himself he said:

"He can go in through the ventilator, and that's all—he gets out of the way." Sergei stared grimly at the soldier. "You'll answer for the kid with your head. If anything goes wrong, I'll pull you all down into the shit."

"Okay—done," the soldier hastened to agree. "In an hour from now the crews will have switched the cars onto track No. 6. I'll meet you there." As he went out into the night and turned around, Vlad saw a predatory face on a squat neck and eyes that were white, like the eyes of an old goose—or so they seemed to him in the dim lamplight. "Track No. 6, don't make a mistake . . ."

Sergei climbed up to the level of Vlad's bunk, silently put his arm around him and whispered in his ear:

"Did you hear?"

For a reply, Vlad sat up and started getting dressed. Then one after the other they climbed down from their bunks and went out into the starry August night. Somewhere above them the universe was roaring and exploding, galaxies were being destroyed and created; around them cities were dying and being born, mountains were arising and melting away; and no one in all creation cared a damn for two tramps walking through the darkness of the Moscow switchyards toward their wretched undoing.

They were already waiting for them at track No. 6. With an occasional flicker of his lantern, the guard led them among the trains until, at the very end of a long row of cars, their way was barred by a dark figure.

"Here."

At first everything went as planned: Vlad was lifted up, and having with difficulty wrenched open the wire fastening, he opened the ventilation hatch and slithered through it into the blackness of the freight car. There, in the pitch dark, Vlad checked out the merchandise by feel. Everything tallied with the way-bill, as the guard had said: bolts of fine cloth, of that there could be no doubt.

But no sooner had Vlad turned to make his way out through the square opening than the silence below him outside the thin wall of the car was hideously shattered:

"Hands up! Don't move!"

Losing his head completely, Vlad hurled himself feet first out of the hatch in a swallow dive, and would undoubtedly have broken several bones had he not suddenly been gripped by a firm pair of hands. Above him a voice croaked with grim satisfaction:

"Got you, my beauty!"

Yet Vlad managed to tear himself away and run. On the way he fell down, picked himself up and fell again, gashing his face, hands, legs, side, and head. From behind came the clatter of boots, rifleshots cracked, signal flares lit up and went out, but all this only drove him onward and onward. Anywhere—but onward!

But fate proved stronger than him, stronger than his legs and his lungs, stronger than his thirst for freedom. For a long while he dodged under the cars, leaped over a dozen brake platforms and raced over switches; but just when it seemed that the worst was over and at any moment he could vanish into the night like a needle in a haystack, an unlit wall suddenly reared up in front of him and there was nowhere left to go. At this he simply sat down on the ground and burst into tears, and gave himself up without resistance to the first pair of hands that came along. Farewell, freedom!

CHAPTER 7

The fortuneteller's cards predict a journey,
A long, long journey to a house of stone:
Maybe that old, familiar place, the jailhouse,
Awaits me, luckless creature, once again . . .

A clear, boyish voice rose and fell in song from somewhere high up on the fourth floor. Vlad started to raise his head in the direction of the voice, but the guard was already prodding him in the back:

"Go on, keep moving, don't hang about. You'll have all the time you want to look around later."

With the smoothness of long practice, the mechanism of what followed worked with enviable efficiency: body search, registration, description of physical defects and distinguishing marks, photographs full-face and in profile, shaving of all body hair, a short stay in the preliminary one-man "boxes," and, finally, as a reward for all the preceding indignities, the cell.

Vlad was pushed into a four-man cage on the third floor, the window of which lacked the usual external sightscreen—an unwritten privilege of underage prisoners. Vlad's future cellmates did no more than cast an appraising glance in his direction and immediately turned back toward the dark-complexioned youth lying on the righthand cot by the window. Apparently staring mindlessly at the

ceiling, he was singing in a high falsetto a song Vlad had never heard
before:

> Day and night my heart spreads tenderness,
> Day and night I'm dizzy with delight . . .

Although the rendering was heartfelt and sincere, the young man's
voice betrayed an obvious note of unease: as boss of the cell, he was
clearly anxious about the newcomer's intentions.

When Vlad began calmly and efficiently to make up the empty
cot, which stood nearest to the slop bucket, the singer was visibly
cheered, and finished his song with evident relief and even a certain
bravura. Then, after a short pause to allow the audience to appreciate his artistry as fully as it deserved, he questioned the new arrival
in a drawling tone:

"Where are you from, kid?"

"From a long way off," Vlad replied evasively, as was proper according to the unwritten laws of the world he now inhabited. "You
can't see it from here, anyway."

"Do you get food parcels?"

"I forgot to fix myself up with a family."

"Just my luck to get one of you tramps." The youth spat with
expressive disgust. "I'll be down to prison rations soon. The Block
Warden keeps me short on purpose so that I'll croak from hunger.
Do you smoke?"

"No."

"Well, thank God for that, at least you'll be some good to us.
That means a bit more for the rest of us to smoke."

Vlad was desperately sleepy, so to put an end to the conversation
he concurred peaceably:

"Sure."

Through the large squares of the grille over the open window the
sultry night air poured into the cell, bearing the normal evening
sounds of the city: streetcars clanged not far away, while from somewhere close, probably a neighboring house, a phonograph sobbed:
"My campfire glows in the darkness . . ." and the ships' sirens
boomed from the nearby Moscow River. For Vlad, life was henceforth divided between "here" and "there," and this depressed him
more than anything else. The only cheering thought was the proximity of Sergei, who was installed on the floor below, as Vlad had already learned on the bush telegraph when he was in the "box." The

thought of blaming his friend in any way never entered his mind. On
the contrary, he was convinced that he, Vlad, had let them down by
not staying put and hiding when the alarm was raised, and thereby
burdening Sergei with a further criminal charge: enticement of a
minor to commit a felony. "I should have laid low," he thought in
self-reproach as he fell asleep, "instead of jumping out in a panic."

Vlad always adapted quickly and painlessly to a new way of life. It
was not long before he was on good terms with his cellmates, while
they in turn accepted him as one of their own and treated him fairly.
Even the only professional criminal among them—Valera, nicknamed "The Singer"—deigned to treat him as an equal.

Apart from The Singer, the cell contained a phlegmatic Bashkir,
who lay on the bed opposite Vlad's. He literally lay there most of
the time, occasionally turning over onto his other side and only getting up to eat or relieve himself—or to do the same things in reverse
order.

The other occupant was an industrial apprentice from Moscow,
who, considering that he was by origin just a country boy from
Ryazan, possessed the strange first name of Lassalle; this he apparently owed to his father's deranged enthusiasm for Marxist ideology. Lassalle was perpetually hungry, and although he received no
food parcels he managed to solve the problem after his own fashion:
he diluted his prison gruel with water from the can in the cell, creating an illusion of abundance that satisfied his bird-brained intelli-
gence.

For days on end The Singer and Lassalle would play games with
cards stuck together out of layers of newspaper and drawn by hand.
The Bashkir slept, while Vlad read as many books as could be borrowed from the library for all four of them, since fortunately none of
the others showed the slightest interest in any form of printed
matter.

Sergei had already announced through the window to the whole
prison that "Vlad the Bookworm" was his partner, which had notable consequences for Vlad's prestige. As a result, The Singer ordered
Lassalle to move over to the bed nearest the slop bucket and offered
Vlad the cot beside the window. He took Vlad's refusal as a threat,
and unabashed by the presence of the others, he simply implored
Vlad:

"Have a heart, Bookworm. Sergei will bash my face in if he finds out that you've been sleeping by the slop bucket. Be a pal, kid—don't drop me in the shit!"

Vlad had no alternative but to move over to the window. Lassalle made a bit of trouble, but was quickly induced to toe the line. Life in the cell resumed its settled course. Thus it is, no doubt, whenever a change of power occurs: at first an outburst of passion and indignant protest, followed by a short period of adaptation to the new state of affairs, with finally a return to the same, age-old routine.

The chief distraction in this monotonous existence was the bath, which took place every ten days. At the bathhouse the inmates of different cells could mix, and it was a time of barter and settling of accounts. Guards in blue overalls fussed around in the infernal bedlam, but their shouting only compounded the disorder: a naked man, for some reason, loses all remaining respect for authority. Standing aloof from the general whirlpool of movement, Vlad enjoyed watching the furious hubbub. And there was plenty to watch!

One day amid the steam and noise he noticed a boy of about sixteen standing under the shower wearing shorts and undershirt. "What the hell is he doing that for?" Vlad wondered. "Is he sick, or something?" Approaching for a closer look, Vlad shuddered: the boy was tattooed solidly in two colors, the undershirt being tattooed in green, the shorts in blue shading almost into black. Since then he has seen many other tattoos, and has even succumbed to the temptation himself, but he was never again to see one that equaled the tattooed boy in the Taganka prison baths.

Before long someone slipped him a tiny note from Sergei, the size of a matchbox top: "Vladka, please say in court it was all my doing. I'll get 25 years anyway. I beg you, for Christ's sake. You have a life to live."

Vlad was bitterly offended. "Oh Sergei, Sergei! Calls himself a friend! What does he take me for?"

Several days later Vlad was summoned to the Block Warden. This gigantic man with the rank of captain (crew-cut gray hair, a row of medal ribbons and three wound stripes on a chest that seemed to be bulging out of his tunic) looked Vlad mockingly up and down and grinned:

"And I thought you were an old lag! Busted for larceny on the railroad—and you're only knee-high to a grasshopper! Okay, you needn't stand, sit down over there. You and I are going to have a talk. Is your mother alive?"

"No," said Vlad, conscious of sinning.

"Father?"

"Killed."

"Where?"

"What d'you mean—where? At the front."

The captain's face wrinkled slightly as though in pain, but then immediately resumed its look of a weatherbeaten figure on a bronze medallion:

"You ought to be ashamed of yourself. A father fighting for his country—and look at his son!" He made a despairing gesture. "I'll talk to you again later . . . Now for another matter. This partner of yours has written a petition to the Supreme Soviet asking for clemency for you, says it was all his doing. Have you known him for a long time?"

"Yes."

"How long?"

"Long enough," said Vlad.

"What sort of a person is he?"

"If everyone was like him, we'd have built communism long ago."

"Like hell! A lot we'd get built if we let you robbers have your way —you'd pinch everything."

"He fought in the war, he's sick, he needs treatment."

"He fought in the war, he fought in the war!" A grim look came over the captain again. "I suppose if you fought it means you can do as you please—is that it? I fought in the war too, and I don't go thieving."

"He hasn't any identity papers—what else can he do?"

"I see you two villains are in cahoots." The Block Warden had clearly lost interest in the conversation. "Okay, you can go now. We'll send on his petition according to regulations, only I warn you —don't count on it doing you any good. The court will decide. Off you go . . ."

As the captain's crew-cut head leaned forward, it was not clear whether he was deep in thought or whether he was simply staring at something on the desk in front of him.

Vlad left the Block Warden's office escorted by a guard. This was probably his first chance to get a real view of the prison in its full extent—to see all its four stories, ringed by galleries with a metal net stretched between them. Like some huge beehive it hummed steadily with hundreds of voices, locked up in their countless cells, each one of which vibrated with an unhappiness whose sound, though barely audible, echoed in the remotest corners of Russia. Strange as it may seem, Vlad felt now for the first time that he was not alone; that alongside him there lived and suffered a multitude of fellow participants in his petty misfortune, a fate ignored by the rest of the world. Each of us consoles himself as best he can.

Hearing the reason for Vlad's summons to the captain, The Singer went almost crazy:

"He'll pull it off, Sergei will!" He was bursting with admiration and enthusiasm. "I'd go through fire and water with Sergei! There aren't many left like him nowadays—you can count 'em on the fingers of one hand. You ought to wash his feet and drink the water, Vlad. He's straight up, that's the only word for it."

Lassalle added his contribution:

"He's tough."

Even the Bashkir came to life, sat up, swung his legs down from the bed, blinked his slanting eyes and laboriously composed the words:

"What a man!"

When Vlad was taken away to court, the send-off they gave him would have done justice to his birthday. The Singer even gave him his own short-peaked cap, which he treasured greatly.

"You'll see—they'll give you a suspended sentence. This is my third time inside, brother, so I know their whole Jewish box of tricks like I know the back of my hand. Once a grownup takes the rap for you, all you have to do is keep your trap shut and squeeze out a few tears. The main thing is to shut up and look sorry. If you get a 'suspended,' then you owe us a food parcel. With as many smokes as you can pack in . . ."

The escorting routine was like a silent game of follow-my-leader, except that after each halt or change of direction a lock clicked shut behind him: slam-click, slam-click, slam-click. Somehow the guards looked less grim than on the day of his arrival. One of them—an older man with a scraggy neck like a turkey cock—even drawled encouragingly:

"You may not even come back here, kid. It happens."

After the gray prison light, the August sunshine seemed even more dazzling than it did through the cell windows or at exercise. Vlad's walk across the summer soil was short, however: no more than three paces that separated him from the steps of the police wagon. A minute later the little tin door with a grille at face level slammed shut behind him. Vlad was driven to court.

The prison lay behind him.

CHAPTER 8

Vlad was somewhat disappointed by the courtroom. He had expected to see a grand chamber, crammed with spectators, but instead
found himself in a shabby little room furnished with a few benches
and a table covered with green cloth that stood in a small raised platform reminiscent of a school stage. A few old women, obvious ha-
bitués of the place, and a couple of drunks who had wandered in to
escape the heat, sat dozing. Everyone looked bored and hot: the
handful of spectators, the little gray-haired old judge, the prosecutor
endowed with an excessively large paunch for his age, and the young
woman defense attorney who threw an occasional frightened glance
in the direction of her clients.

Chief witness for the prosecution was the switchman in whose
quarters they had lodged, and who now sealed their fate in a whole
hour of careful, circumstantial testimony. Then came some lesser
witnesses: the yardmaster, two policemen from the Railroad Security
Section, and finally the checkweighman who had caught the weeping
Vlad beside the station wall.

The judge asked a few pointless questions, leaning gravely as he
did so toward each of the two heat-dazed lay assessors—an elderly
schoolmistress and a bewhiskered workman—who responded with
solemn, understanding nods of the head.

The prosecuting attorney did nothing but breathe heavily, leaning

his paunch on the table. Though making a constant effort to appear
interested and deeply thoughtful, the result looked extremely unnatural, because the heat gained the upper hand and all he could do was
to keep opening and shutting his mouth like a fish out of water.

Only the clerk of the court, a young girl with a black fringe over
her narrow forehead, showed genuine feeling at all the twists and
turns of the case and openly sympathized with Vlad: she obviously
saw him as a mere child, who happened to have been led astray by
an adult criminal.

Counsel for the prosecution was, of course, the first to make his
speech. Shortness of breath predisposed him to brevity. Having rapidly sketched in the circumstances of the crime, and having tinged
his account with suitable political coloring, he considered himself in
duty bound (oh, that heat!) to demand for both of the accused the
maximum penalty laid down in the relevant Decree, namely the
Decree of 4 June 1947, which for the older prisoner was twenty-five
years' imprisonment followed by five years' loss of civil rights, and for
the minor, taking account of his age and the influence to which he
had been subjected, was ten years without loss of civil rights. He
sank heavily back into his chair, satisfied at having finished with a
well-turned peroration.

The plea made by the young female defense counsel hardly
differed from the speech for the prosecution. Indeed, she did not so
much defend her clients as demonstrate how thoroughly well versed
she was in the latest decisions of the Party and the government con-
cerning the struggle against misappropriation of socialist property.
But in the end an access of purely womanly, youthful shame obliged
her to conclude by reminding the court of the good military record
of one of her clients and the extreme youth of the other.

In his final speech in his own defense, Sergei said only a few
words, which made the young clerk of the court blush:

"I beg the court to show indulgence toward my accomplice, whom
I enticed into a life of crime."

Vlad declined to make use of his right to speak.

During the recess, one of the police escort, a wrinkled sergeant
with the Red Star pinned to his tunic, offered Sergei a "Priboi"
brand cigarette through the little window of the cell, and sighed
sympathetically:

"When veterans start going bent, it's a bad sign. Soon they'll be putting us all through the mill. Have a smoke, soldier, you won't get any where you're going."

Sergei countered with a sardonic joke:

"No, thanks, we can always pinch some."

Not to be put off, the sergeant continued:

"Only thing is, though—why'd you have to drag a young kid into it? He's still wet behind the ears, ought to be in school."

"I'm to blame, dad." As Sergei stood chatting by the window, Vlad, seated nearby, could hear every word that was said. "And I'll pay for it."

"Okay, if that's the way you want it," the other agreed, adding as he moved away: "Only they'll throw the book at you for it."

"In for a penny, in for a pound . . ."

They could hear the old women on the nearby staircase knowledgeably discussing the case.

"He'll cop it, and no mistake!"

"Robbery's no joke, you know."

"I feel sorry for the kid."

"Them kids are the worst of all. Only the other day I . . ."

She never finished her remark, for the bell rang to announce the resumption of the hearing. The two friends had long since resigned themselves to their fate, so they allowed themselves to be escorted back upstairs quietly and without any fuss. Sergei, however, could not restrain himself from winking at Vlad and saying:

"Chin up, kid."

The people in the courtroom, as was proper, stood up to greet the trio of members of the bench on their return from the consultation room. After wiping his sweat-dimmed spectacles, the gray-haired judge hooked them around his ears, lowered his nearsighted little eyes and began intoning in a practiced recitative:

"In the name of the Russian Soviet Federated Socialist Republic . . ."

In passing sentence, the court fully satisfied the prosecutor's demands. The escort gave orders to clear the court, and the prisoners turned toward the exit. The last thing that Vlad saw as he left by the side door of the courtroom was the young clerk of the court, her eyes filled with tears.

But a new life had begun for him, a life in which there was no longer any place for gratitude.

CHAPTER 9

After the trial, Vlad was driven away separately from Sergei in the one-man cell of a police wagon, according to the regulations which forbid a minor to associate with adult prisoners. Sitting in his tiny, roasting-hot cage, he pressed his face to the grille with all his strength in the hope of catching a glimpse of the streets and buildings as they flashed past the little window in the wagon door. He managed, in fact, to recognize the corner of Sushchevsky Rampart and Novoslobodskaya Street; the movie theater on Taganka Square, not far from which, on the Bolshiye Kamenshchiki, lived an aunt of his whom he used occasionally to visit with his mother; and the bakery on Krasnokholmsky Embankment. And that was all he was able to see before the prison gates closed behind him again.

This time the tone of the proceedings differed from the two previous occasions. Now he was treated roughly and unceremoniously; the first official to handle his dossier scowled contemptuously:

"Ten years. You'll croak in camp." And he pushed aside the folder with disgust, as if it contained, at best, dried shit. "That's the place for punks like you. Makes the air cleaner for the rest of us."

It got worse as it went on. He was kicked and pushed—always, for some reason, by the scruff of his neck—and if he was spoken to, then invariably in foul language. It was as if he had crossed some invisible watershed, beyond which he ceased altogether to be a human being.

"This is it," he concluded bitterly. "This is where the real thing starts. Up till now it's been roses all the way."

That night, as he was being led along an underground corridor, he suddenly recognized Sergei coming toward him under escort. Just at the moment when Vlad was about to call out to his friend, a sharp command was barked out behind him:

"Face the wall!"

Vlad pressed himself to the wall, but at the last moment he nevertheless managed to flash a look of greeting toward the approaching Sergei, at which a swinging blow smashed his nose up against the wall.

"No turning around!"

Blood spurted over Vlad's face, he yelled with the pain of his broken nose and his cry merged with Sergei's furious roar of anger:

"Hands off that kid, you scum! I'll get you, you Taganka shit-bags, if I have to go to the ends of the earth! What d'you want to bash a kid for? Filthy son of a whore—if only I could've met you at the front, you dirty coward!"

Vlad could hear them twisting Sergei's arm, kicking him, dragging him along the concrete floor, but he went on shouting and shouting:

"Sons of bitches! Cock-suckers! Take it out on kids, would you? Vlad, Vladik, Vladka, don't forget this, don't forget anything! Listen, please—remember it all, we'll pay them back for everything, our time will come! Don't forget, Vladka, I haven't anyone in the world but you . . ."

His voice broke off and went silent, smothered by a gag forced on by the guards . . .

He did not forget, Sergei, and never will forget, but for himself he has forgiven them everything.

Nor will he forget how he stood on a fully lit stage, with a blinding hangover from a week's nonstop drinking, smiling vaguely and miserably at an auditorium full of the usual first-night crowd, and weeping silently for his past, which had just been re-enacted after he had assembled it from memory into a short three-hour play about you, Sergei, about your fate as he imagined it might have been after that bitter parting from you in the Taganka cellars.

He called that play *Man Alive*, and some strangers acted it out more or less tolerably in the small theater on Malaya Bronnaya Street. But however inadequate the resulting play may have been in comparison with your real life, it was nevertheless a grateful testimony to the fact that through all the murk and filth of this existence you bore within your heart, never tainted and never wasted, the Divine Gift of Conscience.

He would have counted himself eternally happy if one day, walking on stage to take the usual bow, he had discerned among the hundreds of anonymous faces your own unforgettable face and had heard the soundless roar of your muffled voice, hoarse with sickness: "You did okay, kid—seems like we had something after all . . ."

But if he unwittingly divined the truth of how you met your end, and you really were sentenced to death for attempted escape aggravated by murder, then may the Lord have mercy on your soul and may the earth lie lightly upon you; and all your unexpiated sins he will take upon himself.

Vlad was awarded five days of strict solitary: four hundred grams of bread and a bowl of soup once a day. Day after day, until he dropped with exhaustion, Vlad paced up and down from corner to corner of his cell, thinking, thinking, thinking. Completely alone for the first time, he seemed to experience anew everything that had happened to him so far. However you looked at it, he had plenty to remember. He rehearsed in his mind countless variations of each episode, but it always turned out that the real-life, original version was, in the last analysis, the only possible one. Four paces one way, four paces back again—how far did he walk like this in the first three days alone? Vlad felt hunger and thirst, terror and despair, pain and suffering, but never once did he feel the need of someone else to talk to. Thenceforth Vlad understood one essential truth: that the person who is bored when he is alone has no right to call himself a human being, for such a person is empty and insignificant.

On the fourth day Vlad was visited in his cell by the Block Warden.

"Aren't you bored?"

"What with?"

"With being in solitary."

"It's bearable."

"Proud, I see." There was a hint of approval in the captain's tone of voice. "But rules are rules, you know: break them, and you get what's coming to you."

"Am I to blame because I was beaten up?"

"Beaten up!" He averted his eyes. "So maybe they gave you a tap or two to keep you in line. This is not a sanitarium, you know. Do you want to be transferred?"

"The sooner the better!"

"Now listen here, Samsonov"—the captain sat down on the edge of the cot—"I'm going to have you transferred out of here tomorrow. It's a good place where you're going, one of the best of the reformatories—but I want to leave one thought with you before you go: quit fooling around. Act sensibly and start studying. You have a good head on your shoulders. I've been looking at your library card, and I've been keeping an eye on you in general. You might become a great man one day, provided you put your hands and your brains to work. I have a couple of kids like you, and if I'd stopped a stray bullet, who knows, they might be where you are now. That's all I have to say to you. And as for that joker"—he nodded expressively toward the door—"I'll teach him to show off his muscle on kids." The Block Warden stood up. "Be ready to move tomorrow night." Then, from the doorway: "Good luck . . ."

A moment later Vlad heard him bawling out the guard who had "baptized" Vlad:

"Strike a child, would you? Bet you haven't any kids of your own. Where's your conscience, Sergeant?"

"He may be just a boy, but he makes more trouble than a grownup. I'm only human, after all!"

The conversation died away at the end of the corridor, but I remembered the sergeant's last words when many years later I read a manuscript story written by a cheerful Moscow scoundrel called Valera Levyatov, which stuck in my mind, and which later, after several retellings, I learned by heart:

Action and Reaction Are Equal and Opposite

"Private Bokarev!"

"Present, sir!"

"Come here!"

"Yes, sir! Comrade Senior Lieutenant . . ."

"As you were! Private Bokarev!"

"Present, sir!"

"Come here!"

"Yes, sir! Comrade Senior Lieutenant! Private Bokarev reporting for duty, sir!"

"About face! Mark time! Private Bokarev!"

"Present, sir!"

"Sit down!"

"Yes, sir!"

"Stand up!   Sit down!   Stand up!   Sit down!
Stand up!   Sit down!   Stand up!   Livelier, man.
Sit down!   Stand up!   Sit down!   Stand up!
Sit down!   Stand up!   Sit down!   Stand up!
Sit down!   Stand up!   Livelier!   Sit down!
Stand up!   Private Bokarev . . ."

That night the soldier wept—quietly, so that no one should hear him. "It's cruel! After all, I'm only human!"

The officer had a wife. "Misha, go and do the shopping," she said. And he went. "Misha, I've a headache"—and he washed the dishes. "Misha, you're as dumb as a block of wood"—and he cringed and looked like a beaten dog.

While his wife often went out, the officer stayed at home alone. He felt sorry for himself, and as he sobbed, he mumbled: "It's cruel! After all, I'm only human!"

When his wife went out, she did not go to the theater. She went to Private Bokarev.

The soldier made the officer's wife give him money. He called her a whore. When she was with the soldier, she turned into a whimpering mongrel bitch.

When later she staggered home, head bowed, humiliated and degraded, she felt like bursting into tears; her lips trembled and she whispered: "It's too cruel. I'm only human, after all."

From above, God looked down upon them. And wept.

In the middle of the night keys rattled in the lock of his cell door, and the familiar, hated voice of the sergeant snapped curtly:
"Okay, Samsonov—out. With your things."
The prison was assembling its regular transfer party.

CHAPTER 10

In the "Stolypin" the underage prisoners were accommodated separately and without too much overcrowding—only two to a bunk.* Among the adult prisoners in the nearby cages, however, the conditions provoked an indescribable uproar of shouting, groaning, and swearing, accompanied by half-hearted abuse from the escorting guards. Not until evening, when the heat had abated and the car was coupled to a passenger train standing at a platform of the Yaroslavl Station, did the prisoners quieten down a little. Human nature is adaptable: it can get used to anything.

Installed on the topmost bunk alongside a thin and totally silent little Uzbek, Vlad was able to peer through the close-set bars of the tiny window. He could see a small area of the asphalted platform, where an old peasant woman was seated on a pile of sacks. Around her played a flaxen-haired little girl of about five, wearing a faded cotton dress and with a brightly colored ball in her sunburnt little hands. Now and again the ball bounced out of her grasp and rolled across the asphalt, at which the old woman would start to fidget on the pile of sacks—though without moving from her perch, being ob-

---

* The "Stolypin" is a specially built railroad car for transporting prisoners; it is named after the prerevolutionary politician P. A. Stolypin (1862–1911), said to have introduced this type of car during his term of office as Minister of the Interior. Although its compartments were designed to hold eight prisoners (in two facing sets of four bunks), the Soviet authorities often managed to pack in three or four times that number into a compartment. (Tr.)

viously more nervous about her hoard than about the mischievous little five-year-old, at whom she merely nagged in a whining voice:

"Behave yourself, Nadya, there's a good girl. Your mother will be here any moment now and she'll be so cross . . ."

As he watched this innocent scene, Vlad's mind was obsessed by the thought that his family was living nearby, in fact no more than two stops away by streetcar; that at this moment his mother had just come home from work, his aunt was fussing around her favorite niece, and that it would never occur to either of them that Vlad was in such close though unfortunate proximity. What fortuneteller could have told them that? No such fortuneteller exists.

A carrot-haired head with a freckled nose shaped like a comma, the face as round and bright as a little sun, poked itself up over the edge of his bunk:

"What d'you think, pal—any chance of us blowing this joint where we're going? I hear some have made it and never been caught . . ."

Without waiting for a reply the head disappeared, and the boy's voice could be heard from down below:

"Hey, pal, I've heard that somewhere up north a whole camp broke out and cleared off, and now they broadcast over the radio from America . . ."

This was greeted with a mixture of laughter and abuse, but the redhead's voice prattled on until the first clicking of the wheels announced to the exhausted, heat-dazed prisoners that they were at last on their way. Relief was followed by apathy, unbroken even by the distribution of rations, consisting of the inevitable piece of salted herring and a mug of heavily chlorinated water.

Among the adults in the adjacent compartments, one man was boring his fellow inmates with the recital of a story that had evidently begun while they had still been standing in the station:

"You know what a thief's life is like, brother—he always thinks he can spot the lady in the three-card trick, but he never can. You can't win. Since 1930 I've done nothing but move from prison to police station and back again. I was only a kid then, but I remember it all like it was yesterday. I come from a village called Torbeyevo, not far from Tula—pretty near, in fact, no more than about forty kilometers. Ours was a fine family: not counting myself there were five kids, Grandma, and my parents. Nine mouths to feed, as alike as nine kopecks. My father was a good craftsman, he could turn his hand to anything—making brooms, making spoons, he could do it all—and on top of that he kept two horses. He never asked charity of anyone, we never had to water the soup, and we lived well. Not like some families: when their father came home he had nothing to put on the table but his prick, they'd bang their spoons on the table and they were so hungry they would've eaten it. It was enough to make you shit yourself laughing. One day, though, someone in the gov'ment got it into his head you can make pies out of shit—and then the trouble started: collective farms! They grabbed hold of my dad and told him to sign on or else. But you can't scare my dad, he's an obstinate old cuss. He told the communists to go and fuck their grandmothers, and he strutted all around the village like a peacock, boasting about what he'd done. But it wasn't so easy to throw them off. Not more than an hour later they drove an old, creaking cart into our farmyard. 'Okay, Gavryushkin,' they said, 'get your whole kulak brood together in what they stand up in. You can take a crust of bread and a pinch of salt for the journey—and it's away with you under guard to the far north!' Mother and Grandma started screaming, us kids were all in tears, but my dad—well, a funny look came over him and his face turned black. 'Why are you doing this to me?' he says. 'What have I done wrong? I've never said a word against the gov'ment and I've always paid my taxes, haven't I?' And then—I remember it like it was yesterday, brother—this pockmarked lout from the local communist headquarters goes up to my dad. He had a pistol on his hip and he was wearing glasses, nose like a duck's beak and big floppy ears he had. 'You've heard of the dictatorship of the proletariat, haven't you?' he says. 'Well, by the law of class consciousness you, Gavryushkin, are a kulak element, and you've got to be shipped out of here into exile.' And he grips my dad by the shirtfront. But Ivan Karpych, my old man, God rest his soul as they say, he couldn't stomach any sort of acting rough. He could bend a horseshoe double, but he thought people ought to be decent and polite, and he fetched that lout a whack across the middle of his forehead. Well, you can imagine: his glasses went one way, his ears went another, and they could hardly put the pieces together again. But as usual, force won the day: they tied up my old man, and took him away in a special cart to district headquarters for assaulting an official in the execution of his duty. We never saw him again. And we were sent away too—only it was three thousand miles farther on. My grandma didn't even make it all the way; she kicked the bucket.

Not surprising either, when even young people were dying like flies.
Later on, in the camps, a man who'd been an engineer under the old
regime told me for certain that in those times when they arrested my
family almost seven million peasants were killed: some were hanged
or shot, the rest starved to death. Sorry, brother, but that's the truth,
and there's no getting away from it. I never did get to the place of
exile either: I escaped in Achinsk, because by then I'd got the message—they were taking us to certain death. I was a desperate lad,
took after my dad, and I didn't waste time skulking around trash
cans for scraps, but I latched on to the real game right away. Soon
they knew me all up and down the main Siberian highway. I became
a pro, and I had plenty of clout in the brotherhood. Did my first
stretch in a reformatory, then I went all the way up the scale from
the White Sea Canal to the camps at Potma. And brother—the people I saw working in the labor gangs on those sites! I had Deputy
People's Commissars running errands for me and fetching water for
me, and ex-generals trailing around after me like spaniels, hoping to
pick up a crumb or two. There was even one famous tenor, Vadim
Kozin, who used to cling to me like a limpet. So don't give me those
hard looks, brother; no use trying to break my heart—I know which
side God's on. Just tell me instead what all those intellectuals of
yours were doing when us peasants were being beaten up and deported, and our frozen corpses stacked up in heaps like firewood.
And not just in ones and twos, or even hundreds—but in millions,
brother! And what for—can you tell me that? For having earned a
crust of bread by the sweat of our brow, bent double over the soil.
We never hurt anybody, never took away anyone else's livelihood—
in fact, we fed them with all they could eat. When my old grandma,
who'd spent all her life slaving on the farm, gave up the ghost in a
cattle car, those intellectuals of yours shouted hurrah: serve her
right, that's the way to treat the kulak monsters. They made up
poems about how happy life was on the collective farms, they rattled
their sword belts and pranced about on parade, and they licked
Stalin's ass. And you think I haven't the right to get my own back on
them, even just a little? Well, for my money there's not one of them
that isn't guilty in some way or other. Of course, sometimes you
come across some real good men, scholars and the like, and I always
felt sorry for them. Even so, there were times when you felt like asking them: what sort of a scholar were you when you went on drinking your sweet coffee and kept your mouth shut while the common

folk were being bled white? What can you expect of us peasants, when educated people were ready to sell their souls to anyone for the sake of their comforts? I didn't play the fool all the time in the camps, you know; there was time enough to spare, and I did quite a bit of reading. If a learned man has a conscience, then he doesn't just keep his mouth shut—he stands up for the truth and risks his life. Jan Huss—ever heard of him? Well, there you are. And he wasn't the only one. But our learned men, it seems, are only in it for themselves and just so as they can feather their own nests; to them we are so much shit, and the gov'ment can do what they like with us. Not long ago, when I was on transfer, I came across a young kid with carroty-red hair and a face so covered in freckles he looked as if he'd been sprayed with dung. Knee-high to a grasshopper he was, and he'd been given five years under the Decree against gleaning. God knows what'll become of him—he's already smoking and drugging himself on chifir.* He's useless as a farmworker now, and when he gets out he'll just drift from one casual job to another, or even worse. As for the people who are still free, well, their time will come and they'll cop it too. Old Whiskers doesn't change his ways; he'll get them one day, even though they may be bigwigs now and making up laws to tighten things up, or writing books about our glorious Soviet youth and composing hymns and cantatas and whatnot. Yet to their way of thinking that red-haired kid is already a criminal, a black sheep, a social reject as they call it. Pen-pushing bastards! There's many of their kind I won't forget. You may not believe it, brother, but I even met that four-eyed punk who arrested my family. Near Archangel it was, in the quarantine barracks. They'd sent us there from Butyrki prison in Moscow to fell lumber. When we were being given our physical, I looked at the doctor's assistant and I thought there was something familiar about him. When it was my turn and he came and peered into my mouth, I spoke up. 'Don't you recognize me?' I said. 'Did we meet on some transfer party?' he said. 'No,' I said, 'it was at Torbeyevo, during the anti-kulak campaign, when you arrested Gavryushkin.' He looked at me, sort of frowning, and turned away. 'It was all so long ago,' he said, 'I can't remember them all.' 'Well,' I said, 'you've still got a scar on your

---

* Chifir is the Russian underworld's slang term for a highly concentrated extract of tannin and caffeine produced by brewing tea at many times the normal strength, e.g., half a pound of tea to half a pint of water. The resulting liquid is a stimulant drug similar in effect to amphetamines. (Tr.)

forehead that my old man gave you.' 'There were plenty of others beside him who beat me up,' he said. 'And did it do you any good?' I asked him. 'Guess it did,' he said, trying all the time to turn away, 'I've had plenty of time to think about it since.' 'We'll meet again inside the camp,' I said, 'and I'll give you some more to think about.' 'Forget it, kid,' he said, 'you're still young, there's a lot you don't understand yet.' And he sidled away out of the room. Three weeks later, though, I did meet him in the camp. Don't look at me like that! I didn't beat him up—I didn't! But one day I cornered him in a dark spot after lights out: 'What price the dictatorship of the proletariat now?' I said. 'Here in the camp,' I said, '*I'm* the prole-tariat and *you're* the kulak and the bourgeois exploiter. And by the laws of my class consciousness I condemn you to death. Say your last word!' 'I'll say it in poetry,' he said. 'Okay,' I said, 'it's all the same to me.' And he began reeling off a whole poem, all in proper verses and in rhyme. It was all about how guilty he was, about the blood of the people, and about the lowdown bastards who made life hell for them. He was so sincere, that son of a bitch, it even brought tears to my eyes, I remember. 'Clear off,' I said, 'and don't let me catch sight of you again—and make sure you get someone to slip me some surgical spirit from the dispensary.' Well, since then, brother, I can't bring myself to hate him; I just despise them—they're such a slimy, slippery bunch. If things were only different, you see, that poem of his would have made up for what happened to my dad and to the whole seven million and he might even have earned a medal. But what made me lose all respect for them was what happened at Kandalaksha. They sent us there soon after the beginning of the war, in the middle of winter, to build a railroad track to Kotlas so as to ship coal to the rest of the country. They drove us out into the open fields in thirty degrees of frost, with a howling wind and nothing all around us except snow and tree stumps. Everywhere you looked there were posters with slogans: 'There are no snowstorms on site!' 'There is no frost on site!' 'The Motherland needs coal!' All they gave us was tents, pickaxes, and shovels, and the order was: 'Get going!' But we knew what that meant . . . it meant—drop dead. As a squad leader I said to my lot: 'Lie down, you guys. Better to lie down and stay alive than die on your knees. The others can build up the roadbed with their bones if they want to.' And they all lay down —thieves and peasants together. Only the others—the politicals—

stayed on their feet, to show how 'responsible' they were. The guards went berserk and started lashing out at us with anything that came to hand, but my peasants and thieves just lay there clutching each other without moving—it was a sight for sore eyes, I can tell you! The guards went on beating them until they got fed up and walked away. But those other swine still wanted to prove their good behavior and tried to make out they weren't just cowards but were acting out of principle. It was just getting dark when five reindeer sleighs drove up out of the darkness, with two men on each, wearing prison officer's sheepskin coats. I watched them drive past and stop somewhere in the middle of the line of prisoners. Well, I thought, they're either going to threaten us or try persuasion. Then suddenly —you could've knocked me down with a feather—I nearly fell over with amazement. One of those jokers on a sleigh stood up with a megaphone and started yelling—better than Levitan the radio announcer he was: 'The Father of All Peoples has telephoned and told us to say he has faith in you!' He shouted this two or three times up and down the column, and then they drove away. And the performance those politicals started then, brother—well, it beggars description. They shouted, wept, and threw their ragged caps into the air. Even some of my peasants began to stir and almost stood up, but I only had to give them one look and they lay down again. So none of my lot got to their feet until they were assigned to another job. But you should have seen those politicals, brother—you should have seen them if you want to know how human beings can turn themselves into lumps of shit. How they slaved! Never in my life have I seen men sweat their guts out like that—I didn't even know people could work that hard! What sort of an ass-licker have you got to be to make a virtue out of breaking records for ass-licking? And you call them human beings—or like they call them in fine big books . . . *homo sapiens!*"

Vlad fell asleep to the sound of this weird saga, and when he awoke it was a bright autumn morning, and the car had stopped; what appeared to be a large station could be seen through the window, the guards were running up and down the corridor and shouting as they went:

"Prepare to detrain! Prepare to detrain! Come on, look lively . . . Move your ass, you mother-fucker!"

It was Vologda—the end of the journey.

CHAPTER 11

Outside the windows of the quarantine barracks the short-lived autumn of the Vologda region was fading away in golds and blues. Pale clouds floated low, dappling the surrounding country with ragged-edged shadows. A damp breeze blew in from outside, sending shivers up the spine. The days dragged slowly by, days spent in daydreams and memories, and in thoughts, cheerless as the weather, about the prospects of life in a prison camp. Ten years! From the limited viewpoint of his seventeen years a sentence of that length seemed unimaginable to the point of horror, its end so far distant that it vanished beyond the limits of comprehension. Vlad could not conceive how he would be able to hold out for half of that ten-year term. Since he now regarded his life as at an end, he was incapable of making plans even for the immediate future. What on earth did it matter what the next hour or the next day might bring him? Just so long as day succeeded day without anyone laying hands on him or bothering him, without trying to worm themselves into his confidence or irritating him with idle chatter and unrealizable dreams.

With a blanket pulled up to his chin, Vlad lay stretched out, day after day, staring mindlessly ahead out of the window, through which he could see the topmost strand of barbed wire against a dazzlingly blue sky. The wire had a peculiarly depressing effect on him. The reformatories in which he had been held before hardly ever

used barbed wire, except around off-limits areas. Raised to the status
of being the principal barrier, it became a menacing symbol of alienation, marking off a Pale of Settlement, a dividing line between life
and nullity, and while his previous escapes had been risky games, any
such attempt was now almost certainly lethal.

Below him, in the space between the rows of bunks, everyday life
went on. The young prisoners fought and made up, then fought
again; they played dice with dominoes, bartered and swapped anything they could lay hands on, and instinctively adapted themselves
to circumstances; Vlad alone remained apathetic and uninvolved.
Vlad had matured much earlier than his fellow inmates, and his per-
ception of reality and all its complexities was far more sober and realistic than theirs. He did not anticipate surviving a ten-year voyage
across the treacherous sea of Gulag, and he therefore preferred pas-
sive drift to pointless resistance.

One day, however, an acquaintance of Vlad's, a young Moscow
pickpocket nicknamed "Chapai" sidled up to him:

"Hey, pal, how about you and me making a dash for it?" Beneath
fiery-red eyelashes, his darting eye gave Vlad a sidelong glance of ap-
praisal. "I did a deal with another guy. He'll raise a racket and the
screws will drag him off to the can. That'll give us the chance to get
out of a window—and then you won't see us for dust." He was literally quivering with impatience. "I saw it when I went for a shit: one
of the latrines is right up against the perimeter. Easiest thing in the
world to get on the roof, and you're as good as over the wire. We
jump over and each go different ways, so at least one of us is bound
to get away . . . Sounds a good idea, doesn't it?"

The dull sky outside suddenly took on the hues of the rainbow.
On the cold breeze blowing indoors there came the pungent smell
of autumnal soil. The world came to life with sounds and voices.
How thrillingly, how quickly hope can arise in an instant from the
ashes of despair!

Vlad had first met Chapai in the "Stolypin." All the way from
Moscow to Vologda the boy had struck up a conversation with each
of his neighbors in turn, and always on the same theme:

"What do you think, pal—is it better to try and skip from quarantine or wait till you're in camp?"

Nobody took him seriously as a rule, but since Chapai's plan was
for them to flee in different directions and not to join forces, Vlad
agreed almost without hesitation:

"Think it'll work?"

"Listen, brother . . ." Excitement made the freckles on his snub nose turn dark and break out in sweat. "We just have to get well away from here, then we can worm our way into any orphanage by crying a few crocodile tears. You and I can easily still pass ourselves off as kids. You know they never make you play the piano in an orphanage.* They just register you under any name you like to give them. We can keep 'em fooled for a couple of months—and then get out for good. It's as easy as pie . . ."

Preparations did not take long. By an unwritten camp law, the others uncomplainingly donated the best available clothing, each one contributed a quarter of his ration from lunch and scraped together a supply of tobacco from his reserves. When they were fully equipped and ready, one of the boys started beating on the door and shouting:

"Officer, they're killing me! Help, they're killing me, officer!"

No sooner had the guards dragged the boy out to deal with him in the corridor, than Chapai smashed the windowpane with a pillow. The glass fell outward with scarcely a sound. A smell of dampness and rotting leaves flowed into the room. For a moment Vlad stood hunched up as he imagined the delicious terror of what lay ahead, but next moment he had flung his light body through the gaping hole into the blue emptiness beyond. Freedom!

Vlad made a frantic, headlong dash across the courtyard, skinning his hands as he clambered up onto the latrine roof, and had just straightened up to his full height in order to jump when he froze with horror: escorted by a guard, two boys were coming straight toward him, carrying the food for the quarantine barracks. Fortunately he did not remain paralyzed for long. Without even hearing the guard's shout, he flung himself almost prone onto the quilted jacket which Chapai had thrown over the barbed wire as padding, and with his last ounce of strength he heaved himself over the fence. Falling on his side, Vlad jumped up, and then, feeling the mossy cushion of the ground underfoot, he set off at a run through the sparse undergrowth toward the distant, dark line of the forest. At first Vlad followed his partner, whose frail little figure was weaving a zigzag course in front of him, but soon his objective—the darkening forest ahead—concentrated his field of vision on that straight line alone,

---

* "Play the piano"—underworld slang for having fingerprints taken. (Author's note.)

and he lost Chapai from sight. The hunt was up and the pursuers were on his traces.

When the first shot rang out over the surrounding countryside, Vlad was already out of breath and having to force his way through thick undergrowth toward the saving darkness of the pine forest. Reaching the first tree trunk he fell down to catch his breath and only then did the sound of rifle fire penetrate his fevered mind. He leaped to his feet again and dashed forward into a thicket, into the protective silence and the pungent smell of pine resin.

As he plunged deeper into the forest, Vlad began to weave his way along the streams, in an attempt to throw the dogs off his scent. He would wade downstream, retrace his steps and then hasten downstream again, jumping out of the water at what seemed to him the most unexpected places. Finally, soaked to the skin and with his clothes in tatters, he reached an open space where a railroad line cut a swath through the forest.

On the far side of the track bed, like a watchtower standing guard in front of a gangers' hut, there rose a neatly made haystack with crisscrossed ropes holding down its tarpaulin cover. The haystack beckoned Vlad powerfully, offering warmth and refuge. Unable to resist the temptation (his strength was already exhausted), he headed straight across the railroad tracks toward it: away with prudence and caution, and come what may!

Having burrowed into the hay, Vlad immediately fell into drowsy oblivion, in which he dreamed of his home and of Mitkovo Station, bathed in the white sunlight of a summer afternoon. Fluff from the poplar trees was drifting in the air, catching on eyelashes and sticking in nostrils. As he walked down the street, someone, most probably Yurka the chessplayer from No. 27 was plaintively calling after him: "Vla-ad, Vla-adka-a!" Golden dreams of childhood. Something was hurting him and something made him want to laugh, and his mother was threatening him from a window.

At first he could only hear a faint whining and the insistent scrape of paws, but that was enough for him to realize it was all over. Only a guard dog, skillfully trained in sleuthing, would act like that. The trap was sprung, resistance was useless. So the dog had picked up his trail after all—but where?

Only when he crawled out into the open and saw the guards clambering down from the track bed did Vlad understand what had happened: the search party had caught him at the very spot where he had crossed the tracks. Guessing it, he cursed his momentary weakness. He should have gone farther into the forest and along the streams without stopping. But there was no time left even for regrets. The guards—one a very young soldier with girlishly pink cheeks, the other a barrel-chested sergeant-major wearing his green tunic unbuttoned—were already standing over him:

"Lousy little pup!" A blow struck Vlad across the bridge of his nose and he fell, but strange to relate he felt no pain, only nausea and the taste of blood on his lips. "The country cares for you, you little punk, and all you want is to go over the wall, parasite. Stand up!"

Staring at the ground and shifting from foot to foot, the young soldier tried to restrain his comrade, muttering:

"Don't, Averyanich, don't do that, he's only a kid, after all . . . You've got kids of your own of his age . . . Stop it . . ."

The sergeant-major had obviously been drinking, and the soldier's remarks only worsened his temper:

"Don't you compare my kids with him! You're too young to be teaching me a lesson. My kids behave proper, they don't go around pinching other people's things or roaming all over the country. If I had my way I'd shoot these young whelps out of hand! The only thing that straightens a hunchback is a coffin. Feeding his sort is just a waste of bread." He took a swing and punched Vlad on the chin. "Get moving, you lousy little slob!"

The guard tried to push Vlad off the track bed toward the forest, but he flatly refused and when the sergeant-major attempted to move him by force, Vlad flung himself prone across the ties:

"I won't go."

"Get up!"

"Kill me here and have done with it."

Vlad knew that once they were in the forest the men could do whatever they liked with him—set the dog on him, beat him half-dead, and finally, having pretended to allow him to escape, they would shoot him down. The railroad tracks, open on all sides and visible to anyone who happened to be in the vicinity, would save him from summary execution:

"I'll go—if you take me down the track."

After a short barrage of blows and curses, the sergeant-major gave in:

"Okay, get moving . . . I don't intend to spend the night out here
with you . . . I'll teach you your lesson back in camp . . . Let's go!"

The way back seemed infinitely long. Doing his best to keep close
to the escort (according to prison service regulations, a distance of
more than nine meters from the guards was enough for them to
shoot him in the back), Vlad was in no hurry as he stepped along
the ties; his stooping back burned in expectation of a blow or a rifle
shot.

Looming ahead in the deepening twilight, the lights from the
watchtowers gave the prison-camp compound an almost romantic
look: a sort of fairground made up of brightly lit cardhouses on top
of a hill. But the nearer they came to it, the more clearly its true nature was revealed—grim huts behind a double row of barbed wire,
the wretched abode of the insulted and oppressed.

In the guardroom they were already expected. No sooner was Vlad
pushed in through the door than a boot kicked him on the hip and
knocked him down.

"Ah, you thieving trash!" The gypsy-like features of the guard
commander, Captain Pisarev, an old acquaintance of Vlad's since his
first day in the quarantine barracks, bent over him. "Where's the
other runaway?"

Vlad could do nothing but roll himself into a ball and shield his
head with his hands. At once blows started to rain on him from all
sides. In their sadistic abandon, the guards even stopped cursing.
Panting and grunting, they beat him up, fully aware of their im-
punity. Vlad felt his body slowly turning into a sack full of pain
which at any moment might burst apart at the seams. Blue swallows
fluttered before his closed eyes, and a smoldering coal burned in his
constricted throat. The last thing he remembered was a short, sharp
kick from a boot heel in his groin, followed by his own shriek, and
then a fall into a black abyss . . .

He felt himself carried away, gently floating. Somewhere nearby,
waves were lapping softly at the shore and someone was singing a familiar nursery rhyme that had haunted him throughout his childhood:

> Boxer, boxer,
> How are things today?
> Not a crust of bread to eat
> The children soon will cry . . .

Then he heard the voice of his sister Nina calling him as though from a far shore: "Vlad . . . Vla-ad, Vla-adi-ik, time for dinner, Mother's calling you!" But when he opened his eyes what he saw was not the courtyard on the Mitkovka but the sea, and himself lying on the shingle beach at Batum, where he and the others were being taken out for a walk from the municipal orphanage. The sky above him was boiling and heaving, while far ahead, exactly level with his eyes, a shining white ship was steaming along with a black stream of smoke curling around its brightly colored funnels. Vlad wanted to get up and walk down the beach to the green water's edge, but at that moment a searing pain shot through him from head to foot. He felt himself pulled by it, and then he was falling, falling into a bottomless chasm, without a gleam of light or hope of salvation.

And then darkness again.

"Vlad!"

"Vla-a-ad!"

"Vla-a-di-ik!"

Silence.

CHAPTER 12

The light touch of a hand brought Vlad to his senses. Bending over him was a thin face with a prominently jutting chin:

"Don't you recognize me?"

By an effort of memory he summoned from the darkness of the recent past his first day in the quarantine barracks: roll call, body search, physical examination. At once he remembered the emaciated prisoner working as a feldsher,* who had joked sardonically with the new arrivals as he examined them:

"How old are you, fella? Seventeen? From the size of your prick I'd have said you're more like thirty-five. Did it grow by itself or did you train it up in your local handicraft class? Okay, move on. Next! Which knacker's yard did *you* run away from? Or have you been on hunger strike? S'pose you thought they'd feed you up in camp. All right. Next!"

Vlad had liked this feldsher from the first. At least he did not lecture them, threaten them, or put on the airs of a big boss. There was something in his way of talking to them that won their confidence, and that made even the prospect of life in a prison camp seem less interminable and less grim.

This man was now bending over Vlad, and through the ineradica-

* A medical assistant. (Tr.)

bly sarcastic cast of his long features there shone an obvious sympathy:

"Lie down, lie down, rest as long as you like. Take your time, you're not going anywhere. Be thankful they didn't kill you—it happens, and no one ever finds out."

The white ceiling floated and swayed before his eyes. Everything around him was white—the walls, the sheets, the windows powdered with the season's first snow—but it was a whiteness dulled by a certain oppressive tinge of gray, the ubiquitous pall of unfreedom. "Solitary!" Vlad grimaced with relief. "Well, at least it means I'm alive!"

"I guess you might say they worked you over with . . . enthusiasm." The feldsher's voice buzzed away quietly over his head. "Some pig even threw a bucket of water into your cell, so we could hardly scrape you off the floor this morning. Those dumb guards really saw red when they caught you. Seems your pal got away; they're looking for him now in Vologda. But you just lie still and relax. The main thing is that you're still alive, and even if they give you an extra two years, it's not the end of the world. You won't have to serve out your full term, anyway; they say that all minors will be amnestied soon." He bent down right next to Vlad's ear, his breathing rapid and hot: "I'd like to help you, but I'm not sure whether you still have the strength to pull it off. Have you ever pretended to be crazy?" He put his own interpretation on Vlad's silence. "Okay, I'll teach you what to do. The main thing is to keep silent and tear up paper. Shut your mouth and tear up any paper within reach. Got it? I'll leave a book on your bedside table . . . Don't worry, we'll do it all properly—it's been done before . . ."

Vlad's first thought was to wonder whether it was a trick, but then he reasoned that the feldsher had nothing to gain by helping him, and he took heart: "No harm in trying—and it might even work!"

The sixth-grade geography textbook left by the feldsher disintegrated slowly but surely in Vlad's hands. A little heap of torn maps and printed pages grew at his feet like a colored mosaic.

Gradually he even started to enjoy it. He liked shredding the greasy, thumbmarked paper, feeling the intoxicating pleasure of a schoolboy's revenge for all the low grades he had once been given for geography. Rip, rip, rip!

Once or twice the feldsher poked his head around the door and winked approvingly. That evening he brought Major Varva, director of the camp medical services, into the room:

"Look, comrade major, he's been doing this all day. When I ask him a question he doesn't answer. Seems like the guards overdid it."

The lame Ukrainian doctor stood beside Vlad, clasping the knob of his walking stick with both hands, and bared his nicotine-stained teeth in a sarcastic grin:

"Malingering, eh, Samsonov?" He lifted Vlad's chin with the tip of his stick. "Aren't you afraid of getting found out?"

How Vlad hated him at that moment! What was he doing it for? What harm had he ever done to this cripple with his stick? Tears of self-pity stifled him, and he tried not to raise his eyes lest he give himself away.

"I'll report this to the camp authorities." The stick was lowered to the ground. "Let them decide. Write up a report on his symptoms. He may be genuinely off his head; it does happen."

Having escorted Major Varva out of the room the feldsher returned, sat down on the edge of Vlad's cot, and said in a low voice:

"Well done, Samsonov. Everything's going fine so far. Just go on keeping your mouth shut. He'll tell the top brass about you now, and then I think it's in the bag. I've been keeping an eye on you since you first arrived in quarantine. The education officer showed me some poetry you'd written; he laughed and said, look—we've got a poet. I write a bit of poetry now and again too, but yours is better. You must study—you have talent, and it ought to be fostered. A talent like yours is only given to one in a hundred thousand, maybe one in a million. It would be a terrible sin for it to be buried unused. It's sort of given to you like a loan, which you have to pay off for the rest of your life. I've spent years in the camps, and I've seen all sorts, I can tell you. If I told you about some of the people I've buried, it'd make your hair stand on end. I remember what one of them, an actor (he had galloping cancer), said to me before his last operation: talent, he said, is given to a person as a reward in compensation for the suffering of others, and so, he said, the man with talent bears a greater responsibility—God demands three times, even five times more from him. I only regret one thing, he said—that I haven't yet had time to repay my debt in full, they didn't let me . . . Don't have hard feelings about Major Varva, he's a decent man, only he got a terrible battering in the war . . . Okay, go to sleep now. You're supposed to sleep, anyway—it's one of the symptoms of depressive reaction."

The feldsher went out and Vlad gratefully fell asleep. When he awoke, almost all the senior officers of the camp were crowded around his cot: There was the commandant, Major Poputko, the education officer Captain Tulupov, Vlad's old acquaintance Captain Pisarev, and a few others lower in rank who behaved with appropriate modesty. Leaning as ever with both hands on the knob of his walking stick, Major Varva was just finishing his explanation:

". . . the symptoms are fairly advanced and absolutely stable, and an early remission is not likely . . . A recovery, that is . . . I think the specialists at Kuvshinovo Hospital will be able to give a definitive opinion." In the light of the single electric bulb his swarthy face with its yellow, protuberant eyes looked kinder and gentler than by daylight. "At all events, we are not in a position to make a precise diagnosis here . . ."

The officers stood around for a little while longer, their blue cap-bands nodding thoughtfully, then they slowly filed out of the room in strict accordance with rank and position. The last to leave was the doctor. In the doorway he turned around, and it seemed to Vlad that a glint of sarcastic approval flashed in the yellow irises of his bulging eyes.

In the small hours of the morning the feldsher brought Vlad his still-wet clothes. With a broad smile he said cheerfully:

"You're to be taken to Vologda for a special medical examination. The important thing now is not to let me down. Do everything I told you to do . . . There you are, you can get dressed. Sorry, but your clothes haven't had time to dry out yet."

The next person to come in was the sergeant-major who had caught him. Shuffling with embarrassment, he turned away toward the window and grunted:

"I'm taking you to the guardhouse. When the doctor's ready, we'll go . . . Don't think bad of me, kid, I was drunk . . . I was beaten up even worse in my time. And a man who's been beaten, you know, is worth two who haven't . . . that's a fact."

They walked through the snow-covered and still-sleeping camp to the guardroom, where Major Varva was already waiting for them. He signed a receipt for Vlad, and they set off into the dark and snow. Out of habit Vlad walked ahead, without hurrying and without turning around. One thing was clear to him: on this day his life was to undergo a radical change, though whether for better or worse was not yet clear. This, no doubt, was the reason why he did not feel the cold. At the end of this nighttime journey waited the unknown.

They reached the station as it was getting light. In the waiting room people stared at Vlad with curiosity and suspicion. A man under guard was nothing unusual in these parts, but even so the sight always aroused a certain interest. An old woman wearing a head scarf that came down to her eyebrows surreptitiously handed Vlad a piece of fish, at which the sergeant-major turned away, pretending he had not seen this blatant violation of prison-service rules.

In the crowded passenger car Vlad attracted little attention, so he spent the journey to Vologda largely unnoticed and able to listen to the other passengers' conversation.

One skinny old peasant was describing the reason for his journey to another equally frail old man wearing a cut-down army greatcoat:

"You see, dad, just getting that permit cost me a small fortune. It's a good thing the chairman of our kolkhoz drinks like a fish, or I'd never have got it at all. And I need it badly, 'cos things are terrible at our kolkhoz. I'm a carpenter, see, and a good one—if you want a house with fancy trimmings, or a boat, I can make it for you. Now I've got my permit I can travel anywhere I like for work. Make enough to buy myself new clothes, help my relations . . ."

His neighbor nodded and made sympathetic comments:

"Yes, you deserve it . . . yes, that's right . . . Now's just the time to find work in town . . . How old are you?"

Facing each other on the top bunks, two traveling lecturers were heatedly discussing the problems of their profession:

"Nowadays they all ask for 'The International Situation,'" said one. "No one wants to hear 'The Moral Image' anymore."

The other disagreed forcefully:

"That's not true! You can't say that! It all depends on how you dish it up. If you give lots of real details from local life and make it really juicy—they'll lap it up."

A rowdy drinking party was in progress in the next compartment, which got to the singing stage and then began to develop into a fight. Only their arrival at Vologda stopped mayhem from breaking out.

Vologda! Even many years later the memory of that town would make his heart beat faster, as though it were a sign, a brand, a symbol of the last of childhood and the beginning of youth.

The town greeted them with a snowbound silence laced with wintry smells: smoke, horse dung, sheepskin coats. They traversed it on foot, and then, after walking across a white field, Vlad could see on the far bank of a frozen river a cluster of dark-red brick buildings, which was shortly to be the scene of a complete and permanent change in his fate.

Feeling faint with nervous expectation, Vlad climbed up a steep slope to the two-story building that housed the hospital offices and the reception ward, while behind him he could hear his escort joking not unkindly at his expense:

"Say, is he in a hurry!"

"Can't keep up with him!"

"Guess he must be frozen."

"So are we, come to that."

"Well, we can warm ourselves up in Vologda."

"Yes, Comrade Major!"

Listening to them, Vlad wondered how it was that these very ordinary and no doubt normally good-natured men could turn on occasion into such savage brutes.

They were met in the reception ward by a little old man in a snow-white coat. Trembling with extreme age, he smiled kindly at Vlad with his nearsighted eyes and whispered in a barely audible voice:

"Good evening, young man, glad to meet you . . ." He paused to catch his breath, then went on: "My name is Abram Ruvimovich . . . my last name is Zholtovsky. I'm the doctor here . . . You and I must have a talk."

Ah, Abram Ruvimovich! He will remember you as long as he lives. You were literally made up of undiluted goodness, although you never used that word. Perhaps he never did learn to love people—that is an art too painful for him to acquire; but thanks to you he did at least learn to feel pity for them . . .

The talk did not last long, and soon a stocky male nurse led Vlad away to another building, where the door of the madhouse closed noisily behind him for a long time.

CHAPTER 13

The lobby at the entrance to the section looked more like a prison cell than part of a hospital. Four men were openly gambling at cards around the tiled stove, in the farthest corner a food parcel was being heatedly shared out, while between the beds a young man with a mouthful of gold teeth was cheerfully doing a tap dance. The resemblance to prison was completed by a hefty, dark-haired man seated on a bench near the door, whose prison-guard uniform clearly showed through beneath his white coat.

No one paid any attention to the new arrival, except for a tall, shaven-headed male nurse who silently pointed out the bed on which Vlad was to sleep, and on which a man was already lying. He answered Vlad's questioning look with a curt explanation:

"Head to tail."

With that he strolled back to the door, where he shared the bench with the prison guard.

His future bedmate looked at Vlad with such glazed indifference that he thought it better to take a walk around the section. It was divided into two large wards and several small ones, which housed, as he guessed, the severely ill patients. The whole section was permeated by a stale, stuffy smell of agelong vintage: a mixture of urine, dirty underwear, and tobacco smoke. A cacophony of weeping, laughing, and singing made up the general bedlam.

As he waited in the lobby outside the toilets, Vlad was joined on the bench by the gold-toothed character who had been dancing between the beds:

"Smoke?"

"No, thanks."

"That's bad. You'll go *really* crazy here if you don't smoke." He threw Vlad a sidelong glance and grinned. "Where are you from?"

"Sheksna."

"I'm from Belo-ozersk myself. That's a work site. The activists don't give you much chance to get bored there. How much did you get?"

"Ten."

"Phew, that's a lot." He whistled. "Which decree?"

"Two, two."*

"I picked up five for dipping. D'you get food parcels?"

"No one to send them."

"Then you're really in the shit." He stared at Vlad and then, dropping his offhand manner, he explained: "In this place they hardly give you any food at all. Some of the staff are okay, and now and again they pass you some scraps—a crust of bread or a potato maybe. I'm okay, 'cos my old lady sends me parcels. So I share 'em out. They sure pulled a filthy trick on you by making you share with that epileptic. You'll never get any proper sleep. He has a fit about three times every night. Next time there's a chance to switch beds, you and I can bunk up together. Meantime, you'll just have to stick it out."

"Guess so. I'm no different from the others."

"If you're like all the others, you'll kick the bucket. Gotta use your head. You stick with me."

"Okay . . ."

"Well, I'll split now. If you want anything, come on over . . ."

"I sure will . . ."

Something about this character made Vlad like him; he was the kind that always said exactly what he thought, and Vlad decided to stick with him for a while and see how it worked out. Thus began Vlad's friendship with Sashka Shilov, the Moscow pickpocket—a friendship he was to remember for the rest of his life. It started off with Sashka rescuing him from the aggressive patients, until he learned to deal with them by himself. Sashka shared his infrequent

* Refers to Section 2, Paragraph 2 of the Decree of 1947. (Tr.)

food parcels with him, and Sashka even found ways of getting newspapers and books for him.

The first night was the worst. His bedmate really did have three
fits, and so before he could go to sleep Vlad had to wrestle three
times with the man to calm him down. This was not, to put it
mildly, an occupation for anyone with weak nerves; but gradually,
night after night, he got used to it and soon was able to handle the
epileptic without undue effort or squeamishness. Afterward he would
fall placidly asleep.

In the mornings the Tartar would feel exhausted and guilty; he also
showed suitable gratitude:

"You see," he said, turning his bright, slanting eyes on Vlad, "I
am like this since childhood. I feel I'm falling, falling somewhere. I
feel so good then and there's a special sort of light all around me—
can't tell you how good it feels, and then I feel bad, very bad . . . If
you ask them, they'll move you to another bed. That cot over by the
window is empty now."

Vlad, however, was determined to stick it out with his Tartar to
the bitter end. Life in the ward was run on prison lines anyway, so
that beds were not allocated by the medical staff but by the gang
which sat around the stove. Their boss was a balding crook nicknamed Cain, who had been brought to the hospital for psychiatric
observation. From morning till night he was surrounded by a noisy
crowd of people wanting to do him a favor and so earn their share of
hospital comforts: a better-placed bed, a less-tattered bathrobe, extra
rations. All day long Cain lay on his cot by the stove, his hands
clasped under his head, issuing silent orders and instructions. He was
under observation for murder during an attempted armed robbery,
and he could expect nothing but the death penalty.

After about a week, Vlad was ordered to report to Cain. To refuse
(as Vlad had learned from experience) was more than one's life was
worth.

Cain greeted the newcomer in his usual attitude—lying on his
back with hands behind his head. He nodded silently toward the
neighboring bed. With a sideways glance of his rabbity eyes he said:

"They say you're obstinate. I like that, I'm obstinate myself.
Aren't you fed up with fighting that epileptic every night?"

"Someone has to do it."

"You're not a Party member, by any chance, are you?" He began to show some signs of animation, if a twisted grin can be called animated. "So you're all for fairness and justice, eh? Well, you'll be disappointed—there isn't any." And straightway, without changing his tone, he said: "I hear you write poetry."

"Well, I do it for fun, to pass the time."

At this Cain turned and looked straight at Vlad for the first time. His face was haggard, with an unhealthy, blotchy skin that obviously came from time spent in prison, but some repressed thought, or rather agony, made it almost expressive:

"If you do it 'just for fun,' kid, you'll never be any good at it. Remember everything you see and hear, kid, make a note in your head, don't forget anything—then you'll be worth your weight in gold, and forever. If you could only write down my life—what a book that would make! Blood and tears . . . Trouble is, this thing on my shoulders isn't a head, it's only a cabbage, or even worse . . . Ah!"—he even gave a sob of uncontrollable emotion—"if only you could write it all down one day!" At once, however, he grew visibly ashamed of his outburst and lay down again on his back. "Okay, off you go. If you want to, you can have the cot next to the window, or you can have this one alongside me. But you can please yourself . . ."

From that day on Vlad's authority in the section became unquestioned; but he stayed with the Tartar all the same, for which he earned the latter's absolute trust and liking:

"You know," said the Tartar, "all people in here are like wild beasts. Pretend to be sick, but never forget their bad ways. Prison-camp rabble!"

"But you're from a prison camp yourself, aren't you?"

"Don't compare me with them—I'm a political!"

"You?"

"Tried to kill president of our kolkhoz. Didn't make it. Pity!"

"What for?"

"He got my brother arrested, got him five years. Brother only wanted a little hay to feed his cow. Cow was hungry, bellowing all time."

"Didn't you feel sorry for him?"

"Who for?"

"The chairman—he's a human being, after all."

The Tartar only clicked his tongue in disagreement and turned away at once, obviously convinced that further discussion was pointless.

Vlad had already seen plenty in his short lifetime, but only at this moment did everything that had ever happened to him, every event and encounter, as though joined up by the final link, fuse into a single unbroken chain, a whole and complete picture. And it took his breath away: what sort of a country was this, what sort of people were those, and how, how could they live as they did?

Ten days later Vlad was summoned for a talk with Doctor Zholtovsky. Given a clean change of underwear and a more presentable bathrobe, he was led through a maze of corridors to the main hospital block.

In the hushed semidarkness of his tiny office, Zholtovsky seemed to Vlad an old gnome, wraithlike and liable to dissolve into dust at any moment. As though waving a feather, the gnome gestured to Vlad to sit down; his voice rustled gently:

"Good morning . . . Tell me about yourself."

"What shall I tell you?"

"Everything."

Although scarcely audible, the word was spoken with such piercing significance that Vlad heard and understood: he really must tell "everything." It was not so much a story as his first confession, with all the revelations and all the fervor that go with it. He told of the first birds flying over Sokolniki. He told of betraying his father and his bitter repentance. He told how everyone had harried and persecuted him, how he had tried again and again to run away, but in the end had never managed to pull it off. And behind it all stood his grandfather Saviely, thin and stooped, a helpless witness to Vlad's persecution.

When Vlad finished, he suddenly felt that the life he had been describing was so long and so bizarre that it was not his own at all, but the life story of some complete stranger. All the while Zholtovsky seemed not to be listening to him. The doctor stared at the lacy patterns of hoarfrost on the window, and only his parchmentlike hand trembled very slightly as it rested on the glass top of his desk. But as soon as the story was over, the hand was slowly raised and lowered in a gesture of affirmation:

"You may go." His voice rose and grew unexpectedly firm in tone. "You're going back home. Ask the head nurse to come in and see me, please."

When she came out of Zholtovsky's office, the head nurse, a short, stout, popeyed woman with earrings, came bustling cheerfully up to Vlad:

"You're to be moved to the section for mild cases, and we're to have you ready for examination by the next review board. You're in luck—must have been born with a silver spoon in your mouth. You're going to be discharged; I know my boss. He seems very upset right now, though—he's actually shaking. Come on—I'll have you fixed up in two ticks."

She led Vlad down the same corridors, then turned off into the section where he had been assigned. Unlocking the door with a key hanging from her belt, she shouted from the doorway:

"Agnyusha, here's a new young patient for you. Take him in, please—chief's orders."

Then Vlad saw her—Agnyusha Kuznetsova, the first woman in his life who would leave a burning trace on his memory for the rest of his days. In looks she was not pretty, nor even particularly noticeable; you would pass her on the street without turning your head. You had to look hard at her to perceive deep in her eyes, beneath their pale lashes, something which caused a long, sad silence to envelop you and from which there was no escape.

"Okay," was all she said, while Vlad felt his heart stand still, "we'll take him in. Why not? Plenty of room in here."

As she made his bed, she asked:

"What's your name?"

"Vlad."

"You're from the city, aren't you?"

"I'm from Moscow."

"My, my!" She now looked him up and down with a certain interest. "When did you leave Moscow?"

"A year ago."

"Are you from a camp, or prison?"

"From a camp. I was in Sheksna."

"My husband's family lives there. Only I haven't seen them for years—since we left to get married, in fact . . . You can get into bed now. Get plenty of rest before you go to the review board, and then we'll see what the doctors have to say. They may even send you home."

Vlad lay down and sank immediately into oblivion. Probably for the first time in all his years of wandering, he was sleeping in a clean bed made up for him by a pair of gentle female hands, in the quiet of an almost noiseless ward and with the hope of returning to Moscow before too long. Now he really believed it would happen.

CHAPTER 14

Kuvshinovo! A place named for a pitcher—*kuvshin*; add a little syllable—*kuvshinka*—and it means a water lily. A word both round and elongated, like a pear, and sonorous as a ritual bell. The taste of a winter's night on one's lips. Slowly, as though unwillingly, snow falling outside a window barred on both sides. And the uneasy signal cries of other men's dreams. What apparitions can they be seeing, out there beyond the bounds of human understanding? What abodes of darkness?

Outside the snow was falling, whirling slowly and gently in the silence. Staring at the darkness and at his own reflection in the glass, imperceptibly Vlad freed himself inwardly from his surroundings, detached himself, listening to the world around him as though from outside. He had the feeling that the hospital ward, like some lonely ark, was sailing through the abyss of night with a cargo of sleeping insanity on board.

Behind him the tiled stove hissed and crackled. The faint smell of smoke scratched at his throat and tickled his nostrils. Shadows thrown by the flames groped their way blindly over the walls, fleetingly reflected in the windowpanes. The ark sailed on among frozen stars, amid a choppy swell of groans and sighs, accompanied by the monotonous sound of a voice beside the stove:

"I shall die on the twelfth, this is my last reprieve." From his in-

corporeal distance Vlad imagined the hollow eyes and heavy chin of
Gena Svirin, the deserter. "Exactly at three o'clock in the afternoon,
right after lunch." With his weakness for food, Gena would never, of
course, have agreed to die before lunch, even in exchange for the
Kingdom of Heaven. "There's another person inside me, and he
foretells everything that's going to happen to me."

"Hark at him—isn't he the lucky one!" Agnyusha, the nurse on
duty, gave an indulgent little laugh which flowed over the sleepy
unease of the ward. "Two whole men for the price of one. So how did
you get here in the first place? Didn't your pal warn you that you
weren't supposed to run away from the Army? Well, here you are, so
take your time . . ."

Agnyusha's voice brought Vlad back to reality. He suddenly felt
the sharp and powerful call of the flesh, he sensed the hot flow of his
blood, heard the beating of his own heart. He even thought he could
detect her smell: a blend of stale hay and washing soap, the smell of
a forty-year-old peasant woman who had never completely left her
farm and the land. Vlad had often sat up all night with her, listening
to her tell stories of when she was young, of her short marriage and
long widowhood.

"I was a good-looking girl in my young days." The words she uttered were solid and round, as though being threaded onto an endless but elegant chain of beads. "There were plenty of handsome
boys chasing after me—a whole flock of them, in fact. But I had to
go and fall for a young fellow who was so poor and so thin you
wouldn't believe it—he was just skin and bone, and all he had was a
little accordion that was fastened by a button. But he was such fun,
it was crazy. And so generous he'd give the shirt off his back to the
first person he met. As for our wedding, well, it was one long laugh—
the bridegroom had to borrow his boots from a friend. We lived like
two lovebirds, we had a song for soup and the chorus for dessert—we
were starving but we were happy. But we only lived together for two
short years. Then my fellow went off to earn big money on a construction site for the Five-Year Plan, and he just vanished there without a trace . . ."

"Yeah . . . it happens." When the conversation was about something that did not concern him personally, Gena Svirin immediately
lost interest. "I'll go and have a last little snooze. You can't sleep in
the next world . . ."

Lord, how slowly and miserably his slippers flapped on the way to his corner behind the stove, what a noise he made as he fumbled around getting into bed, before Vlad heard Agnyusha's steady breathing over his shoulder:

"Why aren't you asleep?" She pressed close against him from behind, and gently bit the skin between his shoulder blades. "Feeling upset?"

"Your winters here are so snowy." His heart went cold and seemed to melt. "It never stops snowing. Looks like everything will be buried."

She pressed against him harder and more openly:

"Not everything . . . a little bit's left showing . . . Why are you trembling so, haven't you ever been with a woman?"

"Yes . . . only it was a long time ago . . . And then not quite."

Gently but firmly she took him by the hand and pulled him to the door and beyond, down the tiled corridor and into the dim semi-darkness of the bathroom. Unresisting, he trailed after her, tottering like a drunkard and whispering faintly:

"Where are you going, Agnyusha? What for? The doctor will be making his rounds any minute now . . . We'll get into trouble . . ."

In reply she only laughed softly and dreamily and went on pulling him after her.

Ah, that bathroom of the manic ward in Vologda mental hospital! He can still remember the peeling green paint on the walls, the cracked tiles on the floor, and even the long streaks of rust on the baths where the enamel had worn away down to the cast iron. Every night when she was on duty, hardly had the last wretch fallen into his phantom-haunted sleep than they would depart, holding hands, for the humble temple of their love, accompanied as they went by the muttering groans of madmen.

There on a bench, which served as both a clothes rack and a block for corporal punishment, they were joined as one flesh until cockcrow. And there was nothing around them but the smell and the silence, nothing but their furious tussling and whispering:

"Quiet, quiet. You're crazy."

"But I'm supposed to be crazy . . ."

"Did you like it that way?"

"And how!"

"You really *are* crazy . . ."

Morning, afternoon, evening all passed for Vlad as though in a fog, until her next spell of night duty. Many were the nights, intoxi-

cating and exhausting, that roared through his body, leaving him
with a calm, clear feeling of gratitude toward her.

It was then that he resolved that, no matter what it might cost
him, he would come back to this place, come back to her. His imagination conjured up the most radiant visions of his return. He
wouldn't just come back on foot, but on a white horse and with a
chestful of medals. He would be cock of the walk, with roosters
embroidered all over his shirt to prove it. Make way, scum—he's on
his way to make Agnyusha proud, to make her the envy of them all.

I should hound you forever, Vlad Samsonov! For twenty years you
fooled around the cities and villages of your beloved homeland, for
twenty years you boozed and bullied your way in and out of every
kind of bar from Krasnodar to Petersburg, for twenty years you gave
first-class service to the whores of nearly a sixth of the globe—before
one day, in an alcoholic stupor, you turned up at Kuvshinovo, a Moscow drunkard in a taxi bought for a fistful of cash, to sit on Agnyusha's grave and down three bottles of port at a ruble forty-seven
the bottle, arm-in-arm with a lunatic you had picked up on the way,
a hospital cleaner.

CHAPTER 15

The river Vologda thawed suddenly and rapidly. Ice floes slithered majestically down the turbid, misty surface of the river, then the water quickly cleared itself of ice; lumber-rafting could soon begin. After the review board, which discharged Vlad unconditionally, he still had to undergo a course of compulsory therapy, which included a promise of work once the rafting had begun. Vlad waited impatiently for the day, and when at last one morning Agnyusha with a triumphant look laid out some shabby working clothes on his bed, he almost burst into tears of joy: "This is it!"

"Go on, get ready"—she pulled him roughly to his feet, but she too was beaming with pleasure—"lumberjack!"

Vlad stepped outside, screwed up his eyes and gasped for breath. Spring in all its fury, raging unheard, was snatching away the drowsy stupor of winter from Kuvshinovo, and the village seemed literally afloat in the joyous, blinding sunshine. Everything around was bursting or collapsing, as though somewhere beneath the revitalized earth huge roots were silently astir. All living creatures seemed to have gone mad: hens, dogs, and jackdaws were racing around the village or in the air above it, their drunken dance suggesting some kind of weird carnival. The streams tinkled and sang. It was spring.

The lumber catchment near the ferry was already full to the edges with glistening wet logs. From the top of the steeply sloping bank it looked like an enormous seine net, in which a vast shoal of fish was gasping and thrashing in an impotent struggle. Walking down the bank, Vlad had a foretaste of the excitement of wrestling with this huge floating mass and he thrilled in advance to the prospect of victory in that duel.

What work that was! Standing in a human chain up to their knees in water, they gaffed the logs with boat hooks and hauled them toward the bank, where loggers piled them up in wet stacks that gleamed in the sun. Agnyusha, being more experienced, stood in front of Vlad; soaked by the splashing water, her face glowed, and as she turned around to him from time to time she would call out in good-natured challenge:

"Well, lumberjack, aren't your knees hurting?"

"Course not!"

"Do you really like it?"

"Sure do."

"After sitting cooped up for so long, you must need the exercise."

"You don't envy me, do you?"

"Like hell! Come on, you'll slow up the work."

"Won't be me that holds it up."

"We'll see!"

Swapping jokes, they passed their catch to each other, while above them floated the springtime sky, and the distant horizon shimmered in an ever-thickening haze.

Vlad never imagined that the herald of his freedom would be Vasya, the disreputable old male nurse from the reception ward. But it was this fallen angel who came down the hillside, dressed all in white, as angels should be, and booming out in his drink-sodden bass voice:

"Samsonov, report to the professor! Samsonov, report to the professor!"

Vlad's immediate urge was to rush toward him, but he swung around and his heart sank: her arms hanging listlessly by her sides, Agnyusha stood knee-deep in the water, her face drained of color, her eyes blankly miserable. Then she gave him a pathetic smile— okay, off you go—and he went, but in going he knew he was leaving behind him far more than awaited him at the top of the hill.

Old Vasya trudged along behind him, panting for breath and giving him an occasional and not unfriendly prod in the back:

"It's the idiots get all the gravy, but in all my lifetime I've never

had one little bit of luck—nothing but trouble and strife. That Zholtovsky always sticks up for you loonies, but for the life of me I can't
think why. He ought to do *me* a good turn for once, and promote
me to *feldsher* . . ."

Wearing a smart new uniform in honor of spring, Major Varva
was waiting for Vlad in Zholtovsky's office.

"There you are, I've brought your discharge certificate," he greeted
him from the doorway. "And I haven't forgotten your rations for the
journey to Moscow . . . Aren't you pleased?"

Getting no response from Vlad, he was noticeably disconcerted,
and to hide his offended feelings he began hurriedly to unpack a
small suitcase and to lay out on Zholtovsky's desk the traveling rations permitted to a released prisoner: a loaf of black bread, fifty
grams of sugar, a packet of margarine, and seventy rubles to buy a
third-class, unreserved railroad ticket home. Doing this, he muttered
sullenly:

"I suppose it's useless to expect gratitude from you. You see yourselves as human beings, us simply as brutes. Anyone would think we
forced you into the camps, but it's *you* who land yourselves there.
. . . Okay, sign here—for the rations and the discharge certificate."
Turning to Zholtovsky he said: "I think that's all that the regulations require, Doctor. According to his discharge certificate you can
either issue him with a passport on the spot or he can get it done
himself in Moscow." Shutting the suitcase, Varva stood up and
briskly took his leave: "Good day to you!"

Only when the sound of his heavy stick had faded away down the
corridor did Vlad recover the power of speech:

"Thank you, Abram Ruvimovich . . . I'll never forget you and
what you've done for me . . . And that's God's truth."

Silently Zholtovsky stood up behind his desk, walked around it
like a sexless shadow, sat down beside Vlad on the divan and laid a
frail palm on his shoulder:

"There's nothing to thank me for, Vladik; I was only doing my
professional duty, as they say. In addition you were a patient who responded well to treatment, and thus you helped me. But I would like
to give you a warning." He seemed to be talking to himself rather
than to Vlad. "Don't trust your first emotional reactions, because
more often than not they are mistaken . . . Pardon my saying so, but
you have just offended that man, who is, believe me, far from the
worst of human beings. He was, after all, sincerely pleased on your

behalf. But one shouldn't necessarily be offensive to bad people either. Regrettable though it may be, it doesn't make them better—if anything the reverse, and they tend to vent their sense of injury on someone else. So the result, if you'll forgive me, is a vicious circle. Relieving your feelings through malice, my dear Vlad, is a dangerous thing to do. Malice destroys a man, and then he becomes my patient. One of them, who is still under my care to this day, is the man who long, long ago killed my own father during a pogrom. I trust you, you see; that is why I am sharing a professional secret with you. What would have become of the man if I had decided to take my revenge on him? But I am treating him, Vlad, and believe an old man when I tell you that I'm always delighted whenever he shows any sign of improvement." With a gentle movement he turned Vlad toward him and they looked each other straight in the eyes. "I am telling you this, Vladik, for a good reason. I believe that more has been given to you than to others: you have a greater capacity for both love and hatred. If you begin to hate, it will enslave you altogether. But if your feelings are of love, you will be able to achieve a great deal. You are a rare kind of person, I expect much of you. Immeasurable gifts have been given to you, but for that very reason an immeasurable amount will be demanded of you in return. Try to be worthy of yourself." Zholtovsky turned away. "I think I have said more than enough, and it's time you were getting ready to go. I have arranged for the hospital to supply you with some rations for the journey, too, and with a few other necessities . . . And this"—a neat bundle of ruble bills emerged from the pocket of his white coat—"is on loan from me. There is exactly a hundred rubles. Pay it back when you start earning."

"What for, Abram Ruvimovich?"

"You're beginning a new life, and believe me, Vladik, every new life costs money."

"If only . . ."

"Go on, take it!"

No, Abram Ruvimovich, he did not repay you that money, nor the warmth with which you gave it to him. He chased after easy money all over the country, he drank and whored, he paid back with spite those who offended him, and he raged beyond measure at all the things he most coveted: women, money, fame. And when the day of

206 FAREWELL FROM NOWHERE

reckoning came, he tried to repent; that is the sum total of his worth to this day, if such be needed for a final balance sheet.

She was waiting for him at the doors of the main building, and they walked through the village to her house, no longer bothering to conceal themselves from the furtive, smirking looks darted at them from windows and gateways, and which only made her hold herself more proudly.

At home, Agnyusha washed and ironed his unprepossessing prison-camp clothes, made him some fish paste for the journey, cooked lunch, put a bottle on the table, filled two glasses to the brim, and, when they sat down, raised hers first:

"Think kindly of me, Vladik!"

Tears choked him while he drank, while he ate, and while he lay down with her afterward in her bed. Still holding back those unshed tears, he walked through the village with her to the ferry, stood hugging her all the way across, staring with misty eyes at the lumber thrashing about in the catchment, and then, still embracing, walked with her to the railroad station.

The agony of parting bore them across fields bathed in sunlight. Beyond the town, the distant country shimmered in a blue haze. To their right the river shone with a dull gleam, breathing out the fresh, young scent of wood and waterweed. Beetles and crows busily raked among the debris of spring. The world was celebrating its rebirth. But something in it had changed—or rather something in them had changed, and no power whatsoever could restore to that world its former solidity and magnificence, its boundlessness and its light.

Agnyusha, this is the first and last letter I shall write to you. It may be that from a distance of twenty-five years I have pictured our encounter as far more idyllic than it really was. Maybe—time does embellish the past. Then why does my heart ache so helplessly whenever I think of you, and only of you? There were many more after you; I won't burden you now with a recital of their shapes and qualities, but not one of them, do you hear, not one of them has ever overshadowed you or obscured from me your slightest feature, your least movement. What else can I say to you in farewell, how can I get through to you? I am grateful to you, Agnyusha, grateful for something which you do not even suspect: for being able to put my trust in a woman. However many times I may be deceived, I will not cease to trust her. And that is all because of you and your purity which you shared with me. However often I may fall, that purity within me will never be exhausted. And that is all thanks to you, Agnyusha, and the strength I drew from you. Whatever defeats I may suffer, I shall pick myself up again. And that, too, is thanks to you, Agnyusha. Now farewell, and forgive me.

Farewell.

CHAPTER 16

Israel! Israel! The night outside was as snowy and black as ever, but something almost imperceptible was already hinting at the faint emergence of morning, somewhere beyond the darkness and the snow. Now every minute was inexorably bringing Vlad nearer to the impending farewell which would separate him forever from those he counted as his last remaining relatives. In some way, this departure to him was as if they were all dying. No doubt because they could never return. Yes, that was the reason: just because they would continue existing somewhere else, the loss of them seemed all the more intolerable. "Come on, let's hurry and get it over with!"

As though to spare his bitter feelings, only the very faintest rustling could be heard on the other side of his barely open door:

"What's the time?"

"Nearly five."

"Time to get the children up."

"Let them sleep till six. That'll be early enough. We can start packing now."

"You haven't forgotten anything, have you?"

"I don't think so."

"Is he asleep?"

"I'll go and have a look."

The silhouette of his aunt was sharply outlined in the doorway.

With an effort she bent down toward him, sat down at the foot of his bed and sighed:

"It's time."

"I'll get up."

"You can lie there a bit longer, we still have to get the children up . . . Take care of yourself now that you're on your own, Vladik. You ought to drink less, you know. Who's going to clear up after you now, with no one but strangers all around? I'm only going because of the children, otherwise I wouldn't be leaving home at my age. We might have managed somehow together, you and I . . ."

His aunt rambled on, stuttering as she choked back her tears, but Vlad realized that she was not really talking to him but to herself, indeed to something within herself, as if words could drown the burning pain which was tormenting her. At such moments one could only listen in silence, so Vlad said nothing, letting his aunt have her say to the end; it was the only way to ease the last minutes before she had to face the inevitable. As far as he was concerned, she no longer existed. All that was left to him was their past life: partings and meetings, quarrels and reconciliations, long silences and rare conversations—and beyond that such an ocean of memorable, heart-rending trivia that if it were all to gush over him at once his heart could not stand it but would burst with pain and intolerable nostalgia.

Finally she stopped, stood up and blindly passed her hand over Vlad's face, as though by this gentle, wordless movement impressing his features on her memory forever.

All the rest—the feverish packing, the taxi ride to Sheremetievo airport, the confusion of farewells and even their plane taking off— remained in his mind as nothing but a necessary though senseless continuation of her last gesture of touching him.

Israel! Israel! Somewhere, over the hills and far away, my nephew is now walking about the Holy Land, my nephew Lyoshka Breitbart —part Samsonov and part (a very little part) Mikheyev. I beg of you only one thing, my dear boy, wherever you may be, on whatever shore fate may cast you up, do not forget your country; it is salted with our blood and our tears . . .

CHAPTER 17

That year Vlad turned eighteen. Youth lay behind him, while the future was so misty that he still had a long, long way to go before he would finally gain some perspective on his life. But he believed in his star. He believed, too, that as it dragged him again and again out of one apparently hopeless mess after another, fate was making him ready for some ultimate and decisive trial. And by degrees, almost unconsciously, Vlad prepared himself for this.

One day, thrown off a train by some drunken conductors, he had found refuge in the lobby of the ticket office at a tiny country station somewhere in Siberia between Kurgan and Petropavlovsk, intending to move on as soon as he felt slightly better. But days went by, the pain did not lessen, the slightest movement cost him a great effort, and the likelihood that he might throw in the sponge became more and more real with every hour. Occasional passengers went in and out, paying no attention to the tramp curled up underneath the one and only bench. When his adolescent body gained the upper hand in the struggle and Vlad began to feel slightly better, he was seized by hunger. The mere thought of food made him flush hot and his head spin with nausea. He dreamed of food from every angle and in every aspect; it persecuted him, asleep and awake, exhausting him with its relentless persistence. Bread—oh, for some bread!

Finally he could hold out no longer and crept out of his refuge in search of something—anything—to eat. As he crawled out, he looked around and froze in dumb amazement at the sight of a miracle. There, right in front of him in the completely deserted lobby, beside a can of water, stood a paper sack, like the kind used for packing cement, in which—he was convinced—there was food, lots of food.

Still not believing his good fortune, Vlad looked inside the sack and burst into tears of relief—for which the several rounds of horsemeat sausage and a loaf of bread were ample grounds. Yet he was ready to swear by all the saints that not a living soul had been into the lobby all day and the cashier had already locked up for the night.

Part 3

CHAPTER 1

"Do you believe in God?"
"I will believe in Him."
"??!"
Sitting opposite Vlad was a journalist—handsome, skeptical, self-assured—in a custom-tailored suit with very slightly flared pants and a tie that toned with his shirt. The toecap of his gleamingly polished shoe wagged steadily in time to his words. As he put his questions, this latter-day heathen with a fat checkbook in his pocket and a leaning toward socialism made no attempt to hide his condescending smile: others might be fooled, but he knew for certain, from an unimpeachable firsthand source, that the world was borne upon the backs of three whales—science, reason, and progress. He could therefore afford to be magnanimous and to extend his sympathy to this ingenuous Russian. He knew, as well as he knew twice two was four, how the world began and how it would end; he had long ago put a price on everything, and nothing could surprise him anymore.

O complacent sheep, ready for the shearing and the slaughter in future social experiments! How many of his kind, once-proud champions of progress, had Vlad met in transit prisons and labor camps—wretched, broken-backed creatures, all semblance of humanity lost, perpetually haunting the trashcans and prison sickbays? What words could Vlad use to bring this pomaded fool in tweeds to understand the inscrutable ways by which he had struggled, through hell and high water, toward that beacon which now illumined his life with its ever-burning light, lending it meaning and hope? How could this little fop, playing at being a free-thinker, ever comprehend the nature and intensity of those grim moments when one's hand involuntarily pinched itself into the three-fingered gesture to make the sign of the cross, when one's soul rose up and was cast down in fear and trembling?

"Just await awhile, my fine gentleman, you strutting peacock from beyond the seas, with your talk of revolution and progress." Vlad smiled bitterly to himself. "Your red rooster will turn on you and peck you in the behind; then you will change your tune, and you will spew up all your fanciful schemes, along with your blood and tears, in the underground interrogation—rooms of your country's prisons. The only pity is that it will be too late for me: I would have liked to have seen you then!

"Those are not my words—they are spoken by Shatov in Dostoyevsky's *The Possessed.* You couldn't have a better description of our Russian Faith. For nearly nine centuries we have lived not by that Faith but in expectation of it. Hence all our history, all its splendors and miseries. Our people move toward Truth by way of a great doubt. But when we Russians do reach that Truth and finally accept it, we will never renounce it. With you in the West, everything has been the other way around."

"You Russians are a strange people." The shiny toecap described a gleaming arc. "You are prepared to argue endlessly about things which in the civilized world have long since been resolved and have been, as you put it, taken off the agenda . . ."

A plague on both your houses! Where do you come from, little man in lacquered shoes? Where is that place, where you have solved all the riddles of existence and taken the Lord God Himself off the agenda? He is indeed gracious, that He allows people like you to take His name in vain and yet still pardons you! His patience may be inexhaustible, but can mere mortals be expected to show such tolerance? Have they the patience to watch and listen while faceless men, sated yet thirsty for ever more power, craftily seduce the mob by promising them yet another carve-up of this world's goods—of which, in the end, the mob will gain nothing? Millions of people shot, incinerated, beaten or starved to death for the sake of "the good of all mankind" bear witness to it from Prague to Kolyma! Is this "good of all mankind" worth it? Is it worth that all the laws of God and man be flouted in its name? That people should lie, slander, and degrade, should force men under interrogation to drink their own urine? What Huns, what Inquisition could have devised such things? Never before, nowhere on earth, even in the most barbaric ages of the past were such things done before!

Vlad felt crushed by silent despair. Try telling this parakeet, this smug bird of passage, about the dreams that have haunted him for years, never allowing him enough peace to relax or reflect . . . and about one dream in particular: it is night, the dim exercise yard of Butyrki prison, a ragged fusillade of shots, cries; and above it all the piercing shouts of the prison warden's eight-year-old offspring, who has been watching the slaughter:

"Let me shoot too, daddy!"

There it is, my fine sir, the price to be paid for forsaking God; for this there can be no forgiveness:

"Let me shoot too, daddy!"

The words burned in his throat with pain and anger. Vlad could only gulp helplessly . . .

"I don't understand you . . ."

"You have it all coming to you . . ." The words formed themselves involuntarily on Vlad's lips. "Yet may this cup pass from you, damn you!"

Vlad weakly closed his eyes. Suddenly he could no longer bear talking to his visitor. Memory, like a whirlpool, dragged him forcibly down into its depths.

CHAPTER 2

For a long time polyglot voices boomed and overlapped each other in the telephone receiver, then came a short pause as though the line had failed, followed immediately by a voice, her voice, his sister's voice.

"Hullo . . ." There was a break in her speech, caused either by emotion or a faulty connection. "How are things with you?"

Vlad kept trying to swallow what felt like a burning coal lodged deep in his throat and finally gulped it down.

"Oh, you know . . . Okay . . ."

Oh, this receiver, the distance, the static on the line! Everything seemed to be conspiring to prevent them from talking to each other. But why, in that case, could he so clearly hear the occasional voices of telephone operators interrupting them? Why did he have such an irritating tickle in his throat? And why wouldn't his heartbeat slow down?

"We're all very worried about you." The words forced their way through the noise in his ears. "You're not sick, are you?"

"I never get sick, except . . ."

"I know, I know, but all the same?"

"If you mean *that* . . ."

"No, no, of course not! You've misunderstood me. It's just that all sorts of rumors are going around here, people are saying God knows what about you."

By now Vlad had pulled himself together and was able to say relatively calmly:

"How are the children? How's Lyoshka? How's Auntie?"

"Lyoshka's being very naughty, he's ganged up with an Argentinian boy and everyone on the block's complaining about them. Ira's going to school, she's starting to talk . . ."

"Auntie, Auntie—I asked you about Auntie . . ."

There was a long pause, broken by an outburst of near hysteria:

"I don't know what I'm going to do with her! She hates us, she thinks we tricked her into coming here . . . But you know what she's like! Write to her, perhaps she'll pay attention to what you say to her."

"Yes, yes, of course I will, but tell her from me . . ."

"I'll tell her, but write all the same."

"Yes, yes."

"Take care of yourself."

"Yes, I will . . ."

"I'll call you again."

"I'll be waiting."

"There's a kiss . . . Do, do take care of yourself!"

"Yes, yes. I'll be waiting for your call . . ."

Click—and once more they were separated by thousands of kilometers, by the no-man's-land of human alienation, which sucked into its darkness everything that they had just spoken and experienced in those three long minutes. The voice had been, as it were, a voice from the black pit of the Beyond. When he replaced the receiver it was almost impossible to realize that his sister was still moving about, talking, doing something, existing in quite ordinary, normal circumstances. To be able to accept things as they really were, Vlad had taken a long time getting used to the fact that the situation ordained for him by fate was irreversible. In the end he was to grow accustomed to it, but never reconciled.

Lord preserve them from harm in the Holy Land! •

CHAPTER 3

Krasnoyarsk in the summer of 1950: a town still half made of wood, with a busy quayside along the majestic river, a sawmill on the opposite bank and cedar-covered hills upstream. Along dusty little streets sloping down to the waterside, log-built cottages, shaded by luxuriant acacias, lurked behind high wooden fences. But this outward look of a dull, provincial backwater was deceptive: hovering in the air was the restless spirit of distant journeys, of easy pickings and quick money, which excited the imagination of newcomers to the town. On almost every telephone pole was tacked a notice, usually scrawled by hand, inviting volunteers to join the next expedition to the Far North, to say nothing of the colorful posters put up by the local Labor Office, promising astronomical wages. All roads, as they say, were open: it was only a question of choice.

Vlad arrived in Krasnoyarsk after a short-lived job at the gasworks in Tula, whence he had absconded after discovering that his first pay packet contained zero rubles, zero kopecks, and had set off to seek his fortune in the terra incognita of the Siberian taiga. By the time he reached Krasnoyarsk he was traveling light, having lost even his belt on the way. Now, apart from the chains of class, he had literally nothing to burden him and nothing to lose.

There was little chance of Vlad getting a job on any expedition:

the "38" in his passport* was enough to scare off any right-minded personnel manager, so he paid more attention to the "Help Wanted" advertisements issued by the Labor Office than to the modest leaflets pinned to telephone poles. But the Labor Office was only offering jobs in logging and construction, and Vlad already knew what sort of a price had to be paid for the high wages they promised.

As he wandered restlessly around the town he nevertheless decided —no harm in trying!—to answer one of the handwritten notices, and found himself in the cool cellar of an erstwhile grain merchant's warehouse, tucked away in a quiet side street near the banks of the Yenisei.

Behind an office desk, resting his sharp chin on his folded hands, sat a tousle-headed man of about thirty, staring into space with a look of boredom. Slightly stirred from his apathy by Vlad's entrance, he lifted his lazy blue eyes toward the visitor and inquired bluntly: "Well?"

"It's about the notice," said Vlad, suddenly flustered. "I see you're recruiting workers for an expedition."

With the same languid air the man stretched out his hand: "Papers?"

Vlad handed over his passport, but without hope. As he had expected, having flipped through the gray booklet the man gave it back with an expressionless face and said:

"No good." Returning the passport to Vlad, however, he bared his teeth in a cheerful grin and winked at him with one hazy blue eye: "What did they catch you for?"

Obviously pleased by Vlad's brief, frank reply, the man seemed to come fully alive and even leaned back in his chair as he inspected his visitor with interest, but in the end he could only spread his hands apologetically:

"Myself, I'd be happy to take you on, but you know how it is: my boss would never allow you to sign on, although I can see you're made for the job. Try somewhere else; you never know—you may have more luck."

This first rejection left Vlad severely discouraged. His fatal weakness was a tendency to panic, and as he went out he saw his future in

---

* Article 38 of the U.S.S.R. internal passport regulations restricts ex-prisoners and other offenders to residence in certain designated cities. (Author's note.)

the most funereal colors. Walking through the gate, he thought dejectedly: "I'm about as lucky as Charlie Chaplin!"

But before Vlad had gone ten paces up the street, he heard the same man's voice calling after him, good-natured but insistent:

"Hey, you hero—come back! D'you hear?"

The curly-haired man was standing by the gate, his long legs planted wide, and his blue-eyed features, the cheeks covered in blond stubble, beaming with irrepressible cheerfulness:

"They can tear my hair out if they like, but I'm going to take you —there's something about you that I like."

The formalities were completed on the spot, standing by the gate: the man simply took Vlad's passport, casually peeled him off five hundred rubles in cash, and said:

"Okay, you're free until we leave. You'll sleep at the back of this place in the hay shed, where all my new recruits hang out. You won't be bored, that I can promise." He called after him: "My name's Skopenko. Remember it—it's an ancient name, famous long ago when the Cossacks were free. Don't forget this address, and don't drink too much—it's bad for you!"

He was a strange man, this Skopenko. Later, he and Vlad were to knock back more than one bottle together, and even more in company; yet Vlad never did quite manage to fathom Skopenko, his first civilian boss. His perpetual clowning, salted with irony, reeked of the graveyard from a mile away. Something deep inside was burning him, only nobody ever found out what it was. At times, in a drunken moment, there would suddenly leap out from the smoky depths of his blue eyes such a white flash of despair that one wanted to turn away or blink.

The shed which housed Skopenko's "recruits" stood far at the back of a courtyard behind the warehouse. When Vlad returned that evening, he found only one of them there, a yellow-toothed little peasant of about fifty wearing a satin Russian shirt. He was seated on a pine log in front of the wide-open door of the shed, and at his feet was a pile of garlic bulbs which he was threading onto a length of stiff yarn.

"Garlic," he replied in answer to Vlad's questioning look, "is the most important thing to take to the Far North. Scurvy is a nasty disease, brother, and once you let it get you, all your teeth are gone before you know where you are."

"Where is everybody? Or am I the only one?"

"Where d'you think they are?" The answer was so obvious to his simple soul that he did not even look up at Vlad. "They're out drinking. Drinking their advance wages. What did you think?"

"And what about you?"

"Know how many mouths I have to feed? No, of course you don't know, or you wouldn't have asked. They're young, too young to work yet, and you can't sit all seven of 'em on one bench. When I was young I was pretty much of a live wire myself . . ." Suddenly, as though returning to the present, he inquired: "And you, I s'pose, are the new one? What's your name? Back home they call me Ivan Akimych. Kalachev's my last name." Short though their acquaintance was, it made the little peasant increasingly genial and talkative: "I've lost count of the times I've been on this job. The money's good and so's the food—wish all jobs were like this. They give you free clothes, too, and the work's okay, no comparison with farm work—plus triple wages, and that's not to be sneezed at. When the rivers are free of ice, you can earn five hundred rubles a night loading barges at Khatanga—think of that!"

Vlad already knew that it was Kalachev and his kind who keep the globe turning, but only now, with all due respect to the Kalachevs of this world, has he come to the sad realization that it is they who also enable all forms of injustice to flourish. We're only small folk. It's no concern of ours. God's too high to help us, the Tsar's too far away. The weakest go to the wall. This is the sum total of the simple-minded truths with the aid of which they drag their yoke through life, with which they shape, renew, and embellish their existence. Blessed are the poor in spirit!

First to appear in the evening twilight was a boy not much older than Vlad. Scarcely able to stand on his feet, he covered the distance from the gate to the shed in long zigzags, and when he finally made it he stopped in front of Kalachev, swaying on shaky legs, and said mockingly:

"How're they coming, dad? What's the plan? What's the orders? What's our socialist commitment? The country's waiting, y'know."

Ivan Akimych cheerfully played up to him:

"All correct, comrade boss! The tobacco plan's a hundred-and-one percent filled, the liquor plan's a hundred-and-two, but there's been a slight hitch in the food plan, couldn't quite make it—we're ten kopecks short on gingerbread." He winked conspiratorially at Vlad.

"Why don't you give us a tune on your accordion, Gena? You always put so much feeling into it."

Gena obeyed and disappeared, and soon the surprisingly harmonious strains of accordion music came floating out of the shed: "Steppeland all around, long the road ahead . . ." The melody filled the quiet evening air and was echoed in Vlad's heart by an irrational sense of yearning: after all, he was no coachman dying of cold out in the steppes, as the song said, and he had no last words to whisper to the man holding him in his arms, yet Vlad only had to hear the tune for his heart to soar to the heights and plummet down again into the bottomless pit—up and down, up and down, up and down.

Soon, as though at the summons of a bird-catcher's call, the members of Skopenko's team began to trickle one by one into the courtyard, and Vlad made their acquaintance: a man from Moscow called Lenya, aged forty, with a complete set of stainless steel teeth and large bald patches running back from his high forehead; a husky, pockmarked Siberian from the Achinsk region, of about the same age but younger-looking and friendlier in manner. Finally there was Zhenya Rotman, a student who had Leningrad written all over him. After stumbling across the courtyard, each in turn disappeared into the darkness of the shed, vanishing, so it seemed, into the very depths of the melody.

"Okay, time for us to take a nap too." Kalachev finished his work, tied the thread into a circle and stood up. "Tomorrow morning they'll all be up on time, fresh as a daisy and rarin' to go—you won't find a better bunch anywhere . . ."

The music stopped, the world fell silent, and in that silence Vlad could hear his own heart beating. His thoughts were borne back into the past, and there rose above him the hazy sky of his native Sokolniki. Then he saw himself walking through a birch forest in his father's countryside. Something seems to draw him on, a far-distant dream that troubles his soul with sweet unease in a presentiment of miracles, of ecstasy.

Next morning Skopenko, with his usual grin, put his head inside the shed and announced:

"Okay, my beauties, we're off today. So eat, drink, and be merry—the trumpets are sounding!"

That evening a little old steamer called the *Nadezhda Krupskaya* carried their team down the river Yenisei and toward the distant smoke of Igarka.

CHAPTER 4

The Yenisei! Many were the rivers that Vlad had seen, from the cascading mountain torrents of the Caucasus to the smoothest, calmest rivers of Central Russia, but such might as this, such sweep, such bends and turns he could not recall. Only amid this thunderous expanse of water was he truly able to grasp the unbelievable size of the vast space, ringed by thirteen seas, in which he lived and which bore the name of Russia.

The steamer took six days to plod its way downstream to Igarka. The banks on either side were high and bristling with conifers. Here and there on the sandbanks were to be seen gravel quarries, where men, stripped to the waist, toiled around wagonettes on narrow-gauge tracks, guarded by riflemen who were themselves wilting in the heat. No, Vlad did not turn and look away at such moments; on the contrary, these sights literally fascinated him. With the terrible selfishness of one who has escaped to safety, at the sight of these men naked to the waist Vlad reveled in his own salvation, all the more because he might so easily have been in their place. Many years later he would recall this and would fear for his soul, which even at that early age had begun to take the first hesitant steps into the wastelands of egotism.

In the hold of the ship, where they were stowed along with the expedition's baggage and equipment, it was crowded but cheerful. Having gotten well and truly drunk, it was as if Vlad's companions had performed some obligatory rite or duty; afterward, they relaxed and seemed thereby to assume their true nature and character. Early in the morning they would draw lots with matches to decide which of them should go up on deck to Skopenko's cabin and wheedle out of him yet another advance of ten rubles, with which they would then buy bread and sugar. With these, together with the free hot water and Gena's accordion, they would fix themselves a thoroughly enjoyable feast.

During the few days of the steamer trip, the person who became Vlad's closest companion was Rotman. A recent high school graduate, he had big, slightly protruding eyes and a touchingly candid expression on a face that was just starting to sprout the fluff of a future beard. Rotman only had to give his shy smile to win one's immediate sympathy. His smile was a kind of visiting card, announcing his hopeless inability to cope with life's problems. To Vlad he seemed like a messenger, a herald, an emissary from another world of which he had long dreamed, a manifestation of a different life which he did not yet understand. Vlad followed his new comrade around like a shadow, while Rotman, who was clearly playing the role of teacher and prophet for the first time in his life, tried hard not to disgrace himself as he delivered a stream of explanations, precepts, and information. It was in these days that a conversation took place between them which was to etch itself on Vlad's memory forever.

"Why, for instance, did you choose to study geology?" Vlad pestered him. "If you'd gone for math or literature, you could have earned much better money when you graduated."

Rotman's dark eyelashes opened wide in amazement:

"But that's immoral, Vladik."

In Rotman's tone of voice there was neither indignation nor question; he was simply making a statement of the obvious, of something that was above mere casual discussion. For a long time afterward Vlad could not discern what it was in his questions that was morally wrong or in any way odd. In those days he saw the world in two colors: black or white, good or bad, yes or no. Nuances, half tones, subtle gradations still eluded him, though they did evoke in him a vague sense of dissatisfaction and annoyance. "Bloodless intellectuals," was his irritated reaction on such occasions, "heads in the clouds!" With the years his perceptions grew keener, the world revealed itself more fully to him, its palette of colors growing ever broader and more complex, until somewhere around the age of thirty he grew more selective in his choice of words and his judgments.

The stop at Yeniseisk was notable for their first bathe, when the heat drove everyone who could keep afloat off the decks and into the water. It was here that Vlad saw her—a corn-gold flash above the glistening smoothness of the river and two droplets of green under a sunny lock of hair. Zinka—a gentle stab of pain in his memory, a sharp highlight amid the darkness of the past, returning as a ghostly visitor to his present-day dreams; cease haunting him for his remaining days, Zinka, because there is no longer a place for you in that life of his.

Vlad swam in zigzags around this blond water sprite, narrowing his circle with each stroke until finally he was almost touching her. Only then, through the buzzing in his ears and the beating of his heart, did he hear her throaty laughter:

"No good chasing me, kid." Her green eyes flashed a challenge from under her wet fringe. "I've got another boyfriend."

"You're a good swimmer."

"What?" She frowned, not understanding.

"I said you're a good swimmer."

"I grew up on the river." As it flew from her lips, her laughter seemed to scatter in sparkling drops, only to settle at once on her face and shoulders. "Try and catch me!"

With rapid strokes she swam hard for the ship, her sharp little shoulder blades twitching visibly under the tight straps of her swimsuit: a golden torpedo on the glittering surface of the water. "Like a fish!" thought Vlad admiringly as he struggled to follow her. "You'd think she was born in the water!"

Later, dressed and sitting on deck, with her hair in a carefully coiled bun under a white head scarf, she told him about herself:

"This town of ours is old, but it's so small there isn't much work. After they've done their time in the Army the boys never come back here, so the girls have taken to going to Igarka to look for jobs. The wages aren't up to much, of course, but we do have fun and sometimes the lucky ones manage to get married. I didn't want to go at first, I was too frightened. People said there was an awful lot of hard drinking there, and the nights are long, but in the end I thought 'nothing ventured, nothing gained,' you can only die once and you'll die one day anyway, why not give it a try? So now I'm on my way there. I don't want to die of boredom in this old dump, and if other girls can make it, why can't I? Our family's small—apart from me there's only my two brothers, Kolunya and Mishenka—but one less mouth to feed makes quite a difference. I may even be able to help them a bit by sending home some of my wages. My dad was badly wounded in the war, he turns out locks in a cooperative workshop, so it's mother who really keeps us all. She does two jobs: she washes dishes in a canteen and then works at half rates as a school cleaner. Somehow or other they made me stay in school through tenth grade, although I haven't a brain in my head and it was tough going. School learning didn't do me much good, though. I'm too stupid, and I could never keep my eyes on a book." She laughed, her yellow eyelashes almost closed and her gaze seemed fixed on something far away, beyond the people and things around her, staring at something that only she could perceive. "If I had my way, I'd just up and run away as far as the eye can see, without ever stopping, and I'd just look and look and look!"

The twilight flowed down from the hills, tinging the river with all the colors of a summer sunset. The forest along the bank grew darker and thicker, the hazy distance ahead slowly came closer, and the soul was imperceptibly overtaken by that eventide melancholy that is like the feeling in anticipation of a long fall, at once heady and exhausting. "The sun is setting in the west. Silence. Slumber overcomes my vain desires." A long life may lie before us, but evening has already brushed us with its touch . . .

Life on board, which had lapsed into dullness as the end of the trip drew near, was suddenly revived as they approached Kureika. In every cabin, in every nook and cranny of the ship, two harsh but highly charged syllables were spoken in every tone of voice: Stalin. And when the famous pavilion, the bluish glass of its windows glinting, came into sight on the steep, treeless bank, all the people spontaneously crowded at the starboard rail: Look—there it is! The man at whose very name, it seemed, all living creatures froze in fearful veneration and nature herself stood tamed, had once lived here, had walked along this bank, had breathed this air, had served out his term of exile like any ordinary mortal; and strangest of all was that in face of such an outrage, such unheard-of sacrilege, the grass had not withered, the sun had not hidden its face and life had not vanished from this sinful earth! From the vantage point of the intervening thirty years, it seemed almost unthinkable.

Trailing along behind the others, Vlad climbed up the high bank, peered without great interest at the half-tumbledown little shack inside the pavilion and at its random contents—a wobbly table, a stool, a fork under glass, two or three facsimiles also under glass—while he listened with half an ear to the patter of the man with a military bearing who acted as guide. For a long time afterward Vlad reflected on the vicissitudes of fate which had raised this failed seminarist to the dizzy heights from which, over at least a third of the earth's surface, he was able to put to death or pardon whomever he wished, while keeping the remaining two thirds in a state of permanent fear. Many were the roads leading from Gori to Kureika, but for Soso Djugashvili many more roads had led away from exile, on a journey that was to take him to the rarefied altitudes of totally unlimited power . . .

Igarka suffocated them with a heat wave of 30°C. and a sun which never set. Hardly had the sun touched the horizon than it started to climb upward again, and its triumphant glare poured down upon the town once more. For several days Vlad and Zinka wandered about this wooden kingdom. At the crossroads, alongside barrels of water, stood notices with the unfamiliar warning: "No Smoking on the Street! Fine for Violation: One Hundred Rubles." Little lopsided log cabins with windows at ground level and two-story barrack-like boxes seemed to float past them in the heavy, humid air that smelled of sawdust and rotting garbage. Fluttering above the rooftops near the port were the brightly colored splashes of exotic foreign flags, promising distant travels and hope. Now and again the sultry silence above the town was shattered by the roar of a seaplane as it took off. A keen sense of the novelty of his surroundings kept Vlad from succumbing to fatigue or boredom.

Toward evening they usually went down to the riverside, and there, sitting on the dried-out quicksands, they indulged in those endless conversations which are forgotten next day, but whose easy, unthinking gaiety stays in the memory for a lifetime . . .

"Do you like it here?" she asked, looking up into his eyes, her mass of straw-blond hair falling to her knees. "It's nice, isn't it?"

"Trouble is, I can't sleep, because I'm not used to the sun shining all night."

"You'll get used to it."

"We're supposed to be in the North, yet it's as hot as it is in Sochi."

"Have you ever been to Sochi?"

"I've been to lots of places."

"Some people have all the luck. Me, I've never been anywhere farther than Krasnoyarsk. I've only ever seen the sea in the movies."

"You'll get there one day."

"If only I do! If ever I get the chance, I'll take it—trust me not to miss it."

"You sound pretty determined!"

"Yes, I am. I know exactly what I'm worth."

Vlad glanced sideways at her and almost choked with astonishment: what had become of the little blond country girl with the look of childish defiance in her green eyes? Zinka's soft features had sharpened, her little freckled nose was pointing upward with a decisive air, her eyes had glazed over as they stared fixedly ahead and at that moment the whole of her figure expressed menace and rebellion. She looked exactly like a little bird of prey about to launch out on its first flight. "Yes," he thought with involuntary respect, "a girl like her will never miss any chances."

The other men on the team reacted in various ways to Vlad's nocturnal walks. Meeting Vlad once after midnight, the ever-wakeful Kalachev treated him to one of his usual sermons:

"You get married, Vladka. Believe me, our Siberian girls make good wives, they know how to look after you. A bachelor's life's a rotten one, you just wear yourself out running from one woman to another. You'll be earning money soon, and that's another temptation. With a wife you won't waste it and she'll make you spend it sensibly. You get married, Vladka, believe me. Remember what old Kalachev tells you . . ."

When Lenya bumped into him, he laughed good-naturedly:

"She's hooked you all right, that blonde has! Watch it, kid—these Siberian girls learn a special grip, they can catch bears with their bare hands. Drop your guard for five minutes and it's goodbye— you'll spend the rest of your life paying alimony."

Only Gena said nothing, but grinned meaningly and gave him a conspiratorial wink whenever they met. In the end he could hold out no longer, and burst into a song for Vlad's benefit, accompanying himself on his accordion:

> Some girls invited me home.
> But I was too shy to go—
> My poor old coat is all in holes
> And my poor little dick's too small . . .

Soon Vlad was called to see the personnel manager. In the school building where they were quartered, Skopenko occupied the office of the deputy principal—a dim little hole measuring nine feet by six, with a single window which looked out onto the blank frame wall of an identical wooden box.

"Okay, Mr. Bridegroom-to-be"—Skopenko's biting sarcasm managed to make it seem as if everything in the little room—desk, bookcase, map of the U.S.S.R., diagrams, portrait of Stalin on the wall—was tinged with a faint look of decay—"your courting days are over, or else I'll have to fix you up with a family home in Khatanga instead of workers' quarters. You're a fine fish"—he shook his curls—"no sooner do you learn to swim than you're looking around for a hook to get caught on." At this he grimaced, as though from toothache, and his next words were almost shouted: "Damn them, they're all the same—they'll all cheat you as soon as look at you!" Skopenko turned away toward the window, controlled himself with an effort, and went on calmly: "You're flying out tomorrow on the first plane. Go and pack, you haven't much time."

How simple the answers can be to all human dilemmas—so simple it's actually funny . . .

Vlad saw Zinka when the boat was already moving away from the quayside. She suddenly appeared on the bank, her figure outlined by her flame-red cotton dress. She flung up both arms and waved them in farewell over her sun-bright head. The sheet of water between them grew wider and wider until, transformed into an impassable gulf through the seaplane's porthole, it separated them completely.

The seaplane taxied over the water for a long way, picking up speed for takeoff, and through the lace-like spray outside the window Vlad once or twice caught a glimpse of a bright spot of color on the bank and two arms waving goodbye: "Farewell, Zinka, little wheaten-haired Siberian sprite—or rather, goodbye for a while, because you and I are destined to meet again!"

Somewhere ahead, waiting for him amid the swamps of the wooded tundra, lay Khatanga, the next stage in Vlad's life.

CHAPTER 5

Seen from the air, the wooded tundra had looked like a diagram of the blood vessels: an intricate network of large, small and tiny arteries on a vast, flat, greenish-gold expanse. Now, however, plodding along the sandy bank of a tributary of the Yenisei, all that Vlad could see in front of him was the fast-flowing river and the faintly rust-tinged foliage of larch trees over the water. Through the mesh of his mosquito net the surrounding world looked blurred and washed-out, as though in an old film.

The rapid, clear waters of the river Meimicha had been venting their turbulent fury upon Vlad for five long days. Harnessed to a tow rope with Gena and Rotman, he had trudged upstream, hauling a boat loaded with prospecting equipment and, as an extra, Skopenko's wife, a radiologist by the name of Irina Mikhailovna. Like the princess in the song of Stenka Razin, by her silent presence alone she spurred them on and fired their imagination. Her mosquito net, which she wore permanently pulled down over her face like a yashmak, only served to emphasize this resemblance. She sat in the stern of the boat, silent and remote, gazing at some point above their heads; her air of detachment, however, only had the effect of heightening the feeling of tension between them.

Whenever they halted she would languidly toy with her portion of the men's stew and then disappear into the taiga, returning only when it was time to move on. Throughout the journey she scarcely uttered more than two words. The men were mystified by this strange woman: what was she thinking about, what was she looking for in the forest? There was something about her that made Vlad involuntarily shudder whenever he met her gaze, and it was obvious that she affected not only Vlad in this way: Rotman always tried to avoid looking at her, while Gena was completely subdued and never even touched his accordion. Sergei Bokov, the guide of the party, looking at them with a perpetual gleam of cheerful mockery in his slightly squinting eyes, would rock with silent laughter and shake his shaggy head:

"It's working with X-rays that makes her like that . . . she's crazy!"

By the time they reached the base camp at Meimichensk, they had all been reduced to a state of self-disgust and could not look each other in the eyes. Vlad, at any rate, had begun to realize why women like this sometimes got thrown overboard—and may God forgive you, Stenka Razin!

The base camp consisted of three wooden boxes—the kitchen, the office, and the storehouse—and a few tents, their sides banked up with turf. Lost in the taiga, it was a nomad encampment sheltering a chance band of strangers, some looking for a fast ruble, some for adventure. Above it hung a lowering, colorless sky, all around was a sea of forest tundra, the leaves just beginning to turn; below, at the foot of a steep bank, bounding gaily from rock to rock, the girlishly skittish Meimicha rushed on its way to the next rapids. Away in the distance, beyond the booming rapids, beyond the bristling expanse of taiga, rose the bluish humps of a low range of mountains, fringed in pink cloud at the hour of sunset. The mountains looked as if they might well be the "edge of the world" described in children's books.

The kitchen, where Vlad was first put to work as cook's help to the slovenly, fair-haired Sima, the camp carpenter's wife, was constantly being invaded by prospectors driven mad by male loneliness; and the cook, to give her her due, refused almost none of them except occasionally, and then only out of congenital laziness.

Her lawful spouse, a crushed and henpecked little peasant of about fifty nicknamed "Cloggy," who sensed rather than knew what was going on, would wander around the campsite with a persecuted look and frequently whined to Vlad in the evening:

"My Sima's not a bad woman, it's just that she was given enough body for two, so she gets a bit restless sometimes. If there's any funny business, you should tip me the wink, and I'll show her the rough side of my tongue."

He felt sorry for "Cloggy," but to act as the guardian of Sima's morals was a task beyond the powers of a whole platoon of nuns, especially since the shameless cook, evidently bored with older men, started making advances to Vlad himself, which left him dumbfounded and unresponsive.

Once a day, in addition to his numerous other duties, Vlad had to take the food in a boat out to the prospectors, who were at work on exploratory panning. He had to tow the boat upstream for about a kilometer and a half, and by the time he reached the sandspit where they were prospecting, he was thoroughly worn out. But once among the familiar faces of his team-mates at the large, busy work site, he actually began to feel rested and relaxed, as his longing to be doing real man's work was satisfied and he was imperceptibly drawn into the rhythm of panning for precious stones.

The process itself seemed fairly uncomplicated: a pump, a buddle (a box looking like a large beehive that contained a series of sieves), and that was all; but there was an element of the miraculous about it, because at any moment the spark of a diamond might flash out from the bottom of that box. Open, Sesame!

According to a tradition of unknown origin, the main pastime after work was a collective drinking party, at which the chief figure was, naturally, Gena and his accordion. These feasts were arranged by each tent in turn, and were prepared well in advance. A week before it was their turn to do the honors, the next hosts in line went to collect sugar from Petrovich the storeman (who could never resist the offer of a free drink) and then brewed homemade beer in two large milk churns. As for the snacks, each tent strove to outdo the others. Canned foods from the camp store counted for nothing, and were treated by the guests with scorn and derision; wild goose was accepted with slightly more favor, and fresh salmon was devoured with enthusiasm, but the only delicacy to be greeted with loud cheers was roast quail.

The festivities usually began in solemn silence, but it was not long before the gentle notes of Gena's accordion could be heard above the chatter and hubbub of generous hospitality. Gena looked so detached from everything around him that none of it might have existed. Sober-eyed, he would sit staring past it all—or rather, his gaze was turned inward upon himself as his obedient fingers squeezed the very essence of his soul into the outside world. That soul of his seemed to forgive every one of them—to forgive their clumsy intoxication, their coarseness, the rancor acquired in a life-time of bitter experience . . .

How it happened, Gena, when and on which day I cannot re-member, but one day the princess who had been our traveling com-panion appeared at one of these parties. She came in, sat down by the entrance, and began staring at you in silence. She only had to look at you, Gena, and you were finished, done for; yes, Gena, you were a dead man even before you were dragged down beneath the thin ice of a late Siberian fall. Never fear, Gena, never fear; it's not such a bad way to go, after all.

More than one pair of eyes, instantly sober, watched you go as the two of you left the tent, but saddest among them were the eyes of Rotman.

It proved to be short-lived and tempestuous, that love of theirs, as though something were driving them on to a rapid and climactic end. Long before Gena's daily shift was over, Irina Mikhailovna would be waiting for him by the forest's edge at the end of the sandspit, and no sooner did the pump stop working than he would hurry to join her. As they vanished into the taiga, the burning silence followed in their footsteps and autumnal gold glowed above their heads.

Skopenko descended on the base noisily and unexpectedly. Tou-sled and unshaven as ever, he strode half-drunk around the campsite, shouting, pestering, and giving out orders:

"Come on, you sons of bitches, you're all asleep and the work schedule's going to hell! God, you've turned this place into a holiday camp—nothing but drinking, whoring, and gabbing. Come on, Pono-maryov, get a crew together, you haven't made a start on the far bank of the river yet!"

The crew boss, whose sluggishness had long since become prover-bial at the base, tried feebly to resist, but it was not easy to make Skopenko change his mind, and soon, with the river already starting to freeze, Ponomaryov and half of the expedition's work force were rowing across the river, taking the base's only radio transmitter with them.

A week later the Meimicha froze across. In vain Skopenko strode up and down the bank, shouting and waving his arms; nothing al-

tered the fact that the base was still without means of com-
munication. When he had run himself to a standstill and sobered up
a little, he lined up the remaining workers on the bank and, thrusting his unshaven chin toward the far shore, asked curtly:

"Who's going across? I'll be generous."

The men were silent. No one, it seemed, was keen to risk his neck
in exchange for the manager's vague offer of reward. Only Kalachev
raised his voice:

"No good trying to get across. It won't hold."

Skopenko gave him a brief, withering glance and again swept the
ranks with a questioning look:

"Well? Will triple rates satisfy you? And I'll add a bonus as well."

Yes, Gena, it was then that she appeared on the bank, as though
materializing from the ground—your destruction, Irina Mikhailovna.
To this day I will swear by the memory of my dead mother that a
minute earlier that woman was not among us. She came and stared
at you with her shaman-like eyes, as though she had not the slightest
doubt about who should make the decision and step forward. And
step forward you did:

"I'll try . . . . Only I don't want the money . . ."

Now it was Skopenko's turn to go pale. In a fraction of a second
he grasped the full import of what had been happening, but the
threat of remaining without communications was more powerful
than his shock of realization.

"Okay, my brave little sailor boy." He gave a pathetic, crooked
grin. "Try it. I'll accept equal responsibility."

Vlad will never forget what happened next. Gena asked for a long
plank, which was immediately produced and put in front of him.
Then he squatted down on his haunches, pushed the plank out in
front of him, lay down prone on the ice and started to crawl slowly
forward, holding his wooden support with one hand. He moved cautiously ahead, while everyone on the bank held their breath and followed his every movement. Vlad glanced sideways at Irina Mikhailovna and was appalled by what he saw: she was staring after Gena
as though she could not see him. A thin serpent of mockery
squirmed between her tightly shut lips. It was the look of someone
who thirsted for revenge, watching their enemy die.

Gena, meanwhile, had reached midstream. It looked from the
bank as though he was already safe, but suddenly the ice beneath
him moved, splitting in a zigzag crack. For some time the plank kept

FAREWELL FROM NOWHERE 237

him on the surface, but in a moment it slithered under the edge of the ice, dragging its victim after it. In the time that it took the watchers to utter a collective groan, everything had disappeared from the white surface of the river except that same hideously jagged crack.

After an outburst of stupid, confused activity, after the noise and shouting—which naturally produced no constructive results— everyone on the bank finally realized that nothing was to be done, that all their chaotic efforts were pointless, and the camp lapsed into an ugly, numbed stupor.

Wandering later through the frostbound woods in a half-dazed state, without realizing where he was going, Vlad reached the prospecting site, and there his dulled hearing was shocked into awareness of stifled shrieks coming from the shore below the steep bank. Then he heard the familiar voice of Skopenko—or rather, not his voice but a rasping, muffled croak:

"Bitch, bitch, bitch . . . You backstreet whore . . . It's all your doing . . . All your fault . . . Wherever did you spring from, you scum, what animal ever gave birth to you? There . . . take that . . . and that . . ."

No, Vlad did not give way to the sinful temptation to look over the bank, but he understood, or rather guessed what was happening down there. Almost knocked out with shock, he lacked the strength to move from the spot and go away, to forget, to blot it all out of his mind.

"Damn you . . . damn you, you slut . . . you've sucked out my lifeblood . . . There, take that . . ."

The reply was a groan and a laugh, in which longing was mixed with hatred.

"I hate you . . . I hate you . . . I hate you all . . . You're beasts, animals, animals . . . Only you . . . animals . . ."

CHAPTER 6

At the beginning of winter Vlad was transferred to Khatanga. On the night when an ancient machine known as a "corncob" flew him to his destination, the frost was so severe that the town was enveloped in a haze. Breathing in that temperature was a unique experience: body and soul were filled with a painful chill, as if one had been dropped into a pit of freezing jelly. One could only try to hold one's breath and grope around blindly and aimlessly. The night was as dense as cotton padding and absolutely pitch black; amid such gloom a man could think of nothing but fire and shelter.

Vlad was greeted at the airfield by Skopenko himself. Shifting from foot to foot, the manager looked searchingly into his eyes and kept thrusting his palm into Vlad's numbed hands:

"You can spend the night at my place, then I'll fix you up tomorrow. It's a poky little hole, so I hope you don't mind a tight squeeze . . . Okay?"

Vlad felt he would almost prefer to stay out of doors all night in the freezing cold rather than spend so much as an hour under one roof with Skopenko, but there was no choice, and with a sinking heart he followed his boss into the burning cold of the darkness. Chilled to the core, his heart pounded out the question: "What can I talk to him about? What on earth?"

The blazing stove in Skopenko's little room gave out a fierce heat.

As soon as he had lit the lamp, the host began to bustle about: he cleared the papers off the table near the tiny window, spread out a newspaper as a tablecloth, and almost at once there appeared four tumblers (two for water, two for liquor), a bluish-gleaming bottle of rectified spirit, and an already opened can of fish.

"Well now," he said ingratiatingly as he filled all four glasses to the brim, "let's drink the first one to your safe landing . . ."

Intoxication made Vlad feel slightly less awkward, but it did not lessen the pain and bitterness of recent events. "Why?" the thought tormented him. "Why did it all have to happen like that?"

"And the second one to friendship," said Skopenko, topping up his glass. "You now have a Siberian winter in front of you, and no one can survive the winter without friendship. Otherwise we'd bicker and nag each other to death. Understand?"

Skopenko never stopped drinking to take a snack; a gulp of water as a chaser, then back to the bottle. He seemed to be forcing himself flat out toward a state of drunken oblivion, but the more he drank, the more his goal eluded him, and this was clearly driving him to despair.

"Do you think I don't know what you're thinking about me?" he finally blurted out. "You have feelings, but I have none—that's it, isn't it? In fact, after that business I'm so shaken up I hurt all over. I should hate him, I should be glad it all ended the way it did, yet my hair stands on end everytime I think about it . . . You're still green yet, green as grass, and you're going to have to learn just what a woman's capable of. She's like a snake—she sucks the very soul out of a man and then simply slithers on to the next one, without so much as a backward glance . . . D'you see? She doesn't even bother to turn around and look . . . And that's what *she* did. Crawled off in search of more prey, God damn her!"

As Skopenko went on talking, Vlad softened toward him, penetrated by a growing sense of understanding and pity; at the same time he was also aware that he was committing perhaps the most unforgivable treachery of his life. "No, no, no!" his whole being protested, yet something stronger than himself forced him to affirm: "Yes, yes, he's right, that's how it must have been!"

Next day—if the vague blue smudge outside the window could be called day—Vlad found a place in the communal bunkhouse, where he was given a campbed right beside the door. As long as the stove kept burning, the atmosphere inside the hut was tolerable enough

to breathe, but when it went out at night—and no one was willing to
crawl out of his sleeping bag to stoke it up again—the wooden box
would be frozen through and through by morning. Thus getting up
every day became an ordeal equivalent to a dash to man the defenses
in battle—once more unto the breach, as it were!

For a month Vlad killed time doing various odd jobs: he unloaded
expedition equipment from an icebound steamer, hacked at frozen
coal, chopped wood for the bosses. And in the idle gaps between
work, filled with nothing but blackness occasionally illuminated by
the Northern Lights, he drank, pointlessly and miserably. He drank
in company and alone; he drank everything, from pure spirit to eau
de cologne; he drank as he would drink several years later, when he
worked on a newspaper, without apparent reason and without even
any particular desire. What price "in vino veritas" now?

The price to be paid, the warning from above, so to speak, the first
sign of Predestination, was not long in coming. One day, before he
could reach the bunkhouse, he collapsed half-conscious into the
snow. It happened exactly as you, Glebka Gorbovsky, my Petersburg
friend and boozing companion, described it in verse:

> Outside the wine and liquor store
> A drunken man lay on the floor;
> A simple man, of Russian race,
> He passed out and fell on his face . . .

That was later, though, much later, and now he lay there, spread-
eagled, and the impassive stars poured down dizziness and blue light
upon him.

Peace and warmth flowed into Vlad's soul; a voice from nowhere
questioned him and he answered silently and with humility:

"Who are you?"

"No one."

"What do you want?"

"Nothing."

"Do you want to die?"

"I don't know."

"And don't you want to know?"

"No."

"But perhaps *that* is the meaning?"

"No, no, no! I don't want anything!"

He was picked up by some belated revelers from the bunkhouse, his sometime drinking companions. Perhaps in that chance rescue there really was some meaning that he did not perceive at the time. But even now—when so many years have passed and Vlad dares to think, having achieved certain powers of insight—sleeping and waking he still carries on that same conversation within himself. Only now he knows for certain with Whom he is talking . . .

This time it was Skopenko's turn to feel superior. The manager beamed with cheerful satisfaction when Vlad, having slept it off, stood facing his bright-eyed gaze:

"So you couldn't stick out one winter, my lad. And I've lived through six winters in this hole. Have you any idea what I've seen here during these winters? What I've had to put up with? How I managed to keep going? And you come along and want to strip my soul bare, prod my conscience, find out the secret of existence. Spinoza and Jean-Jacques Rousseau rolled into one, that's what you'd like to be!" He was positively breathless with triumphant excitement. "Damn you, but I'm going to save you. I'll pay you off tomorrow and give you your pass back to the mainland. Take my advice and don't stop in Igarka—it will finish you off. It's been the ruin of better men than you. Your ticket will take you to Krasnoyarsk . . . Go on, pack your things, cabbagehead."

Ruffling Vlad's hair with a paternal gesture, Skopenko dismissed him with a sweeping wave of the arm and immediately turned his back on him, as though cutting himself off forever from Vlad and from all the painful memories associated with him.

His papers were marked "released on grounds of redundancy," and next evening Vlad was sitting in the freezing cabin of an "Ilyushin" transport plane, the white abyss of the tundra floating past beneath the wing.

To avoid temptation at the airport bar during the stopover at Dudinka, Vlad did not leave the cabin, but at Igarka, where he had to change planes, chilled to the bone after a three-hour flight, he could hold out no longer. He decided to risk one glass and, of course, immediately went off the rails. He started by treating someone to a drink, then they treated him, after which the world started to spin around like a rainbow-colored carrousel that would never stop. Somewhere at the very end, amid the kaleidoscope of faces in front of him, one stood out—a slant-eyed, Tartar-looking face, which later he was to come to know so well.

Vlad woke up in a tiny little room with a low ceiling and a single window looking out onto a blank wall. Leaning over him was the only drinking companion of the day before that he could remember: a Kazan Tartar, a typical descendant of Khan Baty. He greeted Vlad's awakening with a good-natured growl:

"Ah, boy." He clicked his tongue in oriental fashion. "So young, and drinking already. You kick up such a row in airport, almost had to knock your head off. Get up, sober up, and we think what to do next. You even drink all your ticket money, boy." He gave a kindly wave of his small hands, as though to dissipate the fear that had gripped Vlad in a wave of cold horror. "Don't worry, I not kick you out, we find job for you . . . Drink that, it's pure, not diluted . . ."

He was in the house of Mukhammed Mukhamedzyanov, in the "Old Town" at the center of Igarka . . .

Life had to go on, and Vlad had to get up, to think, to go out into the foggy, cheerless world . . .

CHAPTER 7

People say that Igarka is quite different nowadays, but in Vlad's memory it remains as he saw it, first in the summer and then in the winter of 1950: a wooden town, the houses huddled close together, rusty cobwebs of barbed wire looped along the few fences. He knew only too well the kind of life that was concealed behind those fences; but nowadays it seems in retrospect far more menacing and mysterious than it actually did during his sojourn amid its unpretentious reality. Unlike in summer, in winter even at noon you could not see farther than half a block. It had a weird, fantastic look, made up of fragments, details, and props, rather like a storehouse for stage scenery: a shop sign, a piece of sidewalk, the façade or false front of a house—no more. The rest was drowned, dissolved in a dense fog that made it hard to breathe.

Having finally sobered up and come to his senses, Vlad spent his time from morning till evening haunting the offices of the town's labor managers in search of work. But in winter there were at least two, if not three applicants for every job; as outdoor work in the taiga closed down after the summer, a horde of people would lurch back into Igarka, each one intent on fixing himself up with employment until the following spring, which would then scatter them once more to lucrative jobs all over the taiga.

"Ho," Mukhammed consoled him cheerfully, "just fancy—no

work. Are you eating? Are you warm? Do I chase you out of house? No work today—so maybe work tomorrow . . ."

Mukhammed himself was employed as a watchman at the municipal offices; this entailed twenty-four hours on duty, followed by three days of completely free time, which he spent circulating around Igarka's haunts of vice in search of free drinks. This was the time of year when the town's winter residents were spending those same fast rubles, in pursuit of which they had converged on the 70th parallel from every part of Russia and the contiguous Soviet republics.

Mukhammed would come home well after midnight, usually just about able to crawl and more often than not with company. Dasha, his Russian wife, who operated a circular saw at the local lumber works, would simply clasp her hands:

"I don't want these no-good layabouts!" Her small, wiry body tensed itself and quivered; at these moments she looked like an angry hen. "Take them anywhere you like, but I won't let them through *my* front door!"

In the end, though, she always let them in. Having slept off the drink and recovered from their hangovers, the guests would go on their way with polite gratitude. Dasha was clearly pleased by this, being a simple and kindhearted woman.

To this day the mere combination of those two names—Dasha and Mukhammed—has more meaning for Vlad than all the declarations of international brotherhood ever made on this earth. He spent almost the whole winter in the Mukhamedzyanovs' house, and witnessed many occasions when drunkards of diverse Soviet nationalities found shelter for the night and an effective cure for a hangover next morning. Nor was there any particular self-interest or advantage to be gained from their modest hospitality. It simply never occurred to their kindly, ingenuous minds to wonder whether they should take a person in or not. God bless you, Dasha and Mukhammed!

One evening, killing time in the usual joyless fashion with Mukhammed's neighbor, a docker called Sanya Gulyaev (they shared a common passion for spouting their own execrable verse), Vlad and Sanya dropped into the seamen's club on an impulse. A rehearsal was in progress of some trashy one-act "socialist-realist" play, but since there was nowhere else to go, the two friends stayed on to watch until it was over.

In charge of the show was a red-haired man in River Fleet uniform, whom all the others addressed respectfully as "Anatoly Ivano-vich." Hands clasped behind his back, scarcely opening his lips when he spoke, Anatoly Ivanovich paced self-importantly up and down the stage issuing instructions. His efforts, however, had no effect whatso-ever in bringing order into the chaos on stage. Every actor clearly regarded himself as of at least professional standard, so none of them listened to each other and least of all to Anatoly Ivanovich.

Vlad felt his hands itching. Some people might be incompetent, but he, Vlad Samsonov, whose dramatic talents had once thrilled the judging panels of local theater competitions in the very capital of our country—Moscow—was perfectly capable of passing on something of his glorious skill to these provincial clods!

Sanya told him afterward that it had been a sight worth seeing. Suddenly intervening in the rehearsal, Vlad made the ranters tone it down, encouraged the timid ones, told everyone exactly where to stand on stage, threw out a few casual quotations from Stanislavsky and—lo and behold!—the one-acter began to fall into shape, as if it had only been waiting for someone to give it a push and set it going on the right lines.

The miracle which occurred was only a tiny, village-scale miracle, so to speak, but almost two decades later, when attending rehearsals directed by Lyubimov at Moscow's Taganka Theater, he would un-derstand the secret, or rather the mechanism—or, more precisely still, the key to that miracle. The miracle has a very prosaic name—rhythm. When Lyubimov, lathered with sweat and on the verge of a heart attack, would rage away in the half-darkened auditorium, his feverish dissatisfaction would communicate itself to Vlad, and it made him remember that winter, that club, and the first full re-hearsal that he ever conducted in his life . . .

After the rehearsal a thickset man in the uniform of an officer of the River Fleet suddenly appeared from nowhere and came rolling up to Vlad.

"Young man, you aren't from theater school by any chance, are you?" The blond eyebrows on his beetling forehead were arched with excitement. "It does happen, they come here sometimes."

Sanya, standing behind the man's shoulder, gave Vlad the thumbs-up sign and winked encouragingly, as much as to say: Keep your end up, kid!

Fortune turned her beaming countenance toward Vlad. The cherubim of success fluttered their resplendent wings above him:

carpe diem, my boy, a chance like this won't come again in a hurry and often enough it never comes at all.

"No," Vlad glanced modestly downward, "but I shall be going there in the near future. I'm due to enroll in theater school next summer, and meanwhile . . ."

The officer did not even let him finish, but advanced upon him with outstretched arms like a bear seizing its prey:

"Ah, but there's plenty of time till summer, my dear comrade, a lot of water will flow down the Yenisei before summer!" He arched his ash-blond eyebrows again, as though to show just how much water would flow. "Oh, ho, ho! You must stay here and be our club manager. We, the port authority, will provide half your salary, and the shipyard will match it with the same amount—in other words, we won't be stingy. Well, what about it? Shall we shake on it?"

Still unable to believe his luck, Vlad nevertheless found the strength to keep up the cool tone and to prevent his legs from collapsing with joy:

"I'll have to think it over . . . Art is a serious matter, you know . . . You have to give yourself to it body and soul, you can't fritter yourself away. I'll have to think about it."

The officer actually jumped into the air with excitement:

"Yes, that's it! You're quite right, comrade, you certainly mustn't fritter yourself away, you must give yourself to it body and soul!"

Thus began his brief epic at the seamen's club. The man in uniform turned out to be the Political Commissar of the port. Next day Vlad was signed up as the club manager, his salary to be paid jointly by the two organizations, and he was handed the keys to the premises.

In the noisy confusion of his first few days, Vlad paid no attention to a little old woman with bobbed hair who was seen to slip into his rehearsals, disappearing like a mouse into the farthest corner of the auditorium. "The lady who makes the tea, I suppose," Vlad thought unconcernedly, dismissing her from his thoughts. "Probably used to play in amateur theater in her young days before the revolution." About a week later, however, the gray, short-haired mouse emerged from the darkness, crossed the auditorium with brisk little steps, came over to Vlad and curtly introduced herself without a handshake:

"My name's Dyomina. Party secretary of the ship-repair yard."

Ah, how many of them Vlad was to meet in later life—men and

women, old and young, evil and good-natured. He often slept with the women, with the men even more often he drank, but however close they allowed him to come to them, he was always aware of a wall dividing himself from them. All, whoever they were, had one thing in common, an almost innate quality by which, as though it were some special smell, these people invariably recognized each other: a keen, deep-seated mistrust of others. Anyone may turn out to be your enemy—this, broadly speaking, was the crude principle to which their relations with the outside world could be reduced. Vlad sensed immediately that Dyomina belonged to that variety of the species which always had been the most dangerous; sexless, metallic, passed over by life and nature, they are capable of anything. Fear not the apathetic and indifferent, for they are scarcely alive anyway; fear rather the zealots, the activists, for they upset the equilibrium of existence, and that is something more terrible than the plague.

"How is it, comrade Samsonov, that you are preparing the New Year concert and no copy of the program has yet been sent to the Party office?" She bored into him with her gray, opaque eyes which seemed to corrode the object of their attention. "Have you been failing to keep the Party leadership informed, comrade manager?"

Vlad realized that he was facing the first enemy of his "life in art," an enemy "sans peur et sans reproche," sinister and intransigent. "You think you've got problems?" Lyubimov would immediately have said, but you surely know, my dear Yury Petrovich, that the Dyominas of this world are alike at all levels: the amount of blood they suck out of a man is approximately the same . . .

Yet the New Year concert did get put together. The program was a modest one, but not without originality: solo and choral singing, poetry recitals, sketches, a pair of clog dancers—all introduced by an intelligent and witty MC; and as a finale, a one-act play called *In the Steps of their Fathers*, about the life and work of a successful fishery collective. Admittedly there was the problem of an old man—the senior bookkeeper at the shipyard—who kept trying to get in on the act with a monologue about a troika flying along like a bird from Gogol's *Dead Souls*, but Vlad bravely vetoed his attempts to worm his way into the program, even though this was a risky move: this old man was responsible for paying out the salaries. The decisive day drew nearer.

The closer it got to New Year, however, the more insoluble became the problem of the accordion player. For although the holiday audience of drink-sodden dockworkers would probably tolerate the choir and soloists singing "a capella," and, once a rapport had been established between stage and auditorium, might even join in the choruses, no audience, however well disposed, could put up with an unaccompanied clog dance. The potential disaster had to be averted at source.

Feverish inquiries around the town came to nothing, and a tour through the surrounding countryside produced the same result: on the eve of the holiday it was easier to meet a stray wolf roaming the streets of Igarka than to find even the most incompetent musician, no matter what his instrument—fiddle, balalaika, or domra. Little more than two hours before curtain-up, when Vlad was beginning to lose all hope and the ax of retribution was already raised above his head, one of the messengers he had sent to scour the town in search of music returned with a slight but encouraging piece of news: in the women's dormitory of the sawmill an accordion player, a local celebrity called Dima Govorukhin, was lying dead-drunk and sound asleep. And he was not sleeping alone, but with a lady.

Vlad came to life, and the spark of hope drove him into action. At last his own hard-won experience of curing hangovers might be put to a socially useful purpose. Believing that he would succeed, he was borne toward his goal on the wings of this belief. It was not an easy task to find the ill-fated dormitory in the thick, freezing fog of a Siberian night, but Vlad found it nonetheless. Bursting in, he managed without much difficulty to locate the accordion player: a little cubicle in the corner of a big room, screened from indelicate glances by nothing more than a muslin curtain. Here the great musician was sleeping peacefully in the arms of his beloved, scorning the hoi polloi and their petty conventions.

God! No sooner did the dim light from the smoke-wreathed room reveal her familiar face than Vlad caught his breath and his head began to spin: with her flowing hair spread out over the greasy pillow, Zinka, Zinka the blond watersprite, was lying there in front of him, only partly covered by a crumpled sheet. Even the drunken sleep which made her face look so much older could not efface from it the look of a satisfied young female. "Well I'm damned," he groaned bitterly. " 'Death and the Maiden!' I'd like a word with you, young woman!"

Vlad, however, postponed his talk with her till later, and turned his attention to her lover. God alone knows what it cost him, but he brought the musician to his senses and an hour later Govorukhin's somewhat wooden fingers were tuning his instrument backstage at the club.

Vlad's anxiety proved unfounded. Softened up by much drinking beforehand, the audience greeted every number with rapturous delight. Amid the confusion, the old bookkeeper actually managed to sneak on stage with his Gogol recitation, but even he got practically an ovation, such being the power of strong drink to arouse a sense of gratitude in the spectator. Stanislavsky himself could not have wished for a better audience.

After the concert Vlad's bosses from the port and the shipyard, half-drunk themselves, lined up to congratulate him on his success, and even Dyomina offered him a bony little hand as she said goodbye:

"Come and see me after the holiday and we'll discuss a few details, consult the Party comrades, make some comments . . ."

But all this grateful hubbub and chatter passed completely over Vlad's head. As far as he was concerned, the noisy crowd around him might have been drowned in the thick, rancid fog. "Zinka, Zinka," echoed obsessively in his mind. "Zinka!"

At that moment he hated—how he hated!—that idol of the public, Igarka's favorite accordion player, Dima Govorukhin!

CHAPTER 8

Late one night Mukhammed brought home a guest who, though drunk like all the others, was somewhat unusual. Everything about him was odd, from his appearance—tall and slightly stooped, with a bulging forehead crowned by dark, curly hair and a toothless, sunken mouth in an otherwise young-looking face—to the long, tortuous speeches which he made in the intervals between drinks:

"Literature, my friends, in our age—incidentally, in every age as well—is a lethally dangerous occupation, a profession like a sapper's, with practically no chances of survival. Even if a few writers do manage to stay alive, they still end up with something or other missing: their friends, their wives, their health, or, like me, their teeth. I don't bear them a grudge for putting me into a prison camp; Cervantes was a prisoner too, in his time, and who are we, little gray men that we are, to complain? But why do they have to beat us up so much? After all, I signed everything they wanted me to sign. What unfeeling beasts human beings are. You'd think there was nothing easier than to understand your fellow man. You only have to crawl inside his skin for a moment, to put yourself in his place—and you'll always act decently. Then why is it that almost no one, except a saint, is prepared to do that? It's not as if it needs an imagination like Shakespeare's. *That* is the question of all questions, and not 'to be or not to be.'"

He tossed down his drink in one gulp, ran his fingers through his hair and launched again into his monologue:

"Why are you so silent, gray-eyes? Mukhammed tells me that you try your hand at writing now and again. Drop it, kid. Believe me, I speak from experience—drop it. Drop it now, because it's like a drug; kick the habit before it's too late . . . But I'm wasting my time giving you this advice—I know from my own case that you won't give it up. And for that reason you're doomed. Your doom's written all over your face, it's as plain as smallpox. You're doomed because—I can sense it—you're sincere, and in our trade that's worse than cancer, plague, and leprosy all rolled into one. Now is the time of the gray men, the unscrupulous men. Sincerity is at a discount, sincerity is punished under the criminal code with five to twenty-five years' imprisonment, and, in special cases, capital punishment. They arrested me twice; I'm on my way home now, but before long they'll get me a third time, and then it'll be for good. I won't hold out a third time. The worst of it is that we "politicals" have no friends in the prison camps: to the peasants we're people who had it good, the fat cats, and to the professional crooks we're the cause of all their troubles and at the same time we are their legitimate prey; the prison guards see us as enemies of the people, fascists, the root of all evil. It would be better if they gave you nine grams of lead in the back of the neck—*finita la commedia* . . . Don't look at me so wanly, gray-eyes. I'm not afraid of anything anymore, I got over that stage long ago—I've gone beyond fear . . ."

The guest spent three days with the Mukhamedzyanovs, until he was, as he put it, "back in condition" again, having progressed from spirits to milk and tea. He was generous to his hosts, and as talkative as ever with Vlad. After reading Vlad's poetry, he threw the sheets of paper onto the windowsill with cheerful fury. Stooping slightly—the ceiling of the little room was too low for him—he paced up and down:

"Listen to this:

Like a wolfhound our age lunges straight for my throat,
But my blood's not the blood of a wolf;
I'd rather be stuffed, like a hat, in the sleeve
Of a coat: the Siberian steppes.

There I won't see the cowards, the slippery mud,
Nor the blood-spattered bones on the wheel;

Let the blue Arctic fox shine instead all the night,
In its clear primal beauty and grace . . .

"Or this:

When the time comes to bury our epoch
No psalm will be sung at the grave;
No flowers will cover the tombstone,
But nettles and thistles and weeds.
And only the gravediggers hasten
To finish the job. It won't wait!
And quietly, Lord, oh so quietly,
So the passing of time may be heard . . .

"Or this—better still:

All valor, daring deeds, and thoughts of glory
Upon this wretched earth I did forsake,
When, framed within a simple silver setting,
Your countenance shone sweetly in my house.

But when the promised hour did strike, you left me.
I threw the cherished ring into the night.
You gave yourself, your fate, unto another,
And I forgot the beauty of your face.

The days flew by, a swarm of empty pleasures . . .
With passion, wine, I tore my life to shreds . . .
But standing at the altar I recalled you,
And called upon you, as upon my youth . . .

"And you write this sort of thing:

Like a mosquito in the swamps of the taiga
Drowns the plane in the blue of the sky . . .

"It makes me sick to read it. It's all crap, Vladik, crap! I'm giving it
to you straight, because I can see there's a genuine spark inside you.
I don't know why it's there or why it's burning you, but I do know
that the good Lord doesn't give away these sparks for nothing. So
you're fated to do something. It's hard to say exactly what it'll be,
but fated you are; it's like a sentence passed on you by a judge—
there's no dodging it. So while you're alive and feeling, gather your
material: it's all grist to our mill. We writers are a bit like thieves—
whatever we see or hear, we grab and make it our own. But if you

must scribble, at least write about something worthwhile, instead of that junk about mosquitoes . . . !"

After one of the rehearsals at the club, to which Vlad dragged him to show that at least in this he had some talent, he delivered himself of yet another gloomy tirade on the way home:

"You're obviously fated to go through this theatrical phase too. It'll either kill you or cure you. The fact is, the theater's even worse than the writing trade. As a writer you have at least the appearance of seclusion, a sense of autonomy, your own modest little niche. But in theater everything is on public display, everything happens in front of an unblinking eye, so to speak, and every show may be the last. However, there's no point in despairing before you've even begun— time will tell, we shall see . . ."

They slept head-to-toe on one bed in the lobby, which was even smaller than a room. At night, puffing at a cigarette, he would talk to Vlad about everything under the sun:

"I have a friend in Moscow, an artist called Boris Pysin. And sometimes I would say to him: 'How's life, Borya?' And he'd say: 'Well, you know, what with all the drinking and screwing there's no time left over to make a living!' Although that's putting it rather crudely, it just about sums up the pattern of our existence in this country. There are plenty of parties and celebrations but there's nothing to eat. It's a devilishly cunning system—and it would break down if ever there was a surplus of things to buy. In order for it to work, there always has to be a shortage of something—matches, shoelaces, tobacco. The result is that a person's prepared to sell his own mother just to get a pair of shoelaces, and the quality of the tobacco will cause battles far fiercer than the dynastic wars of the ancient clans. It's not even a social system—it's really a sort of mystical process: it converts our human substance into biological clinker . . ."

Vlad still found it difficult to follow his roommate's train of thought, and the essence of what he heard was constantly eluding him, but the transcendent urge to get to the very root of things was already unfolding its timid wings within him. When later he came to realize that to do so was dangerous and impossible, he would nevertheless be drawn toward the edge of the abyss that he discovered that night—even though "much knowledge increaseth sorrow."

When the guest finally recovered and came to take his leave, he patted Vlad patronizingly on the shoulder:

"Don't worry, kid. We're not dead yet and maybe we'll write

something worthwhile; and if we do die, what the hell—there'll be more pickings for the others. If you ever come to Moscow, look me up. I don't know my address yet, but you can always find it through our writers' shop."

And he vanished, disappeared, dissolved into the freezing fog as though he had never spent those three days with them, had never talked, never existed. One moment he was there, and the next he was gone.

Shaking her head regretfully, Dasha said as she watched him go:

"Funny man, that, but nice. The funny ones always are nice. He won't last long, though; he's bound to cop it."

For good measure, so that he would have the last word, Muk-hammed growled:

"Shut up, woman, don't say such things about a departing guest. Where are your manners? There are no more people like him these days, except maybe in prison camps."

After the departure of their eccentric guest, Vlad's work at the club no longer seemed so attractive. He was fed up with all those choirs, those one-act plays, those clog dances to accordion music, to the point where they nauseated him. To make matters worse, Dyomina was on the rampage. She carped at him on any excuse, demanded daily written reports, hounded him at every step through her network of snoopers. Finally he could stand it no longer, and at the next meeting of the club management, in Dyomina's presence he made a number of comments about her which made it clear that she was an old hag, that it was none of her business to teach other people their jobs, that she had been dead from the neck up for some time, and that in general he felt like spitting on her from a very great height. Thus ended Vlad's theatrical career.

As he paid Vlad off, the old bookkeeper (the same Gogol enthusiast who always managed to worm his way into every concert and bored everyone to death with his "Troika" monologue) shook his pink, bald head and sighed dolefully:

"What in God's name possessed you to tangle with Dyomina? Here at the shipyard even the bosses will go a mile out of their way to avoid having to talk to her. Just as you were making the club a success, too—why, it was even starting to make money, and you have to throw in the sponge. Now where's the sense in that, I ask you?"

Having pocketed his discharge pay, Vlad left the aged recitation artist to ponder on the meaning of life, and went out onto the street.

Amid the swirls of mist, winter still kept its grip on every square inch
of exposed surface, but a scarcely perceptible breath of spring was already touching the earth: the fog was thinning out, the clouds were
beginning to part, the outlines of shapes were becoming sharper
and more clearly defined. Spring was in gestation, gathering strength,
storing up its fearful power before bursting forth one morning with
the first, irrevocable thaw. "We're not dead yet," he thought cheerfully, "and if we do die, what the hell—there'll be more pickings for
the others."

First of all, Vlad nevertheless decided to find Zinka. In the rush of
work at the seamen's club, he had forgotten her and the hurt that
she had caused him. Now that absolute freedom from the demands
of "showbiz" opened its golden gates before him, he felt drawn again
to Zinka, to her warmth and understanding. Standing on the threshold of a new start, he forgave her everything: the promises she had
broken, her wounding infidelity, and the disappointed hope that she
might repent of it. "Maybe we can go places together," he thought
optimistically as he set off. "Anything's more fun when you do it together."

Finding the women's dormitory empty, as it was in working hours,
Vlad was greeted by a jaunty, apple-cheeked old woman wearing a
greasy quilted jacket.

"What d'you want, dear?"

"Zinka."

"What's her last name?"

"Her last name?" Vlad was immediately embarrassed, feeling himself blush with shame. "I . . . I seem to have forgotten it . . ."

"What does she look like?" The old woman bared her few teeth in
an understanding grin. "How old is she?"

"Well, she's kind of . . . ash-blond . . ."

"Blond, is she? Know how many blondes there are here? And
they're all called Zinka." She obviously knew exactly who Vlad was
talking about, but for some reason was purposely spinning out the
conversation. "You must have had a lot of girlfriends, dear, if you've
even forgotten how old she was."

"She was just an acquaintance." The old woman's game-playing
was starting to annoy Vlad. "We traveled together on the steamer
from Krasnoyarsk."

"Ah yes," she said, willingly switching tactics. "I know your Zinka.
Everybody here knows her. Only she disappeared a month ago. God

knows where she is now. Maybe her boyfriend, Dima the accordion player, can tell you. He lives just nearby." And as Vlad walked away she added: "Don't be upset, dear. Come back this evening and find yourself another one, there's any number in this dormitory—and half of them are blondes!"

The old woman certainly would have been an ideal procuress, but Vlad only wanted Zinka and no one else. Nor did he want to meet Dima Govorukhin again either, but the desire to find Zinka was stronger than his dislike for the drink-sodden musician. Vlad knew that at this time of the day he would be loafing around in the airport bar, and he set off across town so fast that the frost crackled in his ears.

As soon as Dima saw Vlad, he got up from his seat in the corner and came toward him through the drunken hubbub and the cigarette smoke:

"Hey, Vladimir Alexeyich!" Dima spread his arms in a drunken gesture of welcome. "Fancy seeing you! What is it this time— another concert? Or do you want a drink? What'll you have?"

Embarrassed, Vlad avoided his embrace.

"Not now. Later, perhaps." Every word cost him an effort. "I wanted to ask you where Zinka was."

"Who's Zinka?" His air of low cunning actually suited his Cossack good-looks. "There are lots of Zinkas, but there's only one of me."

"Okay, quit fooling, you know damn well who I'm talking about . . ."

"Forget it, Vladimir Alexeyich. Don't be so boring." Dima tugged at his sleeve. "Why don't we just rinse our tonsils instead?"

"Shut up." Vlad pulled himself away angrily. "I ask you a question as man to man, and you behave like a pig."

This said, he turned toward the door, and Dima's guilty whine followed him as he went:

"So that's why you're leaving us, Vladimir Alexeyich—for a woman. Don't lose any sleep on her account. The only special thing about her was the color of her hair. The rest of her was no better and no worse than all the others . . . Vladimir Alexeyich!"

Vlad went out without turning around. It was now afternoon; the town had finally shaken off its foggy shroud, and for the first time in months it revealed its true aspect. Fluttering from the nearest telephone pole, as though welcoming him like the first swallow of the

coming Siberian spring, was a tiny scrap of paper torn from a notebook:

"Men Wanted for Expedition to the North . . ."

He read no farther, as he already knew the address.

CHAPTER 9

It was when he went to the personnel office of the Northern Expedition that Vlad realized his activities at the club had not passed unnoticed: people had heard about him and he was received with open arms.

"But of course!" The personnel officer, a fair-haired young man wearing the badges of a senior lieutenant, livened up visibly as he flicked through Vlad's papers. "Everybody knows you in Igarka! I kept meaning to go to the club myself, but I could never find the time, and then I went on leave. So you didn't exactly hit it off with Dyomina, eh? I don't know who can get on with that old witch, except a corpse maybe. I can use you here in my office for the time being. A huge backlog of paperwork has piled up here over the winter. We can shovel our way through it together. And you can take charge of our wall newspaper, you're a pastmaster at that sort of thing. So you can sit down right now, and we'll transfer all the data from these application forms into the workbooks . . ."

In this easy, simple fashion began Vlad's employment with the famous expedition. Its task was to prepare the roadbed ahead of Construction Project 503, which was laying the tracks for the Great Northern Railroad from Moscow to Chukotka. Konstantin Ivanovich, or Kostya for short, as the personnel officer was called, improved Vlad's clumsy handwriting and gave him a few lessons in calligraphy. Quickly learning the knack of it, Vlad spent his days bent over the workbooks of the newly recruited batch of seasonal workers, while in his spare time he also managed to knock out some verse for the wall newspaper, such as:

> What need have we of atomic blackmail?
> We boldly march through storm and hail,
> For we've the greatest weapon of them all:
> The mighty tome—Karl Marx's *Capital*.

Meanwhile the sun rose higher every day, chasing the remnants of the wintry fog into dim, dark corners. The first fine droplets began to drip from the ends of icicles. As they thawed out, the ribs of the wooden sidewalks began to show through, the snow was gradually transformed into a crust of bluish ice. Here and there black specks could even be seen on some roofs. Spring was coming.

On one such day Kostya returned from the planning office in an uncharacteristically gloomy mood. He flung his cap down angrily on the table, turned toward the window and said:

"You're to fly to Khantaika, Samsonov, as bookkeeper. As soon as you train a man up to do a job, they reassign him." He swung around to face Vlad, his temper already cooling: "Mind you keep out of trouble. The boss at Khantaika, a man called Solopov, has a character that's no better than your Dyomina's. Watch out, or he'll eat you alive."

"When do I go?" Vlad could hardly conceal his relief: he was getting thoroughly bored with so much paperwork, and had long been feeling the urge to get out to where the first spring heat haze was beginning to shimmer above the taiga swamps. "I'm ready."

"And glad, I see!" For a moment Kostya sounded offended that Vlad was so keen to go, but the mood quickly gave way to an encouraging sweep of his arm. "Hell, yes, I'd much prefer to get away from all this trash too, but when you're in the service you just have to obey orders. You're flying out tomorrow."

Next morning a two-seater "corncob," with Vlad as passenger, took off from the expedition's airfield and flew over the awakening taiga toward a mysterious river with the cheerful-sounding name of Khantaika. After being swept by the blasts of winter, the tundra from above looked sparse and threadbare. The snow had not yet lost its sterile whiteness, the beds of creeks and the ice-encrusted plateaus were just beginning to stand out in clear outline: a snapshot of winter already dipped in spring's developer.

Now and again the pilot, Volodya Konoshevich, would turn around and wink mischievously through the glass of his cockpit at Vlad, as much as to say: "How d'you like it, eh?" Konoshevich had the reputation of being one of the "characters" of the Northern Expedition. Dismissed from the Soviet Air Force for foolhardy behavior, he had survived until now by piloting the flying junk heaps of the Far North. He earned big money, which he immediately spent on drinking and horsing around in every bar from Yermakovo to Tixi, arousing terror among the peaceful citizenry and enthusiastic admiration among his drinking companions. But he was considered a first-class pilot and—even more important under the local conditions —one who never refused a mission, and for that reason the bosses turned a blind eye to his artistic temperament. People who win battles don't get court-martialed.

Enjoying the brilliant sunshine from a clear sky, at first Vlad regarded the slight, intermittent spluttering of the engine merely as an annoying imperfection, an occasional sour note, a trivial lapse in the functioning of an otherwise perfectly adjusted mechanism. But the misfires grew more and more frequent, the plane began to lose height in jerks, as though bumping down an invisible stairway, and the nose suddenly tilted sharply downward. Then the ground reared up and started rushing toward them . . .

In those few seconds as the "corncob" alternately dived and made desperate efforts to flatten out, a jerky film of his life began to unroll before Vlad's eyes, as it had done before in childhood: his father's face reflected in the railroad-car window at night, Agnyusha on the platform at Vologda station, Skopenko's crazy eyes full of drunken entreaty. Then came another scene from his childhood, followed by a mixed-up jumble of images. Flung around the cabin like a rag doll, hitting himself against the sharp edges of the paneling, Vlad threw up violently and abundantly, and in his clouding brain a worn old phonograph record ground out an idiotic refrain: "Farewell, my dear Marusya . . ."

Then Vlad lost consciousness. When he came to his senses, the plane, buried deep in a snowdrift, was slowly cooling off after its attack of fever. The first thing he saw was Konoshevich's face grinning contemptuously at him through the cockpit window:

"You're a fraud! You're only fit to travel by reindeer, but you had to have a ride in a warplane! Serves you right!"

It later transpired that they had managed, by the skin of their teeth, to glide down onto the frozen stream of the river Khantaika not far from the expedition's base camp, and this had saved them: the ten-foot layer of snow had cushioned their impact like a feather mattress.

Admittedly Konoshevich, with both legs and collarbones broken, had to be evacuated from the base by another aircraft, and Vlad had to nurse his bruises and bumps for a long time afterward; but every escape from disaster, as we know, increases one's toughness and stamina, and soon he was clicking the beads of an abacus as he juggled with the figures of the camp's not overcomplicated economy.

At first, life at Khantaika suited Vlad extremely well. Solopov, the commandant, an untidy-looking gnome (who was the absolute double of Andrian Yevtikheyev, the "hairy man" illustrated in the sixth-grade zoology textbook), clearly regarded the new bookkeeper as a protégé of higher authority and welcomed him with benevolent familiarity:

"Well, how's our Kostya, Konstantin Ivanovich? How's Alexander Alexeyevich?" he inquired, cautiously testing the ground and feeling for the shortest way into the new bookkeeper's confidence. "Great comrades, all of them, worked with them for years—this is the third construction project where we've been in harness together. You stick close to me and you won't regret it. And keep your eyes open: we have all sorts here, and some of them are pure crooks . . ."

But the old stool pigeon's inspired appeal produced no response in Vlad. Living as he did apart from the management, in the worker's quarters, he had no desire to be Solopov's informer among them. "I'm not hired for that work," was his mental response. "You're paid to do it, so be your own spy."

The worker's bunkhouse was a square hut with three windows, two-tier bunks, and a partitioned-off corner to the left of the door for a gypsy called Sasha Khrustalyov, nicknamed "Mora," and his wife, Olga, the cook. The hut acted as a safety valve for Vlad, and saved him from succumbing to the stifling boredom of their dreary, isolated existence. Apart from the gypsy, three workers were housed here for the winter: Pyotr Yeryomko, a Byelorussian recently let out of prison, who was a Jack-of-all-trades (groom, baker, and electrician); Alexander Petrovich—retired teacher of literature, a balding, dark-haired man of about forty-five with a voice hoarse from alcohol and the mannerisms of an operatic tenor; finally there was Kolya Dolgov—graduate of the Igarka high school, who had run away from an unsuccessful marriage, which he described with unashamed frankness:

"I was married off one day when I was drunk, and when I wakened I almost threw up: she was as horrible as atomic warfare. For a while we managed to get along okay, I adapted to the situation. When I went to bed with her I used to put a towel over her face and on top of that a picture of a film star. But that got boring in the end. I didn't want a photograph, I wanted a wife, and my own was too disgusting to look at so I signed on for this job. When I've made enough, I'll go back to civilization. She can't find me here, even if she calls in the police—that'll teach her to go grabbing husbands when they're drunk. She won't miss me." In the colorless, almost white irises of his eyes, there gleamed the unshakable conviction of a self-confident fanatic. (Only once again in his lifetime was Vlad to encounter a similarly desperate spiritual void; it occurred one day when he happened to catch the glance of a famous poet of the younger generation, and he felt a moment of horror.) "I've got what it takes. I only have to wink at any woman and she comes running like a little lapdog. I've had so many, I've run out of fingers trying to count them. I had the chemistry teacher in the ninth grade, and she was nearsighted—her glasses were minus three."

The ex-teacher of literature eagerly took up the conversation.

"No, I like 'em young. I'm fed up with all the cute little games that older women play—it's ridiculous! Now a fresh young girl is a different matter altogether. A woman who knows the score just opens her legs, goes crazy, and it's all over in no time, but a young one first acts shy, then she blushes, she wants to and then she doesn't, Mother wouldn't like it, and so on—now *that's* what gives it all a flavor. When I was principal of a village school at a place called Tbilisskaya in the Kuban, I taught literature to the seventh grade and half the class was pregnant by me. I only just managed to wriggle out afterwards, too, although I must say none of the girls split on me. But as for the women teachers, I couldn't stand them, wouldn't have 'em as a gift—I'd rather masturbate."

Listening to their stories, the Byelorussian would sigh to himself on the top bunk, but when he was alone with Vlad he complained:

"How come they're not ashamed to talk about women like that?

Don't they have mothers or sisters? I spent three years in prison, and it was just the same—they're worse than animals. I killed my wife, that's why I went to prison, but it was for love, you see, and I still feel the same about her—I can think only of her. It was some people in a religious sect who put ideas into her head: they told her I was the wrong person for her because I was in the Komsomol. Time and again I went to see her, I wept and begged her, but she flatly refused: either me, she said, or the Komsomol. How can people act like that? She ruined her own life and tried to ruin mine as well. I don't know how it all happened after that—like it was all in a dream. I asked her to come and talk to me outside the village, and when she started singing the same old song again, I guess I blacked out. I've no idea what happened, and when I came to, I was in prison. Of course they took account of my jealousy, my social work, the campaign against religious sects and so on, and they gave me the minimum sentence. When the rivers thaw and the steamers are running again I'm going back home, but how I'll be able to live without her I don't know. Stick my head in a noose, maybe . . ."

Only the gypsy strutted around the camp like a turkey cock, grinning and boasting to everyone with disarming naïveté:

"I have a wife—ah, what a wife! Pure gold-di'mond she ees, what a face, what a feegure . . . and clever, like meenister. And how she love me—ah, my frien', eef I tell you how she love me, you get such envy, you put evil eye on me! She say: I wouldn' change you, Sasha, my golden one, for any prince—that's what she's like . . ."

Ah, Mora, Mora, soul of dove-like innocence, if only you knew that as soon as your back was turned your "gold-di'mond" would run off to Proskurin, the radio operator and storeman. What they did together in Proskurin's hut, God only knows, but they probably did not listen to Morse code or balance the books of the camp storehouse.

When Solopov became convinced that he could not persuade his new accountant to be an informer, his attitude to Vlad underwent a sharp change. He began regularly canceling the payrolls that Vlad filled out, and sending them back to be done again; he made him do manual work; he nagged him about trivialities; finally, he achieved his aim: Vlad went on strike, after first submitting a request for reassignment. But in the conditions of a winter camp in the taiga, any boss can act without fear on the principle that "the taiga is my Law and the bear is my Prosecutor." And that was the way Solopov acted.

Vlad was immediately deprived of his entitlement to free rations, with access to the camp's food supplies only at his own expense; luckily for him, he still had a few rubles that he had saved. He was categorically forbidden to communicate with the outside world. His contacts with the rest of the camp personnel were put under strict surveillance, and, wherever possible, cut off. There was only one thing left to do: to sit in silence, wait until the snow melted, and then make his way on foot through the taiga to Igarka; to wait, thinking to himself: "When will the devil come and get you!"

Killing time by scribbling bad verse, in which, like all poets at his age, he settled accounts with an ungrateful humankind, Vlad stared in boredom out of the window and watched as the ice on the Khantaika grew steadily thinner in expectation of the breakup and the spring flood.

The ice broke up suddenly and noisily. One night Vlad was woken by a rumbling explosion. From outside, two hundred yards away, came the thunder of a veritable cannonade. The building shook and the windowpanes rattled alarmingly: it seemed as if the very ground underfoot was involuntarily floating away into the darkness, thrust by some dreadful, implacable force.

Vlad jumped up, dressing as he went, and ran out toward the river, where several others were already gathered: a tight huddle of seven people come to watch nature awakening from her sleep. Splitting and raging, the ice was bursting furiously through the narrow spillway of the dam, effortlessly smashing the armored surface of the channel in its onward rush. There was something spellbinding in its frenzied rage. Beside this primeval force, man seemed puny and defenseless.

From that night onward the taiga began visibly to change color. The river's high banks, tinged with rust-colored moss, soon turned black, as though charred, laying bare the sad skeleton of the winter-ravaged forest. Vlad began to prepare for his journey. It was about twenty kilometers to the nearest human habitation, where he could pick up a boat to take him the rest of the way, but the journey through the springtime tundra, with its swamps and its streams in full spate, was not going to be an easy one. With his last ten-ruble bill, Vlad tried surreptitiously to buy food from Proskurin, but the storeman, his nearsighted eyes blinking miserably, refused:

"Solopov has forbidden me to do it—I'm not a free man, you

know that. Out here in the wilds you can't get away with anything—just try disobeying him."

Nothing, however, could stop Vlad now.

"I'll make it in two days," he resolved in desperation. "With luck, I won't starve to death—I've been hungrier than this before now." He was actually wearing all his worldly goods, but even so his rucksack was useful: during his enforced idleness he had built up quite a collection of poems and various writings. The beggar, they say, only has to buckle on his belt to be ready for the road, and next morning, watched in complete but eloquent silence by the rest of the camp, he set out. Turn right, turn left—no, better go straight ahead!

Hardly had the camp's roofs disappeared behind the tops of the dripping larch trees when Sasha Khrustalyov emerged from the riverside undergrowth, coming toward Vlad with a loaf of bread and a can of stew under his arm.

"I wait for you so long, I almost freeze to death." As he approached Vlad, the gypsy smiled his usual broad and disarming smile. "Petro sends you bread, and my wife got you this can of stew —she's pure gold, my woman. Don't think bad of us, Vladik, we're only human . . ."

For no more than a moment their eyes met, and Vlad felt a sudden flash of intuition, like a blow in the pit of the stomach: "Yes, he knows, this gypsy, he knows everything—he knows about his wife, about me, about everyone!" So much sadness, so much suppressed pain was flickering there behind his coal-black eyes.

CHAPTER 10

Vlad will remember that journey for a long time. Those twenty kilometers turned into such a lethal obstacle race that when he finally reached the first Volga-German settlement, the route seemed so appalling in retrospect that he wondered how he had ever survived. He had been all but drowned and frozen, and had lost his way. Absurd as it may sound, it was only a passionate urge somehow to get his own back on Solopov and to triumph over yesterday's enemy that saved him from despair and disaster. He laughs longest, as the saying goes, who laughs last.

The settlement seemed deserted. Vlad walked from one end of it to the other without meeting a living soul. The huts which served as living quarters were all locked, and the doors of the kolkhoz office were secured by a huge padlock. He then made his way to the jetty, in the hope of finding at least a boatman on duty.

The only person he saw there, however, was an old man sitting alone on a bollard, his prominent chin resting on the knob of a stick held between his legs, staring at the world from beneath a neatly trimmed fringe of straw-colored hair. His pale, watery eyes had hardened into a look of cold fury from long waiting and seemed to be flashing out a challenge into empty space: "Damn you if you don't come soon!"

"*Ich verstehe nicht.*" In reply to Vlad's question he did not even stir, and only after a long pause did he wave a gnarled hand ahead of him in a vaguely upstream direction. "There . . . chairman . . . fishing . . ."

Vlad looked to see where the old man was pointing, and realizing that he would learn nothing more from him, he set out in the direction indicated. Rounding the first bend in the river, he found himself about two hundred yards from a gently sloping stretch of the bank where the fishing was in progress. At least a hundred men and about twenty boats were milling around in the feverish activity of a big catch. No one noticed him—a lone idler amid the maelstrom of work —until they stopped for a brief smoke break. A thickset, almost square man wearing a sou'wester and rubber waders broke away from a group of fishermen and came toward him. Stopping a little short of Vlad, the man peered nearsightedly, stared, and then recognized him:

"Ah, it's you—the actor! What brings you here? Did you get bored with your club and want to get out into the wilds? Maybe you can help me fix up an amateur theater group—my bosses are always complaining I neglect our education and entertainment out here. I badly need someone like you." He came up to Vlad and thrust out a calloused palm. "Heckmann's the name . . . Come on, let's go. They'll get by without us. Did you walk here, or what?"

Up and down the riverside country from Turukhansk to Dudinka, Heckmann was something of a legendary figure. A former first secretary of the Volga-German Regional Party Committee, he was now chairman of a collective farm of Volga Germans exiled to Siberia, where he managed not only to meet a huge delivery quota for fish but to run a flourishing vegetable farm as well. It was thanks to him that the potato was first grown as a viable crop in these latitudes, which was of the greatest value in wartime and literally saved countless people from death by starvation.

As Heckmann walked slightly ahead of Vlad, his weight swaying ponderously from foot to foot, the impression it made was not so much of a rolling gait as of the earth giving way under his footfall. "You're done for, my friend," Vlad said to himself as he struggled to keep pace.

Heckmann lived in a communal hut that was partitioned off into individual cubicles, one of which, no better and no worse than the rest, he opened with his key. Everything about the place bore the stamp of sound workmanship. Here, man had applied heart and skill to transform an otherwise dull, standard structure: the floorboards were free of gaps and splinters, the well-fitted windowframes were neatly calked up for the winter, the clean, even tone of the whitewash was a delight to the eye. Outside, growing almost right up to the settlement buildings, stood virgin forest. Vlad had noticed this on his arrival, when he had caught sight of a pile of sawdust briquettes stacked up outside a sawmill. "They must be crazy." He had grinned to himself at the time. "That's like living beside a freshwater river and building a desalination plant." But when he glanced over at the far bank to the almost century-old Russian-inhabited village of Plakhino, he saw that in a radius of about five kilometers all around it there was a deforested wasteland where nothing grew but weeds and coarse undergrowth, and he realized that the Germans had not conserved the virgin forest for its looks alone: a wall of conifers, like a fortress, protected them equally from the driving snowstorms of winter and the arid desiccation of the short Siberian summer.

Heckmann opened the door, ushered in his guest and said:

"Come in and take off your things. I'll be with you in a moment." He began to busy himself around the table. "My children are at the boarding school in Plakhino and my wife's out working on a logging team, so I live a bachelor's life." With amazing speed for such a heavily built man, and even with a certain physical grace, Heckmann set the table. A bottle, some bacon, bread, cold potatoes, and onions all appeared as if by magic. "You can wash over there in the corner behind that curtain. Then when you've eaten, you can go to bed."

The strain of the journey made itself felt at once: after his first glass of vodka Vlad felt slack-limbed and drowsy. His host's voice sounded blurred, as though he were hearing it through a padded screen:

"This land cost us dear, I can tell you, comrade. I remember what it was like when they brought us here from Krasnoyarsk in the fall of '41: nothing but forest, swamp, and mosquitoes. They threw us a few axes, a couple of saws, and five sacks of unmilled grain and told us to make the best of it. We're Germans, though, and we're a thorough people. When we put our minds to a job we do it properly. And we survived. We survived, comrade!" Heckmann gently struck the table with his heavy fist and stared searchingly at his guest: hooknosed, with his sad sheep's eyes he looked more like a Jew than a German. "People fell ill and died like flies, we ate tree bark, our dugout huts froze right through, but my little band lived through it all. One thing only I don't understand: the war's been over a long time now, but we're still here. Why? In certain circumstances, in a critical situation, the mass deportation of potential enemies is sensible and even essential. I even said as much to the authorities before they deported us. But now that it's all over, why on earth do the powers that be still keep us here? I've been a member of the Party since the first day of the revolution, comrade; to separate me from the Party would be like cutting off a piece of my own flesh, but lately I can't understand what's going on—I can't figure it out." He poured out the remains of the vodka. "Drink up, lad, and go to bed. I still have to go back to the riverbank."

Against his own will, there suddenly flared up in Vlad's overheated brain a feeling of furious resentment, a feeling which, he realized, had been building up inside him over several years:

"D'you think I'm just a dumb kid, Heckmann, and you don't want to scare me? Now that you've started, why don't you go on and spell it out? Tell me, dear Mr. Party Member, exactly what sort of a wonderful new life you were fighting for and spilling buckets of other people's blood for—and when do you think the fighting and blood will ever come to an end? I've tramped around a good half of Russia and somehow I've never yet found this great truth of yours."

Even through his drunken haze, Vlad could see Heckmann turn pale and his eyes narrow in anger:

"You want the truth, comrade? I could have told you the truth, but I wasn't sure that you could take it. I could have told you how I was hauled off to witness the interrogation of friends that I literally trusted as I trust myself, how they were killed before my eyes before I even had time to say a kind word to them in farewell. I could have told you how we and our families were thrown out of our homes, how we were shipped across Russia in cattle cars without food or water, how the living were piled up in heaps like firewood along with the dead and how only a miracle and our own strength of will saved us once we got here. Yes, it's true that nothing worked out the way it was supposed to, but my conscience is clear. I wanted nothing for myself from the revolution. I thought it would make things better for everybody. But I can't simply wipe the whole of my life off the slate just because some young Russian boy is dissatisfied with its results."

"That still doesn't make it any better for the others." Vlad feebly gave in under the other man's counterblast. "Sorry, Heckmann, it just came out."

"Well, it's called 'speaking one's mind,' I suppose." Heckmann immediately cooled down. "Okay, you'd better get some sleep. Things always look brighter in the morning—although I must say it's hard to tell morning from evening in this part of the world." He gave a good-natured laugh. "What a fabulous country it is . . ."

Next morning Vlad was woken by loud knocking on the door followed by a conversation in rapid German. As Heckmann got dressed without hurrying, he laughed and answered in Russian:

"Don't worry, he won't die of cold. He's made me wait longer than this before now." With a good-morning nod to Vlad, he explained:

"The commandant's arrived. He's come to give me a hard time because we're behind with the delivery plan. Get up and collect your things; you can get a ride to Igarka in his motor launch."

The boat, gently rocking on the water, was moored to the jetty, and a tall, thin, slightly round-shouldered captain in the Security Forces, a white fur jacket thrown over his shoulders, was pacing up and down the landing stage waiting for Heckmann. The latter was obviously used to these visitations; as he walked along he only snorted with irritation and rolled his shoulders self-confidently like a boxer before a fight.

Heckmann did not go down to the launch, but remained at the top of the steps leading from the jetty to the landing stage, which was clearly a long-standing rule in a familiar game. As soon as he saw the chairman approaching, the captain started to bluster:

"What the hell are you up to, you goddam Kraut! What's happened to the plan? Don't give me any bullshit—what about the plan, I say?" He stomped up and down the landing stage, waving his arms and swinging from side to side as though he were on hinges. "We've praised you to the skies, we've coddled you—and you sabotage the plan behind our backs! We knocked the stuffing out of Hitler, so don't think *you* can get away with it . . ."

"The fish won't do as they're told, Captain," Heckmann put in calmly during a pause. "But we'll make the delivery plan." Openly mocking, he clenched his fist behind his back for Vlad to see. "There's a comrade here, Captain, who'd like a ride to Igarka . . ."

"Who? Where's he from?" The captain immediately lowered his

voice and looked worried: he had obviously not counted on the scene being witnessed by outsiders. "What's he doing here?"

"He's the club manager from Igarka." Heckmann's manner was more imperturbable than ever. "Samsonov. Walked here from Khantaika."

"Oh yes, I know him," the commandant said wearily. "He can come aboard. I'll take him. He's chosen a fine time to go hiking, though . . . Now you do your stuff, Heckmann, or I'll get you." For appearance' sake he wagged a threatening finger. "Watch it, Heckmann, or I'll skin you alive." Turning to the boat, he shouted: "Start up!"

The launch made a sharp turn and shot off downstream toward the rapids, while Heckmann, legs planted wide apart and hands clasped behind his back, stood on the shore watching them go. No one knows what he was thinking about at that moment, but to this day Vlad would swear that his mind was on anything but them.

Disappointment awaited Vlad in Igarka: the expedition's headquarters had moved to Yermakovo, so there was no one to whom he could complain and no one to pay him off. He decided against imposing himself again on Mukhammed while waiting for better times. The only thing to do was to press on to Yermakovo on foot.

A well-trodden path led Vlad to the roadbed, along which was strung a temporary telephone line—an infallible guide for the traveler. At intervals of five kilometers stood a patrolman's hut, where any passer-by was a welcome guest: a life alone in the taiga inclines a man to cordiality. Vlad covered the distance in two and a half days of hard walking, and by evening on the third day he was knocking on the office door of the expedition's personnel manager.

This time, however, the once frank and friendly Konstantin Ivanovich did not even look up as Vlad walked in, and said brusquely:

"Nothing for you here, my friend. Solopov didn't consider you as having started work for him at all, so you're not due for any pay. You may get an adverse discharge note under Article 47G,* but I'm afraid there's no money coming to you. My advice is to grab your discharge papers and then get the hell out of here within twenty-four hours, otherwise you'll be in real trouble. Solopov is charging you

---

* Article 47G of the Soviet Labor Code deals with "violation of labor discipline." (Author's note.)

with anti-Soviet activity, and you won't wriggle out of that one. So long . . ."

The chief of the expedition happened to be away on a site tour, so Vlad tried to get an interview with Pobozhy, the chief engineer, but the latter refused to see him. Sitting afterward on the riverbank with a bitter lump in his throat, faced by a prospect of utter hopelessness, Vlad could not possibly have known that fifteen years later this same Alexander Alexeyevich Pobozhy would bring his first literary opus to Vlad for judgment, proving at the same time to be a remarkably kind, simple, and good man.

The only thing that could save Vlad now was for the rivers to melt sufficiently for commercial navigation to begin, which was due to happen any day now. While waiting for the first steamer, he spent his nights in a temporary station building on the future railroad, where the janitor, out of the kindness of his heart, not only allowed him to sleep but even fed his uninvited guest.

"Eat." His crumpled, pockmarked face loomed indistinctly in the semidarkness of the station building. "God commands us to share what we have. I won't miss it, and although you won't grow fat on it, at least you'll have a full stomach. The man who has enough should understand what it means to go hungry. Perhaps one day you'll put in a good word for an old man, and it'll count in my favor."

Two days before Vlad's planned departure, the janitor helped him to avoid a threatening obstacle:

"They say things are terrible in Igarka," the old man warned him. "Crowds of people have been released from the prison camps and they're all waiting for a steamer. You'll never get on board without a ticket. There'll be a police cordon at the landing stage. You'd better go from here to Kureika. There the ship doesn't come to the shore; they bring the passengers out to it by rowboat. My old friend Fedot Yermolayich Savin will put you on that boat. He's well known around these parts. He works as a janitor at the Stalin museum—in fact, he once knew Stalin personally. Once you're on board the steamer you'll have to fend for yourself, but with luck they won't throw you off. Fedot Yermolayich is a man you can trust, and you can spend the night at his place."

With that they parted. "And I set off, treading upon the bosom of the earth, my legs as my support."*

---

* Dante, *The Divine Comedy*. (Author's note.)

CHAPTER 11

The road along the riverbank ran past a string of convict work sites and prison camps. If he could have imagined then how small, how wretchedly cramped this world of ours is! To realize this, there is no need to fly out into space; it is enough to have lived through the forty-plus years of Vlad's lifetime to discover that when hiking along the roadbed of Construction Project 503 he had been, in fact, walking past his own future friends and colleagues, his cronies and drinking companions, his admirers and his bosses. How many of them are now scattered around the globe, having made and unmade friendships with him! How many are still his neighbors, watching with sympathy, pride, or malice as he continues his unequal duel with circumstances? How many are at rest in the Lord, having departed this world before the promised Day of Judgment and the Resurrection? It is hard to know which of them to mention: the erstwhile professional thief Misha Dyomin, now the star literary commentator of Radio Liberty; Sergei Lominadze, once a prison clerk, today a regular critic for *Problems of Literature*—or the boss of them all, the much-decorated Barabanov, who was so ingratiating to special correspondent Samsonov in those days when he eked out his pension in charge of the public waiting room of *Izvestiya*, under the editorship of Khrushchev's mighty favorite, Adzhubei. There are too many to name them all.

The first night found Vlad near a prison-camp compound, one end of which extended right to the bank of the river. He was attracted by the glow of a stove, beckoning cosily through the single window of a hut, which stood slightly apart from the administrative buildings and storehouses at a bend in the river. The door was opened to his knock by a sleepy young man of about twenty-five with a slightly effeminate face and the puffy look typical of prison life.

"Come in." Yawning unceremoniously he stood aside to let Vlad in. "You working on the expedition? Shut the door behind you . . . like something to eat?" The young man gave him a bowl of cold cod, cut off a hefty slice from a whole loaf of bread, and poured out a glass of lukewarm tea from a teapot. "Help yourself—it's only prison food, but there's as much as you want." With that he lay down on a cot covered with tattered blankets, having first thrown an old coat on to the floor for Vlad. "When you've eaten, you can sleep there, and I'll wake you up in the morning."

As he finished his meal, Vlad could not restrain his curiosity and asked his host:

"Are you working on contract?"

"No. I'm doing time. But I'm allowed freedom of movement. I stoke the furnaces at camp headquarters. It's not a bad life. I'm getting out soon—less than a year to go now. Guess I'll stay here, though, and sign on as a free worker. Why should I want to go back to the village I came from? As I remember it, I never had enough to eat and I was treated like dirt. Here I not only get all the bread and fish I can eat, but they treat me decently too. It's 'Vasya, would you mind doing this?' or 'Vasya, be a pal, don't forget to fetch that.' See what I mean? They say to me, 'Vasya, be a pal . . .'! Back home in my village nobody ever opened their mouth except to swear at me. Say what you like, but for someone from a kolkhoz, prison camp is like what a rest home is for other people. You do your work—you get your rations; you finish your stint—you can go take a nap. But in a kolkhoz everything depends on what sort of mood the bosses are in. If they feel like it, you'll get what's due to you—if they don't you won't. Go into the forest and complain to the wolves—that's all the law there is on a kolkhoz."

"But at least you're free."

"What good is that sort of freedom? You can't eat it, you can't drink it. How much freedom did I have in our kolkhoz, anyway? You have no passport, so if you want to go into town the only way to get a permit is to bribe the chairman with a bottle. Step an inch out of line and they kick you in the teeth, and if you try and drown your sorrows, the police pick you up by the short and curlies and fling you in the cooler. No, brother, I wouldn't have your freedom as a gift—I'd rather see it dead and buried. I prefer to eat . . ."

Listening to this confession, Vlad fell asleep, and when he woke up, his host, coughing and swearing, was already stoking up the stove:

"Time to get up, brother. We'll have some tea, then you can be off and on your way and you'll be in Kureika by the evening. It's only a stone's throw from here."

As he was saying goodbye on the doorstep, Vlad asked him:

"What's your name, so I can remember you in my prayers?"

"Forget it!" Embarrassed, the young man brushed the idea aside. "Let's say I've forgotten it. My mother prays for me, and that's enough. See you."

Well, thanks all the same, you weird man, champion of prison food and a fixed working day!

At sunset the pale blue façade of the Kureika museum rose up before Vlad among a cluster of squat peasant huts on the opposite bank. He had to wait a long time before getting a ride across the river in a boat, and having crossed over he found the museum closed. It did not prove too difficult, however, to find the janitor. The first person he met gladly showed him the way to Fedot Savin's house on the hillside.

At first the old man was none too welcoming, but Vlad only had to make grateful mention of their mutual friend from Yermakovo for Fedot to be instantly transformed. His stubble-grown face softened into a delighted grin:

"So the old devil's still alive and kicking! Come in, come in, there's plenty of room. We'll have a bite to eat, then it'll be snoring time. The steamer won't be here till after lunch tomorrow. Don't worry—if he said I'll get you aboard, I'll do it. Everybody on the Yenisei knows Fedot Savin . . ."

Next morning the old man took him on a tour around the lop-sided little rooms of the dilapidated hut, enclosed within its boxlike pavilion, and told his story:

"More times than I can remember I've talked to Stalin face to face, just like I'm talking to you now, when we used to go out hunting and fishing together. He wasn't much to look at, even though he

was from the south. He was short and pockmarked, but he had a
wicked sharp eye—you felt he was burning you up when he looked at
you. He seemed cool enough on the outside, but he was a touchy
fellow underneath it, and if something needled him he could fly into
a temper like I never hope to see again. I was young and stupid in
those days, and if I'd had the sense to know what was what, I could
be rolling in money now. There was his landlord, for instance, Mitka
Kokorev—he was a sickly little man, but he didn't miss a trick. As
soon as they started talking about making this hut into a Stalin museum, way back in the thirties, he named his price as bold as brass:
'Fifty thousand rubles,' he said. That was a crazy lot of money.
Why, this little old shack wasn't worth two hundred in those days.
But he hit the bull's-eye, that son of a bitch, and by God, they paid
up!" He sighed with a mixture of envy and admiration. "Yes, they
paid him! Mind you, he was taking a big risk; they might've just as
easily clapped him in jail, or worse . . ."

When the boat from the steamer tied up at the jetty, the old man
officiously elbowed aside the small crowd and pushed Vlad to the
front:

"This citizen's from the steamship line," he announced, nodding
to the two young sailors with a knowing look. "Comrade Lobastov
knows all about it. Personal order . . . by direct line . . ." Then in a
hasty whisper to Vlad: "Don't hang around, kid, jump in."

The first obstacle was overcome, but the trip to Krasnoyarsk lasted
a further five days, during which he might be unceremoniously flung
ashore at any stop. Everything that Vlad had so far heard about
Captain Lobastov of the *Joseph Stalin*, flagship of the Yenisei ship-
ping line, augured ill for anyone trying to travel without a ticket:
tough, hard on both himself and his crew, he had a reputation up and
down the river as the terror of dodgers and stowaways. While winter-
ing in Igarka he had occasionally dropped in at the club—tall, solidly
built, always well turned-out, with the badge of a deputy to the
Supreme Soviet in the lapel of his uniform jacket—but apart from
the port officials, he never allowed anyone to approach him, and he
openly pulled his rank and acted the big shot. Nevertheless, Vlad
had no alternative: the only person who could save him from being
dumped ashore was Lobastov himself.

To Vlad's considerable amazement, the captain agreed to see him
as soon as he reported himself:

"Yes, of course I've heard of you!" In the small, cramped cabin,
with its thick pile carpet, he looked even more massive and imposing

than ever. "You're the one who stood up to that old witch Dyomina! I used to go to your concerts, and I must say they were very enjoyable. There's been a hell of a row among the top brass at Igarka, all because of you. They're wishing they hadn't fired you now. God, that Dyomina!" His stout figure, his well-cut uniform, even his deputy's badge, all exuded the condescending benevolence of a self-confident man. "She's not a woman—she's a snake. How far are you going?"

"To Krasnoyarsk."

"Without a ticket, I suppose?"

"I hardly had enough money to see me through till spring . . . You know how it is . . ."

"Okay, you can stay aboard." He came out from behind his desk and opened the cabin door: "Hey, you there!" As though at the wave of a wand, the Second Officer materialized in the doorway. "He can eat in the crew's mess. Another mouth to feed won't make any difference." Turning to Vlad he added: "You'll have to work your passage, though. You can swab the decks along with the crew. It'll do you good: you're a bit of a hothead, and too apt to piss into the wind. Fix yourself up wherever you can . . ."

That trip from Khantaika to Krasnoyarsk will long remain in his memory—a journey on which total strangers shared with him their roof and their bread, cheered him with a kind word, and passed him on from hand to hand like the baton in a relay race. There is more, much more, that he would like to tell about that journey, but time presses on. A great poet* has thrown off a few lines, as though casually, in passing, after which any other words on this topic are superfluous:

> Through countless nightmares and through dreams,
> Through towns and villages, through time,
> Past obstacles, past bridges, over streams,
> The road leads on, unswerving, to its aim.
>
> That aim, no matter if the way be short or long,
> Is to persist, to keep on to the end:
> To show the right way, shun the wrong,
> And keep the distant goal in view past all the bends.

And to that there is, as the saying goes, nothing to add, nothing to take away.

* Boris Pasternak. (Author's note.)

CHAPTER 12

There was no question of swabbing the decks on board the *Joseph Stalin:* not a square inch of space was unoccupied. Crammed full, the ship literally shuddered under the strain. Nowhere—in the hold, on deck, in the corridors of the first- and second-class accommodation—was there room to swing a cat. The passengers lay side by side, squashed together like sardines. In secluded corners the scum of the criminal world sat around gambling, brewing chifir and preparing Indian ink to tattoo one another. Prison-camp "mammies"* busied themselves with caring for their little saviors. In the dark passageways around the lavatories, the appealing glances of hungry homosexuals announced that they were ready and willing. An atmosphere of transit prisons and forced-labor camps pervaded the whole vessel. "The sound of roll call and the noise of the camps—once heard, never forgotten . . ."

Vlad was lucky: in one of the first-class corridors amidships, the ship's police detachment broke up a knife fight between thieves, and in the rush to fill the resulting vacuum he was able to grab a place. Only then, stretched out at full length alongside a bulkhead, was he finally able to sigh and say to himself with certainty: "Now I'll make it to Krasnoyarsk!"

---

* A "mammy" (Russian: mamka) is a woman convict released from prison on giving birth to a child. (Tr.)

His immediate neighbor turned out to be a fellow Muscovite, a garrulous youth with big eyes, a broad, flat nose and a grubby peaked cap. No sooner had he settled down than he tried to make friends with Vlad by pouring out a flow of confidences:

"See from your haircut you haven't been inside. Coming back from a contract job?" In reply, Vlad only frowned; he knew this type from his years in reformatories and juvenile detention centers: loud, talkative, oversociable, they always managed to stay out of real trouble in any situation by keeping carefully aside. "I got five years—though with remission for good behavior I only did three. Spent my last year gold-bricking in the prison stores. We were on easy street there, I can tell you—as much chow as you could eat, even a broad or two now and again. I remember once how a bunch of ten of us had a bash at a prison nurse—it was enough to make you shit in your pants with laughing. I got a bucket of water from one of the "politicals" huts, and off we went. That hooker only had time to wash her cunt out between each one but she gave us all our money's worth—I even managed to have a second go at her! Then I took them back their bucket of water and we forced those lousy politicals to drink it— serve 'em right for being anti-Soviet!"

"They're human beings, after all . . ."

"Human beings! They ought to put all those bastards up against a wall and shoot 'em! They're behind bars like the rest of us, but they whine about their 'rights' and demand 'justice.' Always ready to stir up the shit, but when they're caught they can't take what's coming to them. When you land inside, I say you should stop squealing and keep your trap shut—a prison's not a lecture hall. Why are they always griping at the gov'ment anyway? It feeds them, even lets them cheat and steal. At least they're giving 'em stiffer sentences nowadays—all the better for the rest of us." He winked and gave Vlad an ingratiating smirk. "Hey, want a bit of ass, maybe? There's one here—the whole gang of us screws her, and I can fix you a place in line . . ."

Vlad had already seen this girl. Puffy-faced and sluttish-looking, she could be seen lurking in remote corners of the ship, always surrounded by a gaggle of shaven heads and prison-issue caps. The mere thought of physical proximity to her nauseated him. A riffraff of ex-cons was always buzzing around her like flies around a piece of meat, panting with lust, sniggering and swearing. Eventually, when they got bored with her, they would tie the hem of her skirt over the top of her head and douse her below the belt with a bucketful of fuel oil.

"I'll get by without it, thanks." Vlad turned away in disgust to face the wall. "I value my nose too much."

"Okay, please yourself. I'll have a go, though—so what if my nose does drop off?"

"All right, catch a dose if you like . . ."

The gang of ex-prisoners made trouble all the way. By the end of the trip, the ship's cells were crammed with men under arrest, the hard core of whom consisted of at least a dozen candidates for death row. During the five days of the voyage their record cards were filled out with every conceivable felony, from armed robbery to "aggravated assault, to wit: drowning by physical ejection overboard." They would all be summarily dealt with by the courts in Krasnoyarsk, where, to judge by the charges against them, some would end up with nine grams of lead in the back of the neck while the luckier ones would be shipped straight back to Construction Project 503.

In order not to be drawn into this unsavory maelstrom, Vlad made it a rule not to leave his place unless it was absolutely necessary. Scarcely emerging from a state of semi-torpor, he would quickly bolt his free meal in the crew's quarters and go straight back to his corner. Spending his days in a permanent state of near somnolence, he decided that he was dreaming when one morning he thought he saw Zinka at the far end of the corridor. Dressed in expensive crushed velvet, with a fashionable "beehive" hairdo, she was coming straight toward him, her little patent-leather slippers fastidiously picking a way between the bodies and luggage strewn in front of her. She was escorted by a major of the Security Forces, who was gallantly and even somewhat obsequiously steering her by the elbow.

Zinka! At that moment Vlad could not bring himself to call out to you, feeling he looked too wretched and disreputable, but later, in the evening, when the darkness provided some camouflage for his abject poverty, he bumped into you on deck as though by chance, and said:

"So you've got what you wanted, have you, Zinka?"

"Yes, I have," you replied calmly and firmly, as though you and he had parted only yesterday. "Are you jealous?"

"No," he said, but his voice went hoarse and broke off. "Bully for you."

Then he took his hands in yours, put them to your cheeks, burst into tears, and sobbed out to him the rest of your story:

"I've grown a hundred years older in this past year, Vladka. I now know all there is to know about life, there are no secrets for me any longer. When you left me at Igarka, I held out till winter, although there was never a word from you. One day at the "General Delivery" counter in the post office they began laughing at me: your boy-friend's thrown you over, they said, he's found someone else. Well, that day I got blind drunk for the first time in my life. And I started sleeping around. That was when Dima Govorukhin picked me up, and after him I was just passed from hand to hand, my feet didn't touch the ground. Then one day this major found me dead drunk in the airport bar. I still don't know why he fell for me, but ever since that night he's been crazy about me—bought me clothes and shoes, and finally he married me. I should thank God for all he's done for me, but I still can't get you out of my mind. I actually used to come to the club, hoping you might notice me, but you were so high and mighty in those days I couldn't get near you." For a moment she pressed her hot forehead to his, then immediately drew away again. "Obviously we weren't meant to be together, you and I . . ." Her voice broke off on a bitter note. "But I'm hanging on to what I've got now, even though I can't stand the man . . ." In the dark she gave a last, heart-rending sob. "Goodbye, Vladka, it's your own fault —but I'll remember you to my dying day!"

CHAPTER 13

In Krasnoyarsk Vlad made an attempt to take the bull by the horns, and with a mixture of bravery and madness he marched straight into a publisher's office. His outward appearance—a shock of hair uncut for six months, canvas jacket, a bundle slung over one shoulder—obviously created a certain impression. The secretary leaped up with a startled look and immediately disappeared into an office, on whose door shone a nameplate of sterile whiteness: M. Y. GLOZUS. CHIEF EDITOR.

The chief himself, a dark, solidly built, expansive man rolled out into the reception room to meet his uninvited visitor.

"Where are you from, comrade? From the wilds? Verse? Prose?" He rattled off the questions without waiting for a reply, hopping from foot to foot with impatience. "How long have you been writing?"

"I'm from the Literary Institute in Moscow," Vlad lied involuntarily. Realizing that his bridges were burnt, he dived in headfirst: "I took a six-month sabbatical because I wanted to see the Siberian taiga. Now I'm on my way home, so I decided to drop in and have a word with my colleagues. A fresh viewpoint, you know, and all that . . ."

"Forgive me, I thought you were some amateur graphomaniac." With new respect, he put an arm around Vlad's shoulder. "They make my life a misery. Come in, my dear fellow, come in." Benevolence gleamed in the chief editor's dark Semitic eye. "Maybe you can leave us something for our annual anthology. We badly need more lyric poetry—with a suitable political tinge, of course."

As he read the verses which Vlad produced out of his sack, Glozus grunted with satisfaction, excitedly clicked his tongue and nodded in sympathetic comprehension as he paced around his office:

"Good! . . . Very good! . . . Amazingly fine imagery! 'Buzzing like a dragonfly, the airplane melts into the vast blue sky.' Simple and precise! And the most important thing, I notice, is that you cross out a lot of words. That's good. Shows you set high standards for yourself. I see you've crossed out the word 'mosquito.' Of course 'dragonfly' is better and more exact. This is the real thing, this will stand the test of time . . ."

Then he offered Vlad some tea and made a telephone call to someone whom he tried to persuade to come to the office on an urgent matter:

"You won't regret it!" He shouted into the receiver. "This is the real thing, it's classic stuff! He beats our Kazimir hands down! Come on over, I'll be waiting for you . . ."

After about the fifth glass of tea, the man whom the chief editor had summoned with such impatient insistence turned up in the office. Glozus jumped to his feet, fussed around, and danced over to Vlad on his little short legs:

"This is our pride and joy, our classic: Ignaty Rozhdestvensky. You must have heard of Ignaty Rozhdestvensky. I know you two will get on well together." Vlad had of course heard of him, and as he stood up to pay his respects he could hardly believe that he was seeing a real, live poet for the first time in his life. "This, Ignaty, is a young colleague of yours from the Literary Institute, who's passing through town. He spent the winter out in the taiga, and wants to discuss his work with us. He may give us something for the anthology . . ."

The newcomer was a tall but flabby man with an unhealthy yellow complexion. Clutching at his liver, he sat down heavily on the couch.

"Not *another* genius?" he groaned, frowning. "Aren't you fed up with them?" The poet ignored Vlad, openly and without embarrassment. "Not a day goes by without you finding a genius. You pester me with this trivia, and I have my liver to contend with. All right, let's see what your latest child prodigy has to offer."

"No, Ignaty, this time I believe it's the real thing." The chief editor's enthusiasm was waning visibly, and he handed Vlad's sheets of verse to the maestro with obvious misgiving. "Look at that line about the dragonfly! It makes Kazimir look like a beginner."

The poet fastidiously cast his eye over the tattered pieces of paper, dropping one after another on the couch beside him, and with an intensity that grew with each discarded sheet, his yellow face betrayed sensations of unfeigned suffering. When he had finished reading, he let his arms fall lifelessly to each side of his body, like a pianist after the final bars of a concerto:

"What trash! It's terrible, all of it—absolutely terrible!" He stared straight ahead as he spoke. "If only there were one syllable, one word, one tiny spark of talent. Everybody who has nothing better to do wastes paper by scribbling on it. Dragonfly! What the hell is that junk about a dragonfly? They spew out verses—but why, one asks? Why? It's some sort of poetic diarrhea . . . God, the pain!"

The poet closed his eyes and fell silent, as though dead. In the ensuing silence, the embarrassed chief editor spread his hands guiltily as if to say, "Don't take it amiss, my dear fellow!" If only you knew, my dear Mikhail Yurevich, that your visitor was ready to kill you at that moment—but that he now thanks God for his good luck. Now and for evermore, he proclaims to all the world: every beginner should have his Ignaty Rozhdestvensky!

At the time, however, Vlad was in no mood for jokes. Hungry, without a kopeck to his name, and with an adverse discharge note in his pocket, he became a plaything in the hands of fate—from which, as we know, there is no salvation. But despair does not last forever; hope springs eternal, and by the evening a word—a word that was like balm, a word which meant rescue—came into his inflamed brain like a call from childhood, like a distant tocsin, like the far-off smoke of home, sweet home: Moscow!

The five thousand kilometers between Krasnoyarsk and Moscow are engraved on his ribs, his skin, his heart, and his very backbone, so hard was that journey—but somehow he made it. Using every dodge, he flung himself at it and took the distance by storm, until the morning when he breathed in the sourish smell of a suburban railroad station and could sigh with relief: he was home!

CHAPTER 14

If only one of Vlad's relatives or neighbors could have seen him then, the sight would have surpassed even their wildest fantasies. It would have been their ultimate triumph, living proof of all their dire warnings: that Samsonov boy will come to no good! Walking down Gorky Street, Vlad must have looked a truly wretched sight: a filthy hobo with a skimpy little bundle under one arm, his otherwise naked torso covered only by a jacket many sizes too small and fastened at the neck with a safety pin, the long tattered fringes of his canvas pants dangling above laceless sneakers. At the sight of him policemen would at first stiffen like pointers scenting prey, but after a closer look they immediately lost all interest. This was perhaps the most disturbing sign of all: it meant that he had really reached the brink.

It was some time before he made up his mind to appeal as a petitioner to the office of Shvernik, Chairman of the Supreme Soviet of the U.S.S.R. Before that he had trudged from one personnel officer to another, but the discharge certificate issued to him by Konstantin Ivanovich, his erstwhile friend, was about as much use as a piece of toilet paper. With only one glance at this certificate, every personnel officer brushed him away like the devil fleeing from incense:

"Nothing doing, I'm afraid . . . I'd be glad to help, old man, but . . ."

At night Vlad slept in a cranny between a railroad bridge and the back of a beer stall near the Kazan Station, or he took a train out to Ramenskoye, a suburban station. It was one of these trips which finally induced him to make his decision. He was standing that evening in the corridor of a half-empty electric train, where the only other passenger beside himself was a short, fat, clean-shaven man carrying a thin, shabby little briefcase, the handle bound with friction tape. The fat man kept glancing sideways at Vlad, but immediately turned away whenever he caught his eye. They rode on like this for some time, exchanging glances, yet trying not to notice each other, until the man came to his stop and jumped off into the darkness. To this day Vlad cannot understand what prompted him to follow his traveling companion, what force pushed him toward the wide-open door, but everything that then followed is graven on his memory. Lit from above through the doorway, the fat man, with his open briefcase dangling behind him, was following the departing train and offering Vlad a loaf of bread and a piece of cheese. His heart recorded the moment forever: late evening, almost night, a moving rectangle of light, and in it the little man stumbling along the railroad embankment with a loaf of bread in his outstretched hand.

Another knot to tie in your handkerchief, Samsonov!

At that moment he realized that he was near the end of his tether, and next morning, on returning to Moscow, he set off for Mokhovaya Street.*

It was on the corner of Mokhovaya and Gorky Street, outside the main entrance of the National Hotel, amid a crowd that was colorful yet pathetic in its pretensions, that Vlad remembers seeing a man with a dandyish cane under his arm. Wearing a light-colored overcoat, this tall, handsome creature with a luxuriant mustache and a halo of flowing, carefully tended hair moved through the crowd like a visitor from a dream, an emissary of Sheherezade, a vision from another, unearthly world, and the aroma of his well-groomed cleanliness floated behind him like a scarf of the finest material.

You and he will meet again, Sasha Galich, only it will be almost twenty years later, in other surroundings and in very different circumstances, and it is to be hoped that you will both regret that the meeting did not take place earlier!

* The Petitions Office of the Presidium of the Supreme Soviet of the U.S.S.R. is situated at No. 7, Mokhovaya Street. (Author's note.)

It was in the Presidium offices, surrounded by a motley crowd of petitioners and beggars, that for the first time in many days Vlad felt inconspicuous. A bony old woman in a skimpy headscarf was complaining to her neighbor, a morose disabled veteran with a pair of crutches across his knees:

"They can't mean to put him in front of a firing squad!" Her narrow face was tense with perplexity. "Sure, he killed a man all right—but what for? 'Cause he was standing up for me, his own mother, I tell you. That man Spitsyn wasn't a foreman—he was a wild beast, God have mercy on his sinful soul. He gave me such a lambasting with that great whip of his that I couldn't get up from my bed till October. He's drawn blood from more of us wretched women than I can count. And then they tell me my son's a political terrorist. What does my boy know about politics, when his mother's milk's still wet on his lips? No, I'm not one to take this sort of thing lying down—I shall go all the way to Stalin if I have to!"

"Yes, it's a nasty business," the veteran nodded gloomily, "a nasty business . . ."

A short distance away from them, two bespectacled, shabby-looking men were leaning toward one another and discussing their own problems:

"I proved to them that they were obliged to patent my invention, yet they flatly refused to. We're not interested, they said, in engines of that type. Well, I said, who is? No one, they said. But it works, I said! Doesn't matter, they said, we won't patent it."

"Yes, there's bureaucracy everywhere," his companion put in sympathetically. "Take my case, for instance: is a schoolteacher allowed to have a vegetable plot alongside his house? Yes, he is. Is there a government decree to that effect? There is. So I go to the chairman of our kolkhoz and he says to me: 'We got rid of all the landowners in 1917 and we don't need any new ones.' And he, if you please, has three quarters of an acre . . ."

At the head of the line a man was suffering an epileptic fit. An agitated crowd was fussing around the sick man:

"Hold him down by his legs!"

"His head, hold his head!"

"Does anyone have a spoon to put between his teeth? Otherwise he'll bite his tongue off."

"Fetch a glass of water!"

"No need, it'll be over soon . . ."

On receiving the coveted numbered tag from the official on duty, Vlad searched along a corridor for the door bearing the same number; soon he was sitting in front of a hefty woman with a shock of red hair above her white freckled forehead, to whom he gave a rapid account of the stages of his latest odyssey. She listened to him without interruption, occasionally scribbling some notes on a pad and when he finally stopped, she asked him:

"Have you eaten today?"

"No."

"Well, there you are." She opened a drawer in her desk, took out a package wrapped in greasy paper and pushed it toward him. "Take it, take it, I won't starve." Beneath the sarcastic expression on her ugly but gentle features there was a look of embarrassment. "Goodness me, what a tale of woe—it sounds like Przewalski's Siberian expedition all over again. I'll help you, but these things take a little time to arrange. You'll have to wait about two or three weeks. You say you've been in hospital, so you're not afraid of hospitals. That's good. I'll call Yanushevsky at the Psychiatric Reception Center. He'll admit you for a few weeks, you can rest there until you're fit and well again, and in the meantime I'll see about getting your case dealt with. There's ten kopecks for your streetcar fare. Take a B car from the stop near the Red Army Theater. Go to 5 Institute Street. If you really are a Muscovite, as you say you are, you shouldn't lose your way . . . Goodbye. Next!"

Vlad was expected when he arrived at the Psychiatric Reception Center. No sooner did he report to the nurse on duty than she led him to the city's senior psychiatrist, Dr. Yanushevsky, a short, disheveled roly-poly of a man, who seemed to have lost his temper, once and for all, with the whole of the human race.

"Well, let's have a look at you." As he talked he did not sit in his chair, but constantly jumped up and down, flipped through some papers on his desk, twiddled a pencil in his nimble fingers and occasionally wiped his spectacles. "How did you get into such a state, my dear boy? Anyhow, it doesn't matter. Why on earth did you go through all that business of going to the President's office instead of coming straight here? You're a former psychiatric patient, so we are bound to admit you. God, you don't even have a shirt on your back. Okay, we'll find something better for you to wear before you leave." He turned to the nurse: "Lydia Alexandrovna, wash him and put him in a ward . . ."

Much time was to pass before the name of Yanushevsky became a bogeyman of the liberal intelligentsia, a synonym for bootlicking subservience, the mark of Cain for a whole profession; but on that day he appeared to Vlad simply as an aging eccentric with the manners of a man on the verge of retirement.

In the Moscow City Psychiatric Reception Center, or, as some people still call it, Hospital No. 7, Vlad spent a little over two weeks; there he thawed out and was partly restored to his former self. The hospital's chief function was as a staging post for the evacuation of patients from out of town; as a result, there was a constant turnover of occupants, and for that reason Vlad's memory failed to retain a single face or character. Occasionally, perhaps, he recollects the hazy image of a young pickpocket who spent almost all his time in the lavatories, where he would sit smoking; he cleaned the toilet bowls and swabbed the tiled floor, and in the intervals between these activities he would stand by the door and sing prison songs in a thin but not unpleasant tenor voice.

On his third day, as a sign of special trust in him, Vlad was allowed to go for lunch to the TB hospital across the street. Surrounded by majestic old maple trees that shaded the neglected, overgrown hospital park, with its monument to Dostoyevsky, the large, old-fashioned buildings stood on the far side of the fence that surrounded the Psychiatric Reception Center. On his way he often met children of various ages in wheelchairs and on crutches, awkward young creatures with unchildishly sad eyes, but he was not to know at the time that among them was the young man who was to be his future friend and colleague in his ordeals amid the world of the theater and the cinema—Sanya Kuznetsov, a creature of boundless self-esteem and toughness. But the hour is near, Sanya, the hour of our meeting—and of our subsequent bitter parting!

Yanushevsky was as good as his word, and when the time came for Vlad to leave, he was provided with essential clothing which generously included a good, sound pair of army boots, and rations for three days. He was driven to the Kazan Station and dispatched in the direction of Stalingrad with an official travel warrant in his pocket.

Goodbye, once more, Moscow, goodbye until we meet again—in the comparatively near future!

CHAPTER 15

Since Vlad had last been in Stalingrad during the war, the look of the city had changed quite noticeably. The city center was almost completely rebuilt, although the railroad station was unaltered—it was still the same overcrowded wooden building. His train arrived very early in the morning, so he had to spend several hours kicking his heels in the packed waiting room. To the best of his recollection, in every railroad station in Russia that he had ever seen, even the very smallest, a crowd of people was always to be found pushing, shoving, arguing, or simply lying around half asleep with exhaustion. God alone knows where all these restless, bewildered-looking people were going, what urge made them leave their homes and rush off to unknown destinations. It was as if someone had implanted in their minds a perpetual, gnawing doubt: just suppose things are better somewhere else and I'm missing out on it! How he longed to be in the position of most of them: to have a roof over one's head, to be assured of one's daily bread, to have some kind of job, even the roughest! Sokolniki, Sokolniki—he still had a long way to go, dreaming of the down floating from your poplar trees, hoping blindly to come back to you one day! But for the moment his future was wrapped in obscurity, and the omens for the next day boded no good. You never can win all the tricks.

Long before nine o'clock Vlad was hanging around the district police headquarters, and when it opened he was first in the line at the passport desk. A little major, who looked hardly more than a boy, twirled the travel document in his brisk fingers, folded it in two, and handed it back to Vlad:

"Find yourself a job and I'll issue you with a residence permit. That's all. Next!"

Vlad could not allow himself the luxury of launching into that vicious circle: job first, then residence permit, permit first, then job; he had neither the funds nor the time. The only thing he could do was to take the first train south, where he would find it much easier to survive the winter. In order, however, to make the journey which lay ahead, Vlad needed a small stock of bread or hardtack. He had long since disposed of anything that might have had any value for sale or exchange, but still, more out of an old tramp's habit than anything else—maybe something will turn up!—he set off for the local flea market.

Ah, the bitter magic of the Russian bazaars of those days! The dominant color of gray—the gray of ex-army greatcoats and padded jackets—typified the prevailing atmosphere of poverty and misery: beggars, old men, wounded veterans selling their few pathetic belongings such as darned underpants or pairs of down-at-heel shoes. Everything imaginable was being offered for sale or barter—from bent nails to little hand-painted rugs. The competitive atmosphere of the junk market stimulated Vlad's initiative, and soon he had taken off his undershirt and was holding it out in front of him. Unfortunately, the supply of goods of this sort obviously far exceeded the demand: for a whole day he stood around offering his ragged garment, but not a single purchaser was to be found. He was just starting to get desperate, when toward evening he noticed a short, stocky old man among the crowd of peddlers, a grizzled wedge-shaped beard jutting from wrinkled face. Squatting on his haunches in front of a piece of tarpaulin, on which were spread out his modest stock— homemade fishhooks, a bunch of old keys that fitted no known locks, some wire spectacle-frames—the little old man cast occasional appraising glances at him, aimed more at his feet than at Vlad himself. For a long time they exchanged looks in this fashion, the patient hunter and his weakening prey. Vlad was the first to give in, and approached the old man hesitantly:

"Here you are, dad. It's going cheap."

The old man's lined features crumpled like a concertina:

"Don't need that bit of old trash. Got two closets-full of my own. Wouldn't take it as a free gift. Those boots of yours would suit me, though. Won't say I'll buy 'em—can't afford it—but I'll swap 'em for a pair of felt boots, lovely pair, hardly worn, real good prewar quality."

The boots, given to him at the psychiatric hospital, were his guarantee of a safe journey, a sign of his credit worthiness, a pledge of his future. "Anything but those," he protested inwardly, "anything but my boots!" but aloud he said:

"How can I manage without them?"

"Soon be winter, kid—just the time when you'll be wanting felt boots. They'll keep you snug and comfortable all winter, and by the time the warm weather comes around again, you're young and you'll have earned enough to buy yourself another pair of leather boots. It's like the gypsy who sold his fur coat: 'September now, pow, pow, pow—and then it's summer!' Except I don't suppose you can read palms, though."

"Let's have a look at those felt boots of yours." Vlad surrendered listlessly. "Maybe we can do a deal."

"They're at home. You'll have to come and fetch 'em."

"Is it far?"

"As far as a village called Krasnoarmeiskoye."

"How do we get there?"

"On a local train, of course." The old man hastily gathered up his belongings. "It's only a stone's throw from here. We'll be there by nightfall, you can sleep at my place, then in the morning you can be off and away, free as air."

This last argument caused Vlad to give in completely. As Vlad followed him to the station, the talkative old man babbled away.

"Where I live I'm warm and dry and don't even need a residence permit—everyone should be so lucky. Even keep an animal, so I always have milk—it's a goat, you see. The rooms are like a palace, so big you could hold a banquet. For years I roamed around, like you, and never knew where I was going to be from one night to the next. How I lived through it I'll never know, 'cos I'm not big and strong, as you can see. In the civil war I fought for the Reds, I fought for the Whites, and I sometimes joined the Greens, too. Then I did casual work up and down the country, worked on all the Five-Year Plan construction jobs from the Urals to the Amur. Even served as a wagon driver in the last war. After that I spent a long time in hospitals, 'cos I injured my backbone—souvenir of the war, you might say. Now, though, the Lord God has rewarded me for all my trials and tribulations. I live well, I'm my own boss, I've bread to eat and tea to drink . . ." Quickening his step he added: "Better hurry or we'll miss the eight o'clock." To get on board the evening suburban train they almost had to take it by storm, after which for at least an hour they were jostled about in the crowded, smoke-filled car. Then they got off the train, and Vlad's companion led him away into the pitch darkness. It was a mystery to Vlad how the old man, at his age, was able to find the way. Walking beside him, Vlad clung firmly to his sleeve, but even so he frequently tripped and stumbled. Now and again a random light from a window would suddenly reveal a strip of fencing or even a bit of the pavement, after which the way ahead was once again plunged into gloom.

Soon Vlad sensed that they were walking across an open space: there was a bracing chill in the air, the ground underfoot was more even, the darkness seemed to open up and grow less thick. A little later they were obviously standing in front of some vast, dark mass. Even against a background of an almost totally opaque night sky, the huge thing loomed above them in a sort of dull slate color.

"What is it?" His heart turning cold, Vlad slowed his pace. "What on earth is that monster?"

"It's him!" the old man replied with unconcealed pride. "The boss. The old man. Put there to last forever."

Only then did Vlad realize that this was the giant statue of Stalin at the start of the Volga-Don canal, familiar to him from countless newspaper pictures and newsreel films. Instinctively, Vlad's spirits fell: for years now that name had been haunting him—his schooldays, the arrest of his father, the prison camps of 503 Construction Project, the weird pavilion at Kureika—it was all connected with that name. Some horrible power of attraction emanated from those six letters fused into one word, a word which held within it far more than could have been contained inside the short, pockmarked man with a mustache whom the drunken janitor at the Kureika museum had described to him. Rather it was an incantation, a magic key, a sorcerer's "Open Sesame" to set in motion a terrible machine capable of grinding into powder anyone who dared to resist its relentless progress. A few more paces, and they were hidden under the gigantic shadow. In the darkness, Vlad's companion sighed with relief:

"We'll have the stove lit in a moment, then we can make some tea."

Grunting, the old man had to fumble with a lock for a while before a heavy door—made of metal, to judge by the clang—swung open on a black cavern that gave forth a hot fetid smell, a mixture of a pigsty and a flophouse. Even Vlad, long accustomed to every sort of odor, choked in disgust: "How come he doesn't suffocate in here?!"

After some more groping around in the dark, the old man lit a lamp, revealing to his visitor a windowless concrete box, the floor completely covered with rotting straw. An emaciated goat gazed sadly at them from the far lefthand corner. To the right of the animal a stepladder led toward higher, even darker regions.

"This is just my little farm, son," the old man reassured him, making his way to the ladder with lamp in hand. "I live there, on the upper level. The smell's a bit thick at first, but at least it's warm." He disappeared through a hole in the ceiling and invited his visitor to follow him. "Don't be afraid, she doesn't bite, just climb straight up!"

Above, in a kingdom of rags and trash, it was indeed somewhat easier to breathe, but the odd thing about the room was its strange oval shape: overhead, its hollow, arching form disappeared out of sight, while its length and breadth were disproportionately short for its height.

"Where are we?" Vlad asked nervously.

"In the boot, of course!" the old man replied casually, rummaging about among the junk. "Don't you see? We're inside Comrade Stalin's boot. This is how much the bosses trust me."

"Why? What for?"

"I'm the guard here!"

"But what on earth is there to guard? No one's going to pinch the statue, after all."

"I have to guard the storehouse across the canal, too. Lots of valuable stuff in there."

"Valuable stuff?"

"Barbed wire."

"Who wants to steal barbed wire?"

"Ah, I can see you're green as grass, kid." He emerged from the heap and threw at Vlad's feet a patched but apparently sound and wearable pair of felt boots. "Everyone steals nowadays. Why, they'd

even pinch shit if they found some—and as for that barbed wire, it's
in terrible short supply, ask anybody you like. Last year a freight
train ran off the track. Well, everybody from all the villages hereabouts came running along with buckets, scooped up the diesel oil
that leaked out and carried it home—but if you asked them what they
wanted it for, they just said as how they were going to keep it for a
rainy day and how you never know when it might come in handy
around the house." The old man watched intently as Vlad tried on
the felt boots for size. "Well, how do they feel? They don't pinch,
do they?"

The felt boots had come just at the right moment. After the stiff,
tight-fitting army boots Vlad's feet positively luxuriated in the
softness of the well-worn felt.

"What did I tell you?" the old man cackled with satisfaction.
"I'm an honest trader, I am, never sell shoddy goods. Wear 'em and
be thankful to me. What's more, I'll throw in a loaf of bread and six
rubles as an extra; I know what it's like to be roaming around without a place to go." Skillfully he made a place for his visitor among
the rags. "You can lie down and sleep there, kid."

For a long time after he had put out the lights, the old man still
went on moving about, wheezing, and telling his stories:

"This statue, brother, is something amazing, fabulous—you
couldn't describe it if you tried. They used a hundred freight cars of
metal alone, and it's got more kinds of special, cunning machinery
than a secret factory. They've even fixed up a death-ray machine in
his cap, so the birds can't shit on his head: they drop dead right out
of the sky. That's one of my perks, too. I pluck 'em and throw 'em in
the pot; they make pretty good soup, rich and fatty. Never a day
without meat for my dinner, that's me . . . Ah"—here the old man
actually groaned in the darkness—"now if I'd gotten to the top of
the heap the way Stalin has, I'd show a few people who's boss. He's
too good and kind, the old man is, just too easygoing by far . . . No,
you've got to use the big stick and weed out all the troublemakers by
the very roots!"

Next morning the old man showed Vlad out, and as he flung open
the door, said to him cheerfully in farewell:

"So long, kid. Remember what I said: you'll thank God for the
rest of your days that an old man let you have those felt boots for a
song—and with a free gift thrown in, too. Off you go now, and if you
ever pass by this way again, just drop in!"

The weather promised to be fine. Feathery clouds swirled above the frost-covered roofs; as it rose above the edge of the horizon the bright sun colored them with a pale pink tinge, and wisps of blue smoke from the chimneys floated peacefully upward in the still air. Vlad's feet felt warm and comfortable, which made the journey before him seem bearable. A man doesn't need much to be content!

When he reached the village he turned around. The huge statue towered above the canal, dwarfing everything around it by the total lack of proportion with its surroundings. Behind its back the bare steppe, parched almost to a red color, was smoking with the morning mist, and one could imagine that the statue had just walked here from over the horizon, leaving behind it a lifeless expanse, sheer emptiness, dust and ashes.

The express trains, it turned out, did not stop at the village station, so Vlad, frustrated, set out to walk along the ties of the railroad track toward the nearest junction. But the higher the sun rose and the softer the tar grew underfoot, the more uncomfortable he felt in his new footwear. His felt boots were, in fact, disintegrating before his eyes: the soles were splitting away at the toes, the uppers were flaking off and falling apart. "The old prick cheated me!" Vlad almost burst into tears. "He palmed me off with some rotten old junk from the trash heap!"

Forced to take urgent action to save the situation, Vlad turned off the track toward the first house that he happened to see. Just as he reached the front step, the door of the porch opened and a little woman, a dark head scarf down to her eyebrows, gently invited him: "Come in."

Vlad followed her through the dim porch, from whence they passed into a large but very sparsely furnished front room with a Russian stove facing the door. A large, ponderous man with a wooden leg, wearing an old army jacket over his undershirt, rose to greet the visitor:

"Come in, come in." Patting Vlad on the shoulder with a weighty palm, the man gestured to him to sit down on a bench beside the stove. "I saw you through the window, and I thought, 'Here's a visitor who wants to use the toilet—we ought to ask him in.' You must have a bite to eat—there's some potatoes left over from yesterday."

As Vlad, nervous and somewhat confused, was explaining the reason for his enforced visit, his host got up without a word, stumped over to a far corner, rummaged around a little, and returned a minute later to offer Vlad some waxed thread, a needle, and a cobbler's awl:

"There you are, better fix your boots or you won't get very far." Turning to his wife, who was standing timidly by the doorway, he added: "Let's give ourselves a bit of a treat—serve the potatoes, Manya."

When he had grown used to the room's semitwilight, Vlad glanced around him as he worked and noticed that countless children's eyes were staring brightly in his direction from every corner, from behind the stove, and even, it seemed, from underneath it. "I wonder how he managed to father so many?" Vlad thought to himself in amazement. "He's not all that old yet!"

Later, when his entire brood was seated around the table, the host said with a genial laugh: "Lord, what a lot of kids I seem to have!" He glanced lovingly round the table. "They may not all be mine, but we're all one family, and they'd go through fire and water for their old dad." Grinning, he gave them all a conspiratorial wink. "Ain't that so, kids?"

Busily gobbling their potatoes, they gazed at him with dumb adoration and loyalty, and their different-colored heads nodded excitedly, as much as to say: "He's great, our dad!" Their mother, who was tirelessly ladling out potatoes from a saucepan onto their plates, glowed with gratitude, but she remained timid and silent as though burdened with some perpetual guilt.

Unembarrassed by his wife's presence, Vlad's host told his story between mouthfuls:

"When I left home for the war, there was only one on the way, but when I came back in '44 she already had three. 'Where did you pick up all these,' I asked her, 'under a gooseberry bush?' 'Life was too hard for a woman to live alone, Vasya,' she said, 'you couldn't expect me to manage all alone.' 'Okay,' I said, 'let's have some kids of our own now—the more the merrier.' So off we went; a new one almost every year; we ruin ourselves paying for all the christening parties but we have fun, we get by, there's never much to eat but we keep each other amused and it helps to pass the time . . ."

To this day I'll never understand him, that weird but wonderful man!

Vlad felt he could not depart without leaving something in token of his gratitude, and as he walked out through the porch he surreptitiously left two three-ruble bills on top of a stack of firewood—the

298 FAREWELL FROM NOWHERE

"bonus" that the old junk dealer had thrown in with his felt boots: I'll get by somehow or other, and the kids can get something nice with it . . .

Vlad had already put quite a long stretch of the railroad track behind him, when from far away there rose and grew louder an urgent little treble voice:

"Hi, uncle! Stop . . . wait!"

Vlad turned around and froze in astonishment. Wearing an enormously outsized pair of rubber overshoes, one of the little girls was clumping toward him along the ties, a dark head scarf, obviously her mother's, flapping around her like a raven's wing. A warm lump came into Vlad's throat, he gulped and ran back toward her, picked her up, hugged her, and immediately felt the convulsive beating of the little heart.

"Hey, what's this, running out half-dressed!? You mustn't do that! You'll catch cold, you silly little thing!"

Insistently, she kept shoving the two crumpled three-ruble bills into the front of his shirt, repeating as she did so:

"Papa told me to . . . so did Mama . . . we have enough . . . Papa told me . . . Mama too . . . we have plenty . . ."

"What's your name?"

"Nastya," she said, relaxing in his arms, "Nastyushka . . ."

Well, Nastya, Nastyushka, let me write you down in my list of names to remember in my prayers!

CHAPTER 16

The sky emptied itself onto the earth in a smothering deluge. Steaming like fresh milk, the rain hung suspended almost noiselessly above the town. The heavens, it seemed, were finally and forever merged into one with the earth. Through the open doors of the baggage room, Vlad stood gazing out at the station square as it was soaked by the smoking torrent. The square was empty, except for a lone female figure standing under the checkerboard sign of a taxi stand—a bright dab of colored stuff woven into the muslin curtain of rain. For some time the woman stood motionless, enveloped in rain, looking like a flower that by some miracle had grown through the asphalt, until suddenly, as though waking up, she started briskly from the spot and plunged across the square. Vlad gasped as the fringe of black hair about her pale, biblical profile briefly flickered past him. Wondering what a girl like her was doing in this place, he immediately forgot about her. Although his memory obligingly relegated her to one of its remotest nooks, it was a long time before the emotional shock caused by that sudden thrill subsided. Ah, Lyalya, how often he will recall that day, that rain, that moment of delicious pain which seared him as he stood in the baggage room of Krasnodar Station, after several miserable, lonely years spent in prison camps, hospitals, and the Siberian taiga. On another occasion, almost a quarter of a century later, when on the street in another town he chanced to meet her again—or rather a sad facsimile of her, a shadow, a blurred copy of former glory, with a molting chignon in place of the raven-dark fringe—he would again gasp, but this time out of mawkish pity for himself and his own past: "God, oh God, how long ago, how agonizingly long ago it was!"

Now, though, having completely forgotten about her, Vlad sat down on a window ledge in the corridor of the baggage room, greedily inhaling the intoxicating smell of a bakery which was floating in his direction from behind some nearby roofs. The aroma flowed, spread, pervasively enveloped him, causing him to feel mild nausea and giddiness. Vlad was irresistibly drawn toward that enticing drug, but the soles of his felt boots, which had brought him here from Stalingrad, though hastily fortified with twine, were scarcely holding together; to go out into the rain would mean being finally reduced to walking barefoot, which did not suit him at all. His felt boots were the last outward sign of his erstwhile respectability, the sole witnesses to his status as a property-owning citizen. The rest—canvas pants, an undershirt branded with the hospital stamp, an almost useless quilted jacket, a cap that was just a shrunken, crumpled lump of cloth on top of his bare, shaven head—had long since rotted and was only held together by a miracle. With impatient longing, Vlad waited for darkness to fall. In the dark he could make his way barefoot to his cherished goal without running the risk of being arrested by the first policeman.

So slowly and imperceptibly did the daylight change its color and intensity that the darkness seemed to be growing inside Vlad himself instead of around him. The interminable day tightened itself around his throat like a noose, causing him long spasms of breathlessness. When finally the darkness did close about him, he took off his felt boots, stuck them under one arm and raced away, so hungry that he was determined, at whatever cost, to overcome all obstacles between himself and his objective. Vlad ran, flew, floated through the delicious smell of bread and the noisy hammers of success pounded in his temples. The surrounding world consisted now of nothing but that aroma and that sound . . .

His sense of smell led him to the low, white buildings of the bakery, in front of which a freshly dug trench stretched along the whole length of the street, like a line of defense which he had to take by storm. Without a moment's thought, Vlad flung himself into the assault with the fury of desperation. Three times he fell back from the very top of the far side and slithered down into a mush of wet clay before the hostile trench surrendered to him, and the grayish-white façade of the bakery, with its many windows, rose before him like the wall of a palace in one of the tales told by Scheherazade. Instantly Vlad saw what he was looking for, as one notices a woman in a faceless crowd, a lone star in a pitch-black sky, a goldfish at the bottom of an otherwise empty pool. His field of vision was narrowed momentarily to the dimensions of an open windowpane, where, on top of a pile of rejected scraps of bread, there proudly shone in all its glory a whole, plump loaf with a slight crack along the edge of its top crust. He walked, or rather he tiptoed furtively toward it, as though stalking a wild animal or an alert bird that he feared to startle by a careless rustle or crunch. He seized it quickly but noiselessly, like the magic flower in a fairy tale, and then, clutching the still-warm booty, he flew, as though weightless, into the darkness and the rain, back to the safety of the slushy trench. Many were the times after that that he was to assuage his hunger—the hunger of a day, an hour, a minute, hunger that seemed unendurable—but no subsequent occasion could compare with the stilling of his hunger that night. He did not so much eat as engulf that loaf, and it went into him in the way that a woman goes into a man—totally. When he was finally sated, and he began to perceive the world around him again—the rainstorm, the night, the wet clay underfoot—nothing seemed so terrible any longer. He felt able to cope with it all—and not only with that, but with everything else that made life worth living. And in the bright, distant, rainbow-colored prospects which arose before his mind's eye, amid the spectral groves and the castles in the air Vlad suddenly saw her, the girl with the raven-black fringe above a biblical profile, and probably for the first time in his life his heart melted with tenderness.

He pushed himself away from the slimy wall of the trench, took one light and easy jump, and he was on the top. With buoyant tread he strode back to the island of light on the station square. From his previous place by the baggage room, his whole being transformed, Vlad cheerfully studied the faces around him and tried to guess their status and occupation in this world. Now, each one of them seemed interesting and even dear to him. They milled around him, the old and the young, the dull and the lively, good-looking, ugly, alert and lethargic, the prosperous and the beggars, uniformed or civilian; they circled around him until one—sharp, wrinkled, slightly drunk—detached itself from the carrousel of faces and loomed up in front of him:

"You just out of jail?"

"Sure, I've done time." Vlad was still full of cocky good humor. "Why? Want to write it up in the newspaper?"

"Uppity." The face crumpled into a mocking look and its flabby mouth opened in a half smile, revealing a row of strong, nicotine-stained teeth. "Aren't you scared?"

"Scared of what?"

"Here in the Kuban we don't like uppity strangers. They get busted under some new law and put away."

"That happens in other parts, too."

"You're right, it does. Where are you headed?"

"Looking for a better boss than the last one."

"Found one?"

"Not yet."

"Waiting for a good job to turn up?"

"Something should come along anytime now."

"Thought so. Want to come and work for me?"

"I'm under restriction; I can't go just anywhere."

"To hell with that! Want to come?"

"Where?"

"To our kolkhoz. Work in the brick factory."

"Okay—if you're on the level." Vlad was inwardly tense: fickle fate had already held out several tempting possibilities, but all of them had collapsed, one after another, like houses of cards—on his release from prison camp, the discharge papers issued to him by the authorities were extremely restrictive. "Just be human, boss, that's all I ask . . ."

As though suddenly sobering up, the man gave him a long, sad stare, then gripped him firmly on the knee:

"I'll be human, my son." And something shifted in his metallic, creased features; something softened, as though deep within him a fire had broken out which smelted his whole being anew into a different cast. "I was doing my best to be human, son, before you were even born. In those days there was such a famine in these parts that I was stacking up our kolkhoz peasants in heaps with my own hands. And because I still tried to give them a crust to eat, I got my first spell of prison. And so it went on . . . I don't want to tell you about it, and you don't want to hear. Well, to cut a long story short,

I'm now a Party secretary not far from here, about twenty miles out of town at a village called Plastunovskaya. Six collective farms, one of them's mine, called "The Bolshevik." Take the first train. I reckon you can manage it without a ticket. Anyway, I don't have any money on me right now. Been at a Party meeting in town and I drank it all. You can spend the night here in the station, then come and see me tomorrow. Ask for Kosivtsov. Okay?"

"Thanks, boss."

Kosivtsov sighed deeply and his face took on again its previous rigid, harsh, expression. "Okay, I'm off now. I know one of the barmen here, he'll give me something for my hangover . . . See you tomorrow."

The whirlpool of faces swallowed him up, and Vlad could hardly suppress his passionate desire to follow him, in order not to lose that magic of human contact which had given such a lift to his spirits.

Vlad did catch the first local train next morning. As he stood in the corridor of the departing train and watched the last lights of the town flickering past the rain-lashed windows, he was full of new hope and bright expectation, yet somewhere deep inside him he also felt a sweet pain, a sense of loss. Loss . . . of what, of whom?

Only many years later would he realize that there is no end to such losses, but that they also enrich the heart and soul.

Don't forget me, Lyalya!

CHAPTER 17

Who are we? What are we? Whence have we come and whither are we going? Or are we really only "anchorites in this world" who have "given it nothing, taken nothing from it, added not a single idea to the sum of human thought, contributed nothing to the perfection of human reason and distorted everything which that perfection has conveyed to us?"*

When we stand at the Day of Judgment and we are asked to say why we lived and what memorial to ourselves we Russians have left behind, what shall we reply? Shall we say that for centuries we drenched our own land with rivers of blood and tears, that we ruthlessly persecuted the weak and slavishly fawned upon the strong, that time and again we subjected ourselves to the will of alien pretenders and vagrant dreamers? Or shall we tell how many lies and how much perjury burden our heart, what an infinity of sins both open and secret have besmirched our soul, or with what a multitude of evils we have clouded our reason?

No doubt we will remain silent—silent with shame and fear, with sorrow and repentance. And perhaps then, amid the general silence, one of us will step forward—a thin, gray-eyed boy dressed in cheap

* Quotation from the *Philosophical Letters* of Pyotr Chaadayev (1794–1856). (Tr.)

cotton, with straw-filled sandals cut from an old car tire on his bare feet, and with a rotting pair of felt boots under one arm. He will step forward and say:

"May I reply, All-Highest?"

The silver trumpets and the choirs will be silent, an attentive hush will fall and an impassive voice will graciously pronounce:

"Speak."

"Forgive us," the boy will say, "and absolve us in the name of Thy Son. If what we have suffered is not enough for Thee, then allow me to take their sins upon myself and alone to answer for them all."

"Do you know what lies ahead?"

"I do."

"You are not afraid?"

"If I were afraid, I would not have asked."

"Indeed! Then go . . ." And the boy will walk away in silence into the darkness, which will open out before him. His tattered sandals, stuffed with last year's straw, will leave a damp line of footmarks along his predestined route. His thin adolescent body, twisted with rickets in childhood, will shine through the holes in his cotton garments amid the slate-gray silence of Oblivion and Eternity.

He will refuse to give his rotting felt boots to those who remain behind, to those who will be forgiven, for he still has far to go and they may yet prove useful on his journey.

Perhaps, who knows, something may cause the One above to shudder, and He, moved by the suffering of His Son, may call out after the boy:

"Stop! Stop, boy!"

We know not how it comes, or when, but the most priceless gift to man from above is . . . Hope.

I am already dreaming of foreign lands, and my heart, shedding its outworn plumage, is falling, falling, falling, into the empty abyss!

Part 4

CHAPTER 1

A list of names for Vlad to remember in his prayers.

"To pray for the well-being of: Maria; Yekaterina; Alexei; Irina; Yury.

"To pray for the repose of: Fedosya; Saviely; Akulina; Alexei, soldier; Dimitry, soldier; Anna; Mikhail; baby Nina; baby Leontii; Anna; Georgii; baby Alexander; Varvara; Maria; Olga; Tikhon; Axinya; Martha; Lavrenty; Nikolai; Vasily; Ivan; Konstantin, soldier; Sergei, soldier; Lyubov; Alexander, soldier."

Notification: "Your husband Samsonov, Alexei Mikhailovich, born in the Village of Sychevka, District of Uzlovaya, Province of Tula, was reported missing believed killed while on active service in February 1942. This notification serves as entitlement to institute a request for a pension. Signed: Lieutenant-Colonel Fokin, Military Commissioner."

No, he has no objection to this version, dear Lieutenant-Colonel Fokin, especially since it gave the right, as you state, to a pension—the pension which only saved them from dying of starvation in that it was enough to keep them in matches. In reality, though, Alexei Mikhailovich Samsonov was killed—and there are living witnesses to prove it—at the very beginning of the war near Sukhinichi, when he and many others were abandoned to their fate by their officers. God forbid that his son should now wish to settle accounts on this score; he only wishes to record this fact in the interests of establishing the objective truth.

Death Certificate:

Citizeness Samsonova, Fedosya Savelievna, died on 24 October 1956. Cause of death: compression of the thoracic cage, which cause has been duly entered in the records of the Registry of Civil Status under entry Number 1627. Place of death: Moscow, Province of Moscow, Russian Socialist Federated Soviet Republic. Place of registration: Sokolniki District Office of the Registry of Civil Status of the City of Moscow.

Signed: Illegible.
           Registrar.

How many secrets lie hidden behind those smooth official turns of phrase over their illegible signatures! "Compression of the thoracic cage" sounds so much more decorous than "under the wheels of a train," but we shall never know whether it caused Fedosya Savelievna Samsonova to feel any better for it. That's just the way it goes.

As Vlad leafed through that long martyrology of lives cut short and hopes unrealized, his heart went out to that other branch of his family which was still flourishing on this earth: "How are you over there, my dears, how are you managing, and is the bread of that distant exile not too bitter?"

He could envisage them all clearly, each and every one of them; he talked first with one and then with another by telephone, but an awareness of the abyss dividing them never left him, threatening them with the oblivion that comes from habit and acceptance. "No, no, never!" Vlad would protest mentally at the thought. "Never!" But something, some worm of doubt in the innermost recess of his soul undermined that protest: "Yes, yes, yes!"

CHAPTER 2

The brick factory was a long, rectangular, thatched wooden building above a tiny lake, where a bristling stubble of cropped rushes stuck through the ice-smooth surface of the water. Two kilns under sloping tiled roofs stood below the factory at the foot of the high lakeside cliff, while all around there was nothing but the steppe, sparsely dotted with farms and Cossack villages. In the evening, when little points of light began to gleam in nearby farmhouses, the vast, resonant spaces became as vibrant as a taut bass string, and the heart was gripped by an uncanny feeling evoked by the distant past. Somewhere out there on the steppe, one felt, there galloped headlong a Don Cossack captain with the summons to revolt on his wind-chapped lips and the ends of his cowled cloak flapping behind him like wings. O Lord, see him safe! Each light in the growing darkness might be the one that was lit just for him, offering him warmth and shelter. Any sound amid the silence—the distant hoot of a locomotive, the bark of a dog, the call of a bird—might be an agreed signal to him on his way, and every star a secret guide.

At the factory Vlad found four other roving spirits, devotees of the joys of vagrancy and distant wanderings. One was Vitek Yeryomin, who had dropped out of technical school, a restless lad of about seventeen with pale-colored pupils to his eyes; then there was a dopey Ukrainian kid called Levko Savchenko, a face like a pancake strewn with huge freckles, almost a professional runaway from the plow; Vovchik, nicknamed "Melon," an orphan from the fringe of the criminal underworld; and Petrovich, a taciturn old man with a matted beard that grew almost up to his eyes, a little pewter cross on a piece of twine showing through the open neck of his extremely ancient undershirt. Such was the company.

The single hut was divided into two halves, in one of which lived Vlad and his companions, in the other the foreman Frol Parfyonich with his vast wife, who doubled as the factory cook.

"I can't face it, I'm going to work at a dairy farm or a pig farm instead," she would complain tearfully, exhausted by the insatiable greed of her clients and her fierce, dark eyes would grow moist with suffering and self-pity. "Whatever I cook for you, however much I make, you just gobble it all up like geese."

The size of their appetites, however, did not stop her from robbing them shamelessly. Every Sunday when she set off to visit her family at their farm, she would load up the little two-seater buggy until it was about to collapse under the weight of provisions from the factory storehouse—provisions that were intended to feed the brick workers. Even her husband the foreman, who had difficulty in finding room to sit among all the cans, cartons, and sacks, blushed with embarrassment all over his bony face and muttered to her:

"That's enough, that's enough, Mother, there's not exactly a famine at your folks' place." He was an "outlander"* and consequently greatly respected his wife and was even a little bit afraid of her. "Get in, now, and sit down . . ."

Having nearly starved on his long journey, Vlad really did eat enough for three, being quite unconcerned about the mental equilibrium of the thieving cook. Each new morning he felt his muscles noticeably filling out, his bones strengthening, and his skin growing taut and resilient. For the first time in a long while he felt that he was twenty years old, that life was in front of him and that his battle for a place in the sun was only just beginning. The reviving flesh required a suitable outer covering. Vlad spent almost all his spare time repairing, patching, and darning his ancient clothes, trying to adapt them, however slightly, to his new circumstances and the coming winter. An object of his special concern was the new pair of sandals cut out of old car tires that had been issued to him at the fac-

* Derogatory Cossack term for a person living in a Cossack region but not of Cossack stock. (Tr.)

tory. Clumsy though they were, they turned out to be an ideal sort of footwear for the impassable Kuban mud. Every day he changed their straw stuffing, made fasteners to keep them tightly closed and was never without his cobbler's thread for a moment. They were not so much scrap-rubber sandals as seven-league boots straight out of Grimms' fairy tales!

The bricks in the kilns had already been fired during the past summer, so the work to be done was simply to get them out of the kilns, lug them to the roadside, and there stack them in pyramids. Each morning they divided up into teams of two and set to work. Petrovich, being the fifth and odd man out, got the easy job of loading up their wheelbarrows. The tempo of the work increased slowly, but as a rule toward lunchtime it gradually turned into a competition to see who could carry the most. Getting into the spirit of the race, Vlad mentally cut himself off from the outside world. Through the salt sweat which clouded his eyes he saw nothing but the thin ribbon of planking in front of him, at the end of which stood the goal—the red blob that was the pile of bricks. As his strength grew within him, the weight carried by his wheelbarrow grew daily heavier: forty, sixty, eighty, a hundred, and finally a hundred and twenty bricks! All at one go! Arithmetic for first-graders: a hundred and twenty times two and a half—three hundred kilograms and not a gram less! His eardrums rang, and by the end of the shift his lips and eyelashes were covered in the gritty brick dust.

They pushed uphill in a line, each one with his wheelbarrow, but when the kilns were half empty the teams were obliged to split up into single units: one to load the bricks, one to cart them away. Even with this slight complication the work soon got into a steady routine again, but as the end drew near it was every man for himself. On the rare occasions when he stopped by to keep an eye on them, the foreman grinned, sighed, and grunted at them:

"Old Dobbin getting worn out with pulling uphill, eh?" His diabolical eye winked sarcastically. "Bit different from sitting around in railroad stations and catching fleas, ain't it? Ah, you greedy-guts—call yourself workers, you mother-fuckers . . . !"

During the long autumn evenings they played cards, and on Sundays they feasted, trading corn stolen from the nearby field for moonshine liquor from the farmers, thanks to the fact that the foreman and his better half were away from the factory for the day. Food to go with the liquor was literally running around under their feet: the foreman kept rabbits, which he allowed to run loose, so he never knew how many there were; this meant that Vlad and his comrades only had to entice one out into the open in order to have the wherewithal for the weekly orgy.

There is one great advantage of getting drunk when young: a young man wakes up next morning as though newborn, with a crystal-clear head and pure intentions, ready, as they say, to laugh and sing like a child. But that dread beast the hangover is slumbering somewhere inside him and one day it will awake; it will stretch out its claws and seize its prey, dragging him through all the nine circles of infernal suffering. How many times, after getting dead drunk, plunging into false chasms and soaring to deceptive heights, will he wander amid the convoluted labyrinths of delirium before reaching that invisible boundary, beyond which there is no salvation!

As a rule they drank hard, passing the bottle around just to see how quickly they could reach a state of oblivion or total liberation. Then when reality, as though stirred up by a stone thrown into it, split apart and began to ripple and shatter into fragments, the triumphant ego burst its bounds and flooded out into the open.

First to jump up was Vitek.

"Yee-ee-ow!" He pranced around the table like a lunatic. " 'On the hilltop stands a donkey, waves its ears and starts to prance.' " The eloquent pause that followed was taken up with a virtuoso display of dancing. " 'Seven drovers beat the donkey—you should see that donkey dance.' Strike up, brothers!"

And the brothers struck up, using bowls and spoons, knives, combs, the palms of their hands and the soles of their shoes—an orchestra that made up in volume for what it lacked in harmony. Vitek was, it must be said, a brilliant dancer. To the accompaniment of the makeshift instruments he bounded around the earth floor with a rhythmic drumming of his feet, his eyelids lowered in semi-oblivion:

> And slam, slam, slam, slam,
> Now the gang is having a bang—
> Ass in the air, head down, hey!
> Communism's on the way . . .

"Okay, hold it, you guys, gotta stop, I'm knocked out . . ."

"I could've done with him at Igarka," said Vlad with alcoholic enthusiasm. "We'd have shown 'em something at my concerts!"

Finally, tired of laughing and shouting, they would fall into an

exhausted silence, overcome by a dull sense of depression and maudlin self-pity. As their throats tightened in bitter spasms, this new
condition prompted its own remedy and one of them would break
into song. The others enthusiastically picked up the words:

> In the garden where I roam
> Loudly sings the nightingale:
> And I, abandoned, far from home,
> Forsaken, let me tell my tale . . .

Each one of them knew perfectly well that he was not "forsaken"
and not "abandoned," that his family had set the police searching
for him all over the Soviet Union, that he was an orphan by choice,
and that his "gravestone in a distant land" was something that lay in
a misty, conjectural future, but the sentimental enchantment of the
song had captured them, wringing from them the sweet sorrow of
drunken tears.

The foreman was obviously aware of a great deal that went on, but
he said nothing, preferring a guilty mutual dependence to a good
quarrel, which might cost both sides dearer than an uneasy peace, especially since he had long ago lost count of his rabbits and the corncobs stolen from the collective farm were no concern of his. Occasionally, though, he would break out in envious spite:

"The police may not have caught you stealing corn yet, but don't
you try and pinch any of the stuff that belongs to the factory—I
know you young punks, there's no holding you!"

But cards and booze soon palled. Once constraints were slackened,
their energies demanded adventures of greater scope and desperation. From his past experience Vlad knew that they were nearing the
point where, in such circumstances, a general brutalization would set
in, and then, by the inevitable pressure of collective involvement, he
too would be drawn into any crazy escapade they might think up.
Once more the specter of the prison camp loomed ahead of him.
Danger makes a man inventive. It was now that he found a use for
his skill, acquired in his long spells in reformatory and prison, as a
storyteller or "novelist." Vlad's memory had retained dozens of
"novels" to be told by installments, made up as he went along and
recounted by him during long, dreary evenings in the cells. It was no
great effort to refresh his memory, brush the dust off these stories
and put them to use. And Vlad plunged headlong into the task.

Ah, those "novels," cooked up during long prison nights! How complex and tortuous their intricate plots, how subtle and detailed their psychological conflicts, how strong and boldly drawn their characters! Poison and dagger, vampires and princes, noble ladies and dwarfs, transferred from story to story at the will of the narrator—all were caught up in a vertiginous pursuit of fame, riches, and love. Death was annulled by miraculous resurrections, nobility triumphed over perfidy, passion overcame all obstacles. The names alone were a thrill: Princess Margo, Count de Polignac, Zabello the robber chieftain, Zara the witch, and Charlie the pubkeeper—there are too many to remember them all now.

Vlad exulted in it. Quickly finishing their supper, the gang would settle down comfortably on their bunks to hear the latest installment of a free drug that lulled them to sleep. Vlad strained every nerve to sing his siren-like song for them, as he dreamed up ever new twists of plot embellished with the most fantastic endings. A more grateful audience he could never have found—an audience which demanded only one thing, but in that demand was inexorable: there had to be a happy ending! The author needed no asking; even the great Hans Andersen would have envied his dénouements. A happy ending, please, gentlemen, with a kiss into the camera!

Vlad, too, found himself being drawn into this game. Like a funnel, the world of illusion sucked him down into its enervating trap; words floated like soap bubbles in the darkness, lending it a deceptive atmosphere of comfort and well-being. One day, though, waking up in the morning he looked around him and saw the shabby, dirty room, the fly-blown poster on the wooden partition advertising a set of reproductions of Bryullov's pictures, his companions asleep under their fusty rags, a patch of bare steppeland outside the window, and he suddenly felt the delicious stab of a burning idea: "But why don't I write stories about all this? Why not? Surely it must be of interest to somebody?" Within him, the instinct of self-preservation still protested, craftily putting forward saving excuses, objecting that this locale was abnormal and untypical, but a spark of doubt had already caught his growing urge for self-expression and the fire that it lit was warming his heart: "Yes—I must write about this and nothing else. Everything else is just lies!"

He knew by heart, line by line in countless drafts and variants, the entire store of poetry that he kept hidden inside his straw mattress, but now Vlad could no longer bring himself to recite a single line of it. In comparison with the insight that he had suddenly acquired into his present surroundings, his doggerel about the romance of the taiga and the struggle for peace now seemed a monstrous outrage against the true nature of things. To sit for nights on end by a kerosene lamp, holding the stump of a pencil, amid the snoring oblivion of his ragged companions, after prison camps and endless casual nights spent in squalid hovels—and then from all the raging sea of language to land nothing better than a half-dead little goldfish of hollow words, worn-out clichés, and borrowed names! God, what a perversion of his gifts!

To his later regret, this state of mind did not last long. Daylight came and with it the comforting excuse: "You're not the only one; other writers have shied away from the ugly truth before now. Cleverer people than you keep their mouths shut, so there must be good reason for it." The approval of his audience also helped to bolster his belief in this rationalization.

"Good stuff," Vitek pronounced authoritatively, as though applying the official seal, when they listened to him declaim his windy, inflated verse. "Just like in the paper. You're as clever as the whole council of ministers put together, Vladka."

Levko, with typical Ukrainian sentimentality, agreed obsequiously: "It's good, very good! There was a guy in our village who made up poems. They were good, too, and they were even broadcast on the local radio."

"Why waste time talking?" To Vovchik's credit, his thinking always worked on practical lines. "Take the stuff to Krasnodar. You'll make a heap of money and we'll all have a night out on the town!"

How many times afterward was he to hear the same remarks, only slightly camouflaged with high-sounding terminology—and to how many people, by no means untalented, did they bring disaster, serving so often as excuses for treachery and bad faith.

Old Petrovich said nothing, but just went on wheezing and puttering away in his corner; no one could make out whether he disapproved of the sinful project or was really looking forward to the possibility of a free booze-up.

Vox populi, vox Dei. Petrovich didn't count; he was a cranky old man, and anyway he wasn't quite right in the head. The casual suggestion of making a poetic raid on the regional capital began to grow in Vlad's mind and soon matured into a definite decision: come what may, he would do it!

They prepared Vlad for his trip with more care than a prima

donna before a première, pooling resources on the principle of the old Russian proverb: with a thread from each house in the village, a beggar can have a piece of string. Vitek lent him his still thoroughly wearable overcoat from his days at technical school. Levko contributed his one pair (unique in the whole factory) of unpatched pants, while from his more than meager personal wardrobe "Melon" provided a fairly sound pair of shoes. Even old Petrovich was not too mean to rummage in his belongings and hand over a dirty, crumpled three-ruble bill:

"Take it, you'll never manage in town if you don't have a kopeck in your pocket. Then when you get rich you can pay me back with interest . . ."

Make sure you don't forget that day, Samsonov: 2 December 1951. The morning mist over the frostbound steppe. A cold thrill of excitement in the pit of your stomach and a whole career ahead of you. Carthage will be destroyed!

CHAPTER 3

A dry cold was chasing shoals of fiery-red fallen leaves across the asphalt. The smoke of stoves hung in layers over the roofs, wrapping the town in a floating blue haze. Through the lace-like tracery of leafless plane trees, the sky looked lowering and damp. Winter was bending tenacious autumn to its will, sweeping its last traces and relics out of every corner.

On reaching Krasnodar in the evening, Vlad spent an uncomfortable night in the station waiting room, and soon after dawn he set off to explore the town. It was empty and clean, as though it had been closed to the public for shooting a film. The rows of good, well-built houses were linked by a succession of high fences, behind which leaves fluttered noiselessly to the ground in old, well-tended gardens. Obviously the people here lived in solid comfort; they had settled in their homes with a view to permanence and had bequeathed their acquisitions from generation to generation. Everything—the ornamental shutters, the brick-paved paths, the solid metal latches of the gates—spoke of a confident awareness of durability and prosperity.

Vlad's circular meanderings gradually narrowed until they brought him to the town's center of activity—its belly, the so-called Green Market. In contrast to the barren, mean little markets of Central Russia, the local bazaar was amazing to a newcomer for its wealth of choice and lush colors, but the most striking thing about it was excess—excess in everything and everywhere. If there were watermelons, then they had to be in a mountainous pile; if grapes, then grapes by the basketful; if poultry or fish, then in great solid heaps. The abundance of the region displayed itself garishly, even arrogantly, as if to show off.

After pushing his way through the usual maelstrom—amid the familiar surroundings of buying and selling, the competitive urge for mutual gain—with the approach of nine o'clock Vlad started to make his way out: somewhere, down one of the streets leading off the marketplace other concerns and other interests awaited him.

The editorial offices of the local newspapers were accommodated in a rather gloomy, two-story, converted private house on Krasnoarmeiskaya Street, the location of each one within the building corresponding to its status in the official hierarchy—the young peoples' newspaper on the first floor, the Party newspaper on the second. Vlad pushed open the door nearest to the hallway, and found himself in a large square room densely packed with desks. Behind one of them, near the window, he noticed a hunchbacked man bent over a drawingboard. Without looking around toward the intruder, the hunchback continued to sketch something on the paper in front of him with broad, sweeping strokes.

"Er . . . good morning," said Vlad earnestly, clearing his throat and trying to be as dignified as possible. "I should like to see somebody from the arts and literature department."

Instantly the hunchback turned a piercing eye on him, and through the dim wintry light of the room, rays of sunshine seemed to sparkle, leap, and flash from his cheerful, mischievous, challenging gaze:

"Poetry, I suppose? Yes, I guessed at once—poetry. Sit down, give your feet a rest. Gogin will be here soon and he'll take a look at your poems." He turned full-face toward the visitor, grinning sarcastically: "He's a *great* expert!" The narrow, finely-chiseled features with an aquiline nose quivered with good humor. "Belinsky's nothing to him!"

Essman, Essman, unforgettable Boris Essman! If he had known then how much he was fated to drink with you, how long you were to live together under one roof in your tiny little garret with the skylight in the ceiling on Ordzhonikidze Street, how many hours he and you were to talk together! Ahead of you were two years of encounters and partings, laughter and tears, quarrels and reconciliations—and then your death, when, coming out of a bar, you fell face down on the asphalt with a heart attack and a soundless cry on your bluish lips.

Vlad wanted to reply to the hunchback, to keep the talk going, and perhaps to conduct a preliminary reconnaissance by means of a carefully steered conversation, but his opening words died in his throat. The door slammed, he turned around, and while he did not exactly recognize her—he would have needed more time for that—his whole being sensed her. The pale, matt features beneath the pitch-black fringe, the sharp toss of her head upward and sideways at the same time were indelibly imprinted on his memory from that rainy day at the station. Yes, Lyalya—once seen, never forgotten.

The rest happened as though in a dream. The woman went out into an adjoining room, came back in, spread some papers out on her desk, stared absent-mindedly past Vlad and then got up and went out again. All this time he was in a cold sweat and a hot haze was floating in front of his eyes: "Who is she, what does she do here, what's her name?"

Gogin appeared, a flabby, owlish little man wearing a blue, semimilitary tunic thickly sprinkled with dandruff. The hunchback introduced them, whereupon Gogin led Vlad into his office and began examining his poems; after much humming and hawing, he wrinkled his nose in distaste and said abruptly in a lisping voice:

"Not much imagery . . . no, not enough imagery . . . you lack experience of life . . . got to work on your language, too . . . Read Mayakovsky . . . and Pushkin. We can't publish this stuff . . . Reads too much like prose. Come back later and bring some more. We'll read it. Goodbye."

Of all this waffle, the only thing that penetrated Vlad's distracted consciousness was the verdict: no good. This, however, was enough to make the floorboards tilt and swim beneath him. Sitting with his back to the door he somehow managed to convince himself at that moment that his failure, his shame and defeat were happening before her eyes, in her presence, and because of this he was ready to sink through the floor, dissolve into thin air, vanish, evaporate, cease to exist. As he walked past her on his way out, he discovered for the first time in his life that the ground really can burn the soles of one's feet.

Down the steps, along the street, past houses and fences, through the December wind he was borne along by a despair which would not let him stop or think. I can't! I can't! I don't want to! I don't want to do anything! Drop it, forget it, throw it all away!

Later, Vlad never did manage to discover why he nevertheless stopped and drew breath just when a shabby signboard above an unprepossessing doorway came into his field of vision: "Krasnodar Regional Book and Magazine Publishers." Fate, destiny, chance? Call it what you like—it may equally have been one or the other, or all three—but the fact that he stopped to catch his breath in front of that sign was to have decisive consequences. It was all or nothing.

Having climbed to the second floor and walked along an unheated gallery, he found himself in front of wide-open double doors, beyond which stretched some premises which looked suspiciously like a warehouse converted into offices: windows with external bars, a concrete floor, and a ventilation duct along the cornice. The desks, pushed one up against another like goods awaiting dispatch, only increased this resemblance. Here, to judge by the accessories on the desks, was the entire staff of the publishing house, from the editorial director down to and including the bookkeeper. An elderly typist sitting almost right beside the door, wearing a pince-nez and looking like some *grande dame* in an old-fashioned photograph, nodded haughtily toward the far end of the room without even waiting to hear what the visitor had to say:

"Over there, please."

Following her glance, Vlad met the eyes of a fat, generously built man, who was staring at him from a desk in the farthest righthand corner of the room. Puffing at a pipe, the fat man smiled at him wearily and guiltily, as though apologizing in advance for a possible rejection.

"I've written some poetry." Vlad sat down on the silently proffered chair. "Would you mind looking at it?"

"That's why we're sitting here, dear boy, that's what we're here for." The fat man pushed away a large manuscript, and leaned confidentially toward Vlad.

"The trouble is"—reaching into his pocket, he realized only now that in the heat of the moment he had left his sheets of poetry at the newspaper office—"I seem to have . . . lost them. No, I forgot them." At once, as though plunging headfirst into the deep end, he decided that the situation could not get any worse: "Can I recite them aloud?"

"Oh, really!" The fat man held up a pudgy hand in protest. "I can't take it in by ear. Literature is a sensitive business, you know. The eye is essential. Come again another time . . ."

By now, though, Vlad was not to be fobbed off so easily. Head down, he raced for the precipice and no reasonable objections could stop him.

"I'll only recite one or two," he said, vowing to stick it out to the death if need be. "Please let me!"

"All right, if it's really only one or two," the fat man sighed resignedly, giving in to Vlad's persistence. "Go ahead, then." Even today Vlad can reel off those same pieces of doggerel, but the memory is too painful. On that winter's morning, however, like a wood grouse giving its mating call he was deaf to all else: intoxicated by every line of his verse, he spouted them under the crossfire of nearly two dozen eyes staring at him. "Lyre," of course, rhymed with "fear," "battle" rhymed with "bottle" and "believe" with "leaf," and the whole lot was dedicated to Nazym Khikmet, the temporary favorite of capricious fate, the idol of widowed lady editors and balding, would-be bards. Burning his bridges behind him, Vlad pressed on, and the specter of ultimate failure gave him courage—the courage of an escaping prisoner.

Secretly Vlad hoped for success, believed in his luck—anybody risking his all on one throw must have a store of hope somewhere in reserve—but even so the turn of events that followed his recital came as a complete surprise: he was applauded! Yes, with slightly embarrassed smiles the office workers actually gave him a subdued but friendly round of applause. It was victory—his first victory in a new and alluring field. Vlad was now ready to bless even the disastrous Gogin of the local newspaper, who had unwittingly paved the way to his triumph. Oh, but if only *she* had seen him at that moment: he could have wished for nothing more!

"Splendid, dear boy, splendid!" Deeply moved, the fat man actually came out from behind his desk and stretched out his hand. "My name's Vasily Popov. I really work in the prose section, but it's part of my job to keep in touch with poetry, so to speak. Sit down in my place, take some paper, write down everything you've just recited and we'll see if we can print it in our next anthology . . . Take a seat!"

Vlad literally bathed in the smiles and excited whispering. To this dizzying accompaniment he wrote out his poems, gratefully took his leave and walked away; even on the street the verses still resounded in his head, fluttering around him like radiant, seraphic wings.

Moral for beginners: knock at every door, and one of them will open . . .

He positively flew to the railroad station, his feet not touching the ground. The town no longer seemed so grim and forbidding; on the contrary, the houses, the fences, and the trees behind them now seemed positively welcoming. The wisps of blue smoke floating over the clean, tidy streets gave them an air of kindliness and comfort, the fiery-red leaves on the asphalt now crackled deliciously, the prospects before him were bathed in all the colors of the rainbow.

The station had just come into sight at the end of the street when on a corner, outside a wine bar, his path was blocked by the hunchback from the newspaper office:

"Ha ha! Whom do I see?" Already noticeably merry, he was shaking with good-natured laughter and clutching the sleeve of a tall young man on crutches, with a black forelock above the face of a handsome bandit and his empty right trouser-leg pinned up to his waist. "Well, what is it—thumbs up or thumbs down? I hear you had no luck at our place, but what about other ports of call? I sense a certain animation, so does that mean you struck oil somewhere? Where? Upstairs at our place? Or at the publishers? Okay, we'll hear all about that later. Allow me to introduce the financial wizard of the publishing house—Seryozha. He is a connoisseur of free drinks and good talk—remember that for future reference. And this, Seryozha, is another new victim for you . . . Sorry, I didn't catch your name . . . and how much ready cash do you possess? I'm Boris Essman, artist."

When the brief introductions were over Vlad extracted from his pocket Petrovich's three-ruble bill, Seryozha gloomily chipped in with the same amount, and Essman added ten rubles, remarking briskly:

"Enough for a glass apiece and even a snack to go with it. Follow me, musketeers—John the tavernkeeper awaits us!"

In between toasts, Vlad regaled his companions with the epic tale of his publishing debut, which aroused their unfeigned enthusiasm mingled with admiration. On the strength of it Essman held a whispered conversation with the bartender, placed another bottle on the table and made a speech suitable to the occasion:

"Ladies and gentlemen! Today, 2 December 1951, the light of a new, rising star was first seen to gleam in the firmament of Russian literature. The great poet Vlad Samsonov has set out, cudgel in hand, on the rocky road to literary fame! Allow me to propose a toast . . . and so on and so forth." With one gulp he downed his drink and shook his curly head, almost suffocating with uncontrollable laughter. "He's a smart guy is Vasya Popov, he'll make some useful political capital out of this now. And how! After all, he has found, cherished, and fostered a bard of the people, you might say, a Homer of the collective farm taken straight from the plow . . ."

The outcome was, as always on such occasions, that they managed to get well and truly drunk: on the way they quarreled, made it up, quarreled again, but it all ended with them swearing an oath of eternal friendship. It was late evening when Vlad, noisily escorted by his new friends, reached the station; here Essman tearfully begged the conductor of the local train not to lose his best friend, the conscience of the nation, the treasure of world literature.

The hunchback's emotional, tear-stained face haunted Vlad's alcoholic dreams all the way back to Plastunovskaya.

CHAPTER 4

Life at the brick factory went on its usual way. After his successful trip to Krasnodar, Vlad's authority was visibly strengthened. His companions hung on his every word, always hungering for him to give them an order or utter some revelation, ready at his slightest sign to go through fire and water. Through him these boys had suddenly been made aware that they too were part of a larger world, from which they felt they had hitherto been unjustly excluded. The conviction that each of them might have some talent, and might also, when the moment came, win himself a place in the sun, transformed them: they grew bolder, became more self-assured, physically less awkward and wooden.

"Ah," said Vitek, stretching reflectively, "with these legs of mine it's time I joined the Red Banner Dance Troupe. All I do here is get sunburned and screw that old woman. I'm getting in really bad shape . . ."

The almost unnatural liaison that had developed between Vitek and the foreman's wife was enough to perplex anyone. No one even noticed how and when the forty-year-old peasant woman had managed to train him, still almost a boy, to satisfy her needs. Vlad could not help smiling whenever he tried to imagine them in bed together —the rather masculine Cossack woman with more than a hint of a mustache on her upper lip, and Vitek, the undersized child of the wartime blockade, the runt from Leningrad with his pimply, spotty face. He obviously found the relationship a strain, but it was more than he could do to refuse her services: the temptation of extra food proved stronger than his distaste for her. Axinya, the woman in question, could not take her eyes off him; in her efforts to please him, she secretly fed him with titbits out of sight of her husband and the other workers in the brick factory. In fact, the foreman guessed that something was up, but the only sign he gave of it was to be more often drunk when he appeared at the factory.

There is no saying how long this might have gone on, had not Vitek disappeared after one of the usual Saturday night booze-ups, taking with him all twelve hundred rubles of the foreman's savings. For the rest of the factory's inhabitants, the whole business threatened to take a very nasty turn: in such cases the Cossacks are swift to exact revenge. At a general council it was decided to fetch the foreman from his wife's farm as quickly as possible, so as to establish their innocence. Levko was sent off, and within an hour the foreman's buggy was back at the factory.

"Well, my fine-feathered friends"—he gave off a strong reek of moonshine liquor—"so you've been shitting on your own doorstep, have you? Now you'd better find him for me, otherwise you'll have only yourselves to blame for the consequences. We'll split up into pairs, two of us will go off to the station at Plastunovskaya and two to Dinskaya. He can't have gone far, so he must be skulking around at one or the other. Okay, get going! No sense in hanging around here doing nothing."

Across the steppe, occasional gleams of light from farmhouses shone through the frosty night. Seated alongside the foreman in his buggy, Vlad could already sense that something terrible was fated to happen that night, of which he was bound to be, if not a participant, then a witness. Nagged by a feeling of impending horror, he could at last restrain himself no longer and said:

"Let him go, Parfyonich, he's only a young boy. We're all human and we're all God's creatures."

"And God will be his judge." The foreman's voice faltered. "I don't mind about the money, kid. I've got another score to settle with him."

"Don't do it, Parfyonich. Whatever he did, he's a living soul. What's done is done, and it'll cost you dear if you destroy another human being just for that."

"Why are you so soft on him, kid?"

"If you'd lived my life, Parfyonich, you'd be a bit easier on him too."

"And how do you know what *my* life was like? Were you with me in those German POW camps? Were you felling lumber alongside me at Kolyma, or squashing lice in those filthy prison huts? That's the way it is, kid—life's been hell for every one of us, and that includes me."

"Sorry, I didn't know. But I still feel bad about that boy. He's so young, he can't even wipe the snot off his nose."

"Okay," the foreman said grimly, "we'll see about it when we get there. He'll have another sort of snot to wipe off his nose when I've finished with him, though—it'll be red . . ."

Dry and frosty, the night rushed toward them, and as he stared into its immeasurable vastness Vlad sighed to himself: "Why can't people live together in peace? There's space enough for us all, why do we have to squabble and fight each other?" And then he thought: "So many people on this earth, and almost every one of them has some riddle, some enigma hidden within them—and what a riddle!"

They drove through the village without stopping, and when the lights of the station showed in the distance, Vlad's heart began to ache again. Fear of the inevitable seemed to make him shrivel. "Let's just hope to God he's not there," Vlad prayed to himself. "Let's hope he's had the sense to go to Dinskaya! At least it will be our guys who find him there, they'll just give him a token punch-up and let him go."

At the station the foreman pulled the buggy up sharply, tied the horse to the hitching post and said as grimly as before:

"Okay, you wait here, since you're so softhearted. There's no guts in you young slobs when it comes to the crunch. I'll have to rattle that young bastard's teeth myself."

Vlad hoped and prayed that Vitek would not be there; after all, only an absolute fool would come here after such a theft, but Vitek apparently hoped that the foreman would not come back until morning and the others would not catch him, or that if they did catch him they wouldn't hand him over. But for them to have acted with such chivalry was tantamount to signing their own death warrant: the men from the local Cossack village would have first mutilated them and then beaten them to death. The boys had no alternative.

Now as he sat in the buggy, Vlad listened intently for the slightest sound coming from the station: a door slamming, occasional voices, the noise of the buzzer in the dispatcher's office. He was just beginning to feel that all might be well, when the darkness was rent by a piercing, childlike shriek. It was Vitek, screaming with a sound that was almost inhuman. From the noises that Vlad could hear, Vitek was being dragged outside and beaten up at the edge of the nearby wood. Suddenly the foreman emerged from the darkness, leaped up on the seat, and gasped hoarsely:

"Let's go!" When they were already on the way, he added: "I didn't touch him. Those are the Cossacks beating him up. I didn't do what I came to do—I just took back the money."

Vlad threw down the reins:

"I'm going back, otherwise I'll never forgive myself for the rest of my life." And he jumped down. "I can't help it, Parfyonich—if I let them do it, his blood will be on my hands."

"You fool, they'll finish you off as well!"

"It's no good, Parfyonich—let them kill me too, I can't just stand aside."

"Damn you, you soft slob, get back up here: you're going back there with me, otherwise they'll break your neck along with his. What the hell makes you so obstinate?"

When they returned, a bunch of men were gathered around Vitek, who was not even groaning any longer but simply gulping convulsively. The foreman pushed his way through the group of Cossacks and said quietly:

"Okay, boys. Leave him alone now, he's only a kid, after all."

One of the men barked angrily from the darkness:

"Gone soft, moskal?* We oughta string up all you moskals from one tree."

"You know me, Cossacks. I've lived here among you all my life and I've never done you wrong. You've blown off steam, so let him be. He's my responsibility now. He'll be put to bed back at the factory."

"All you moskals are made of mush. Here, take your bricklayer."

Together the foreman and Vlad laid the fragile, apparently boneless body in the buggy and set off, leading the horse by the reins. After a long, uncomfortable silence, the foreman said to Vlad:

* Moskal (derived from Moskva = Moscow) is a contemptuous, derogatory Cossack term for any Russian who is not an ethnic Cossack. (Tr.)

"I don't know where people like you spring from—maybe it's your kind that keeps the world together, otherwise we'd all have torn each other to pieces long ago. You shouldn't be working at my factory. I'll talk to the chairman tomorrow, and he can find you a more worthwhile job."

They walked the rest of the way to the factory without speaking. There was simply nothing more to be said about the events of that night.

CHAPTER 5

The dirty white snow outside the window filled the room with a dismal twilight. In the school for tractor drivers, whither Vlad had been transferred at the foreman's request, he stuck out like a sore thumb. The other students, hefty and warmly dressed peasant lads, looked at him askance, avoided him and hardly spoke to him. He lived in the bunkhouse on a pig farm, where he was also treated with suspicion, the attitude of the Cossack villagers being that he was a tolerated though unwanted interloper. The local inhabitants had no love for outsiders, especially if they came from Russia, and automatically regarded them as enemies.

From morning until late afternoon Vlad listened to a thick-tongued instructor lecturing on carburetors, pistons, and oil feeds. The instructor, too, looked on him with some disdain, as though Vlad were the mangy sheep in this rosy-cheeked flock of young Cossacks.

The spring of that year was notably damp, with chill winds blowing, and Vlad in his threadbare jacket was cold even in class. He now had to mend his rubber shoes almost daily, but in spite of that they still leaked, so that Vlad never had dry feet. As he gazed out of the window at the damp, gray spring weather his future looked immeasurably joyless. While the instructor was mumbling away about the chain-drive system, Vlad was wondering what he was going to do next, how he was to keep body and soul together.

It was at that very moment that there came a turning point in Vlad's destiny, after which his life was launched upon a dizzy, spiraling race in pursuit of the specter, the fata morgana, the mirage of success and recognition. At first Vlad did not even realize what had happened, but a presentiment, a hint of forthcoming events induced in him a sudden, tremulous glow of anticipation as a new Pobieda car stopped outside the window, and a minute later three men marched noisily into the classroom. The first was known to everybody in those parts who was not totally blind: Berezhnoi, secretary of the District Committee of the Party. The other two were among the dozen-odd leading figures in the locality—Sivak, the chairman of the collective farm, and his Party organizer, Vlad's protector, Kosivtsov. The class froze into silence, while the instructor took up a pose and rolled his eyes in a display of thrilled expectation.

Everything about Berezhnoi—his green uniform à la Stalin, his striking features that seemed just about to be perpetuated in a stone monument, his fearsome glance—expressed power and the habit of command. With a haughty eye he glanced around the classroom and barked abruptly:

"Which of you is Samsonov?"

Vlad stood up, trying to control his nerves and guessing that the district Party secretary had not paid a visit to the tractor school just to pass the time of day.

"I am . . ."

Never in his life, before or afterward, did Vlad ever experience a look of such fastidious contempt. Having obviously decided to wither Vlad with a glance, Berezhnoi spat out with equal brusqueness:

"So you're the writer! Right, follow me."

As Vlad took his seat in the car, Kosivtsov secretly gave him a friendly wink, as if to say: "Don't be scared!"

Berezhnoi gave an order:

"To the clothing store!"

The servility of the sales people surpassed all the bounds of politeness. They gazed in doglike devotion at the distinguished visitor, as though ready to do the impossible.

"Suit, underwear, shirt," he ordered through clenched teeth, staring over their heads. "Overcoat, shoes—no, better make it boots. Send the bill to the District Committee." Then turning to his retinue: "Now give him a bath!"

At the public bathhouse Vlad was scrubbed by the manager himself, after which he was driven to have his photograph taken and then to the police station, where his out-of-date identity card was exchanged for a new one. After that, in a private room in the local teahouse, the First Secretary deigned to engage him in conversation:

"Now, Samsonov, the District Committee is showing great confidence in you: we're sending you to the regional writers' conference. So see that you don't let us down and don't make a fool of yourself. When you return we'll find you a job on the cultural side. Off you go now to the local Party committee office and get yourself a travel warrant. I've given the order. The collective farm will advance you a little pocket money. That's all. I still have to go to the Machine Tractor Station. The others will tell you everything else you need to know. Goodbye . . ."

And with that Berezhnoi vanished as suddenly as he had appeared. Sivak briefly explained the situation to Vlad. A telegram had come from the regional branch of the Writers' Union with orders to send the young poet from their collective farm to the conference.

"Well," Sivak went on, "we at the farm office racked our brains for a long time wondering who that could be. Luckily the foreman of the brick factory realized it must mean you. We've already found a job for you—we badly need an organizer at the village's House of Culture. We'll pay you on a basis of forty-five workdays, and you'll be given board and lodging at the farm's guesthouse. Now go and get your things ready, the conference starts tomorrow . . ."

As they were saying goodbye, Kosivtsov took him aside, put his arm around Vlad's shoulder and said:

"I guess I made the right choice when I picked you, kid. Now your future's in your own hands. Make sure you don't do anything stupid, because if you fall on your face one more time, you won't get up again. Come and see me when you get back and we'll have a chat . . . Well, so long!"

How happy, how inspired he felt at that moment! If only Vlad had known then what a heavy, almost unbearable cross he was taking up! Yet now, when fate has made that all too clear to him, if he were to live his life over again he would not exchange it for any other, even with the knowledge of all its tribulations.

He went to Krasnodar full of hopes and expectations. Practically

everything on the journey delighted him—the railroad car, the other
passengers, the steppe outside the window. This sudden, rapid transformation in his life seemed to foretell something even more
significant that lay ahead. Sitting alongside him in the compartment
was a glum, half-drunken little man wearing a shabby overcoat, who
now and again took a pull at a bottle that was sticking out of his
pocket. After several nips, he said to Vlad:

"Well, son, I suppose you don't approve? Your turn will come,
sure as fate. I used to work here on the local newspaper. They fired
me, so now I'm looking for another job. You don't know what it's
like in our trade: if you don't tell lies, you don't survive. As soon as
you tell the truth, they hit you over the head with Article 47. So here
I am, bumming around the country. It's high time I came to my
senses and started turning out the same sort of junk that everyone
else writes, but I just don't seem able to do it. Last piece I did was a
feature exposing the manager of a grain elevator, and he turns out to
be a member of the governing board of the paper. So yesterday they
sacked me and I'm on the move again. Maybe something will turn up
in Stavropol . . ."

At the time, in his puppyish excitement, Vlad did not believe the
little man, reckoning that he had been fired for drunkenness, but
later, after losing his own job on a newspaper for exactly the same
reason, he had cause to remember him.

The people in Krasnodar made a great fuss of him, vying with one
another to show him off to a succession of officials, to whom they introduced him loudly and brashly:

"This is the peasant poet from a collective farm! Be kind to him
and you can commission a poem to order, all about life on the Soviet
farm."

Vlad was intoxicated by it all, never suspecting that he was simply
being made use of as eyewash for the Party bosses, who urgently
needed to be able to prove in their reports and speeches that they
were fostering genuine talent from among the peasantry.

When Essman met him, the artist chuckled patronizingly:

"Ah, the untaught genius himself! Greetings, greetings! Take care,
or they'll kill you with kindness, and even then you won't escape.
You'll do much better to split a bottle of Kuban wine with me."

The thrill of his success made Vlad generous. He treated Essman
unstintingly to drinks, ordering glass after glass, and as the artist
quickly grew drunk he said loudly:

"Ah, my boy, so you're longing to become the Djambul* of the Kuban, are you? A real poet would be sickened at being labeled a 'peasant poet'! Do you know what a real poet is? 'Had I but known when I began, The fate that is a poet's lot, That for his verse they'll hunt a man, Put him to death and let him rot.' Now there speaks a real poet! Vladik, Vladik—how can I explain that if you go the way you're going now you'll find nothing at the end of the road except disaster, shame, and oblivion? But right now you're like the wood grouse in the mating season—you can't hear a thing. Have another drink!"

Indeed, Vlad did not hear him, taking Essman's remarks as nothing but the usual alcoholic drivel. As he was dragged from one tedious official reception to another, it was as if he were attending the first funeral wake of his lifetime. Then something happened which wiped out the rest of the world for Vlad, and even the thrill of success and recognition retreated into the background. He met her. She was covering the conference for the young people's newspaper. From that moment onward, the words that were showered on him from the rostrum lost all significance: Vlad could see only her and think only of her. She actually came up to him to ask for a short interview. Gulping for breath, Vlad mumbled something or other, which he instantly forgot, while she, unaware of the state he was in, put questions to him and made notes; then as she said goodbye she briskly introduced herself:

"My name's Lyalya Tvorogova. Stop by at the office and sign the proofs of your interview. It's the rule."

At the newspaper office she behaved toward him with the same directness and brisk efficiency as before, softening her manner a little only as he was leaving:

"Have you had supper yet? We have a good canteen here in the building."

He felt dizzy. To sit near her, to see her close to himself—what more could he ask for?

At table she asked him about his life, about the work he did on the collective farm, and he felt justified in saying that he was in charge of the farm's House of Culture. Later, when Vlad escorted Lyalya home, they spent a long time walking around her house while he talked and talked and talked. That evening he told her absolutely

* Djambul Djabayev (1846–1945), the national bard of Kazakhstan is regarded in the Soviet Union as the prototype of self-taught poetic genius. (Tr.)

everything, the whole truth about himself, and when the time came to say goodbye she now looked at him with unconcealed interest:

"All that's behind you now, Vladik." She gently stroked his arm. "I think you should succeed in everything you choose to do. I would love it if you'd come and see me whenever you're in town . . ."

Walking to the station, Vlad almost sang aloud—perhaps he really did sing, but he was so excited that nothing of those moments remained in his memory. Life seemed full of meaning and all the past was simply a dream—a bad dream, but prophetic.

Who could know then, who might have supposed that the path which began for him at that obscure Cossack village, and which was to lead the hero by tortuous ways through the intricate labyrinth of two decades, across the Caucasus, across Central Asia and back to the place of his birth at Sokolniki, would eventually lead abroad to a little town near Paris, whence it would summon him again into darkness, night and uncertainty?

But on that distant February day, gasping with excitement, Vlad saw his future as uncomplicated and cloudless, like a child in front of a Christmas tree. In the late afternoon twilight the surrounding steppeland seemed even more transparent and resonant than usual. Lined with ridges of snow, the cooling fields exhaled a faint, pale lilac-colored mist, in which the lights of the nearby farms winked and gleamed enchantingly. Vlad's lungs swelled with the resilient air, and the evening star shone ahead of him. Star of the fields, star of his homeland.

If only he had known that evening how rough was the road he was about to tread and that within twenty-odd years the Star of the Fields would become for him the Star called Wormwood.

CHAPTER 6

The old agronomist from whom Vlad took over the charge of running the House of Culture was clearly aggrieved, and vented his ill humor on him:

"It seems we're to have our own writer on the payroll. Any minute now we'll find ourselves being written up in some history book, I suppose."

Vlad tried not to get drawn into an argument with him, as he appreciated that the old man had good reason to feel offended in the circumstances: here was some young Johnny-come-lately arriving to rob him of what was a lucrative sinecure. Vlad tried to bring out the funny side of it, laughed politely and even told a few suitable jokes, but it was not easy to mollify the old man; his offended feelings were literally boiling inside him and now and again they would bubble over the top:

"So we're such millionaires that we can't manage without our own writer. It's all eyewash. As if we'd produced a homegrown Pushkin —what a joke! Of course the fact that this Pushkin doesn't know buckwheat from oats is unimportant. Nowadays there are plenty of collective-farm chairmen who can't tell a pig from a pumpkin either, but they go around giving orders all the same."

They completed the handover, though hardly on amicable terms. Vlad, however, was not particularly worried about sparing the old man's feelings. For the first time in his life he had a place, even though it was an official one, where he could read and write as much as he liked and on whatever subject he liked, in total solitude and without being disturbed. He was not exactly plagued by visitors: the peasants were well able to plow and sow without his help, the place was kept up more for show than for educational purposes. Admittedly the building was used once a week on Saturdays for political instruction lectures, but people came to these unwillingly and only because the sessions were compulsory.

This verbal farce was acted out by a tally clerk from the Tractor Brigade, Nikolai Gorobets. In tortured, mispronounced Russian he hastily reeled off to his listeners extracts from the columns of the local newspapers, after which lecturer and students departed, with feelings of mutual satisfaction. At first Vlad tried to help him by marking the stress on the correct syllables, but soon he stopped bothering, and even derived secret enjoyment from some of the lecturer's more crass mistakes.

The only innovation which Vlad permitted himself was to start building up the library, for which purpose the farm management was fortunately generous with its funds. They harnessed a horse to an old carriage for him, and he set off on a book-hunting expedition to the nearest town, where he was greeted as a welcome customer by the local bookstore: his purchases were infrequent but large, and every visit from Vlad meant that the bookstore manager fulfilled his monthly sales target.

It was these books which started it all. Vlad suddenly noticed that for the first time he was starting to get visitors, mostly schoolgirls. They would come in, shuffle their feet in embarrassment, then mumble, blushing:

"I'd like to join the library . . ."

They returned their books with exemplary punctuality, but, as Vlad observed at once, unread. Conspicuous among them was a short, plump creature, a typical Cossack girl with fat cheeks and sharp brown eyes. After school she would sit for hours in his library bent over a book or a magazine, but Vlad could see quite well that her glance was merely sliding absent-mindedly over the pages while her mind was occupied with something quite different. At first Vlad paid little attention to her. In the almost intolerable tedium of village life people would naturally be drawn to a lighted building where a newcomer was to be found—and not only a newcomer but a poet, who to these people was a strange, exotic creature. But youth asserted itself, and before long he was casting surreptitious glances at her, feeling a reciprocal attraction. Being a stranger, the Cossack tabu on relations with "outlanders" had a sobering effect on Vlad, and this silent courtship might have gone on forever, had she herself not made a direct approach to him out of the darkness late one evening. She came up and said in a matter-of-fact voice:

"Don't be afraid, Vladik, I won't tell anyone . . ."

Lyalya, Lyalya, forgive me—you were so high and unattainable for me and I was so weak and defenseless against the demands of the flesh that I could not resist the temptation, and, as the saying goes, I fell. I fell, cursing myself for my weakness. The only thing I can say in mitigation is that I have paid dearly for that fall. Over many long, painful years I have paid for that moment of seduction, and the paying of that debt, like a curse, is still with me to this day.

In a Cossack village, though, nothing ever goes unnoticed; soon the whole of Plastunovskaya knew about their affair, which was regarded as a forbidden liaison. It was not in itself a particularly heinous violation of the established rules: young people in those parts regularly lived together before getting married; what was really scandalous, however, was for a pure-blooded Cossack girl to live in sin with someone who was not only a no-account moskal but an ex-jailbird to boot. The girl's mother, normally a mild and good-natured woman, was so caught up in the general indignation that after a few days she came bursting in upon him at the library uttering threats and lamentations:

"Whatever have you done to us, you young scoundrel!" She dabbed at her dry eyes with the corners of her head scarf. "You should be ashamed of yourself, ruining a pure young girl, shaming her in front of all the village—and her still only in tenth grade! Why, I was ready to do away with myself from shame, only I've got two more to care for! Didn't you ever think you should have spared a poor girl who's still only a child?" She stood for a long time beside his desk, swearing at him up hill and down dale, then ended plaintively and almost peaceably by saying "You can get married if you like . . ."

To get married was easier said than done. His three-month passport had long since expired, and they were in no hurry to give him a new one, obviously fearing that given a valid passport he would not stay in the village. The thought of losing the celebrity, whom they had found by happy chance in their midst and to whom they would proudly refer in their periodic reports, was more than the local leadership could bear. Vlad's position was also complicated by the fact that in the farm guesthouse he was now living from hand to mouth: as a mark of solidarity with the rest of the villagers, the manageress was refusing to feed him, and there was no question of his moving out of the guesthouse to live in a cottage as a lodger. The boycott was enforced by the method of collective responsibility.

Seeing no way out of the situation, Vlad fled for help to Kosivtsov, who listened to him, grunted understandingly, pouted with helpless exasperation and sighed:

"Ah, you young people—get yourselves in a mess and then come yelling for help! I've heard about your trouble, and I've also heard that her mother's kicking her out of the house. Believe me, brother, the village grapevine spreads news faster than a priority telegram. Obviously you've no hope of renting a room. No one in the village would give you one—that's the way people are here." The Party organizer stroked his pointed chin thoughtfully. "Okay, on my responsibility you can move into the storeroom at the House of Culture for the time being, then we'll think up something better. Off you go . . ."

Their joint possessions—a sack of flour given to him as an advance in lieu of salary, and a little bundle containing her few clothes—barely took up half the space at the back of the buggy in which they drove through the village to their first home. Hundreds of eyes, staring out of windows and gateways, paved the way for them with hostility and malicious glee at their plight. The dust of that village street has penetrated his inmost being to leave an ineradicable mark of humiliation and insult. This, no doubt, was exactly how prisoners of war must have felt when they were made to file through the streets of an enemy town.

It is too difficult, and anyway pointless now, to try and judge who was right and who was to blame in undertaking their aimless and unplanned spell of cohabitation, the sole result of which was a daughter, now a twenty-year-old girl, a strange rootless creature with no particular bent or talent; but looking back now on the past, he is prepared to forgive you everything for the way you endured that drive through the village, and to ask your forgiveness.

Thus began their life together, which was so short and so bitter that it would have been better had it never taken place. Their entire stock of food—one sack of flour—melted before their eyes, which was not surprising, since in the brief intervals between working and making love they devoured enormous quantities of dumplings, with the insatiable greed of hungry youth. Dumplings, dumplings, and more dumplings! Those lumps of flour, boiled in water with practically no seasoning, seemed to him then the most delicious meal on earth, the food of the gods, beggars' ambrosia. And when his unlegalized mother-in-law secretly brought them a bottle or two of sunflower-seed oil with an onion as a bonus, the simple dish gave off the aura and aroma of a veritable Belshazzar's feast.

A modest addition to their meager rations was also provided by some of the exhibits from the agricultural museum that formed part of the House of Culture. More and more gaps began to yawn in the stands and display cases. Apples from the last crop and last year's record-sized corncobs, huge pumpkins and the seeds of dead sunflowers, sugar beet and even buckwheat, all went into the pot. Unfortunately, the scarcer and more perishable kinds of produce—tomatoes, cucumbers, peaches—were preserved in liter-sized jars of Formalin, otherwise a use would have been found for them too. In the fall came watermelons, and Vlad earmarked them for exhibition in the House of Culture in quantities that would have sufficed to fill a medium-sized pavilion at Moscow's Permanent Exhibition of the National Economy. Necessity is indeed the mother of invention.

Nadya was now eating for two. Her belly swelled, her cheeks grew hollow, her features sharpened and came out in patches of yellow: the breath of life of another being, as though burning her from within, made her waste away outwardly as well. It can hardly be said that Vlad had ever really loved her, but when at night he listened to the barely perceptible heartbeat of the little lump of flesh that he had begotten, he felt something like tenderness toward her. The realization that he would soon become a father filled him with a sense of responsibility, compared with which all his past problems now seemed insubstantial and trivial. Something that was a part of himself was about to come into the world, yet different in appearance and with another, separate destiny. What would that destiny be?

After a dry, lingering fall, winter crept up on the village unawares: starting with a light dusting of hoar frost in the mornings, the steppe froze; the roads and the cart ruts turned hard as iron, the streaks of smoke above the roofs grew denser and longer. One morning Vlad came out of the dark storeroom in which they lived and blinked; outside all the windows of the old farmhouse which housed the museum and the library there gleamed the whiteness of snow. Like a fluttering veil, the typically thin snow of the south was floating lightly to the ground, but behind that lightness there was also a certainty that it was permanent. The snow was presenting the Kuban with its first visiting card.

There followed many days of sharp but brittle frosts and a thaw in the afternoon, which by evening turned to slush. Around this time, after deduction of advances, Vlad received his annual pay and their life in the storeroom visibly improved. There was enough flour and oil to last until spring. Nadya grew more lively and cheerful and was no longer irritated by trifles. Her erstwhile friends began occasionally to visit her; in spite of itself, the village seemed gradually to be coming to terms with their continuing liaison. But the inevitable day was approaching . . .

Suddenly one night in early February she started screaming and would not stop. Vlad tried to light the lamp, so that he could see to pull his boots on, but when his shaking fingers refused to obey him he gave up the attempt and rushed off to the fire station, running barefoot through the February slush of mud and snow. Without looking to right or left he raced past houses and gardens toward the light shining outside a shed, and the thrill of fear over what was happening at home helped him on his way. The marathon that he ran on that night in February is another thing that he will never forget.

The fireman on duty, Stepan Stetsenko, was practically his worst enemy in Plastunovskaya—he was a distant relative of Nadya—but from the moment that he saw Vlad appear in the doorway of the fire station, he instantly grasped what was happening and somehow he relented. He began running, bustling around and gabbling in an attempt, to judge from his voice, to calm himself rather than Vlad.

"Don't worry, brother, don't worry! I've had three kids myself, I'll be ready in a moment and we'll get there and back in no time. The main thing for you now is not to worry!" He backed the best gelding into the shafts, then harnessed and bridled the animal (who was accustomed to emergencies). "Everything will be fine, brother . . . got three myself, this is nothing new to me . . ."

On the way back, puffing at a cheap cigarette in the damp night air, Stepan grunted to Vlad in a tone of conciliation:

"Don't be offended at us people here, brother. We're used to our own kind, but an outsider—well, to us he's as prickly as a hedgehog under your shirt. You'll find the village people won't bother you anymore, 'cos like it or not the baby will be a little Cossack, whether it's a boy or a girl, and they'll accept it." He drove the cart right up to the front porch of the House of Culture. "You run in now and warm yourself up—you must be completely crazy, coming out barefoot! And I guess you could do with a drink too!"

He saw you, Tatyana, on the very next day, through the glass screen of the maternity ward, held in your mother's arms. Then you were still just a tiny bundle of flesh, without a name and without a fate, for the Lord had not reached out and touched you through Baptism.

Long before Nadya was discharged from hospital, Kosivtsov called Vlad to see him:

"Congratulations on your daughter!" He came out from behind his desk, embraced him, gave him a seat and sat down facing him: "The farm management was going to give you a present, but the District Committee has ordered us to transfer you to work on the local newspaper, so you'd better start packing. Go to Dinskaya, find out all about the job, rent a room and take your wife straight there. You've had about as much as anyone can take from the people in this village. I'm sorry to see you go—if we had maybe two or three young lads like you here, we could really do something. Oh, well . . . Don't think badly of us, come and see us whenever you can."

When you accompanied him to the door, Nikolai Gavrilovich, and closed it behind him, the bond between you was broken forever —or rather its visible, physical aspect was broken off, but the bond itself is still there to this day, reassuring him that some people are indeed human beings. Nor is it party allegiance or political views that divide them, but only the light and the darkness contending within them for dominion over the heart. What matters is which of these two wins—for upon that depends how a man lives and acts. And to have learned that lesson from you, dear Nikolai Gavrilovich, is deserving of gratitude! Farewell . . .

Next morning Vlad went to Dinskaya, the district center, to begin another and not unimportant stage in his life.

CHAPTER 7

"What is the press?" The editor looked at Vlad through his spectacles with the triumphant defiance of someone who already knows the answer. "The press is the sharpest, the most deadly weapon that our Party possesses. Who said that? Comrade Stalin. Have you ever seen Stalin?"

"Yes, I have." Vlad was somewhat dumbfounded by this onslaught. "When I was a child . . . at a demonstration. In films, too."

"At a demonstration? So you're from Moscow, are you?"

"Yes, I am."

"Ah, you Muscovites!" He stood up and the dandruff cascaded like powder from his green uniform tunic.

"At a demonstration! Why, I've been as close to him as I am to you now and I've shaken the great leader by the hand."

As though afraid that his visitor might run away, the editor barred the door with his body, and this enabled Vlad to examine him in some detail: a tall, graying man with a rounded, slightly effeminate face, wearing the Party official's plain military-style tunic and a pair of captured German leggings. On him, the leggings looked particularly absurd.

"I was secretary of the Novorossiisk Party Committee at the time." He was, as Vlad later discovered, an inspired liar who sincerely believed his own lies. "For some reason Mikhail Ivanovich

Kalinin, our beloved President, came to the town one day. 'Are you,' he said, 'Roman Zamyatin?' 'Yes,' I said, 'I am.' 'Roman,' he said, 'how come you're the Party secretary here and you haven't finished the reconstruction of the port yet?' 'Sorry,' I said, 'comrade President. We'll do it.' 'I give you,' he said, 'three days in which to have it done, then I will personally check on it.' As you know, there are no strongholds too great for communists to storm and capture. Do you know who said that? Comrade Stalin said it, remember that. Well, to cut a long story short, I mobilized a group of activists, youngsters, townspeople, I tracked down some unutilized resources and did the job on time. I didn't let the old man down, and I kept my word of honor as a Bolshevik, too. He had a good memory, did the old man, and he came to check up on me as he said he would. 'Well done, Roman,' he said, 'you didn't let an old man down.' I was leading him up the gangplank to a motor launch, because our President thought he'd like to inspect the port from the windy side, so to speak, when he tripped up and fell into the water. I went in after him fully clothed, and although it's not very deep there, I had trouble enough getting him ashore. Well, there was first aid, an escort and all the rest of it. The dear old man was driven off under special medical observation. Before the water had time to drip off my clothes, I saw three cars drive up to the very pier where I was standing: whoosh, whoosh, whoosh. Guards tumbled out of two of them, and Stalin himself got out of the third one. 'Where is Roman Zamyatin?' says he. Well, I commanded a division in the Far East, I know the rules of the service, and I jumped to attention. 'Comrade Stalin,' says I, 'I am.' And would you believe it, he didn't say another word but just walked up to me, bowed down his proud head, took my hand in his two hands and shook it warmly. He didn't say a word, you see, just took my hand and shook it. Took it and shook it." His eyes shining with a beatific gleam, he seemed to get stuck at this point, like a needle jammed in one groove of a worn-out record. "Took it and shook it. Took it and shook it." At last he came back to earth with a jerk and ended patronizingly: "And you tell me you saw him 'at a demonstration'! Off you go to work now, and learn the ropes . . ."

Some good, however, came out of this: the shock that Vlad experienced during this first conversation with his editor somewhat cooled the ardor which first had been aroused by the idea of his new job, and he went to work devoid of the awe and veneration he had previously felt for the Soviet provincial press.

Vlad was put in charge of the paper's Arts and Literature section, which had previously been handled by the managing editor, Ivan Gerzhod, a melancholy converted Jew whose curly red hair tumbled almost down to his eyebrows.

"Did he ask you, 'What is the press'?" Gerzhod met Vlad as he came out of the editor's office. "Tell me honestly."

"Yes, he did."

"Did he tell you his Stalin story?"

"Yes."

"And did he tell you how he met Voroshilov?"

"No, he didn't."

"He will."

Gerzhod looked at him with mocking eyes, put an arm around Vlad's shoulder and led him away to his own cubbyhole. "If you have some poetry to give us for a start, I'll publish it in tomorrow's issue." An amateur versifier himself, the managing editor knew how to gain the allegiance of a new colleague. "This folder contains all the material for your section: reports on local events, amateur shows, schools, poetry by the kilometer and by the ton. And give me your own stuff right away; if we leave it till after lunch it will be too late for tomorrow's paper—our printers can be rather temperamental."

Next morning Vlad held before him a fresh copy of the paper, in which his first published work, set in six-point nonpareil, graced the third page. His poems were, of course, incredibly bad, but at the time, burning as he was with an author's vanity and almost speechless with delight, he found them, if not the peak of perfection, then at least no worse than others which he read almost daily in newspapers and magazines. And they may well have been so—if that is any excuse.

What is the secret of it? The alphabet is the same for everyone: twenty-six characters, a, b, c, d, e, and so on; yet why, how does it happen that in one case they can be arranged into: "A wondrous moment I remember," and in another: "Oh how vast my own, my native country"?* What Good Spirit inspires a man so that he can turn a combination of these letters into Love and Revelation—and

* The first quotation is the opening line of one of Pushkin's most famous lyric poems; the second is the start of a patriotic song that is generally regarded in the Soviet Union as an extreme example of tasteless jingoism. (Tr.)

what is the Evil Will that can twist the selfsame letters into a piece
of unbelievably banal drivel? One day Vlad will learn about this, but
will it not then be too late?

On the very next day he received a visit from his first admirer, a
globular lady of well over sixty who turned out to have been teaching
Russian at the local high school since before the revolution.

"You are a poet," she declared peremptorily, sinking into a chair
like a ball of uncooked dough. "No, it's no use contradicting me—
you are a poet. I felt it as soon as I read your poem. I write too, and
I know what I'm talking about, believe me." She was forcing the
pace of the conversation with lightning speed. "I thought you might
like to read some of my work." She handed him a rolled-up exercise
book. "There you are."

His head began to ache after the first few lines. Later, this was to
become an almost pathological symptom: whenever he had to read
trash, his feelings about it were registered by a headache that acted
like a barometer. All this aging madwoman's suppressed complexes,
all the things which she would never have dared to utter aloud in
real life, had been poured out onto the lined paper with a sort of aggressive shamelessness. "I stand before you bare: Oh kiss my breasts,
my hair, We'll sin now with each other, As you sin with another . . ."
Or: "Forget vain hopes, wake not the slumb'ring beast, My clothes
you shall not tear, nor see my breast." And so on and so on, in
the same spirit and with much emphasis on "breasts" in various
aspects and situations. Looking at her, at her virginal features devoid
of any trace of passion or maternity, it was a safe bet that if she had
ever "sinned" it had only been on paper.

Many were the memorable graphomaniacs of different ages, pro-
fessions, and temperaments who were to pass before him in the years
to come. They were to cause him little but headaches and boredom,
yet in the end, having tasted to the full the rich variety of garbage
that does get into print, he actually came to feel a certain sympathy
and liking for these sincere fanatics: at least they were honest about
this mania of theirs . . .

"Not bad," Vlad mumbled in perplexity, making a feverish mental
search for an acceptable formula of rejection. "The trouble is . . . er,
this newspaper . . . is the political organ of the District Committee.
We really need something topical . . ."

The lady rose majestically:

"You have misunderstood me, young man. I'm not interested in anything so vulgar as publication. I came to you as one poet to another." She took back the proffered exercise book and swept out with a parting remark of condescending magnanimity: "Even so, you are a poet! Yes—a poet!"

Long after she had left, the room exuded an aroma of cheap perfume and powder. "Yes," Vlad sighed heavily, "the old girl's an obvious nut. God—how many more like her will there be?"

Gerzhod put his head in through the open door and gave a mocking wink:

"Well, how was it?"

"How was what?"

"That creature."

"So it was you who unloaded her on to me, was it?"

"Of course." Gerzhod roared with delighted laughter. "Don't worry, you'll get used to that sort of thing. In time you'll even get immune to it. After all, I deserve a rest from her by now—you're still young, you'll survive, but I can't take it any longer."

So saying, he disappeared into the neighboring office in a cloud of tobacco smoke.

Imperceptibly Vlad slipped into the everyday routine of a newspaper office, and that routine, by a natural process, became part of his own life as he was drawn into the daily round. For days on end he would hitchhike around the region, or more often travel on foot, gathering news, writing, polishing, correcting proofs, hurrying to deliver his allotted two thousand words of copy before the deadline.

Roman Zamyatin ran the newspaper on principles that only he understood, but it is a curious feature of any publication that whoever runs it and whatever it prints, it somehow always keeps on coming out. Zamyatin himself could not write and had no wish to, so he spent most of his time playing chess with some of the free-lance contributors or visitors to the office. Although a man of phenomenal ignorance, he was nevertheless regarded as one of the best chessplayers in the locality and even entered in regional competitions. His only personal contribution to the newspaper was a column entitled "Do You Know?" which he had invented and of which he was extremely proud. He kept an incredibly tattered old notebook, whence he extracted the aphorisms, proverbs, and snippets of information that went into his column. Since the notebook contained an enormous number of quotations of the most varied sort, it was not uncommon for Zamyatin's column to include, side by side, such utterances as:

"Study, study, study" and "In one month a louse can lay 3,350 eggs." The leading articles, which the editor was supposed to write ex officio, were actually composed by the various departments according to subject matter, and as a rule he never even touched the paste-up of each issue prepared by Gerzhod. He did, however, have a weakness for displaying his authority now and again and would alter somebody's copy for the sake of appearances. For instance, from a headline that read: "Farmers Slow in Fall Plowing," he would remove the last word, explaining his reasons by reference to Chekhov: "Brevity is the sister of talent," and although the sister in question had absolutely no connection with Roman Zamyatin, one had to accept his correction in order to cut short his enthusiasm for excursions into literature. "Who said that? Chekhov. You should know that, you're working for a newspaper, not a flour mill."

It so happened that before he had been in his job for six months, Vlad brought the editor an article about a school hiking trip at one of the latter's moments of writer's itch. Zamyatin read it, frowned, made a few marginal corrections, and then leaned back in his chair, scattering a shower of dandruff all around him: "Not bad for a beginner." He gazed at Vlad through his spectacles with the look of a weary master craftsman obliged to teach a novice the rudiments of his trade: "Only a lot of things need changing. You write here, for example: 'The transparent expanse of the valley opened up before them.' What do you mean—'transparent'? A hole can be transparent, a pane of glass can be transparent, or an excuse can be transparent, but an expanse—never. Throw it out. Or this, for instance . . ."

"No, Roman Nikolayich." Suddenly, as though touched on a raw spot, Vlad was sickened beyond toleration by Zamyatin's schoolmasterly lecturing: "I won't change it."

"What do you mean?"

"Quite simply that I refuse to make that correction and that's that —because in writing there is such a thing as imagery, of which you appear so far to be totally unaware." From the rapid change of coloring on the editor's face Vlad observed with satisfaction his rapid metamorphosis from perplexity to incredulity, followed swiftly by unconcealed fury:

"Listen to me, boy." As soon as Zamyatin started talking, Vlad could instantly smell the stuffy air of a prison-camp hut and hear the rich flow of obscenities as one professional criminal told another exactly what he thought of him. "I eat little horrors like you, buttons and all. Go and write an application for dismissal 'at own request' while I'm still in a good temper."

"And you can go to . . ."

Knowing now that Zamyatin was all bark and no bite, Vlad did not spare his words. On top of this, his family life was not working out, having lately kept going only on habit and inertia. Vlad had been offered a contract for a book of poems by the Krasnodar publishing house, which grew daily more and more tempting. "Come what may," he said in desperation, "I'm getting out!"

Within an hour Vlad had resigned from the newspaper and collected his back pay, without ever hearing the editor's story about Voroshilov promised by Gerzhod. To Krasnodar!

CHAPTER 8

Boris Essman was famous in Krasnodar for possessing the happy knack of always being the first to meet anyone who had just received an advance of royalties. Coming out of the publisher's office Vlad bumped into his artist friend, just as though Essman had been standing there and waiting for him.

"Aha!" said the hunchback, shaking with soundless laughter. "Who's this I see! Are congratulations in order?"

"Yes, I got my advance."

"I do not ask how much. I ask—where shall we go?"

"What do you suggest?"

"One brilliant thought occurs to me." Essman scratched the back of his neck thoughtfully. "Today at the 'Kuban' our veteran author Adrian Rummer is baptizing the proof copy of the second edition of his novel *The Sea*. All of our elite, so to speak, will be there, and it's time you got to know them."

"Lead on." Vlad was quickly getting used to his position, and so restrained himself from showing too much enthusiasm. "Let's go and have a look at your elite . . ."

They found the party in full swing. Several tables had been pushed together, and in the middle of a dozen or so guests sat an elderly man of massive proportions, with a mane of gray hair above a high, deeply lined forehead and cornflower-blue eyes blurred by an alcoholic haze, who was announcing to the room in a stentorian voice:

"It takes more to live your life, you know, than to cross a field. What a deal of eating and drinking it has been—and foot-slogging, too, with one's belt tightened to the last hole. I remember how I walked from the Caspian to see Maxim Gorky, with nothing but a knapsack and a pair of ancient, down-at-heel shoes . . ."

As they joined the company, Essman gave Vlad a mischievous wink:

"Stick it out—it takes him a long time to tell this one."

From the weary tolerance on the surrounding faces it was obvious that they had heard this story many times before and were well and truly bored by it, but the occasion obliged the guests to be polite and so, as though fulfilling some traditional duty, they adopted expressions simulating interest while waiting in tense expectation for the next toast. The host's excursion into the past went on and on, everyone was feeling the tedium, and in order to rescue the party from collapse Essman seized on a momentary pause and interrupted Rummer's long, rambling effusion:

"Just a minute, Adrian, I have an important announcement to make!" He laid his hand on Vlad's shoulder. "Here among us is our new comrade, the poet Samsonov, of whom I trust you have all heard. He has just got his first advance, and you know what that means . . ."

The resulting enthusiasm, fired by the prospect of finally getting back to the real matter in hand—drinking—was indescribable. If Pushkin had walked live into the room at that moment, he would have aroused less interest than did Vlad: immediately glasses were filled and toasts drunk to the talented newcomer, to the new luminary on the Kuban's poetic horizon. One toast followed another as everyone present conscientiously strove to earn his share of Vlad's advance.

Vlad's righthand neighbor, a thin young man with small but expressive features, with a dead cigarette in his wet lips, muttered into his ear:

"My name's Zavalov. Do you know Zavalov? Everyone knows Zavalov, never been such an actor before and never will be again . . . got it? Let's get the hell out of here and go back to the hostel where I live, the girls there are fantastic . . . Shall we go? We'll fix up a foursome, play 'push me, pull you' and all the rest of it. You won't regret it. Zavalov's the name, Georgii Zavalov—got it?"

Strangely enough, that chance acquaintance somehow lasted throughout the next twenty years. Drink-sodden and sinking lower and lower, the erstwhile star juvenile lead of the southern Russian theater would later come and see Vlad in Moscow every August (when actors come to audition for the new season) invariably drunk and accompanied by a new girlfriend. He was ingenuous, was Zhora Zavalov, ingenuous in everything—in his infidelity and perpetual lying, in his debts and his deceitfulness, in his maniacal self-esteem and his total unreliability. Rich is the land of Russia in this worthless but charming breed!

In the drunken hubbub, hemmed in by the noisy circle of guests, Vlad did not see her until the moment when she firmly made a space for herself at the table between him and the actor. Also finding a place was her companion, a tall, dandified man with a look of inbred arrogance on his complacent features. The newcomers' irruption was greeted with general applause:

"Lyalya!"

"Make them stand a round of drinks for being late!"

"Just a little one—enough to fill a little horse trough!"

"Ah, Lyalya," said the host, summing up the general feeling as he gazed at her with bleary eyes, "if only I was younger!"

After their first meeting, Vlad had several times met Lyalya briefly, in her office or on the street, and they had even talked, but the distance that separated them was too great for him to permit himself anything more. Every time he met her Vlad was overcome with confusion and could only find enough breath to say a few hollow, meaningless words. Now, sitting beside her, he inwardly shriveled into a feverishly pulsating little lump, afraid that a careless word or movement might betray the torment that was devouring him.

In the hope that it would help him to loosen up a little, relax and feel slightly less constrained, Vlad was just reaching out for a bottle when at the same moment, like an electric shock, like a burn, he felt her hand on his elbow:

"You shouldn't drink any more, Vladik," she said without looking at him and scarcely moving her lips. "And you'd do better to go away from here . . . Would you like me to come with you?"

The sudden rush of joy to Vlad's heart sobered him up instan-

taneously and sharpened his hearing and awareness. He caught the
barely audible sound of her casual "I'll call you" spoken to her companion, noticed the latter's haughtily offended nod in reply and was
just tensing himself with hostility in readiness to start a fight, when
he found himself being pulled after her across the room, out into the
September night, into the lights of the town and the starlit streets.

They walked aimlessly, down alleyways, while Lyalya held his
hand in hers and it seemed to Vlad that he was not walking but
floating over the ground, and that the earth was being unrolled toward his feet like a carpet.

"That sort of life is not for you, Vladik," she urged him softly, accompanying each phrase with a gentle squeeze. "It's not for you.
Why follow the example of those walking corpses? They're just a
bunch of failures, whose only hope of self-assurance is to look for it
out here in the provinces. They're nothing but clowns, aging provincial clowns!"

"If you don't want me to, Lyalya, I won't. I never will, if that's
what you want, I promise you."

"Ah, Vladik, don't be silly. I'm years older than you are. In ten
or fifteen years I'll be an old woman and you're only just starting to
live properly!"

"Without you—never."

"You silly, silly boy . . ."

"Never, Lyalya, never!"

"My God, how stupid you are . . ."

"Lyalya!"

And he kissed her. Everything within him froze, only to explode
the next moment in a blinding sense of the richness and beauty of
the surroundings: through the gently rustling leaves of the plane
trees shone the star-misted sky, from the river Kuban came the barely
perceptible chill of a breeze; from behind garden fences the pungent,
heady smells of the approaching fall caressed his nostrils.

Words now meant nothing, yet they flew from their lips unbid-
den, heightening the unique, unrepeatable flavor of the night:

"If only you knew, Lyalya . . ."

"Quiet, Vladik, be quiet . . ."

"I can't."

"Why not?"

"I want you to know . . ."

"I know it all anyway."

"How?"

"A woman always knows . . ."

"Does she feel it?"

"Of course . . ."

"Everything?"

"Yes—everything . . ."

Somewhere at the very end of the street, or farther away still, the bright streak of a new day was just to be seen, yet they walked on and on around the town, holding hands and noticing nothing around them. O moment, stay awhile!

CHAPTER 9

There is something primal, elemental about autumn: that shifting season, the fall. The translucent glass of empty skies. Vlad was treating Essman to drinks on a cafe terrace in the city park, among fallen leaves and avenues drenched in cold sunlight, amid the deserted silence of an October afternoon. Although growing drowsier from glass to glass, Essman kept trying to tempt him:

"You're turning me into a solitary drinker," he said reproachfully after each drink was served. "That's no way to behave. Come on—let's have at least one together!"

"No, Boris." The buoyancy of spirit which had recently lightened his life was still worth more to him than the illusory freedom of intoxication. "I won't, and don't try to persuade me. I'll order you another one if you like, but I won't drink myself."

"Oh, come on, Vladik!"

"If you keep it up, I shall go, Boris."

"All right." Essman obediently gave in. "Maybe you're right—provided, that is, you manage to stick to it. But here in this God-forsaken backwater, it's a hard thing to do, very hard. Sooner or later they all crack up and start going downhill. Take Rummer, for instance—what a fine figure of a man he was when he first came here; you could have used him as a model to paint some legendary hero like Ilya Muromets. Now he's just an alcoholic ruin on two legs. As

for his novel *The Sea*—you know how he never stops telling everyone, "Gorky praised it"? Hell! Gorky praised anything that was
shown to him; one of the usual signs of senile decay, that's all. It
doesn't make *The Sea* a better book. It's another of those vast novels
about the problems of a fishery collective caused by the mechani-
zation of labor-intensive processes! God, what unreadable crap!
You're doing the right thing, Vladka, by steering clear of us. We're
the leftovers of art and literature, a worked-out seam, ballast. We go
on acting as if we were doing something real, but we're just playing
meaningless games. Real artists, real writers live a different life, Vlad,
totally different. They don't just live, their life and their art are one;
they don't die, they simply dissolve into their work. Death for them
is a culmination, nothing more, so when death comes the true artist
always takes it calmly because he knows he has done something
worth dying for. I remember, there was an old artist who taught at
our art school and he used to tell us a legend—Georgian I think it
was, or it may have been Armenian. Anyhow, its origin doesn't matter, that's not the point . . ."

The Story of the Master Craftsman
Who Knew

"It all happened God knows when, nearly five hundred years ago,
somewhere in the Caucasus. A certain robber prince, who had, to
put it in modern language, made himself a handsome pile by raiding
and robbing his neighbors, took it into his head to redeem his sins
before the Almighty by building a church whose magnificence would
eclipse everything else of its kind that had ever been built. Ah yes,
it's an age-old weakness of tyrants to light penny candles to the
memory of the people they have slaughtered, in the form of
churches, pyramids, and monuments! But when the tyrant commands, the satrap's job is to obey. A Master Craftsman was needed,
the like of whom was not to be found in any of the neighboring prin-
cipalities. And that Master Craftsman was found, at once. Such men
are always a pain in the neck to others, and they get rid of them at
the first available opportunity. On the very next day he was taken
into the august presence of His Robber Highness. When the prince
had declared his will, the Master Craftsman asked him: 'You will
not interfere, will you?' 'No,' replied the prince, 'I give you my
word.' 'Then I agree.' 'Why don't you ask me about your pay-

ment?' the thieving prince could not help asking. 'Have you no requests, no wishes? Ask me!' 'I know what reward awaits me, prince,' the Master replied. 'What is it?' inquired the prince in surprise. 'Death,' answered the Master. The brain of the noble robber could not follow this logic: 'Why?' 'Because when I have finished, you will not want me to build a better church for anyone else.' 'Yet you accept all the same?' 'I do,' replied the Master. 'What makes you do this?' The prince was dumbfounded. 'Tell me.' 'God,' the Master answered calmly. 'Very well, then—begin.' The royal bandit smiled ominously. 'And may God, as the saying goes, be with you.'

"The work began at a furious pace. Day and night, alongside his apprentices and slaves, the Master lived with his creation, guiding the work as the church grew and broadened. Day and night, winter and summer, spring and autumn, for many years the Master Craftsman never left the scaffolding; he worked hard enough for four and no one ever saw him eat or sleep. 'Madman!' the common people whispered in corners. 'He is driving himself to his death!' But the Master knew that the remaining life allotted to him was just as long as it took him to complete the building and therefore he did not spare himself, for that was in the hands of the Almighty. The prince meanwhile grew aged and enfeebled, looking with envy at the unflagging energy with which the Master Craftsman worked; but even in his old age, plagued by ills and malice, he tried yet could not understand the secret of the Master's zeal. 'What is this?' he wondered petulantly, comparing the Master with his own wretched, exhausted condition. 'Obviously he has been keeping something from me, a secret that gives him some advantage.' The Master, however, had no time to spare for the prince's complexes; he worked on, and under his guidance there grew his greatest creation, the like of which was indeed not to be seen for a thousand miles around. When to complete the magnificent structure there remained but to erect a suitable spire, the prince again summoned the Master Craftsman to an audience. 'Will you not stop now?' he said, insinuatingly, to test the Master out. 'You only have three more days of work, therefore in three days' time you will die.' 'I know,' replied the Master, 'but permit me to go, the work cannot wait.' 'You and I are old men,' the prince began to weep, 'I am satisfied with your work, but let our children finish it and let you and I die a natural death.' 'You are magnanimous, my lord, but I must finish my work myself.' 'But you belong to me and I can order you to do as I wish!' 'My life belongs to you, my lord,' said the Master with a deep bow, 'but only God has power over my soul.' 'Go,' said the prince, 'and be accursed!' For the final three days the Master Craftsman wholly forgot what it was to eat and sleep as he put the final touches to his masterpiece, and when on the fourth day the scaffolding was taken down, before the gaze of a vast concourse of people there arose the magnificent church. The divine perfection of its proportions harmonized ideally with the mountainous background and with the river that meandered picturesquely through the valley. Until the very last moment the prince did not know—or rather, he was not sure—whether or not he would execute the Master Craftsman, but he only had to catch sight of the miracle that had arisen in front of the battlements of his castle for all his doubts to vanish. 'This proud man must die,' he commanded, 'for he will not rest until he has made something even better, and I have so many enemies!' And the Master died. He died, as might have been expected, on the executioner's block, in front of the same crowd of people which only yesterday had hailed his genius with such delight: the mob has a short memory, it lives only for the day. But the old rogue of princely blood was not fated to celebrate his triumph: he gave up the ghost at the very same moment as did the Master Craftsman, only far less heroically; for the prince died of premature senility, brought on by an evil disease which in our day is known merely as syphilis. They were buried at the same hour on the same day, each according to his rank and station: the one with weeping and lamentation in the family vault, the other we know not how nor where. Time has long since removed all trace of both their graves. But the church into which the Master Craftsman put his very life stands to this day, while not even the name of the prince has been preserved. True, it is said that some fanatical nationalist grubbed around in the archives and wrote a master's dissertation on the royal robber, in an attempt to prove that this prince had once existed, but the dissertation, it seems, was not accepted. And the church still stands, Vladka, and what a church! . . ."

"Is that story meant for me, Boris?"

"Yes. For you to remember." The hunchback finished his brandy and sniffed a corner of his napkin. "For all your birthdays at once."

"I will bear it in mind."

"It would be a good thing if you did."

"Would you like another drink?"

"Order me one more, and go. I'd like to sit alone for a while. It's a good idea, once in a while. In a certain sense solitude is a kind of exercise in mental hygiene . . ."

At the corner of the avenue Vlad turned around. In the autumnal sunlight, amid the dazzling colors of the fallen leaves, he suddenly saw in Essman's hunched little figure so much sorrow and hopelessness that a momentary, piercing stab of pity made him involuntarily frown: there, quite alone on the cafe terrace, a man was drawing up the balance of his life, and the results, by all appearances, were unconsoling.

CHAPTER 10

Krasnodar was drowning in the March slush. The low-lying sky seemed to have fastened itself to the roofs, never again to rise higher, while the surrounding world had dissolved in the damp, flu-laden murk of early spring. Visibility in the street was reduced to the length of a block, beyond which all else only loomed indistinctly in the wet mist. Even the people looked hollow and somehow permanently sodden.

Vlad was sloshing through the foul weather toward the publishers' office in the hope of finding out something about his long-promised book and, if possible, getting another advance on royalties. The day-to-day reality of literary life had long since become a tedious routine. What had begun as a festive carnival was gradually losing its color, growing dull and frayed.

The publishing offices proved to be almost empty, and only Vasily Popov, his first benefactor, was seated at work with his inseparable pipe in his mouth, although without the customary Rabelaisian smile on his thick lips. He looked somehow shrunken, with a colorless, lackluster air. Even his pipe, on this occasion, was not puffing out smoke with its usual locomotive-like energy. Offering Vlad a chair, he greeted him with no more than a nod.

"What progress with my book, Vasily Ilyich?" Sensing that something was wrong, Vlad played it in a low key. "Isn't it about time it was coming out?"

At first Vasily Popov said nothing, but simply looked at him with an expression that would have conveyed to a blind man that Vlad was utterly contemptible and had better leave—or rather, get the hell out of the place—before he was murdered on the spot. Only after this eloquent pause did Popov boom in a sepulchral voice:

"What book, comrade?! . . . Stalin, our leader, is dead!"

As Popov resumed puffing at his pipe and the cloud of smoke enveloped his face, he seemed thereby to be finally shutting himself off from Vlad, who had ceased to exist as far as he was concerned.

Walking out, Vlad found that he could not define exactly how he felt about this sudden news. He had never been greatly thrilled by the figure of the mustachioed generalissimo who headed the Soviet state. Stalin had existed on such an exalted plane that Vlad had perceived him as something outside the normal scale of values. At that moment he felt nothing but a vague indifference. To him, the fate of his book was a far more real source of anxiety.

In the doorway of the office he bumped into Rummer, who was already half-seas over, and behind whose back Vlad descried a tall man of about thirty, wearing a shabby but well-cut raglan coat.

"Vladka, well I'm damned—someone I'm always glad to see!" As usual when drunk, Rummer was cordial and expansive. "Seryoga, let me introduce you"—he turned to his companion—"to our young hope, the poet Samsonov. The hell with seeing these damned publishers. Let's go and have a drink instead, the newspaper paid me my retainer today . . ."

They set off through the slush and soon were comfortably ensconced in a private room of the town's best-known restaurant. Rummer—especially Rummer on the spree—was a favored customer, so the table was quickly and superbly set for them.

"Now, Vladik"—it only needed one drink for him to launch out in his most pompous style—"look at this man and remember him. What a personality, I tell you, what a personality! A veritable mine of information and experience, you might say. His life has been more like a novel than a life. I'd write it myself, but the bastards would never publish it!"

The human novel looked, in fact, like some battered but proud bird, gazing out with sadness at a world grown wearisome to him. There really was something otherworldly about him; he had the air of a noble hawk contemptuous of the petty bustle that seethed below him.

"Yes, I've lived it up in my time." Only after his third drink did the guest deign to speak. He drank without eating the usual snacks between drinks, but he gave little sign of getting drunk except that his eyes glazed over with a sort of melancholy fury.

"Would you like me to tell you a story for the fourth drink?"

Instead of a reply, the ever more expansive Rummer only clapped his hands in approval.

The guest proudly bowed his head in token of gratitude.

The Ballad of the Bartered Camel

"I was fated, friends, to be born the son of a famous old Bolshevik who joined the Party long before the revolution. Yes, yes—that's the one! None other! This was undoubtedly the beginning of all my misfortunes. I was raised, as you will appreciate, in hothouse conditions. At home there was literally everything that anyone could want. My parents spoiled me, and so I grew up never having to refuse myself anything. They say I was an infant prodigy: I could draw well, I wrote poetry, and I even sang in international juvenile competitions. My only failing, in my parents' eyes, was laziness. I would remark, in parentheses though, that to this day I regard the attribute of sloth as a gift from God, which has saved me from the dubious temptations of a career and from unjustly enriching myself at the expense of the gullible taxpayer. For as long as I can remember, my elder brother was always held up to me as an example. A modest, hard-working boy of mediocre abilities, everyone was touched by his assiduity and neatness, thanks to which he earned himself a silver medal in school and thereafter a gold medal when he graduated in documentary film-making. Now he is wallowing in official fame, pulling in a fortune from making films about how happy the natives are in the era of socialism, while your humble servant remains in a state of indigent yet noble idleness. When my respected papa was cast down from the heights of ministerial office and dispatched into outer darkness as ambassador to some Pyrenean cesspit, he took me with him. Before he reached his destination, however, my papa was unable to endure the affront of his political demotion, and he joined his Maker, as they say, in a Paris hotel room, hoping that he would at least be accorded a suitably grand funeral. One must give our government its due; it is never tightfisted over cremating the bodies of deserving old revolutionaries, and my father was indeed given a first-rate funeral and his ashes were immured in the wall of the Kremlin.

"After my father's death, my mother, my brother, and I stayed on in Paris for a while, where we were caught by the war. We came home in 1946 on a wave of émigré patriotism. Like the majority of such innocent returnees, we would undoubtedly have been sent off to live in the back of beyond with a residence restriction in our passports preventing us from living in the big cities, if my brother and I had not been adopted by an old friend of my father, a famous art historian who at that time was in charge of that pawnshop of the Peredvizhniki—sorry, I mean the Tretyakov Gallery.* My respected brother quickly adapted himself to the new situation, clicked his heels, regularly brought home A grades, took an active part in political life, climbed doggedly up the ladder of success to the lush uplands of official recognition, while I, in the meantime, set off along another path in search of delights of a different kind. Among the social outcasts of the bohemian world, I quickly became close friends with a couple of stalwarts of underground, unofficial art, two selfless devotees of the muses who liked to live life to the full. Ah, where now are the golden days of boisterous youth, the rose-strewn time of hope and longing, the springtime upsurge of ardent inspiration? What a life we led, what fun the three of us had together, what prospects beckoned to us from the hazy distance! The feasts on Olympus, the nights in ancient Athens pale beside our pagan orgies. The enterprise was financed by Erik, the youngest of us, but who had already fought at the front and tasted the delights of prison, a sculptor of genius—I must stress, incidentally, that this is no exaggeration and he has proved it in his work. Musical accompaniment and mass culture was provided by Lyosha, author of several masterpieces of risqué and downright indecent lyrics such as 'Othello the Moor,' 'He Lunged for her White Breasts,' 'In the Caucasus There Grew a Cherry Tree,' and many more equally memorable hits. I supplied the intellectual atmosphere, the elegiac mood, the stimulating talk and

* Founded in 1870 by the painter Kramskoy, the Peredvizhniki was a group of painters who cultivated a realistic style and an anecdotal, moralistic approach to subject matter as a means of social criticism. Active for twenty to thirty years, the Peredvizhniki and their works were later accorded great respect under the Soviet regime as being the exemplars and forerunners of "Socialist Realism" in art. Until the mid-1950s, the Tretyakov Gallery in Moscow was largely filled with their works.

so on. Together we made such an ideal trio that we might have been envied by Vasnetsov's 'Three Knights,' by the brothers Rayevsky and by the Fyodorov sisters. But alas, harmony is unthinkable in the dark ages we live in, happiness is short-lived and fortune is fickle. My adoptive parents were alarmed about my future and sounded the tocsin. One fine day, as the saying goes, Nemesis in the shape of a policeman and a janitor took hold of me in their lily-white hands and took me off to the purgatory for alcoholics on Radio Street, to undergo a course of compulsory treatment and rehabilitation. A very fashionable establishment—all cleanliness and tiled floors, chicken bouillon and heartfelt lectures on the dangers of fuel oil. I was in distinguished company—from Bulganin's son to the famous airman Vodopyanov. You might think it was fun—nothing to do but lie around and eat as much as you liked, but I felt homesick. Oh, how I missed our close-knit little brotherhood, our nocturnal vigils with the obliging ladies who frequent the Kazan Station, the lecherous verse we composed in the intervals between other activities. Occasionally my faithful friends and comrades-in-arms penetrated to my place of incarceration. With the kind blessing of the nurse on duty, we would retire to a secluded spot and knock back a bottle or two. Each one of us felt that our splendid little community was coming to an end, that we were at a parting of three ways where we should have to head off in different directions, and that life was moving to a close, toward its sunset. Our sadness was pure and unclouded, our parting short and laconic. Thanks to the efforts of my new father I was packed off to Yaroslavl, with glowing references, to take up work in the local press; for some reason my family thought I had the makings of a great journalist. Coming from Moscow, I was greeted in the ancient city of the Varangians in first-class style—after all, it wasn't every day that they welcomed the son of a man who had been an Old Bolshevik and a people's commissar. The chiefs of the aborigines arranged a dinner in my honor, at which the wine flowed like water and the food reminded me of one of the prewar window displays of Yeliseyev's delicatessen store. After my spell of enforced monasticism on Radio Street I was unable to resist such temptation, and I fell on the free food and drink with all the enthusiasm of someone just escaped from a besieged city. Of course I went beyond the bounds of permitted behavior, ran off the rails and over the embankment. Even now I have only a vague idea of what happened to me that evening. I believe I asked for more vodka, and when they wouldn't give me any I offered to perform 'The Dance of the Gnomes'—a splendid dance, by the way—and I think I even managed to dance the opening steps before I was seized and bound. Next morning your humble servant awoke in the sterile whiteness of a hospital ward, whence I was soon accompanied to my place of residence by an escort of two hefty male nurses. My family had hysterics. At a council of my relatives it was decided to place me under the moral tutelage of my elder brother, who by then was already making a name for himself in documentary films. That year, as it happened, he was scheduled to make a movie about the cultural renaissance of the wild tribesmen of Central Asia after the overthrow of their hated exploiters, the feudal landowners and the obscurantist mullahs. The council did not last long, and it was no sooner said than done. A few days later the Moscow–Ashkhabad express bore me away, together with an impressive crew of film-makers, to the exotic remoteness of the back of beyond. My job, it transpired, was uncomplicated but responsible: I was put in charge of a portable gas cooker, on which, according to the director, the culturally reborn nomads, having forever abandoned their primitive campfires, prepared their food in the sparse oases of the desert. In Ashkhabad the crew acquired a sizable herd of camels, rented from a collective farm just outside the city. I was allotted a middle-aged monster, quite tolerable as camels go but arrogant and evil-tempered in the extreme. I cannot imagine why he didn't like me, but he had a disgusting habit of spitting whenever he cast his contemptuous gaze on me. Every morning the sleepy film crew would plod off into the Karakum desert, where they were awaited at the nearest nomad encampment by a mob of extras, hastily recruited from the local layabouts, who for thirty rubles a day gladly pretended to be peaceful herdsmen seated around my gas stove, holding cattle goads and newspapers in their hands. A caldron full of rice pilaf steamed away on the stove, and an eagle circled in the sunny skies above. These pastoral scenes were supposed to impress the mass audience with the prosperous life of the dwellers of the sands, their thirst for knowledge and the fulfillment of their love of freedom. The result was a piece of eyewash in the best traditions of the unforgettable Dziga Vertov; it not only met all the criteria for Soviet home consumption but was also capable of tugging at the heartstrings of progressive circles in the West. I didn't waste my time, either. Having struck up friendly relations with the local press, I sent them a series of deeply felt pieces about the daily working routine of the film expedition, which enabled me to maintain my accustomed lifestyle. But our circus act was constantly being delayed: you know how it is in movies—either the light is wrong, or the director is out of sorts. Soon the demand for my journalistic output began to fall catastrophically, and a yawning gap opened up in my budget. There was no question of getting a loan: only someone like Wolf Messing, or at worst Quillot, is capable of borrowing a ruble from a member of a film crew. The effects of alcohol withdrawal were attacking me in their full delirious horror, the ground was giving way under my feet, and green devils were doing their mocking dance around the top of my head. When it got to the stage where I could not sleep and life itself became unbearable, I had a brainwave—a simple idea of genius. Incidentally, it is an axiom that all the best ideas come closest to genius when they are most simple. Next morning, as though accidentally, I slept through the crew's morning assembly and missed the daily caravan. Later, when I set off to catch them up, I made a detour to the bazaar, where after a heated but fruitful bargaining session I traded my monstrous beast for a similar, if slightly older one, plus a solid payment in cash. After all, friends, what difference is there between one camel and another? Two humps, a dirty tail, a slobbery jaw—they're all the same. What administrator would ever think of checking up on the color of their coat? What's more, the collective farm was getting the same amount of rental whatever the age of the beast. The deal, it seemed, caused no one any harm, and it literally saved me from death by unquenchable thirst. Unlike the camel, I could not go for more than a day without some suitable liquid. Having cured my hangover in the nearest dive, I stowed a couple of spare bottles into my saddlebag and set out to catch up to my comrades engaged on this ghastly documentary. No sooner, however, had I left the city limits and plunged into the desert than the camel collapsed beneath me and fell over onto its side, almost crushing my leg with its weight. In vain I swore at it in the filthiest language, in vain I kicked the animal, the camel would not get up. Before my eyes its soul parted from its body, its flanks subsided, its eyes glazed over and grew vacant. A minute later it expired forever. 'You fell as a victim,' as the song says, 'in the fateful struggle.' It was only then that I realized I had been cheated. I had been basely, pettily, treacherously swindled. Anyone in my place would have given up the struggle, but I am a man of duty; with me, duty comes before all else. Heaving the accursed stove onto my shoulders, I struck out across the Karakum desert in the wake of the departed film team. That, I'm telling you, was something of a hike! Alexei Maresiev, Hero of the Soviet Union, had nothing on me: let him try and survive in that diabolical inferno! Fiery balls expanded and burst inside my poor head, my mouth and throat felt as if they were lined with emery paper, my feet slowly but surely turned into burning coals. Through the salty haze in front of my eyes I could no longer distinguish anything but a whitish-yellow glare, pierced by a roasting sun. I thought at the time that I had lost my way and had crossed the entire desert from end to end at least twice. When I finally realized that I would never get out of that frying pan on my own, I lay down and gave myself up to the will of fate. I don't remember how long I lay there like that, baking in the sand like a pie in an oven, but in the end I was found by a drover, who had been specially hired by the expedition and was looking for the lost camel. When I came to, I saw above me a pair of slanting Asiatic eyes, silently asking me: 'Where's the camel?' 'Dead,' I replied equally silently, and nodded over my shoulder: 'Back there.' Without a word he picked me up and dragged me along the way I had come, snarling at me as he did so in angry, and, I suspect, obscene terms. It turned out that I had managed to go no farther than a kilometer from my fallen, four-footed comrade. In the meantime the camel had become noticeably more shrivelled and desiccated, and I even began to feel genuinely sorry for this luckless toiler of the desert. 'No,' said the slit-eyed drover, clicking his tongue, 'wrong camel.' I could only feebly insist on my story. 'What d'you mean—wrong camel?' I said. 'I tell you it's the right one. What more do you want?' He then lifted the hind leg of the deceased and I saw to my chagrin that I had been doubly cheated. Not only had they fobbed me off with an animal that was at death's door in exchange for an arrogant but healthy camel, but that carcass turned out to have been a female camel into the bargain.

"There is no limit to human perfidy! Deaf to my feeble excuses, the drover sat down on the sand, rocked back and forth and lamented and bewailed the stiffening corpse of that wretched beast. I confess, friends, that never before or since have I ever seen such unfeigned grief. People only mourn like that for some close and dearly beloved creature, after whose death life becomes empty and pointless, like eating without drinking. I couldn't stand it, so I took out a bottle and waved it in front of his eyes. At first he shook his head, but at my prolonged insistence he responded to the invitation and took a sip. His pupils moistened, as they say, his Tartar-Mongol eyes clouded over with a watery film: his soul released its liquid essence. My son of the steppes, my socialist Central Asian started to mumble and then burst into song. I naturally joined in, our voices blended in a charming duet of two suffering souls amid the sultry wastes of Asia —or rather, among the mudhuts of suburban Ashkhabad. It was this that saved us. The combination of his oriental lyrics and my rendering of 'Stenka Razin' drew the attention of some passing natives, we were picked up and that evening we were delivered, complete with portable gas stove, to police headquarters, from whence I was released next day by the manager of the film unit. There was a colossal scandal and they wanted to prosecute me for embezzling socialist property, but out of consideration for my elder brother's services they confined themselves to putting a stamp in my passport that restricted my residence to my place of work. Since then, cursed by my family and hounded by fate, I change my 'place of work' as often as possible, being unwilling, for reasons of principle, to pay for the baseness of my fellow humans. Really, it was too much—palming me off with that trash, and a female too! I shall continue my search across the wide, wide world to find a refuge for my injured feelings!"

Vlad listened with half an ear as the eccentric newcomer told his story, while staring with morbid curiosity at his face, his movements, and his gestures. For the first time in his life he was seeing a Russian who came from "outside." This man had been "over there," had breathed the air "over there," had met people who belonged "over there." This visitor seemed to him an emissary of another world, a legend come to life, a messenger from a different dimension.

"You've lived *abroad?*" He was almost breathless with a burning sense of prophetic foreboding. "What's it like 'over there'?"

The man only gestured limply in reply:

"Like it is everywhere, my young friend, like it is everywhere. Much the same, only more so. It's not worth talking about. How about that fourth drink?"

The drinks came during the ensuing moment of silence, after which, in an attempt to correct his faux pas, Vlad said hesitantly:

"Stalin's dead . . ."

Again he had to endure a painful moment of embarrassment, only this time of a different kind. The two drinking companions looked at him with disdainful pity, which made him feel like a naughty, badly behaved little boy.

With a mirthless smile the visitor said:

"My condolences . . ."

Rummer did not even deign to comment. He merely turned toward the door and gave a loud order:

"Another bottle!"

After that they drank on for a long time, but the two older men's subsequent drinking seemed to go on separately: Vlad was demonstratively excluded from the company, they hardly spoke to him, and carried on a cryptic conversation between themselves. This boycott made Vlad suffer inward agonies, and that evening for the first time he got dead-drunk.

He dreamed a dream in which he was flying above a huge deserted town, crisscrossed with a dense network of little streets, and no matter which way he looked he could see no end, no boundary to that town. Tiring, he came down to earth but some terrible force picked him up and carried him aloft again. Thus, rising and falling, he flew onward into a grim unknown until Essman's kindly laughter interrupted his flight:

"Get up, Vladka, time for the hair of the dog!"

CHAPTER 11

Every town in Russia has really only one street. Krasnodar is the same, especially in summer. The street is called "Red"—Krasnaya Street. Vlad loved that street, its colorful, ever-lively crowds, its lights winking through the leaves of the plane trees, its cellars and dives. He loved to lose himself in its human torrent and watch the ebb and flow of colors and generations. Toward about six o'clock in the evening the gray color of the more elderly inhabitants and the visitors from out of town began disappearing into the adjoining streets and alleyways, making way for the rainbow-bright carrousel of youth, until by seven o'clock the younger generation, with its carnival brilliance, had completely taken over Krasnaya Street until far into the night.

Vlad usually met Essman around nine. At the first open-air bar they would drink an "Adrianovka"—fifty grams of vodka diluted with colored soda—and then set off for a meeting in person with the inventor of this cocktail, Adrian Rummer, in his usual restaurant. Rummer would already be waiting for them, either in a private room or in the crowd out on the terrace (depending on his credit worthiness), always surrounded by several admirers and drinking companions, and with his faithful Sancho Panza, one-legged Sergei, the publishers' accountant, close at hand.

"And they call themselves writers nowadays!" he boomed, sweeping the company with the patronizing glare of his alcoholic eye. "Things have come to a pretty pass when Syomka Babayevsky and Yurka Laptev are called classics! Now in our time there was a whole cohort of *real* writers around the unforgettable Maxim Gorky. Lyoshka Tolstoy—what power, what imagery! Lenka Leonov, Sashka Fadeyev, Mishka Sholokhov! Splendid fellows one and all! And Maxim himself in our midst, an old falcon in a flock of young sparrow hawks. Like the words of that song: 'Around there wheeled in flocks the falcon's young.' He taught us the most important thing of all for a Soviet writer—socialist realism. Socialist realism, my friends, is . . ."

In his fifty-five years the old cynic Adrian Rummer had been through so much hell and high water that he probably knew the true price of everything on this earth; this loud but insincere praise for the sacred cows of Soviet literature was his way of utilizing any secret-police informers who might be present, and thus "planting" evidence of his loyal, orthodox views on the appropriate authorities. I can imagine what he really thought about socialist realism, when only two years later he tied a noose around his neck and hanged himself in his own bathroom.

Excited whispering, stimulated by the prospect of free drinks, accompanied the verbose speeches that he made "for official consumption":

"Adrian has a head on his shoulders all right!"

"The man has the divine spark!"

"When he says something he means it!"

"And that man has seen things worth remembering."

"What a life he's had."

"Learn from him while he's still alive . . ."

Having successfully cadged some drinks, the hangers-on would fade away, and when Rummer was left alone with Vlad and Essman he became caustic and morose:

"I met Zhora Sokolov this morning. The son of a bitch was running to trade in some empty bottles on Sennaya Street. 'What's the hurry, Zhora?' I said. And he said: 'I'm having a tough time of it, Adrian. All last night I only kept going on beer. I'm having a controversy with Sartre.' How d'you like that, Boris? The son of a bitch doesn't know his ass from his elbow, he'd sell his own mother for five kopecks, yet he has the effrontery to polemicize with no less than Sartre! I nearly split my sides with laughing. This is no life, Boris, this is no life—we're drowning in shit! Here we are in the lousiest city in the country and the lousiest hack in the place imagines he can argue with Sartre! About what, I should like to know?"

Later, toward midnight, when the evening's show was over at the theater, Zhora Zavalov appeared, as usual with some new girl. He freshened up the flagging party with a couple of bottles and the drinking revived, the actor now adding his share to the conversation: "I could hardly get through it—God, what a terrible play, it makes you want to throw up." One after another Zhora downed all the drinks awarded him as "fines" for coming late, and when he felt himself "in form," as he put it, he leaned back in his chair in a picturesque pose. "Why are you keeping us on short rations, comrade writers, by giving us such lousy stuff to act? Where is the real thing? Where are the good plays, the tragedies and comedies, for heaven's sake? You can't *act* with the garbage we get . . ."

Zavalov, too, was talking "for effect," except that he was doing it to impress the girl he had brought along. He was, so to speak, introducing her into "society," showing her "a bit of class." When they began to see double and tears of maudlin sentimentality started to choke him, for no good reason Rummer started to sing:

"The Cossack girls were gathering . . ."

In the way that he sang it, this favorite song of the Party leadership was so distorted by Rummer's malicious sarcasm and contempt that Essman immediately turned bright red and gasped with soundless, delighted laughter, and Zhora spread his arms in admiration:

"Brilliant, old man . . ."

It was a signal, a trumpet call. Instantly the maître d'hôtel materialized at their table, his hands clasped on his chest in entreaty:

"Comrade Rummer! Adrian Vasilyich, I beg you, we're closing! Comrade Zavalov, please!" The imploring look in the eyes of this former political prisoner, who knew what such pranks might cost him, flashed signals of fear and pleading. "Come again tomorrow, but please . . ."

They parted on the corner, each going his own way, only to meet the next day and start it all over again.

In the provinces, a town has only one street.

CHAPTER 12

Where his book was concerned, matters had unexpectedly come to a standstill. Back in March, after his conversation with Popov, Vlad had sensed that the attitude toward him was slowly but surely changing for the worse. In the editorial offices of the local newspapers, there was not a trace of the former cordiality. The tone, when anyone spoke to him, was now querulous and chilly, as though they were talking to a tedious graphomaniac who was disturbing their work. At the publishing house almost everyone stared straight through him, and only the legless Sergei, glancing nervously around, offered him a few uncertain words of consolation:

"Hang on, old man, just hang on a bit and it will work out. Things are a bit tricky at the moment, there's the usual panic . . ."

Life, however, grew harder every day. Vlad was in debt to everyone, including his landlady, who, although a kindhearted woman, was beginning to drop hints about it. The approaching crisis pushed him into taking a dangerous step. Deciding to cut the Gordian knot, he presented himself before the grim eyes of the local Party boss in charge of propaganda. Although he agreed to see Vlad, he did not invite him to sit down and merely grunted through clenched teeth:

"Well?"

As soon as he started talking, Vlad saw, sensed, understood that he was expending his energy in vain as he attempted to get through to the great man; the latter was simply not listening to him, being occupied in doodling on his notepad. This cretin, who had a master's degree in philosophy, yet who in a public speech had used the word "liberty" instead of "libretto" and referred to the Eiffel Tower as the "Eifiole" Tower, did not even think it necessary to listen to him! It was, perhaps, at that moment that Vlad's fastidious distaste for this particular breed turned into an almost physical aversion.

"See here," he grunted again when Vlad finally stopped talking, "go back to your collective farm and work. We won't stop you, there's nothing more for you to do here." The official was staring over his head as though giving orders to empty space rather than to an individual person. "That's all. You can go."

In that moment everything that was lurking in the depths of Vlad's soul—his father's needless death, hunger, his fights and escapes, jail and prison camp—coalesced and focused itself on that uncouth, pockmarked face. No—I'll say it all, God damn you!

"Scum." Tensing himself as though before leaping into a chasm, Vlad rapped out the word distinctly and repeated it: "Scum."

"Wha-a-at?!"

"You are scum."

Vlad turned and walked out, expecting to be stopped, bound, and hauled off to the appropriate place, but all remained quiet behind him and he marched into the street unhindered. Clearly the unexpected shock had proved stronger than the boss's anger.

It was now that Vlad was forced to admit to himself bitterly that he had only been of use to the Party leadership as an ideological titbit with which to add flavor to the periodic reports and speeches in which they accounted for their activities. As an autonomous individual he had never figured in their calculations, had never existed, and this was the most insulting thing of all.

Vlad only came to his senses when suddenly, on the street outside the municipal park, he came face to face with Frol Parfyonich, the foreman from the brick factory. Looking at Vlad with embarrassed deference, the man clumsily shuffled his feet and mumbled:

"Well, I never expected to see you, Vlad, of all people! Heard all about you, but never thought I'd meet you. You've sure changed— one of the bigwigs now. You did the right thing and I'm glad . . . The boys all remember you." As though he suddenly guessed what Vlad would be pleased to hear, his unshaven features broke into a beaming smile and he went on: "Our Vitek's working at the Machine and Tractor Station as a mechanic. And he's married, too! His wife's due to have a baby any day now—nice girl she is, an 'outlander.' I'll be glad to give them your regards." Then he added hastily, as though fearing the specter of that experience which they had shared: "Well, let's shake, we may not see each other again!"

Of course they never did meet again, but as he watched him go, Vlad caught himself thinking that he could never forgive the foreman for what had happened on that night they both remembered so well.

Another surprise awaited him at home, and not a pleasant one. Just as he reached the gateway, from out of it appeared a totally unexpected visitor—Nadya, his wife.

"Hello . . ." She touched him pleadingly. "I decided to come and see how you were getting on," she said, then immediately began to make excuses for herself: "I came into town to deliver a load of cabbages from the farm, I'm working in the farm office now, in the produce department."

"How's Tatyana?"

"Oh, you'd never believe it"—she was clearly delighted by his question—"she's growing up to be so bright, just like you. She can already say 'Mama,' 'Papa,' 'Nana,' and she's even started walking a little. When she grips on to a stool, you just can't prize her loose from it! Why, only yesterday . . ."

She chattered on shyly, and for a moment Vlad was seized by a thought that was as simple as falling into empty space: "Perhaps that is the sort of life for you after all? Why not? Live a normal life, raise kids, get a job like everyone else, and give up all this ambition." He immediately rejected it, however: no, anywhere but there, anywhere but that hellish place where a person is dogged by contempt and hatred just because he's from another part of the country.

"What are people saying back at the farm?"

"All sorts of things." She gestured vaguely. "But it's all just talk."

"No, go on—tell me honestly."

"They just laugh." Suddenly Nadya began to weep soundlessly. "They're laughing at me. I don't really mind, after all, what I went through before was worse and I can't blame you. Only it would be nice if you could come and shut their mouths."

No, Nadya, you didn't succumb or go under, did you? Fifteen years later you came to see him, with cheerful impudence, to show off to him with photographs of your new home, your new husband, and your new child. The market trader overcame the woman in you and you outdid everyone else in greedily stealing any sort of farm property that you could lay your hands on, and you soon stopped regretting your youthful indiscretion with the susceptible young librarian. To each his own! Even so, I can never be forgiven for the tears you shed on that chilly evening, standing in a dark street in Krasnodar.

Vlad accompanied her back to her hotel and as they were saying goodbye she impulsively seized his hand, pressed it to her cold cheek, and blurted out:

"Will you come and see little Tanya sometime, maybe?"

"Maybe," he agreed unwillingly, knowing in advance that he would not and that this was their last meeting in these parts. "If you like."

"See you soon, Vladik . . ."

"Sure . . . So long."

On his way back, out of habit Vlad set off for Lyalya's house on the corner of Sennaya Street and Ordzhonikidze Street, but he quickly stopped short and remembered: the evil he had done to his wife was now coming back at him like a boomerang. He now saw that other woman rarely and usually in secret. Lately she seemed to be embarrassed by him and tried not to be seen in his company by people they knew. The humiliation which he felt at this was gradually destroying his self-confidence, his aims and plans. Yet even while aware that the end was near and inevitable, he still hung on her every word and gesture, her half smile, in the faint hope of bringing back the past, that brief springtime, that holiday which had long since come to an end. Do not ask pity of a woman, she lives in another world!

CHAPTER 13

Together with the first snow came the first rumblings of thunder. Early one morning, a violently agitated Essman burst into the house where Vlad lodged, with a fresh copy of the newspaper in his shaking hands.

"Read that." Having marked a paragraph at the bottom of page three with his fingernail, he handed the paper to Vlad. "It's started!"

In an article entitled "Greater Artistic Skill and Higher Ideological Standards Needed," a short but pregnant paragraph was devoted to him: "In the final analysis, the premature adoption of professional status can only have bad results. Vlad Samsonov, the peasant poet from the village of Plastunovskaya, whose early work was extremely promising, having abandoned his family and his work, is now living a bohemian life and is pestering every editor in town with verses that leave a great deal to be desired." A certain clumsiness in the style was outweighed by the extreme clarity of the article's meaning, which was simply: get out.

Vlad had foreseen, indeed knew for certain, that he would pay for his talk with the propaganda boss and that the day of retribution was near, but when it suddenly came to pass, he lost his head. In a little town like Krasnodar an article like this meant that a line was drawn under a person's career. The ring had been closed.

Much later, when he was the target of abuse and hostility on a far bigger scale, Vlad would laugh skeptically at his youthful fears, but that morning, alone with Essman, he was in no mood for laughter. He had been forcibly driven into a corner, and at the same time deprived of any chance of hitting back, because the enemy was faceless and invisible and the wall behind him was transparent and unsafe. He had not even been offered an opportunity to capitulate . . .

You should have been at my side then, my dear Andrei Sakharov, but I have a long way yet to go until our meeting!

"What are you going to do?" The hunchback anxiously watched Vlad as he feverishly got dressed. "Where will you go?"

"I don't know yet."

"Don't do anything stupid."

"I'll try not to."

"Shall we go together?"

"Why?"

"It's more fun . . ."

"What about your 'mental hygiene'?"

"See here, Vlad . . ."

Essman was hanging around uncertainly in the doorway, as though expecting Vlad to change his mind, but at that moment Vlad was not in the mood for his friend's anxiety and sympathy, and as soon as Essman realized this he silently disappeared.

He had to straighten himself out, come to his senses, and collect his thoughts in order to make the right decision. Vlad set off walking aimlessly, circling around the outer reaches of the town and instinctively avoiding the center for fear of meeting someone he knew. That would have been the most unbearable thing of all. Even so, he was not able to avoid an encounter.

Suddenly, out of the semidarkness of a bar in some remote suburb, the figure of Zhora Zavalov emerged, already half-drunk:

"All hail to the hero of the day!" Zhora flung himself at Vlad with outstretched arms. "Why so downcast?" He already knew everything. "Laugh and tear it up. In Rostov, I remember, they gave me such a lambasting it made my hair stand on end. Don't worry, it happens all the time. You can't scratch every midge bite and you can't please all the fools all of the time. Why don't you come with me? We're doing *Cyrano* tonight—it's the first night, in fact, so that means there'll be a party afterwards. We'll have a drink, pick up some girls, and fix up some 'push me, pull you,' eh? And of course you can see what sort of a Cyrano I make. Follow me, maestro!"

Vlad suddenly ceased to care about anything. The theater was as good a place to go as anywhere else—what if people did see him? He might as well be hanged for a sheep as a lamb. Anyway, the entertainment might distract him and take his mind off his problems, help him to relax and regain his equilibrium.

Zavalov continued his tour of the haunts of vice, dragging Vlad after him and treating him to a barbaric mixture of drinks ranging from muscatel to beer, until they reached the theater, where the actor suddenly pulled himself together and sobered up:

"Wish me luck, Vlad, and I'll tell you to go to hell. You never know, you may have luck in your hands . . . God bless us!"

Although Vlad has had some connection with the theater, loves the stage and knows a few of its simple secrets, he has never succeeded, though his hairs are now gray, in grasping the mystery of that transformation. An actor who only half an hour ago, it seemed, had been blind-drunk, was suddenly able, once on stage, to sigh with unrequited love and jealous fury and make the audience sigh and suffer with him. May the devil take you, Zavalov! And may God preserve you!

But Vlad was unaware of what a blow was still to strike him. As the curtain slowly descended at the end of the last act and the applause broke out, from his seat at the far back of a box his glance involuntarily strayed over the audience as it gave a thunderous ovation; suddenly he went cold and his heart plunged into a bottomless abyss: on the far side of the orchestra seats, in the third row back, her shoulder touching the good-looking man whom he had first seen coming into a restaurant with her, stood Lyalya, and her eyes, looking up at her companion, were glowing with pleasure and devotion, while he in his turn was gazing down at her with a look of satisfied condescension.

With a bitter lump in his throat, half-choking with pain and tears, Vlad rushed for the exit and out into the night. He saw nothing except an iridescent, lace-like pattern in front of his eyes amid total blackness. Someone called out to him, but he fled into the dark without turning around, and nothing could stop his agonized flight. Reality was conspiring against him. He had been struck down, as the sick or wounded are stricken while they drag themselves on their painful way. Lyalya, Lyalya, why did you have to do this to me?

Silence.

CHAPTER 14

Despair carried Vlad through the late autumn night toward the block where, on the corner of Sennaya and Ordzhonikidze, there stood the single-story red-brick house in which she lived. He could not explain what he was hoping for, or why he had convinced himself that she would come out. Intuition alone made him take up the almost senseless vigil: she must, she had to come out! It seemed to Vlad that the intolerable burning which was consuming him from within could not fail to communicate itself to her at once, otherwise there was no justice in this world. He had the feeling that he was walking on the edge of an abyss with only a single gleam of light in the depths—the clear-cut outline of her window.

Much water was to flow away down the glittering rivers of time before Vlad would grasp the simplest of truths known to the male sex: do not chase a woman who is leaving you—you will never catch her up. You will become her shadow; she no longer sees you.

The tiny mustard seed of his faith sprouted, and Vlad was rewarded: the miracle happened. She came out. Without greeting him or looking at him, she said:

"I've been talking to your wife." Lyalya stressed the last word, as though once and for all defining the extent of the distance which now separated them. "You must go back to your family, Vladik."

"But you knew about that!" he half-shouted, half-croaked. "You knew everything!"

"You have a daughter, Vladik." She seemed not to hear him. "And you must take care of her. In any case, you ought to go away from here for a while, until it has all blown over."

"What are you saying, Lyalya?" He could hardly hear himself speak for the noise in his ears and the frenzied beating of his heart. "Think, Lyalya, think what you're saying!"

"I have no more to say to you." She turned around and the light from a nearby window flickered over her tense, matt-white profile. "Don't follow me."

"Lyalya!"

Life ebbed away from him in time to the click of her heels fading away into the darkness.

"Lyalya!"

It was an entreaty, a cry for mercy, a call for pity and compassion, but she did not respond, did not hear, would not condescend.

Of their own accord his legs took Vlad to the actor's hostel where Zhora lived, to the boundless oblivion of drunken intoxication. When he arrived things were already wild; he slipped easily and unobtrusively into the artificial whirlpool of the party and was instantly, after one glass, dissolved in it like salt in alkali.

And away it went. Faces, bodies, clothes swirled before him in a carnival of nonstop drinking. People came and went, like sentries whose duty it was to change the guard beside him. Women stripped, put the light out, and then they were gone. Zavalov sang a sentimental song and wept, crawled over to kiss him and sang again. In rare moments of utter blackness, Vlad suddenly heard a voice, as he had once heard it in Igarka.

"Are you all right?"

"No."

"Then why all this?"

"What else am I to do?"

"Get up and go."

"Where to?"

"I'll show you . . ."

Once more the mist exploded before his eyes. Inside a circle outlined in glaring light the insane, reeling carousal continued, in which he was an invited guest and everything started all over again. Reality laughed and cried, disguised as a soggy cucumber and a salted herring. A rich man's farce was being played out within the humble confines of an actor's meager salary.

Toward the close of the party Vlad finally collapsed into total unconsciousness and did not get up again. Delirium, like a horrible film, unrolled in his head with capricious inconsequence and speed. Perhaps this will teach you, boy, not to do this again!

From the disjointed fragments of his delirious visions there was formed the likeness of a deserted city: the black holes of windows, smashed or boarded up crisscross, the yawning chasms of doors and passages, blind alleys from which there was no way out. Walking in thick and sticky mud, he was forcing his way through this lifeless realm, overcoming countless obstacles, falling and getting up again, in a feverish search for at least one living soul. But all around there were only deserted houses, buildings without doors or windows, blank walls with only loopholes at the corners; and not a soul amid all this hollow decay. How afraid I am, O Lord! Then he thought—oh wonder!—that he saw the outline of a painfully familiar figure in a distant window; breathless, he ran toward it, but the shadow vanished, having been only an optical illusion. "O Lord," he cried dumbly, falling into the saving dark of his own blindness, into the warm pit of awakening, "save me!"

Year after year that delirious dream would pursue Vlad whenever drunkenness began to rage within his fallen soul, trying to crush his soul, to turn it into a rotting vegetable. But the Ever-present Hand did not abandon its weak servant and time and again would grant him strength to rise up.

When Vlad eventually opened his eyes he saw Essman's anxious face leaning over him and almost burst into tears in a burning rush of gratitude. The hunchback only waved his short arms in an embarrassed gesture:

"Get up, Vlad. Time to go. Try as you may, you'll never drink all the wine there is, you've got to leave some for the others." Then with male clumsiness he helped Vlad to dress. "Come to my place, you can sleep it off there."

As he walked through the snow-powdered town, Vlad took a decision which—so he imagined—would bring about a final, sharp change for the better in his life.

"To Moscow!" he repeated bitterly to himself all the way. "To Moscow, to Moscow, to Moscow!"

CHAPTER 15

A winter so hard was a rarity in those parts. The frosts struck as early as November, and from January onward the snowstorms continued almost without interruption. Vlad hardly went out at all but sat indoors in Essman's lair. For days on end he struggled with his friend's ancient radio in a vain attempt to extract something faintly intelligible through the howls of jamming. Once or twice a few words did break through, but it was impossible to connect them up into anything coherent, and he soon got bored with this occupation. Boris kept no books, on the principle that "people would pinch them anyway," so, being left to his own devices, Vlad's thoughts willy-nilly returned to the cheerless subject of Lyalya. He now realized that the affair could have ended in no other way; he had nothing to offer her except a future of total uncertainty. For all that, she had nevertheless had to make a choice, and now, on sober reflection, he was forced to admit, hand on heart, that the comparison was not in his favor. Unfortunately, though, this did not make him feel any better.

Each piece of news that Essman brought him was less comforting than the last. The young people's newspaper had talked about the possibility of Vlad writing a short story for them, but nothing had come of it; the publishers had finally decided to tear up his contract; and in his speech at a conference on ideology, the Party's regional

propaganda boss had gone so far as to call him a "shady character."
Tactfully, the hunchback said nothing about Lyalya.

"That's the way it goes, old man." His sympathy was genuine and
unfeigned. "But don't be downhearted. It'll all come out in the
wash. I know these Party shit-eaters: they yell their heads off, and
then before you know where you are some new 'campaign' is under
way, someone else becomes the scapegoat and they don't give you another thought." Sensing, however, that this was not the real cause of
his friend's depression, he added encouragingly: "All is not lost,
Vladka, all is not lost . . ."

Ah, Boris, you blessed soul, you of all people knew perfectly well
that he hadn't a chance, that nothing could put matters right now
and that all really was lost, but by your nature you were incapable of
being cruel to be kind at that moment. Accept this, then, as your ep-
itaph from him, Boris Essman: a master craftsman who never lived
to see his own church spire!

From time to time Zavalov would drop in, as always with a bottle
in his pocket and his latest passion in tow. Bursting noisily into the
room, he would slam the bottle down on the table and immediately
give Vlad a smacking kiss:

"Vladka, my friend!" The reek of liquor on his breath was as
heavy and persistent as the smell of mold in an old cellar. "We'll see
them all dead yet, the bastards! Forget the whole thing and look
after Number One. Have a drink and mix it with a little water—but
only a very little, mind!"

Then he would sing, knowing Vlad's weakness for old gypsy songs.
Zhora's pleasant if slightly tremulous and alcoholic tenor voice
would fill the room with the illusion of temporary peace. Although it
helped to calm Vlad's nerves, no sooner did Zavalov stop singing
than the feeling of misery rose in his throat again and he rudely
pushed the actor off the premises:

"Clear off, Zhora, I'm not in the mood."

With an understanding wink to his girlfriend, Zhora disappeared
uncomplainingly, only to return a week later with the same props
and the same lines . . .

Meanwhile winter raged about the town. A solid layer of frozen
snow covered the skylight in the ceiling. The rare visitors who came
brought in with them a cold gust of frosty air. Vlad never stopped
thinking of his plans for a dash to Moscow, but he had no money
and there was no hope of getting a loan. Had it been warmer, he

would have made up his mind and traveled as of old, without a ticket, but how could anyone ride the rods in this freezing weather? In any case, it was probably colder still in Moscow, and he had no prospect of shelter in the capital. There was no question of turning up on his family's doorstep: he would only have dared to do that if he could arrive with a success story. Sokolniki would never see him come home as a failure!

Vlad's hesitations were cut short when one day Essman came home even more hunchbacked and gloomy than ever:

"D'you know what?" He sat down heavily on the edge of the bed. "They refuse to give me any more work." Vlad had never before seen his friend so downcast. "To hell with them!" For a moment, Essman flared up. "We'll starve together, you and I, and with a bit of luck we'll survive the winter!"

This Vlad could not allow. All his worldly possessions were on his back; it only remained to pack his collection of poems into something, which they did by their joint efforts, using old newspapers for the purpose. Boris—admittedly without total conviction—still tried to persuade him to change his mind, but he firmly cut short his friend's moral wavering: "No, Boris, no." A vengeful determination was slowly growing inside Vlad. "This time I'm going to show 'em. It is not yet eventide, gentlemen! The real show is only just beginning! Let's go."

Outside, the cold was clearly too much for his light overcoat and thin cap. With his ridiculous, tightly rolled bundle tied up with string held under his arm, Vlad immediately felt he was back at Igarka again, looking like a scarecrow, a third-rate actor in a lousy show touring the far north—a sort of grasshopper who had squandered the summer in singing when instead, like the industrious ant, he should have been toiling away to make sure of keeping warm in winter.

They were, of course, unable to resist the nostalgic temptation, and stopped off in the same basement bar where they had first made friends and drunk their first bottle together. Neither of them, however, suspected that this conversation amid the hubbub and tobacco smoke would be their last, that they would never meet again and that this time they were sharing their last bottle of wine.

"Forgive me, Vladik, I've only managed to scrape together a very little money for you." The hunchback hastened to deal with the business side before they started drinking, as he counted out a few grubby five-ruble bills and pushed them toward Vlad. "This will be enough for you to take a ticket as far as Tikhoretskaya, then you'll just have to see how things pan out—with luck they may not throw you off and you can make it to Moscow. From Tikhoretskaya it's only another twenty-four hours, anyway. Well, good luck, Vladik, and may the wind keep blowing in your sails, as the saying goes." As usual when he got slightly drunk, Boris livened up and sparkled, grew talkative and outspoken. "Do you remember that story I told you about the Master Craftsman? To be honest with you, I would gladly die too if I were only allowed to see *my* masterpiece, but I know I never will: I've sold myself to the newspapers for a mess of potage and the chance of getting a picture or two in local exhibitions. Ring down the curtain, finita la commedia! I've lived out my life, Vlad, and you're only twenty-three. Don't go the way I went; you still have almost an eternity in reserve, and never be afraid to start all over again from zero. At your age, Picasso was sleeping under newspapers, Walt Whitman was almost a beggar, and Cervantes was being hounded from one debtor's prison to another—so never be afraid of starting all over again. I believe in you, Vladik, you *will* build your church—only don't ruin yourself on the way, don't buckle under, don't give way to drink, and then one day you will see *your* masterpiece and die, for that is the law: he who sees it must perish. But what a wonderful moment to die! Don't be afraid of death; dying is a simple matter—the only things to fear are lies and failure . . ."

Warmed by drink and talk, the two friends no longer noticed the cold on the way to the station, where Vlad bought a ticket for a train that stopped at Tikhoretskaya. Before he climbed aboard, a force far stronger than mere custom brought them into each other's arms and for a moment they were joined in one essence where all was indivisible: thought, breath, and spirit.

"We'll meet again, Boris, remember that . . ."

"God bless you, Vladik," Essman said quietly and hopelessly, as though sensing his own approaching end. "God bless you!"

From old habit, Vlad climbed up onto the top bunk near the heating pipe, and until Rostov no one disturbed his fitful sleep. Then, however, the conductor, a nearsighted little man in a quilted jerkin, caught him on the way to the toilet:

"Hey, stop, young man—weren't you supposed to be going to

Tikhoretskaya? Yes, that's right—I've got you marked off in my ticket register. We've gone long past Tikhoretskaya by now!"

This time, Vlad's usual frankness let him down. The little man listened, blinked his myopic little eyes, and interrupted him waspishly: "Fired you from the newspaper, did they? Wrote lots of articles and went on trips for the paper, I suppose, and now you're trying to bum a free ride to Moscow, is that it? I'm not a hard man, but I'm not the boss around here: you'll get me into so much trouble from the inspector that I won't hear the end of it for a year. Okay, I'll let you go the rest of the way, only out on the back platform, if you don't mind, and nowhere else. You can stoke the heating furnace if you like, it's a mite warmer in there."

He was clearly playing a nasty joke on Vlad. Only a polar bear could survive the journey to Moscow out on the platform in that cold, but obviously the conductor had to keep on the right side of his superiors, and Vlad had no choice. Clutching his rolled-up newspaper, he moved into the little furnace compartment, where he roasted on one side and froze on the other.

Vlad, however, still had something to learn about the great Russian people, who are, it seems, a crazy mixture of goodness and filth in roughly equal proportions. The conductor proved to be very inventive in his ways of amusing himself at Vlad's expense. From time to time he would bring mostly drunken passengers along to the back platform, open the door of the furnace compartment, and show Vlad off to them like a freak in a circus:

"Used to work for a newspaper"—he would have made a first-class tourist guide—"and got the sack. Now he's off to Moscow, no less, to make his fortune. Look at all that paper he's got with him—guess he's going to try and palm it all off again on someone else, that's the sort he is . . ."

Oh, how he hated, Lord forgive him, how he hated that man! Everything in him seemed to burn with agonizing hatred. It was then that he understood how a living man of flesh and blood could squeeze the trigger without hesitation. How many bursts of machine-gun fire did he mentally loose off at those grinning drunkards, while his soul was almost dissolved into outer darkness! Again he sinned in his heart, and again . . .

Somewhere past Kharkov another "stowaway" appeared—a stocky youth in a quilted jacket with a typical prison-issue cap on his shorn head. At first he tried to squeeze in beside Vlad, but there was simply not room for two. Out of a sense of solidarity, Vlad came out, and for the remaining seven hundred-odd kilometers they took it in turns to exchange places.

The lad was talkative, and hardly stopped for a minute as he described his familiar odyssey:

"They let me out, but with my passport marked so that I have to live at least a hundred kilometers from a big city, so no one wants to give me a job. I'm going to Gulag headquarters in Moscow now—let *them* find me a job, or I'll spend the rest of my days shuttling back and forth across the country like a lump of shit in a tin can. I'm an orphanage kid, see, so I got nowhere to go. Got ten years inside and five years' loss of rights, then they let me go on the amnesty—go where you like, they said—only nobody wants me. They take one look at my papers and I'm out on my ear—we don't need your sort here, they say. Our soldiers fought and died in the war, but there still isn't enough to go round, so get the hell out of here . . . Wanna bite to eat?"

He took out of his pocket a congealed lump of bacon about half the size of the palm of his hand, wrapped in greasy paper.

"Don't you have a knife? Okay, you take first bite. I haven't got a knife either, but I'm not fussy."

"Nor am I . . ."

By turns they wore out their teeth on the old, gristly lump of bacon, and the spirit of prison-camp brotherhood hovered over them in the shape of the steam from their own breath. Share and share alike! Gone but not forgotten—where are you now, my onetime traveling companion?

Suddenly the Moscow skyline appeared in a melted patch on the little window: Moscow, vast, frostbound, the occasional white spires of skyscrapers piercing the mist. His heart stopped and immediately rose up in his throat: now, now I will either storm you or I won't, my eternal fortress, my magic castle, the love and the curse of my life! Sokolniki!

CHAPTER 16

Jerusalem, 11 March 1972

My dearest Vladenka,

We have written again and again, but still absolutely nothing from Moscow. How are you, what are you doing, what's happening, how do you feel? We think of you so much here, we're getting very worried. There seems to be no good news from Moscow, either on the radio or in the papers. Do write and tell us about yourself, even just a few lines. Life here goes on normally. We are studying the language terribly hard. Yura talks it very fluently now, of course he makes mistakes but people correct him and they can understand him. I'm getting on better with the language too. The other day Yura and I talked with an official about the chances of getting work. After the end of this academic year, in June or July, I may be able to enroll in a special six-month language course for teachers of mathematics, physics, and chemistry. That would be very good. I've handed in my papers to the university, but there's very little hope, the entrance requirements are very tough, although they are largely of a formal nature.

I've already written to tell you that we've had several letters from Europe, including one from Georgii Yevgenievich. He has gone to a lot of trouble on our behalf, and has invited us to stay with him. It's too early for us yet, and too expensive, although we very much want to go. But I hope that if we succeed in getting jobs, we shall be able to go. We think you will probably soon receive the first present from us and from Auntie. By the way, I had a very serious talk with Auntie yesterday, and I shall have to talk to her again—to dot the i's and cross the t's, as they say. There's absolutely no reason for her to make such a fuss and act the martyr all the time. If it gets absolutely unbearable, we shall have to think up some solution. In general, a lot of things here are complicated and difficult, the most trivial question becomes a huge problem. But Yura has passed the crisis, I think. He has become much more relaxed and less strung-up. That's about all for now.

Do write to us. Give our regards to absolutely everybody. Lyoshka misses you and often talks about you. A big, big hug and a kiss, we'll always remember you. Keep well, take care of yourself. And *do* write. Another kiss.

Katya.

That was all. The last page was rustling in my hand. That chain of apparently random yet divinely interconnected events which is life breaks off in yawning emptiness. You do not know, cannot know what will become of you in a day, an hour, a minute, a moment, whither and into what channels your destiny will flow, but whatever happens, we—you and I—are forever inseparable, linked by the blood bond of shared memory.

Until we meet again, dear one.

CHAPTER 17

Dear Katya!

Today I went back to our old house. Nowadays it is surrounded on all sides by multistory boxes, which look down in faceless arrogance on this little island, this lonely oasis, the frail ark of our past, the only remaining guardian of our ghosts and our sighs, of our insatiable memories: a snow-covered little plot of ground, hedged in on all four sides by the adjoining buildings, with the long extinguished boiler room in the righthand corner and two frail wooden fences along the lefthand side. Like the prodigal son I stood before the threshold of my father's house, except that no one was waiting to welcome me with love and forgiveness. The empty windowpanes stared at me with indifference; behind them seethed a dark, strange, hidden life that was unknown to me—if you can call it life, that nomadic existence of those alien hordes of temporary invaders, transitory seekers after happiness in the capital city. Everything here, I thought, looked so utterly familiar—the path from the gateway to the main entrance, the rusty hinges of our battered front door, the worn steps leading upward—yet in the whole house, in its fundamental essence I had a sharp sense of collapse, corruption, and decay: a shabby stage-set, covered in a fine layer of ash, after the run of the play has ended. All around was emptiness, silence, and cold. I stood before my tiny Mecca, my personal Carthage that had, at last,

been conquered, at the gates of my own Jerusalem, but I felt no joy
of conquest and encounter; instead I could only weep. I wept for
those whose ghosts still haunted the place, for those who did not survive, whom time swept away, whom I should never meet again.
"Farewell! No planes fly there, no trains arrive from there!" Through
time and across the years, in the sunlight of childhood I descried
their faces: my dead little sister, Tonka, Leonid Durov, Natalya
Nikolaevna, Sarah Itkin, Uncle Volodya, and many, many others
from around and about. The faces swam toward me from their vertiginous distance, overcoming oblivion with all the ease of immor-
tality:

NINA: Don't worry, Vladka, we'll survive; go on living, I don't
want to. But why did Mama ever bring me into the world at all?

LEONID DUROV: Perhaps we'll have a bit more luck at the next stop,
Vladik; we *must* be lucky—we've deserved it.

NATALYA NIKOLAEVNA: If only I knew what will become of my
boys, if only I knew!

SARAH ITKIN: I don't care who he looked like, Samsonov, but I only
wish that Karl Marx had suffered as much trouble as my Solomon!

UNCLE VOLODYA: I drove five people's commissars to the firing
squad, and I'm still going strong. I'll be waiting to see what becomes
of you, Vladka—keep your chin up, son . . .

CHORUS: And whichever of your parents you take after, Vlad, don't
feel sorry for yourself, go ahead and live your own life like everyone
else . . .

"I can't live cooped up in this lousy city of yours, there's more
sense in my ass than in all your heads, you slobs from Mitkovskaya
Street . . ."

"My head isn't made of tin to be stuck in the oven and baked. Let
Nikiforov go and fight, if his head gets shot off they'll give him a
new one at the Lubyanka. I'm going to sit out this war on the home
front, I don't have any quarrel with Hitler . . ."

"How much longer are you going to torment me, curse you? How
can I get away from you, you monsters—clear off, get out of my
sight! God, the pain, the pain!"

"Vladik . . ."

"Vladka . . ."

" 'Boxer'!"

"Samsono-o-ov!"

Can you hear them, Katya? We cannot brush them aside or leave them behind us as we go away to another part of town or to distant lands. On the contrary, the farther we go away from them in time and space, the closer and more tangible becomes their presence alongside us. Down the steep spiral of this bloodstained century, through the minefields and barbed-wire entanglements we have followed behind them, and, therefore we owe to them, at the very least, our lives. Their mistakes and blunders, their sins and errors, and, finally, their unrecorded deaths live on in us, imparting to us a wisdom we have not deserved and a warmth which we squander. They are like the little knots in the living lacework of this world: without them, all the threads of existence and memory would have long since fallen apart. Like burnt-out stars they still beam out their guiding light for us in the darkness and cold of our earthly existence. They are like the echo in a seashell, bringing to us the roar of surf whose sound died away long ago. Without them we do not exist, without them we are nothing, without them there will be no salvation for us. "Say not, my friend, 'they are no more,' but say with gratitude, 'they were' . . ."

A frosty mist crackled and billowed above me. The courtyard flowed around me from all sides with its hollow silence, and I had the strange feeling that I was crumpled into a ball and beginning to dissolve into that silence, merging with its sadness and decay. From every nook and cranny there fluttered toward me the brightly colored birds of my memories. Over there, in the gap in the wall between the boilerhouse and the old stables, which were later converted into a library, Lenka Tsaryov, nicknamed "The Snake," shot it out with the police after a raid on the ration-card office of the local housing administration. And there, near a gate, stood the shack belonging to Shilov, the janitor, in which were my two or three bricks that went to eternity along with the janitor and his shack. And here, in the second-floor window of the wooden annex, for nearly a decade, there lurked, as though in a portrait frame, the gaunt figure of Uncle Volodya Tselikovsky, ex-chauffeur to five unlucky people's commissars, who joined his Maker through drinking polishing fluid and was buried by his drinking companions at the expense of the housing committee. I weep and sob. My soul mourns. Ghosts, ghosts, ghosts! They have been crowding around me, firmly and loudly announcing their right to a word of reminiscence or a brief episode: a rushing kaleidoscope, a glittering carrousel, an iridescent streak from the past. Nothing is forgotten, nothing! We are like the leaves of a tree: even when we fall, we retain within us its image and likeness. I am yours, yours forever, my courtyard, my house, my Sokolniki!

Through the freezing mist above Mitkovskaya Street, above its hooting and clanging, above its weathervanes and railroad warehouses there rose up the vast, many-layered mass of the city. From there, one looked upward at Moscow from a lower level, and therefore it looked even more overwhelming than usual. There, behind the walls of those boxes of varying age, in the quiet of laboratories, in the mechanical roar of workshops, in the furtive talk in offices the fate of the country was being decided, a country that breathed for thousands of miles around, that existed within a circlet of a dozen open seas, in the domes of empty churches and rusting rockets, drunken and holy, gentle and savage, falling and rising again. My country. Our country, Katya!

She has rejected us, her obstinate stepchildren, and watched us go without regret. In her temporary deafness, she is still unable to hear what it is we are calling for in our bitter love for her. But in her arrogant incomprehension can already be sensed the agonizing question: where are you going? And we will return, we will most certainly return, to give her an answer in the hope of finally being understood. Therefore I do not say now "farewell," but just "goodbye."

Until we meet again, Mother!

Amen.